STRANDED

DON J. O'DONNELL

Between Lake Superior and the prairie's edge lies a region known as "the Quetico." This is a landscape of tangled lakes and rivers, of rocky islands and towering granite cliffs, of misty mornings and splendid sunsets, of beaver, moose, and loon.

—Bruce M. Littlejohn
"Quetico Country: Part 1: Wilderness Highway to Wilderness Recreation."
Canadian Geographical Journal, Volume 71, Number 2, (August 1965)

Quetico and the Boundary Waters are reminders of the past, when the world was wild and woolly. The Lord only knows how the original explorers found their way through the "Land of the Great Pierre." Without maps they must have foundered many times, for maps are the tools of survival in the parks. If you can't read a map and relate them to the land, you better travel somewhere else.

—An Ely Outfitter

I study the parks before I ever go up there. My group looks at maps of the whole area, memorizes the lakes and routes we intend to use, and makes damn sure we can navigate into and out of both the Boundary Waters Canoe Area Wilderness and Quetico Provincial Park. Can't leave a trip up there to chance. In this day and age, you can even look at Google Maps to find good views of both parks—just put in the name Ely, MN, and then add the name of a destination lake, like Moose, Knife, Darky, Argo, or Brent Lake, and decent stuff shows up. From there, you can move the cursor around to look at either park or just put in the name of a lake in the directions category, and it will locate it, and give you directions from Ely. Also, the Outfitters sell detailed maps that show actual portages and routes between lakes, so we always take those. I love the parks, but they are remote, and can be dangerous, so you have to be prepared.

—An Experienced Visitor

To my father, who spent most of his life setting a wonderful example for his nine children. He loved fishing and camping and joined me for a trip into Quetico when he was seventy.

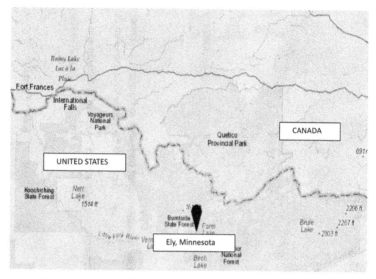

- Map services and data available from U.S. Geological Survey, National Geospatial Program."...

Map 1 – Quetico Provincial Park in Canada is shown north of the United States border. The town of Ely is shown (illustrated by the marker near Farm Lake) south of the U.S. border in Minnesota.

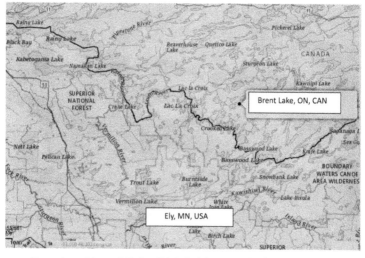

- Map services and data available from U.S. Geological Survey, National Geospatial Program."...

Map 2 – Brent Lake in Quetico Provincial Park in Ontario, Canada is shown north of the border between the United States and Canada. Also shown is the town of Ely, Minnesota located on State Highway 1, (MN1), and The Boundary Waters Canoe Area Wilderness.

CHAPTER ONE

A red-tailed hawk screeched from above. The *kee-eeeee-arr* call caused me to grab a pair of binoculars from my canoe and sprint forward to the edge of a small waterfall to look for the bird soaring above. The wilderness sky was empty, but what I did see after shifting my view to the area below me was startling—a woman with nothing on. And she wasn't alone.

Rarely did I see people in the outback of Canada's Quetico Provincial Park; in more than ten trips into the park, I'd seen few couples. None of them were nude, let alone making love.

I moved slowly back from the edge and slipped behind some brush less than three hundred feet away from them. I let the field glasses hang down from a strap around my neck. They deserved their privacy, for a few more minutes anyway.

When I returned my gaze through the binoculars the lady was sitting on the man's lap, facing him, her body swaying with the gentle rocking of the rope-net hammock supporting them. Her back was glistening with sweat, and I noticed a tattoo on her right butt cheek—a butterfly. They needed a little more private time.

On most trips, my team of campers and I only encountered other people on the days we entered or exited the park, usually at forest ranger check-in points. The parks are so vast that visitors can scatter in the wilderness after admittance, and one might never meet or even see other people. On occasion, I did observe folks in the wilds, but it was unusual. Now, accidently seeing people where they weren't expected, especially when they weren't here four hours ago when I had passed by this campsite, was astonishing. The lovers were at a place marked on maps as Brent Lake Campsite NE. It's actually located on a small island. I'd stayed at the site many times in previous trips and it was my favorite in Quetico. My three friends and I were staying at the another site on Brent Lake, about two miles to the west. My buddies had remained behind while I went fishing alone.

With the binoculars I noticed the woman had stopped moving and was slumped against her partner. He was sitting sideways in the hammock, perpendicular to the way it was hung, feet on the ground, back and shoulders buried in the netting. She covered his chest as he balanced them both, and I wondered if they'd fall out after their glorious workout. But they clung together, locked in a steamy embrace. How long would I have to wait here until it was civil to paddle past them? I'd been fishing in a tiny lake above their campsite and my canoe was still in it at the shoreline behind me. My plan was to leave by reversing the route I used on the way here—this time, hoisting my canoe by rope down the waterfall, rather than up— and entering the main section of Brent Lake directly behind the lovers' position.

The couple stirred in their hammock, but the man's feet were still on the ground beneath them, and the woman was pasted to his chest, clinging to his neck like a sleeping child. What luck. *Dammit, I had to get past them.* Putting down my field glasses, I glanced around. Bright sunlight sparkled off the water as it splashed over rocks, and I watched the cascading rivulets, thinking of some innocuous phrase to pose to the pair like, "Sure is a warm day," or "Hope you two are well-rested."

I reached for my sunglasses, patting my shirt pockets. They weren't there, but halfway down the incline, just the edge of the eyeglass frame was visible in the path beside the waterfall. It would be tough to manage without them—headache-inducing—so I decided to inch down the slope to get them. After I retrieved the glasses, I'd climb down the waterfall with my canoe, whether the lovers were ready or not. As I was about to go, a glimpse of movement from below caught my eye and I froze in place.

From where I was located on the precipice, I could only see part of the campsite and just the upper halves of two tents set up in the area. The amorous couple was thirty feet behind the site in a clearing. Using the binoculars, I observed two men carrying fishing rods moving toward the firepit and the tents. Both were dressed in T-shirts and blue jeans.

Who are these guys?

They looked inside both shelters and checked around the entire site. One of them spotted the hammock, and they approached the lovers. A dry feeling caught in the back of my throat. In seconds, the two men were standing near them. The men halted before one reached out with a fishing rod and tapped the lady on the shoulder. She bolted upright in her man's arms and tumbled backwards toward the ground as her partner tried to hold her. They flipped out in a heap and the lady slammed the turf as the guy fell on top of her. In an instant the naked man was standing upright, yelling at the fishermen. Arms were flailing and the men were jumping around like cartoon characters in a silent movie.

The nude guy and one fisherman were standing toe-to-toe,

screaming. Muted yells ricocheted through the woods, but no actual words reached me. A pushing session started and the fighters were able to fend each other off until the lover without clothes fell backwards over the hammock from a violent shove. The fisherman looked down and started shouting at the lady. She seemed to be stunned, and he suddenly kicked her in the stomach with his boot.

Damn. What's going on here?

The naked man jumped up and leapt at him. They grappled in a wrestling hold then twisted off to the side and fell to the ground, thrashing for half a minute; I focused the binoculars on them and zoomed the viewfinders in tight. The nude guy was squirming on the ground, holding his genitals as the fisherman rose to his feet.

A glint of sunlight flashed in my eyepiece, and I saw a gun, something like a chrome-plated pistol, in the hand of the fisherman. The nude guy was on his knees now, trying to stand up. The intruder stood over the fellow without clothes and pointed the gun at his temple. In slow motion the pistol erupted and the face in my viewfinder distorted, wobbling to the left, looking like a Viet Cong prisoner executed on a television news report years ago. Blood spewed out like a geyser from the man's head before he hit the ground.

I moved slowly backward and crawled deeper into the underbrush beside the waterfall. Until this moment, I'd made no sincere attempt to hide. Now all I wanted to do was evaporate, to slink into the wilderness and vanish like an echo in the wind. The need to report this assassination to the park rangers was now a driving force in me. The dead guy was slaughtered like an animal and didn't deserve his fate. He needed someone to tell his story. It was the same thing as the famous question, "If a tree falls in the woods and nobody is around, would it make a noise?" only with a murdered guy in the wilderness, but I'd heard his silent scream.

I hunkered down behind a small pine tree and peered back at the campsite, thanking God my clothes were in camouflage hues—a bush shirt in dark olive and mottled brown, along with tobacco-tricolored jungle pants with multiple pockets. My baseball cap was a speckled brown camouflage pattern. None of the colors would stand out at this distance, and I could carefully poke my head through the leaves and branches to look below.

The woman was still on the ground on her side, and the two fishermen were arguing. The murdered guy was sprawled out like a slaughtered chicken, head drenched in a pool of bright red blood. The men walked around in circles, talking, quarrelling, and gesticulating toward the lady. They looked crazed to me.

The fisherman who had done the shooting was tall, well over six feet. He had a bushy head of black hair, a full beard, and a swarthy complexion. Lean, muscular biceps popped out from beneath a dark blue T-shirt. A tattoo edged out under his right sleeve and down his forearm—a snake or something. He was in his mid-to-late thirties, and maybe a hundred eighty to two hundred pounds, about my weight. His partner looked to be about the same age but chunky, bordering on fat, with a shiny bald dome. He was much shorter than the shooter and had "Hard Rock Café" printed on the front of his yellow T-shirt.

The lady was somewhat younger, between twenty and thirty with long slender legs and shoulder-length blond hair. She was sitting up on the ground now, still naked, arms clasped around her thighs and shins. Her face was buried against her knees, and she was shaking—crying probably—and in shock if my hunch was right. Dammit, I wanted to help her, but I couldn't confront two villains without any weapons of my own. The best way to rescue her was to get to the rangers as fast as possible, tell them what happened, and let them deal with the killers. It didn't feel good to leave a person in such distress, but it might be the only way she would make it out of the park—if I could get to the authorities fast enough.

The tall guy grabbed the woman by her arm and pulled her to her feet and toward a tent, slapping her brutally on the head a couple times, and again on the buttocks as she stepped carefully over jagged rocks and tree limbs on the ground. Without shoes she couldn't move quickly, and the guy jerked and slapped her repeatedly. She finally fell, but he dragged her the last few feet toward one of the tents. He threw a flap open and pushed her in the shelter, but I couldn't see inside. The chubby guy went to a second tent and disappeared, but within a minute or two, he came out of his tent with a blue tarp, a small shovel, and two short pieces of rope.

He went to the corpse and kicked it several times, then shook the tarpaulin and laid it out. With the shovel, he scooped the blood-soaked dirt around the dead guy's head and tossed it on the tarp. Then he rolled the figure inside, tying the sheet at both ends with the ropes. Although it hit me as a grisly thought, the shape looked like a giant piece of saltwater taffy in a candy wrapper—the poor bastard. When the fat guy finished, he left the tarp on the ground and went back inside his tent. Nobody came out.

After ten more minutes I took a chance and scrambled to the top of the waterfall where the path was, entertaining the idea of going down with my canoe, paddling quietly past their camp and hightailing it back to my own campsite. If I could sneak by them, getting some help would be possible. But if they saw me, they might try to shoot me with the pistol. Or if they wanted to confront me, it would be difficult to outrun them on the water. I had to assume they had a canoe—how else would they have reached the Brent Lake campsite? Two people are usually able to paddle a canoe much faster than one person alone.

I made myself calm down, took deep breaths, and concentrated on what I did know—my precise location at the top of the small waterfall on the north side of Brent Lake. Below me, several hundred feet away, was the occupied campsite. One key fact in my favor was that the killers didn't realize I was up here and had seen the murder.

The terrain around here was familiar enough to me, so escape was possible after plotting a course to safety. The park rangers could do their duty after I reported the crime, and save the woman if they could get to her quickly.

My watch read 2:31 p.m. I had planned to be back in my camp by 4 p.m. Nightfall in Quetico Provincial Park didn't happen until around 9 p.m. at this time of year, late June, so my friends would probably come looking for me if I didn't make it back at the appointed time. I needed to get moving now to make my arrival time. Our group had a standing order—if you got lost or injured, you stayed put until help arrived. Period. But one standing order had already been broken today—going out alone. You were never supposed to do that, but since I wasn't going far from camp and had insisted on leaving by myself and my three buddies knew exactly where the little lake was located, they had relented. The other guy traveling in my canoe, Chuck Renfro, had suffered cramps in his calves this morning after some grueling portages through the park yesterday and wanted to rest and fish near our campsite. So much for standing orders.

Knowing my camping buddies would come looking for me for sure, my biggest worry was their safety. They knew my plans, and I didn't want them to run into these assassins and get executed. I had to prevent that no matter what. No firearms are allowed in Quetico, and I certainly didn't have any. But the killers did—at least one. No telling if they'd brought more.

Another twenty minutes passed. The camp below was still and I studied the track up the incline I had used this morning. After attaching a long rope to my canoe's bow hook, I had climbed up the waterfall, wound the rope around a tree, and hoisted it to this upper lake. The path the canoe had made in the grass as it slid through the brush and weeds was barely visible. The rope was still attached to the bow hook, and I entertained the thought of lowering the craft down. I would have to take care not to hit a rock. Aluminum canoes sound like bass drums when you hit rocks. I tried desperately to find the courage to make an attempt to slip past the killers, but finally decided it wasn't an option. It would require a different route to evade them.

I pulled out a map from my trousers pocket and opened it up. The Boundary Waters Canoe Area (BWCA) is in northern Minnesota, and it adjoins Quetico along the US-Canadian border. Between the parks there are over two thousand lakes, most of which are accessible, but only by canoe since motorized boats are restricted to a few select lakes. The parks are isolated and intended to be that way, dedicated to rugged campers and fishermen who paddle into the wilderness with just canoes and backpacks in search of beauty and solitude. And there is an endless bounty of both, splendor in the majestic bald eagles flying overhead, thought-provoking miles of unbroken shoreline where no human foot has trod, and countless streams and rivers that burble over rocks unscathed by anything but the Ice Age. It is nature at its purest. The parks are unspoiled, untamed, and unforgiving. But for me and many of the campers lucky enough to be awarded an access permit into Quetico each season, fishing is the temptation that entices people to forgo the conveniences of the modern world. Pike, bass, walleyes, and lake trout abound in the pristine waters, so plentiful in places that any lure cast near them will evoke bone-jarring strikes. It *is* paradise to those who love freshwater fishing.

This was my fortieth birthday celebration trip. My best friend had planned our camping and fishing excursion months ago, back in January. *Great way to commemorate the big four-oh and get you to forget the tragic death of your wife.* It had worked so far, until I witnessed the gruesome murder of a naked guy and the abduction of his spouse or girlfriend. What were the odds of seeing that? I was almost in the center of the two-million-acre (or thirty-five-hundred-square mile) joint preserve, and the probability of even encountering other campers, let alone witnessing a slaying, had to be less than getting struck by lightning. What horrible luck.

I reconfirmed my position on the map. It was miles in any direction to an exit point—those designated areas where roads touched the perimeter of the parks and cars could be left, or where outfitters who arranged camping equipment and supplies had pick-up points or commercial lodges for their customers. My partners and I had used an outfitter, Bill Pec of Ely, Minnesota. His base camp and lodge were situated on Lake Lac La Croix, over twenty miles away. In my opinion, it might as well have been on the moon for how long it took to travel that distance in this rugged terrain.

Lac La Croix and a few other lakes are authorized for motorized vehicle use—boats with outboard engines that dropped campers off with their equipment and canoes at remote points and returned at a designated time to pick them up when the trip was over. After being dropped off on Monday, June 24, and checking in at the Canadian ranger station on Lac La Croix, it had taken us two days to reach our campsite on Brent Lake. We had ten and a half days left until a Pec employee was to meet our group at an outbound rendezvous point near Minn Lake.

A clanging noise rose from below, like a pot or a pan being dropped on a rock. I searched diligently with the binoculars, scanning the grounds and the waters nearby, but nobody was visible near the firepit, the tents, or anywhere else.

The one thought that continually plagued me was, *I've got to get away from here and warn my friends before they come looking for me.* The killers might shoot them if they came searching around. I should have bolted down the waterfall after seeing the lovers resting in the hammock. I could have offered an apology for interrupting them and been politely on my way. Instead, I'd gotten myself stranded on the waterfall, with killers below, and no easy route back to safety.

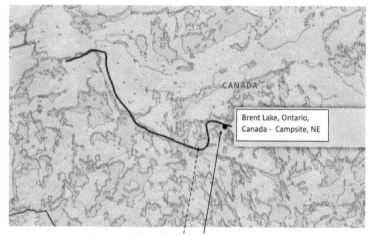

Brent Lake, Ontario,
Canada - Campsite, NE

- Map services and data available from U.S. Geological Survey, National Geospatial Program."...

Map 3 - The area of Quetico Provincial Park on Brent Lake where Roger and his friends intended to camp and fish during their trip into Canada (highlighted by the arrow.) The dashed arrow shows where Roger and his team did camp.

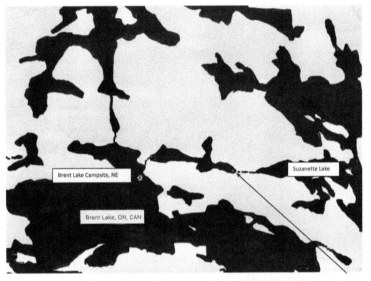

- Map services and data available from U.S. Geological Survey, National Geospatial Program."...

Map 4 - A view of the Northeast campsite at Brent Lake (marked with an X) and The Little Lake (unnamed on Park maps) and a portage between it and Suzanette Lake.

CHAPTER TWO

After observing the campsite for half an hour, my eyes were weary, and I pulled the viewfinders away and rubbed my eyelids. I never saw anyone the entire time, but the noises continued. They were there.

I reconsidered my escape plan while looking at my map. It was easy to see I was at least ten miles from the most heavily traveled section of the park—Crooked Lake. The BWCA and Quetico are crisscrossed with countless lakes, streams, and rivers, but a few large lakes dominate the landscape and are used as main routes by people heading into and out of various sections of the preserves. I was literally out in the middle of nowhere. But that's why my team had come up here.

The small lake I had been fishing was not technically part of Brent Lake, but an unnamed offshoot that was trapped above a rock cliff and a waterfall about fifty feet high. Huge sections of Quetico are so remote that human beings never christened them with titles. It's the same with about half the tiny streams and lakes in the park.

It was impossible to call my camping buddies or the park

rangers. Cell phones didn't work in this section of the park. Coverage was spotty at best anywhere up here, but once you got into the Canadian side—and in the middle of the area no less—there was no signal at all. A few cell phone towers were scattered around the edges of the park, mostly on the US side, but there weren't many of those. I didn't even have my personal cell phone, which I had intentionally left in my main equipment bag back at camp, to recharge for taking photographs. But if the phone had been with me, it might have been possible to record the murder or take photos of the aftermath. In a word, there would have been some proof of what I had witnessed. Stupid me.

Our outfitter had offered us a GPS device that was capable of sending out an SOS in case of emergency. The unit even allowed a person to text a message to someone at a specific time, like once a day at 6 p.m. There had been massive technical improvements in communications since my buddies and I first started our journeys into the parks in the nineties, and even though we debated it for an hour—because we are old hardheads—we declined any new devices. "We can read maps," my partners said. "We're not taking any of this high-tech horseshit with us. We're having two weeks of uninterrupted nature, with no screens, no messages, and no phone calls." It had sounded good at the time, but I'd have given anything to have a cell phone or emergency GPS with me now. Help could have been on the way at this very moment. How could we have been so foolish?

A scream from below broke the silence. The two men began shouting at each other, yelling and cursing, using words I couldn't understand from this distance, but they sounded really pissed off.

With them still in the campsite, there was no choice but for me to consider making my escape across the small lake I'd been fishing and on through a stream to my east and into Lake Suzanette. It would be the long way back to my campsite, and I guessed the stream might actually be turning into a bog, and be impassable. I had never tried to use the route, but knew biological change from a crystal-clear Canadian Shield lake into a putrefied swampy bog is a normal event in the evolution of northern waters. It usually took thousands of years, but if beavers took up residence and blocked the flow of water it could happen in decades, not millennia. I saw one of the furry rodents swimming near my canoe earlier in the day.

Below me, the yelling had definitely ended. The place looked deserted, but they were either out of view or in their tents. *What had these guys argued about? And where were they now?*

Since my canoe was behind me and still in the water, I knew it couldn't be seen from the lower campsite. I pushed it into the little lake and paddled east along the southern shore for about five hundred meters. As I suspected, beaver dams choked the waterflow as it entered the east end of the lake. Piles of rotting tree limbs blocked my path. It could take hours to get through. What if the villains came up here with a pair of binoculars while I was struggling in the bog? I'd be in plain view from the top of the precipice. I turned the canoe around and paddled halfway back to the cascade.

Returning to my observation point at the waterfall, I studied the campsite carefully, using the binoculars. I remembered it well from previous stays there. It's one of the most beautiful in the entire park, situated on a tiny island made mostly of rock and surrounded by dense brush. And it was high over the water, offering a place to dive fifteen feet down if you wanted to swim. From my vantage point, I could only see half of it: part of the firepit, some of the logs arranged as seats, and about half of the backs of both tents. The one bad thing was the canoe landing for this site was directly south of the main area, hidden by pine trees, so it couldn't be seen from my position on the waterfall.

Without warning the trio came out of the tents. The woman was dressed in jeans and a dark long-sleeved shirt now, her hair pulled back in a ponytail. The tall guy led her to the firepit and pointed at a log fashioned into a seat. It was hard to tell, but her wrists appeared to be bound in front of her. At least she was still alive and hadn't been murdered in one of the tents. It was something to feel good about.

While the woman sat on the log, the men went to the body and pulled it along the ground, sliding it toward the canoe landing. They struggled but finally lifted it, each one holding an end. They carried it down the hill to the south, out of view. I hoped they were heading out and moving across the lake away from me. But in a few minutes they reappeared. The lanky man went to a tent, ducked inside, and came out holding two shovels. He went to the firepit and spoke to the lady. It looked like she was crying.

The campsite had been vacant when I passed by before mid-morning. *So who was the dead guy?* Was he some poor fellow with his wife who'd been attacked by two rogues? Or was he a member of this party, or somebody else who had stumbled upon the campsite, like me? No. I found it hard to believe a woman would make love to a stranger who appeared out of nowhere. The dead guy was either an unfortunate stranger camping with his wife or girlfriend, or someone in the killer's party. Either way, he was finished.

A loon called out. Its melancholy tune echoing across the lake was an eerie, cheerless, and isolated sound. Normally the noise was enthralling, but now it chilled me, making me realize how alone I was, completely stranded, with no way to warn my friends who might come to this campsite at any second. *What would the tall guy do if he accidentally spotted them?*

I steadied the binoculars, hoping that question would never be answered. I watched as the lanky guy talked with the woman before he disappeared with her into a tent. When he came out, she wasn't with him. He and the chubby one talked near the firepit. They picked up the shovels and walked toward the south end of the camp and vanished over the hill. They were going to bury the body.

I watched desperately for several minutes, wishing their canoe would appear beyond the outcrop, heading south, or east, or anywhere but toward this little lake. But when they reappeared, they had spun north, heading toward the waterfall and me. My mouth filled with cotton balls. I crawled along the ground into heavier brush and started moving toward my canoe. It was about three hundred meters from the precipice to its hiding spot. My heart was pounding, and my ears were ringing with the incessant thumping of my own pulse. I didn't want them to know I was up here. I rose into a crouch and scurried along a mat of pine needles and twigs, branches whipping my face. *What if they came up the waterfall and saw my sunglasses in the grass?*

At my canoe, I lay down in the brush and trained my binoculars on the precipice. Only a portion of it was in view, much of it obscured by tree limbs and weeds. It took an eternity, but finally the tall guy emerged from below. He stood on the waterfall, surveying the small lake. Thank God I hadn't tried to traverse through the swamp a few minutes ago—I might be slogging through the muck in clear view. He looked around the shoreline, then down at his feet. All my trampling around may have left mushy tracks, and the canoe could've left a wide swath in the weeds and brush. The tall one studied the bushes and ground for a minute, but never came in my direction.

Finally, he turned away and went back down the slope. Minutes later he and his partner returned to the top, carrying the tarp. They struggled, nearly dropping it into the waterfall before heading off into the woods on the far side of the lake, away from me.

I almost lost sight of them in the undergrowth, but they didn't go far from the precipice, and the chubby guy's yellow T-shirt was partly visible through the branches and leaves. Shortly, sounds of digging and scraping hit my ears, and I knew what they were doing—burying the body. Unfortunately for me, every ten or twenty minutes the tall guy came back to the top of the falls and looked around, checking the little lake as well as Brent Lake below. It kept me rooted in place.

They worked in the thicket for nearly two hours as I held my position, figuring they'd see me if I tried to slip down the incline. I had no plans of letting them know I was up here, and certainly had no way to confront them without a weapon. I was just praying they'd leave their campsite when the burial was complete.

Without warning, a paddle clanged against a canoe nearby. My temples throbbed as I strained to look back into Brent Lake, but the afternoon sun was in my face, causing me to squint. The foliage around me masked the water below. *Who was in the canoe? Could it be my friends, the woman, or somebody else?* I started inching toward the falls, crawling on my belly until some of the lake below was in view. But there was no canoe anywhere. The brush shook and the tall man's head almost poked out of the branches, but he didn't step out into the clearing on top. "What's up?" he yelled, looking below.

"Looking for a friend," came the reply. It was my camping partner, Duke Johansen. A retired shipping company executive, he lived in my neighborhood in Atlanta. It was his idea to plan our celebration trip. *God, Duke, the guy's got a gun. Don't come up here.* "See anybody up there?" Duke yelled.

"No. Been fishing here all day. Nobody up here but us."

"When did you go up there?" shouted another voice from below. It was my other partner, Larry Wadkins, who lived in St. Louis. He'd joined us in Minneapolis for the trip.

"After breakfast," the tall man lied. "We're camped over there, behind you. I saw a canoe pass out in the lake, headed east, couple hours ago. Along the far shoreline."

"How many in the canoe?" Duke asked.

"Couldn't tell. Looked like one, but there could have been another. It was a long way off. Why?"

"Our friend was supposed to be fishing in this lake above the falls today. He's missing."

The tall one spun around and glared at the lake. He looked closely along the far shoreline, then down at his feet. His eyes tracked toward me. "There's some animal tracks up here, but I haven't seen anyone since we got here other than the canoe across the lake. That was probably him." He answered in a way that said he didn't want to talk anymore. He stepped further back into the leafy cover. I wasn't sure Duke would buy his story.

"You say it looks like somebody was up there?" Duke yelled.

"Not really, no footprints, just some tracks and shit in the trail, probably a moose or a deer."

I realized the tall guy was throwing them off, on purpose. He had no way of knowing if I was up here or not, but he didn't want my buddies coming up and snooping around and possibly seeing the body. I didn't want that either, and was ready to stand up and yell if Duke decided to come up to the precipice and look around for himself. Suddenly the tall one cried out, "What's the guy's name?"

"Roger. Roger Cummings," Duke responded.

"Hold on a sec." The tall guy walked away from the top, out of site. "HEY, ROGER, YOU UP HERE? ROGER, ROGER CUMMINGS, ARE YOU UP HERE?" The words reverberated around the lake. The voice was louder than a bullhorn, but my ears were so alive a whisper would have sounded the same. He screamed my name a couple more times.

"Nothing, buddy," the guy yelled down to Duke.

"Thanks, man." Duke hollered back. "By the way, we're staying over to the west on Brent at another campsite on this lake, couple miles away. If Roger comes by, tell him we're paddling back there."

"Yeah, I'll do that," the tall man said. After a second, he asked, "Hey, what's he look like?"

Duke shouted back. "He's forty, in pretty good shape, maybe a hundred eighty pounds, six feet tall, red-blond hair, fair skin."

"I'll keep an eye out for him."

I bet he would.

"Thanks," Duke yelled.

Shit. Now the guy knew where we were staying and what I looked like. He even learned my full name. But he only had a suspicion I was nearby, based upon the comments of my pals, so my description and name wasn't worth much, unless he suspected I had witnessed the murder.

Paddles clanged against the canoe in the lake below; they sounded closer than before. My heart pounded while I prayed Duke and Larry were turning around, not deciding to land and come up the waterfall and look around themselves. Although it sounded like they were satisfied and leaving after the discussion, you never knew with Duke; he could be extremely headstrong and was prone to making rash decisions. But there was an unwritten rule in the BWCA and Quetico: you could talk to people when you saw them in the bush, but it was verboten to paddle up and land at a campsite or fishing spot when others were there—a curious courtesy everyone obeyed. My partners knew this. Most people stopped their canoes in the water when they encountered others, chatted, and paddled on their way. I suspected my pals hadn't landed at the fishermen's campsite, just as I guessed the lady had been killed, or tied up, or somehow incapacitated in the tent. She would have been screaming at my friends if she could. But who knew?

My binoculars confirmed Duke and Larry were making their way back into the main channel of Brent Lake. They didn't stop at the campsite below. It was almost 7 p.m. and they wanted to be back before dark. They would hope I had fished somewhere else, then moved on, and maybe circled around the south side of the lake where they couldn't see me. Thank God they hadn't come ashore.

A loud curse reached my ears. I'd lost track of the fishermen, but within seconds I realized they were traversing down the waterfall, back to their canoe. One of them let out a nasty yell. Must have slipped. I prayed he hadn't fallen on my sunglasses—that'd be a sure giveaway. I snuck through the brush to get a clearer view. They were at the bottom, pulling their craft into the water and jumping aboard before paddling back toward their campsite.

When the men popped into view above the canoe landing, they were running. The tall man raced to one tent, tore open the flap, and then raced to the other. He ripped that flap away, then kicked at the second one. The chubby guy ran to his side, and they flung their arms around wildly. My bet was the woman was gone. They ran back toward the landing and out of view, and their canoe was not visible out on the lake. They could be anywhere. I watched for two hours until darkness enveloped me. *Where had these guys gone? Could Duke have spotted the lady in the campsite and taken her with him? Or could he have run into her out on the lake and helped her reach our campsite?* If he had, the killers might be after them now, and my friends could already be dead.

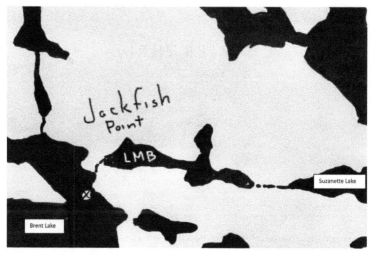

- Map services and data available from U.S. Geological Survey, National Geospatial Program."...

Map 5 - The Little Lake (unnamed on park maps) above the waterfall and a landmass called Jackfish Point written by Roger on his maps. The small waterfall is noted between The Little Lake and Brent Lake. LMB means Largemouth Bass as written by Roger to indicate they are found in The Little Lake.

CHAPTER THREE

I lay near my canoe and tried to rest, but it was impossible since my buddies might be in serious trouble and could be facing two killers in the dark. While hiding in the underbrush with a pounding heart and a head full of questions, it wasn't easy to think of my situation as safe. *Hidden* might be a better choice.

Through the binoculars I looked in the direction of the campsite. There wasn't a speck of light coming through the forest. Not so much as a flicker from a cigarette lighter, a beam from a flashlight, and certainly no fire in the pit. It would have been noticeable from a mile away, and there was no sound. The place seemed abandoned.

How many people had been in the campsite below? There were three for certain. I reminded myself there had been four. Transporting four campers and enough supplies for them wasn't possible in only one canoe. There were some versions large enough, like nineteen footers, that could handle three people and their gear. But the people today—either from one group or two—had started out with four folks, so there had to be a second canoe. Maybe the lady had paddled off while the fishermen buried the body? From the waterfall you couldn't see the landing, so she could have slipped away. It made sense, judging by the reactions of the fishermen when they returned from burying the naked man. But my buddy Duke hadn't mentioned seeing anyone when he talked with the tall guy.

A million scenarios flashed through my head. *What if the lady had escaped, and the tall guy caught her out on the lake and killed her?* Then he'd disappear and I would probably never see him again. But what if he couldn't find her? He might come back to the camp and wait out the night. What if the woman had paddled west and found Duke, Larry, and Chuck? Or what if she hadn't escaped and was dead in her tent? There were so many *what ifs.* I knew nothing. . . just had guesses.

What facts were real and important? For one, the tall killer had certainly tried to keep his identity hidden from Duke and Larry. He had prudently remained concealed when they talked at the waterfall, and to me, that meant he was planning on fleeing. He probably guessed it would be impossible to positively identify him, and the BWCA and Quetico were so vast, discovery of the body would be a long shot. The odds of somebody stumbling upon the corpse up here had to be infinitesimal. If I hadn't seen the shooting and known approximately where the body was buried, it was conceivable the naked guy wouldn't be found and his disappearance never explained.

My other concern was the murderer had seemed irritated that two people had appeared in the lake and seen him at the waterfall. He was rather brusque in his discussion with Duke and Larry. If a search for the naked man was conducted, somebody might listen to Duke's account of their meeting, and check out the top of the waterfall. And since Duke had told the tall guy where he was camped, that meant my buddies were at risk.

The one thing I was certain about there were only two witnesses. The chubby guy didn't count, since he was in this almost as deep as the shooter. That left me and the lady. The tall guy didn't know I'd seen anything, but he had reason to worry about the woman. *He'd have to do something about her.* And my guess was she had escaped—big problem for the tall guy, but one for my friends too. What if she paddled off and found them? They'd take her in, undoubtedly. If she talked about the murder, Duke would break camp and bolt to a ranger station in a heartbeat. He was an excellent outdoorsman and was capable of navigating in the dark. He was also clever enough to know that if the woman had escaped from a killer, the bad guy probably wouldn't be far behind. Without weapons to protect himself, he'd be on his way to a ranger station one second after she opened her mouth and told him. *What if she didn't?* I tried not to imagine it. But no matter what, my job was to stay alive, evade these monsters, and get back to my buddies before someone else got massacred.

To keep from losing my focus, I inventoried my canoe. Inside was a canteen, a bottle of iodine tablets, a small tackle box, a fly-fishing vest, two spinning rods, two life vests, two paddles, and a backpack loaded with my maps, a pencil, a heavy-duty flashlight, an extra pair of sunglasses, and two Baby Ruth candy bars. Laying on the floor was a spare T-shirt, along with an extra pair of heavy-duty socks. Next to them was a hundred-foot length of rope with an attachment you could affix to a canoe bow hook. In my pants pocket was the ultimate Swiss Army knife—every device and tool offered. On my wrist was a plastic watch, one with a host of buttons for different functions and a face that glowed in the dark. I pushed a button on the side, and the watch faintly illuminated. It was 9:53 p.m., Wednesday, June 26. My sparse assemblage of gear wasn't much to defend myself with, or to survive in the woods for a long period of time. Still, it gave me the ability to drink potable water, catch some food, and find my way to safety.

Visions of my son and daughter danced in my eyes. They were the epicenter of my life, at home in Atlanta. Forcing them from my thoughts all afternoon had worked in the daylight, but now in the darkness, the need to get back to them was overwhelming. My kids, the twins, had already lost one parent. I couldn't allow them to lose a second. Ricky and Crystal were not really kids anymore, since they had graduated from high school this past spring. I recalled us standing together at their graduation party, arm in arm, drinking root beers. Ricky was my pal. . . my buddy. . . my comrade. Crystal was more aloof, but she garnered a special place in my heart after the death of her mother. Although she had a perpetual scowl on her face since the passing of my wife, Sherry, she told me she did not blame anyone anymore.

My predicament with the killers kept forcing its way back into my thoughts, overshadowing concerns about Ricky and Crystal. The immediate problem was my partners, their safety, and my need to reach them. Now, the tall guy knew where they were camped. Duke and Larry would have searched for me until an hour before darkness prior returning to their tents. If my pals had accidently run into the killers (who could be hunting for the lady), they might have been shot and may well be dead already. It was a grisly thought.

A snorting noise startled me. I tried to get an accurate bearing on the noise, but sound is elusive at night, and it was hard to pin down. It was coming from across the small lake, not nearby—a black bear. There were plenty of them in the parks. They're notorious scavengers and can smell rotting garbage miles away. If the naked guy hadn't been buried at least six feet deep, the beasts might be digging him up already.

More snorts came from across the lake. Damn. If wild creatures were rooting around over there, they might uncover the body in no time, and it wouldn't remain intact for long. In a day or two, it could be stripped to the bone and strewn all over the forest floor. The thought of a mangled corpse a little over two hundred meters away was chilling, but so was the thought of black bears so close. Few outdoorsmen consider them dangerous, except a sow with cubs, but they can be scary. I've had run-ins with them before. Normally, the animals are not very aggressive, and making a racket by slamming pots and pans together will chase them off. But they are persistent bastards and will return if they think food is at hand, like giant rodents, annoying pests who will raid camp supplies if you are not careful. Seasoned campers know that once the creatures get interested in an area, a family of them might linger around a specific campsite for the whole season. The park rangers and equipment outfitters are always quick to inform inbound campers of this fact. When my buddies and I had come into the park three days ago, our outfitter had mentioned that there was a bear problem around Argo Lake. That wasn't far from here. The beasts had been scaring campers since late May. Nobody wanted to run into a four-hundred-pound monster in the dark, and I wished I'd chosen Hawaii for my fortieth birthday celebration.

Weariness was tugging at my eyelids, pulling at them with a relentless urge. I had to sleep. For me, rest was one thing and sleep another. To make it through the day tomorrow would take real energy from a couple of hours of slumber. I lay on my back and gazed at the cloudless, star-dotted sky above the little lake. There are no big city lights within a hundred miles of the parks and the sky gets as black as space. Millions of stars bunched together like strands of miniature pearls blinked and pulsed. The Milky Way appeared so close you could almost touch it with your fingertips. I started to doze, caught in that state between sane sleep and insane thoughts. Visions of my son and daughter reappeared as I thought about them attending college in the fall. They were about to leave and start a life of their own, and I had to be there to support them—couldn't get caught by these killers. After the death my wife, I thought life couldn't get any worse. Now I wasn't so certain.

A snapping branch awoke me. It was loud, and close by. My heart pounded so hard my ribs throbbed. I rolled over, searching the darkness beyond. *Crack.* It happened again, ten or twenty feet away. I pulled my buttocks tight, trying not to soil myself. *What was out there?*

In the distance, well beyond the noise, was a flicker. It was a fire in the fishermen's campsite. I tried not to focus on the glittering flames. A faint smell smacked my nostrils, not smoke, but I couldn't classify the odor. Something was close. I thrust my face near to the ground, scanning left and right above me, trying to catch a shadow. Beside me, less than ten feet away, a silhouette moved.

I didn't dare budge or breathe for a minute. My breath was stagnant before I started sipping miniscule sips of air through my lips. Then the silhouette moved again. *Crash.*

The rasps of crickets and locusts or whatever makes those god-awful sounds at night filled the sky. Between the fusillade of chirps, weeping sounds poked through: low, deep weeps, like a wounded animal. To my front was a shape. My eyes registered it before my mind could. Then the shape came straight at me.

A foot stepped within inches of my face. Out of fear I snared an ankle and began wrestling the creature to the ground, tackling it as my arms involuntarily grabbed a calf, then a thigh, then an arm, and finally a torso. I aimed for the head, pulling with all my might, hauling the body down as my hands sought out a mouth. A yelp started, not loud, but gaining in volume as I covered it in a wrestling hold, squeezing a face, and finally a mouth. It was a warm mouth, a soft mouth, and it trembled. In the darkness was a woman in my grip, sobbing so hard we both shook. I held her tightly, suffocating her cries. We lay on the ground for what felt like hours.

"Who are you?" I finally hissed, releasing my death grip.

"Janeene," came a soft reply. "Please don't kill me." She was limp in my arms—a rag doll with no muscles or bones. She passed out for a minute as I clung to her like an angry bobcat. Slowly, her eyes blinked, the whites visible through the darkness.

"Are you the woman from the camp below?"

"Y... y... yes. How did you know?"

"I saw you today, in the hammock, before the murder."

Warm tears streaked my fingers, and I knew she was crying before I heard it. She sobbed in my hand, lips trembling against my palm. "You saw the shooting?" she finally mumbled.

"Unfortunately. One of the worst things I've ever witnessed."

She sobbed again, tears running over my fingers in a torrent. I slid my hand down to her chin. "Shouldn'ta done it," she said.

"Done what?"

"Made love with Bobby."

I waited for her to stop shaking. "Who is, er... was, Bobby? Your husband?"

"No, a friend of Hank's."

A friend of Hank's? "You all knew each other?"

"Yeah. We all came here together. I was... sort of Hank's girlfriend."

I thought about what I'd seen today in the campsite. Hank must have been the shooter, Bobby the naked guy who got killed. If this lady and Hank were a couple, he had a right to be mad about the hammock escapade, but it didn't give him grounds to execute the man.

The woman was breathing easier now. My pulse was still racing, but not pounding as it had been. I realized now that Duke and my buddies were not in danger, not tonight anyway. Glancing around, the blackness didn't seem as heavy as it had a few minutes ago, probably from my growing night vision and the realization I wasn't going to die at this moment. I looked more closely at her face. Her features were coming into focus— a delicate nose, an oval face, heavy, thick eyebrows and large eyes. I couldn't make out the color.

"Why did he kill him?"

"Because of me. Hank and Pete went fishing. They were supposed to be gone for a couple of hours, and I got stupid, and a little drunk, and egged Bobby on. I'd been flirting with him for weeks before we came here." She took a few deep breaths. "Hank told Bobby to leave me alone, but I seduced him, and we made love. We must have fallen asleep 'cause the next thing I knew, Hank was back, and the fight started." Her words were a soft whisper. "I shouldn't have done it."

"Nobody should have done what they did," I said, "me included."

"What'd you do?"

"Observed. . . saw everything. If I hadn't pulled my damned binoculars from their case, I wouldn't have witnessed you and your friend, and got myself stuck on the waterfall trying to be polite. I would have been heading toward my camp long before the asshole, the person you call Hank, shot the guy."

"Not *the* guy, or *a* guy, a person. . . Bobby. His name was Bobby." She sniffled again and stiffened in my arms. I let her be silent for a minute. Silence sometimes makes people talk more freely, always worked on me.

"No, it's me who's to blame," she said. "I lied to Hank about my feelings. We weren't real lovers. I'd been seeing him on and off for about six months and liked him, early on, but didn't love him. After the lottery, he wanted to get serious."

"Lottery?"

"Yeah. Hank won one of those *Fantasy Five* things. He got over eight hundred thousand dollars from it, after taxes, and we started seeing each other more often, a lot actually, and then he wanted to do this camping trip."

"Why camping?"

"To get away from all the people begging him for money— like his mother, brother, and his ex-wife. Since he won the money two months ago, the calls haven't stopped. Hank even quit his job at the plant. He said people were hitting him up for a loan all the time, even one of the VPs. Nobody can bother you up here." After a second, she added, "Wish to God he'd never won it. I was getting ready to leave him, then. . ." She settled down in my arms, body still limp. She was lying on her back, me crossways over her like a TV wrestler. I released my hold on her chin and mouth, but kept my arm wrapped around the back of her neck, just in case.

"Tell me about the other guy."

"Pete? Why?"

"Because he's teamed up with a killer. I'm planning on getting out of here and the more I know about him, the better."

"Pete's not a killer."

"Might as well be. He's Hank's partner."

She kept quiet after that remark. Finally, she said, "Pete's been Hank's friend since they were kids. They worked at the plant together, live pretty close to one another, and they've just been close friends. Hank took care of Pete at the plant. That's all I know."

"You said, *worked*. Did Pete quit his job too?"

"Yeah."

If both were out of a job, they could definitely be a team, the sort of team where one would help the other, no matter what. I'd seen evidence of that this afternoon. It wouldn't surprise me to learn they were planning on escaping together now—Hank and Pete on the run with a nice bankroll.

"What type of plant?"

"What do you mean?"

"Like what did it make? What kinda jobs did Hank and Pete have?"

"The plant makes fishing rods. . . special ones. Some sell for hundreds of dollars. They're called Magnums, and the name of the company is Magnum Fishing Rods."

"I know 'em, real high-tech gear."

She settled in my arms, seeming to think I'd been satisfied with the answer.

"What was Hank's job?"

"Does it matter? I told you he quit."

I was beginning to dislike this lady's attitude. "It matters because I need to understand the man. He killed your partner today, in cold blood, and I want to learn everything I can about the monster who might come looking for you."

She sniffled and moaned and after a brief cry looked directly at my face, although the color of her eyes was still hard to see. "Sorry, I'm tired and scared, and want to go home to my daughter." After a few seconds, she said, "He had a great job with the company, Manager of Engineering. . . been there since he graduated from college at Perdue. I don't know what he did at work, can't even guess. I'm an accountant, and work for a different company, so I don't know much about engineering stuff. Besides, he didn't talk much about his actual job, just how angry he was at being pestered for money at the plant."

I pondered her answer. Apparently, Hank was fairly well-educated, and so was she. "What did Pete do?"

"I only know this because they talked about it yesterday after supper as we sat around the campfire. Bored me to death. Pete was a rod maker or builder, I think they called it; anyway, he was the guy who made the fishing rods and got them ready for others to finish up."

"Finish up?"

"Yeah. Put on the things that the line passes through and the handles and all the other stuff."

I'm facing an engineer and a highly-skilled craftsman. They should both know a lot about tools, along with many other technical things. They might be tough adversaries, and I already knew they were cold-blooded, fully capable of killing, and probably desperate to eliminate evidence of their crime and escape no matter who got hurt.

"Did you see any other people today?"

"Like whom?"

"Like my friends, two guys in a canoe who came looking for me. They talked with Hank at the waterfall."

"Don't know what you're talking about."

I thought for a second. *Maybe she didn't? Or was lying? Perhaps I shouldn't trust her at all?* "I saw the tall guy, Hank I guess, pull you inside a tent after the fight. Then he and the chubby guy came up the waterfall and buried the naked guy. What happened to you? I never saw you come out of your tent."

"I did come out."

When? I replayed the events in my head, realizing there was no certainty about when all the things happened. I was getting groggy and tired, and probably confused like any eyewitness who saw something terrible. "Okay, now I remember, you were sitting outside by the firepit, with your hands tied. Right?"

"Yeah, they were. Hank. . . raped me in the tent, then tied my hands." She whimpered a little, then said, "Hank told me he'd say I killed Bobby. Shot him with a pistol." She started to whimper again.

"Go on."

"Then he told me to dress and go outside. Next thing I knew he ordered me back in the tent and tied me up again. This time he tied my mouth and feet as well. I waited there for a while, but was afraid he'd come in and rape me again or kill me. He's a violent bastard. I worked the knots loose and got free, and when I looked around, he and Pete were gone. I didn't know where they went, so I snuck down to the canoes. One was missing. I took the other and tried to get away. . . but, but I heard a paddle banging nearby."

"You couldn't tell where the noise came from? Like a canoe in the lake?"

"No, I couldn't see anything, and thought it might be Hank after me. I couldn't get far and was afraid he would catch me, so I pulled it up on the shore and hid. I heard some yelling, but it sounded far away. I almost got back in the canoe, but then started walking instead. Wanted to get as far away from that bastard as possible."

"How'd you end up here?"

"I don't know." She started sniffling. "Was lost. Then woods got dark, and about an hour ago a campfire lit up and I moved near it, but it was them. I could hear Hank talking and I just started moving the other way."

Walked in a giant circle, I thought. Not uncommon for somebody inexperienced at hiking in the woods at night. It was the best thing that could have happened to her, though. If she walked a straight line, say directly east, she might have perished before she found help. There were only a few official campsites on Brent Lake and most of them were west of her possible route. "When you left in the canoe, which way did you go, east or west?"

"I don't know."

"Let me rephrase that. When you were standing at the canoe landing looking out at the water, did you head to the left or the right?"

"To the left."

"East then. How far did you paddle?"

"Not far. . . I moved for maybe ten minutes when the yelling started. I was afraid they'd come after me. There was a little crack in the shoreline, like a stream or something, so I pulled the canoe up into it. There was a small pond nearby."

"Did you pull it far into the woods?"

"Yeah, tugged it up a tiny hill and hid it behind a tree. It's halfway to the pond; I also put some branches over it."

"I assume it's an aluminum canoe, right? Silver?"

"Like gray-silver, not shiny. Are there other kinds?"

"Yeah. Some are made of Kevlar and they're usually dark green. They're much harder to see in the brush. You think it's hidden well?"

"Did the best I could."

Now for the important question. "Think you can find it again?"

She looked at me. I still couldn't see the color of her eyes. "From the water, maybe, not from the woods, though."

I had a rough idea where her canoe was. From studying the maps all afternoon, I'd memorized the terrain for about a thousand meters in all directions. Southeast of the fishermen's campsite was another little lake, like the one I fished today, but it was truly landlocked. There was no exit into Brent Lake. It sounded like she pulled her craft near that spot. I didn't want to yank my flashlight out and check the map, especially if that was Hank and Pete down there by the fire, like she said.

"When did your group come into the park?" I asked.

"Five days ago. We were supposed to stay for another week."

"Just the four of you?"

"Yes."

"Where are you from?"

"Around Minneapolis. I live in Chanhassen, Hank and Pete live near Minnetonka. Bobby lives downtown. I'm not exactly sure where."

I didn't correct her and remind her that Bobby had moved. Permanently. "So, nobody would be expecting you home for another six or seven days?"

She nodded but didn't answer. I quit asking questions, thinking about her replies. My party wasn't due back for a long time either, more than a week. This wasn't good. Nobody would have reason to search for either group now except Duke, Larry, and Chuck. But they would probably give me another twenty-four hours or so to show up before they headed to a ranger station, and the trip out would take them a day at least, moving quickly. The rangers might take a long time to get back here. The woman and I would have to survive for half a week at least before help might come. The only thing that could alter that would be if Duke and Larry flagged some other campers heading out and reported me missing. There was a high probability that might happen. Although the parks were remote, people were up here, coming and going across the lakes as their schedules dictated, just not many in Brent Lake. But even if a party was heading back, it still might take more than forty-eight hours to notify the rangers, and the forest service was not known for reacting with lightning speed to missing people in the BWCA or Quetico. It happened all the time. We were looking at a minimum of half a week to a week in hiding, with exceptional luck.

I slipped my arm out from behind her back and propped myself up on my elbow, facing her close enough to knock her out if need be; didn't know for certain where her loyalties lay.

"Sorry I attacked you."

"I'm sorry you *had* to attack me," she returned. "This whole thing is my fault."

I really couldn't disagree with her. I'd never been around people who could be sleeping with one person in the morning, and another in the afternoon. It didn't make sense to me. Then again, in my corporate days I'd worked with people dedicated to work, honesty, and family. Or so I thought, until it became apparent more than a few of my former coworkers would screw somebody in an instant, in the literal or figurative way. Morality was a perception of the holder and mine was no more righteous than the next person's.

"Don't want you to think I'm a slut puppy," she said, like she was reading my mind. "Normally I'm only with one guy at a time, and they're usually much better people than Hank. I should have left him long ago." She paused, almost in tears. "That was wrong today, with Bobby, and I got him killed. It was stupid and selfish, but I don't want to die for it."

"You're not going to die."

"Promise? I have a six-year-old daughter and need to get back to her." She leaned up on her elbow, putting her face within a foot of mine. "I'll do anything you say."

"Good." I sat up into a cross-legged position. "You can start by telling me more about Hank and the chubby guy."

"What else do you want to know?"

"Have they got more guns than that pistol I saw today?"

"Yeah. Some handguns and three rifles."

"Rifles? How they get them past the rangers? They're supposed to check for things like that."

"Hank said they wouldn't check. They asked some questions, looked over our camping gear, but didn't open anything up. We packed them in the sleeping bags. Hank brought rifles you can break in half; calls them Dakotas. He gets a laugh out of that—same name as his pickup truck."

Some manufacturers like Dakota and Sauer made rifles that had detachable forearms to reduce the length of the stock, in classic takedown fashion. She let out a long sigh and rolled over on her side and pulled something from behind her back. "I took a pistol with me." She brandished a dark shape in her left hand, and I almost passed out.

"Shit, you could have killed me." I never thought to frisk her, guessing she was too puny to try anything against me.

"I don't want to hurt you. You're the only real chance I have to get home and back to my daughter." She offered me the weapon. "Here, you take it."

CHAPTER FOUR

I was too tired to move anywhere, so we stayed in place for the night. Janeene was asleep ten minutes after she petrified me with the gun, a Ruger semi-automatic .45-caliber pistol. Because it was dull black in color, it would not reflect sunlight as the gun that killed Bobby had. Not being chrome plated was a godsend, but it was a blessing with just two bullets in the clip.

The campfire in the distance was dwindling as I scanned the scene many times. Once or twice a person passed through my line of sight and seeing the silhouettes gave me reassurance. I knew their location, and they didn't know mine or that I was watching them. And because they were back in the camp, I suspected they hadn't murdered my friends; they'd be long gone if they had. For some reason they felt safe for the night. I didn't understand why, but my one worry was that they might have found Janeene's canoe, figured she hadn't gone far, and were going to track her in the morning. That was a bother. But I'd run so many scenarios through my head it was impossible to deal with them anymore. It was satisfying enough to have a fix on the fishermen. Now there was time to make a plan.

I slept soundly until 5:30 a.m. A squirrel rustled in the bushes and awoke me.

In the binoculars a thin trail of smoke was rising from the campsite firepit toward the treetops. The air hung limp, as still as a morning meadow. I tapped Janeene on the shoulder. "We've got to get moving. I want to try and get into Lake Suzanette again." She nodded and sat up without speaking. In the twilight, I got a better look at her face. The left side was badly bruised, like a boxer's after losing a fight. Swollen, bluish lumps almost poked through her skin and she had the puffy eyelids that people have after sleeping in the open woods. Still, she was pretty. Hazel-green eyes peered at me, perched above a thin, aquiline nose and thick, full lips, all set in an oval face. Her eyes were large, slightly almond-shaped, reminding me of a newborn colt. Streaks of dirt smeared her face like misplaced mascara. Her dark green shirt was rumpled and open; beneath it a matching halter-top garment. Her blond hair was pulled into a tight ponytail. She looked wonderful, mostly because she was alive and I was not alone.

We moved to my hidden canoe and put the things I had taken back inside. We pushed it from the bushes into the water, but didn't launch it, and I went and looked at the campsite again. Nothing moved. I directed Janeene into the front seat, took my place in the back and shoved off with a paddle. In twenty minutes, we were moving in the creek toward Lake Suzanette. We were not actually in a stream, but a swamp, and we soon lodged against a rotting tree stump. I pushed against it fiercely, trying to gain enough resistance to propel us forward. We moved a foot or two, but it was slow going. Beavers had built enormous dams at the mouth of the swamp. Logs were poking out in all directions, packed with mud where they had been pasted together. Every few feet there was a break in the logjam—a crevasse of water where I could dip the paddle straight down trying to find the bottom. In places it was deep, over my head. No way we could get out and walk and push the canoe through. Moving across this bog would take days. It was impossible to step out of the canoe and onto the logs. They were floating, not secured to anything. A canoe is not stable to begin with and, perched on floating logs or clumps of swamp grass, it's tantamount to a circus high-wire act. "This isn't working," I said. "We'll capsize. Let's back up and head over to the shoreline."

Paddling us out of the bog, we landed near where we started and pulled the canoe into the brush and sat on the ground. "Dammit" I said, "we're going to have to carry it on our shoulders to get through the portage."

"Okay."

Okay? She had no idea what that meant. Between most lakes in the park there were portages: trails that led from one lake to another. They were clearly marked on the maps, and campers used them like roads to carry all their gear back and forth. In the Canadian park, the portages were more rugged than in the American area since fewer people used them, but most were passable. They might have steep sections or be so overgrown with weeds or underbrush they were difficult to traverse, but you could walk them with a canoe on your shoulders. Here, at the mouth of the swamp, there was no portage. There was *supposed* to be one a quarter of a mile farther on, but it probably hadn't been used in a century. To even reach it—if I could find it—I'd have to carry the canoe over mushy deadfall, logjams, and slippery rocks. The deep pockets of water were something to contend with too. I was afraid it couldn't be done. My watch showed 6:55 a.m., and we'd gone nowhere in an hour and a half. "You thirsty?" I asked her.

"Yes."

I handed her the canteen. "Drink all you want; water isn't our problem."

"Did you treat it?"

"No. I only use iodine pills when there's no choice, like when refills come from a bog. But the tablets make it taste like crap. Most of the water in the parks is potable; you just fill your canteen from a big, clear lake. I scooped it out of Brent yesterday." She looked toward the swamp. "Didn't get it from there, don't worry."

She sipped a little and I drank the remainder when she handed it back. "I'll check their camp," I said. "You wait here."

I slithered back to a vantage point and aimed the binoculars carefully. Below, nothing was happening; then I noticed movement in the bushes. The tall guy stepped back from a tree and wiggled while pulling up the zipper of his jeans. He walked to a tent and kicked it. A minute later the chubby guy came out and went to a tree and did the zipper dance. *What are you guys up to?*

The men seemed to dally. They built a fire, put on a pot of coffee, and started making breakfast. *Christ, they're acting like normal campers.* I heard a noise behind me and turned around to see Janeene. "Couldn't wait there alone any longer," she said as she crouched beside me. "What are they doing?"

"Nothing. Absolutely nothing. Can't believe it." She leaned close to me to try and look through the eyepieces. I gave the binoculars to her. As she watched them, I studied the little lake and swamp, judging how far we'd made it earlier and how far we needed to go to be out of sight from the precipice—a long way, maybe more than a quarter of a mile. It would take hours to reach a point where the swamp narrowed between two ridges and became a mass of thick green vegetation. And I had no idea what lay beyond that. The map indicated a portage, and farther, a slough of Lake Suzanette. My bet was the whole distance was mushy, deep, impenetrable swamp. I decided the Lake Suzanette escape route was out of the question.

"We need to go to the other side of this lake," I said, pointing to the far shoreline, about two hundred yards away.

I pulled my maps out and put one on the ground. It was a very detailed view, and I showed her where we were, where the waterfall and precipice were, where the fishermen's camp was, where her canoe was, and where we needed to go. She noticed the name "Jackfish Point" printed with a black grease pencil on the mass of land to our northwest.

She asked, "Why is 'Jackfish Point' written on your map?"

I laughed at her question. "Jackfish is an unofficial name for an eastern chain pickerel. It's a fish with a lot of teeth, and people who grew up in the South call them jackfish. I caught one once in the little lake and wrote the name on my map in grease pencil to remember where I caught it. The land directly behind the waterfall is what I call 'Jackfish Point.' It's where they buried the body."

She paid no attention to my comment. "You have a lot of writing on your map."

"Been used a lot."

"What do these letters mean?"

"They're abbreviations. *W* means walleyes, *SMB*: small-mouth bass, *LT*: lake trout, and so on. The outfitters will mark them to show you where to catch each type of fish. I've come here often enough to have added some spots of my own. You see this," I said, pointing to the letters *LMB*, "that means large-mouth bass. Wrote it myself, not certain anyone else knows they're here. That's why I came to the little lake. Not many places in the parks with these fish.

She pointed. "You have a circle on the place where Hank

and Pete are." A large red grease pencil mark encircled the campsite. I'd drawn a star in the circle as well.

"It's been one of my favorites for years. If my team hadn't arrived in Brent Lake so late in the day, we would have tried to stay where you did, but we came in at the southwest end of Brent and it was getting dark, so we decided to stop there. It's not a good idea to travel at night if you don't have to." I didn't tell her if we had gotten to her site first, none of this would have happened—to me, anyway.

"Shouldn't we stay here?" she asked, pointing to the side we were on now. "We can walk to my canoe if I'm reading this right."

"You're a pretty good map reader. Yeah, I'd like to stay on the south side, but I'm getting worried."

"About what?"

"Them." I pointed below. "They act like they have all the time in the world." She studied my eyes. "What are you saying? You think they found my canoe?"

I didn't answer, but that was precisely my worry. "Is the tall guy, Hank, a good hunter?"

"Guess so. He goes all the time."

"What about the chubby guy?"

"Pete? They go together."

"Great."

I glared at the map. Of all the places to fish in the park, I pick a place where I'm stranded. "Was either of them in the Army?"

"Hank was. He was in ROTC in college and went into the Army as an officer for a short time after school. I don't know any more than that."

"How old is he?"

"Thirty-eight, will be thirty-nine in two months."

"What about Pete?"

"About the same age. He was in the Air Force after high school. He wasn't in long either."

This was getting worse. All three of us spent time in the service of good old Uncle Sam. But their service was a long time ago, and they hadn't spent as many years in as I did, or performed the same duties I had. "We have to go to the far side, the north side of this lake," I said, pointing at the map. "If they did find your canoe, they might be able to track you back to here. And even if they didn't find it, the body is up here, and they might want to check on it. Or move it. They didn't have time to bury it all that well or deep enough. And yesterday the tall guy might have seen my tracks in the mud. He could come checking around." I thought about my sunglasses dropped at the waterfall. If either of those guys saw them, they would know for certain I had been there. "We're only. . ." I picked my head up and looked back toward the waterfall, "three hundred fifty meters from the top. Worn out our welcome in this place is my guess."

"What's a meter, exactly?"

"A yard, for all intents and purposes. If I say something is five meters away, think of it as five yards away. That will make it easy for us to understand each other. It's what I tell everyone to do that has no experience with meters, just yards, and feet or inches."

"Why do you use that word *meter*? Were you in the military?"

"Yes, for ten years, a long time ago. The Army. Captain Cummings, Armored Cavalry, at your service."

She studied my eyes for a second. "Should I salute you?"

"No, just don't argue with me."

* * *

Around 8:30 a.m., I refilled the canteen from the little lake, added an iodine tablet, and put it in the canoe, pushing the craft into the water, leaving its aft end on the shore with Janeene in the front. "You hold it here; be right back."

From my vantage on the precipice, only one of the men was visible. The chubby guy was tending the fire, making something in a frying pan, but Hank wasn't in sight. I scanned the whole campsite and the lake below. He was nowhere to be seen. This was the moment I dreaded most, not being able to spot one of the killers. *Where is he?* What was he doing? Sleeping in his tent, relieving himself in the bushes, or sneaking up to my position? A sudden movement to my right answered the question. Swinging the binoculars along the crest of the camp and toward the open water revealed a canoe with one paddler—Hank drifting out from behind the rock outcrop. He was leaning over, filling a canteen. He finished with one and filled another. But instead of turning back toward the landing, he started to slowly paddle toward the waterfall.

"We've got to hustle," I hissed, pushing our canoe from the bank. "Hank is headed this way."

We stroked across the little lake, about two hundred meters (or yards) from south to north, like Olympic rowers. We made it in minutes. Janeene threw her paddle out on the bank as I ran the canoe aground and jumped into knee-high water holding my paddle over my head, pushing and shoving the canoe as hard as possible to get it out of sight in the brush. She pulled the bow. The shoreline was rocky, and we made scraping sounds with the hull before I lifted it in my arms and carried it up a small hill and hid it in a pine thicket.

"Why didn't we just hide on the other side?" she asked.

"Just don't trust it. I've been traipsing all over that bank. Can't push our luck." I didn't tell her it felt much safer with two hundred meters of water between him and us. The tall guy was a killer, a hunter, and possibly well-armed.

"Wait by the canoe and don't sneak up on me like you did before. Stay with it until I come back." I moved ten feet down-hill to a stand of bulrushes at the water's edge. Poking the binoculars through the weeds and surveying the top of the waterfall, Hank appeared at the top. He was holding binoculars himself. He gazed in our direction. God, I hoped he hadn't heard us. He looked back and forth along our shoreline, the flash of sunlight glinting from his lenses a time or two. The sun was in his face, but it was behind me, so I should be safe to look. Twice he stopped and stared for a long time. My insides churned since our canoe wasn't hidden very well. He lowered the binoculars and turned around and picked something up from the ground. He slung a small backpack over his shoulders and reached down again. This time he picked up a rifle.

In an instant he disappeared in the brush, heading in the direction of the body. He was gone a long time, maybe twenty minutes. I was getting worried he might be circling around the little lake from the west, coming toward us, when he returned to the top of the waterfall. He knelt on the ground, partially hidden in the weeds. He stood and followed a course along the ground with his eyes and started moving slowly along the south shore of the little lake. He was following my tracks. Damn, I'd moved back and forth so much there must have been a muddy trail the size of the Cumberland Gap. And I'd plowed my canoe into the bushes several times. There'd be a lot of beaten-down weeds. And after Janeene encountered me, even more. There was a chance he would think it was a moose trail—when they frequented an area, they trampled paths like bulldozers—but since this guy was a hunter he'd recognize animal trails, and if even one clear footprint of a boot was visible, my chances of remaining an unexplained mystery were gone.

Near where I had hidden the canoe the day before, he crouched, rifle at the ready. He slung off the backpack and pulled something out. He held a dark object to his mouth. I couldn't focus well enough to see it clearly but had a guess. I turned and slipped back up to Janeene. "Did Hank bring a radio with him, like a walkie-talkie?"

"Yeah. He and Pete each have one. They used them to talk to each other when we were paddling in the lakes."

"Wonderful. In the old days you weren't allowed to bring that kind of electronic stuff in the park." I realized how stupid the statement was the second it left my lips. There were a lot of things you were not supposed to do in the park, like bring in booze, or carry guns, or kill people. These guys didn't follow any rules.

"Do they have any other stuff I should know about?"

"I don't know, like what? Told you about the guns."

I thought for a second. If they had radios, they might have miniature GPS devices that could pinpoint your position within fifty feet. "Did they bring special electronic stuff, like radios or other gadgets?"

"What do you mean, gadgets?"

"Small things, like cell phones about this size." I made an oblong shape with my hands a couple of inches across. "Or did they have something that looks like a funny watch, or a big—"

"Wait. Hank did have something like that. Pete too. I remember them saying they could always tell where we were, but I never looked at the gadgets."

"Damn," I muttered. Small GPS units could be purchased from hunting or sporting supply stores or rented from the outfitters. They were becoming quite popular. With Hank's newfound wealth, he probably purchased one or two. I knew how the devices worked but wasn't sure how they could be used to locate your position in the BWCA or Quetico. They had the advantage over me.

"Do you need a gadget to move around?" she asked.

"No. A good map is all you need. A compass helps too."

"You have one?"

"Maps, but no compass." I felt like an idiot. In my haste, it was left it in my main pack back at camp. "As long as we stay around Jackfish Point, we won't need one. And if we get out on Brent Lake, I can get us to safety. I know this area of the park pretty well."

"Don't understand how everyone doesn't get lost up here. All the lakes and woods look the same to me."

"It does to most people. Come on, we have to move," I said, grabbing her hand to help her stand.

"Why?"

"Because they'll be searching for us any minute now." I glanced around the pine thicket. The canoe wasn't very well-hidden, but it would have to do. "Janeene, without making any sudden moves, and *no noise*, get everything out of the canoe. Put all the small stuff in the backpack and the big stuff on the ground, then wait here until I come back. I'm gonna watch the little lake for a while. Don't come down there." She gave me an imploring look. "Just do as I say, please. Wait for me here, so I know where you are." I went back to my observation post in the bulrushes.

As feared, Hank was standing at the precipice. Ten to one he'd called the chubby guy on the radio, and he was on the way. When the fat bastard popped up atop the waterfall in another five minutes, I knew they had found Janeene's canoe. There was no other way he could have gotten to the precipice from the campsite. He wasn't wet, so he hadn't swum over, and Hank used the first canoe. It also explained why they were in no hurry when I watched them this morning. They knew

Janeene couldn't go far. And now, if Hank had seen one of her footprints, they had an idea where she might be. Damn, one canoe down, one left.

They huddled at the waterfall, talking. After a while, the chubby guy disappeared back over the edge. *Sending him back for supplies?* Hank stayed at the top, working his binoculars back and forth. I went back to Janeene.

"We need to hide these," I said, looking at the paddles and life vests. Nearby, eighty to a hundred feet away was a thicket of briars surrounding a lone pine tree. It could be recognized easily, even in the dark. I gathered the equipment and crawled off to the thicket, which was so dense you couldn't see inside, and slid the paddles, life jackets, and the bow rope on the ground into the bushes and covered them with pine straw.

Back with Janeene, I whispered, "We'd better E&E."

"What?"

"Escape and Evade." I was thinking in military terms now. At this moment I knew exactly where we were, but in an hour or two, I might not. "You wear that little backpack, Janeene. I'll carry the other things. Now let's go."

We started away from the lake on a gradual ascent up a hill. It was at least three-quarters of a mile to the first slough on Suzanette and working our way through the deadfall and rugged terrain would take half a day. But I had no intention of heading to Suzanette, at least not until we knew what the killers were doing. We stopped under a stand of pine trees, and Janeene lay down.

I pulled the pistol from the backpack, cleared the weapon, and inserted the magazine with a click and chambered a bullet. Two rounds. Only two stinking rounds, barely enough to piss a man off. It would take a clear head or chest shot at ten meters to make good use of them. *Shit.* The loaded gun went into my fishing vest, safety on.

Grabbing my binoculars, I maneuvered around to get a partial look at the small lake below. Pine trees obscured the view, but it was easy to tell we were about three hundred meters above it. My worst fears had come true: A canoe with one guy in it—Pete—slipped slowly around the far side. A second person was walking the bank near where Janeene and I had hidden last night. It was Hank slinking along the shoreline, carrying a rifle. Both were moving carefully, taking no chances. Any thought I had of ambushing them vanished.

They poked around for a long time, then suddenly the canoe turned directly north toward my side of the lake. Hank lay down on the ground, aiming his rifle past the canoe at our shoreline. They were coming after us in a frontal assault. The enemy craft was closing at a steady pace. It wouldn't be long until bullets might be ripping into the trees where we'd landed. I pulled Janeene to her feet and started up the hill again.

Twenty minutes later, as Janeene rested against a stump, I stood watching the little lake. She drank about half of the water from our canteen, but that was fine with me. I needed her in the best shape possible. We could survive from the abundant water in streams and lakes; what we couldn't do was reach safety without a canoe.

Pete wasn't visible anymore since he was hidden under the tree line below me, but I could see Hank. He was still holding his rifle. *What was Pete doing down there?* I strained with the binoculars to catch a glimpse of him, but no luck.

"See them?" Janeene asked. She was rubbing her knee.

"No. How are you feeling?"

"Tired. Aerobics class is nothing like this."

I tried to laugh. At least she had some spirit. Suddenly, a loud metallic clang carried up the hill.

"What's that?"

"An axe chopping up my canoe I'd say."

"Oh shit."

The banging continued for fifteen to twenty gut-wrenching strokes. My life had just gotten worse, and I knew it wouldn't be long until they came up after us. Damn, we were outnumbered, outgunned, and out of the ability to move on the water. *Stranded, in other words.* Suddenly, I saw Hank get up, wave, and run toward the waterfall. He disappeared over the top. Now what the hell was he doing?

A billion more scenarios flashed through my head. Why had Hank left? Gone back for more supplies or weapons, or had he decided to paddle around to Lake Suzanette to envelop us? They had radios. It was possible. But envelopment would take a long time. If they decided to track us, Pete would have to hide his canoe first and come after us on foot. "I'm going down below for a minute."

"Roger, don't leave me again."

"No time for discussions." I looked around, studying the features. A toppled oak tree lay within fifteen meters of us, its branches splayed out on the ground like a garden rake. I could find this place again. "Be right back."

I went downhill about a hundred fifty meters, much closer to the lake than intended, but I couldn't see anything. Finally, I spotted Pete stashing his canoe near the edge of the swamp on the north side of the little lake. They were going to track us, not try the encirclement maneuver. Marking the canoe's position with some funny-looking trees, it would be easy to find, and I hustled back toward Janeene. *Thank God we held the high ground.* It was the most important military tenet of all, next to secrecy and surprise. But I had those elements in my arsenal as well. Too bad there weren't some weapons and ammo to go with them.

I urged Janeene to get up. "We have to move."

We carefully crept up to the highest ridgeline. It took four hours, and I couldn't shake the feeling a bullet would be slamming up our rear ends the whole time, but we never heard or saw anything from Pete.

From the ridgeline, parts of Lake Suzanette were visible. The vegetation was so dense only glimpses of shiny, barren water came through, and certainly no teams of forest rangers in canoes coming to our rescue. For a minute, my heart sank to my knees, followed by the dry heaves twisting my stomach into hemp rope.

"Do you think they're behind us?" Janeene asked, interrupting my thoughts. She was sitting on the ground, massaging her thighs.

"Don't honestly know. They don't know where we are any better than—" It suddenly occurred to me that Hank and Pete didn't know a hell of a lot more than I did. They weren't even certain there was a *we*. They may be thinking they are only chasing me, or just Janeene. Even if they'd seen two sets of boot prints, it wasn't definitive proof we had teamed up, just that we had both been at the little lake. I could have made mine yesterday afternoon, hers last night or today. All they knew was I hadn't left by canoe before they carried the body up. *That's all they really know.* I stood up, feeling better. They were flying partially blind, like me.

"Is this what you did as a soldier, climb until you were exhausted?" Janeene asked.

"For many years. Lot easier when you're younger."

Her fingers continued to knead her thighs. "Seems like you're in pretty good shape to me."

"Exercise a lot. . . and as a hobby, I still box." I made fists, took a fighting pose, and said, "Taught the sport to my son and his high school friends."

"Don't work out as much as I should," she said. "At a time

like this, wish I hadn't quit smoking. Could use a nice nicotine buzz right now."

"Me too."

"You smoke?"

"Not for last twenty years."

"Good habit to quit. It's nasty. Hank smokes like a fiend."

"What about Pete?"

"He smokes, too, but not that much."

One of them smoked last night at their camp when I watched them. It was difficult to tell, so I'd disregarded it, but a lit cigarette could be seen from over a thousand meters away at night in an open area. In a dense forest the distance would be much less, but it could be seen if they weren't careful. I'd watch for the faint red dot, since they were both smokers. What other habits did these guys have I should know about? "Hey, you said these guy hunt together. When do they go?"

"What do you mean?"

"What time of year?"

"Fall mostly. Hank really likes to hunt deer. And he goes out west to hunt something big—bigger deer, I think."

"He ever mention hunting elk?"

"Yeah, that's what he goes for."

Elk were difficult to hunt and sometimes required a long shot, an accurate shot at long ranges. Hank was probably a good shooter.

"What about Pete?"

"I'm not an authority on Pete."

"Yeah, but does he hunt more than Hank, or less?"

"More. He goes all the time—spring and fall. Hank doesn't go as much in the spring."

Pete was probably a turkey hunter. Spring was the primary season for them, and they were tough to hunt. Stalking was the best way until you found a good place, then you ambushed. Or better yet, called them in. This was beginning to make sense—a stalker and a shooter combining forces.

"Would you call Hank a gun freak?" I asked.

"Guess so. He's got twenty of them."

"Rifles?"

"Mostly. He likes pistols, but not as much."

"Does he consider himself a good marksman?"

"Very."

"Wonderful." They were going to be a tough team to outwit. Although Janeene didn't mention it, I wondered if they had military-style weapons. "Did you see them bring any rifles that looked like machine guns?"

"No. Pete said something about only being able to shoot single rounds with the rifles they brought along, like when they go hunting." I thought about her statement; it was good news if it was correct. "Do they have semi-auto or fully automatic weapons at home?"

"I don't think so. There's a range in Minnetonka where they can shoot all kinds of stuff, but I think other people own the guns they shoot when they visit. They rent the guns and buy the ammunition."

"You said both of them were in the service. Do they talk about that much?"

"No. Neither of them liked it. Hank said he was always in trouble and hated it. Why you so interested?"

"Because soldiers are taught a lot, whether they're good ones or bad ones. They'll be coming up here sooner or later." The value of the high ground was pounded into soldiers from day one. They were coming.

"Other than hunting, what other hobbies do Hank or Pete have?" I needed to know as much as possible about these guys. "What else do they like to do?"

"Don't know much about Pete, like I told you." She seemed

to think over the question, though, and finally said, "Hank likes to fly his drones."

"Drones?"

"Yeah, the things like model helicopters with cameras so he can take pictures."

I considered this while she looked at the grim expression on my face. "Does that bother you, that he likes to fly drones?"

"It does if he brought one up here with him." I thought about the possibility of infrared cameras. They would be almost impossible to hide from if Hank could fly them around our area and pick up our heat signature in the woods. They were getting cheap enough he could have one with special features. And he should have enough money now to buy a very sophisticated model capable of spotting missing hikers in deeply wooded terrain. Shit. Another major problem to deal with.

"He doesn't have one with him, if that's what you are worried about."

"How do you know?"

"Because he was pissed off that his good one was damaged right before we came up here. He flew it into a barn or something and smashed up the camera."

"No chance he didn't bring another one on the trip?"

"I don't think so. . . didn't use one at our first campsite, and he was complaining about the time it took to repair the damaged one. He said that was his favorite."

I couldn't shake the possibility that the asshole had a drone. Hadn't seen or heard anything to make me think he did, but it was something to keep in mind. Even a drone with just a simple camera could be fatal. One photo of us on this hill or near the ridgeline would confirm our position and could lead them to us. I'd have to remember to use camouflage whenever we moved, like sneaking under tree branches, avoiding open areas, and sleeping under leaves or ground cover whenever possible.

My head was spinning as I pulled out a map and glanced at it, remembering the Conmee Death March. It gave me an idea: lure them away from us. "Take off your boots, Janeene, quickly, please."

"My boots?"

"Yeah." While pointing at a dead pine lying just below the ridgeline fifty meters away, I whispered, "Take them off and then walk very carefully over to that tree. Don't break a twig or leave a footprint on the way over. And wait for me there."

She unlaced her hard-soled hiking boots. I strung them around my neck then crested the top of the hill and started down toward Suzanette. Every few meters I picked a muddy or barren spot and put a print or two of her boots. After a few more paces, I'd put one of mine. Nothing too garish, but enough to persuade a good tracker that we'd been hurrying this way—together or separately, they'd have to decide. I stopped in a creek three hundred meters down the hill, sat on a rock, took my boots off, and gingerly climbed out and started away at a right angle, careful to step only on fallen leaves and no branches. I went a hundred meters, sat down, and put my boots back on. Thirty minutes later I was back with Janeene.

"Here," I said, handing her boots back.

"My feet are really sore," she said, massaging her toes.

"Another major rule in the military is to take care of your feet." Mine were sore, too, and wet from carrying the canoe out of the water before, as well as crossing the small creek. Rummaging through the little backpack I found the spare socks. "Take your socks off and give them to me." She did as directed. Her feet weren't wet, maybe a little damp, but they would dry. Her toenails were painted a light blue color. They were chipped, like they hadn't been manicured in some time. "My daughter uses a color like that," I said, tossing the socks to her. "Put these on."

"Won't you need them?"

"No, I'll wear yours after they dry a little more."

"Phew, don't you want to wash them first?"

I smiled and put her socks in my bush shirt pockets, one in each, and buttoned the flaps. They should be completely dry in an hour or two.

CHAPTER FIVE

The late evening sun was casting long shadows and melting dark areas into hazy patches as we were heading southwest away from Lake Suzanette and the ridgeline we crested earlier in the day. Moving back toward the little lake, a small creek that cut across our path formed a ravine. No deeper than forty feet, it was extremely steep for this area. Other parts of Quetico and the BWCA had much harsher terrain, some with waterfalls, cliffs, or canyons hundreds of feet high or deep. But this section of the park was relatively flat by comparison, supposedly scraped level by glaciers from the Ice Age.

I climbed up the steep, damp, mossy crevasse, moving one foot at a time with the patience of a watchmaker, helping Janeene, careful to point out hand- and footholds with every move. She didn't need to slip and twist an ankle.

Jagged rocks and broken limbs protruded at uneven angles, making climbing slow. The ravine afforded a natural barrier for our defense. A position on the southwestern side of the obstacle could be used to ambush a pursuer—and if I'd have had anything other than a pistol with two measly rounds, it might have worked. But we'd have a better chance escaping if we could avoid Hank and Pete altogether. So far it worked. . . hadn't seen nor heard them since the canoe bashing this morning. Once near the crest of the high ridgeline, I smelled the tell-tale sign of cigarette smoke in the breeze, but it was only for a second. We'd hit the ground and waited for half an hour; I searched the woods with the binoculars. I didn't tell Janeene why and never saw anybody. If a burning cigarette was that close, the smoker could have had us in his gunsight, which was way too close to ignore. But we never spotted anyone, and I hoped if my nose had been correct, my planted boot prints had led the stalker down the other side.

Before coming out of the crevasse, I poked my head carefully over the sight line, surveying the woods all around me. It would be hell to spend half an hour carefully traversing it and then pop up like a target in a shooting gallery. "Come on, Janeene, we still have a long way to go." She was tiring but had quit complaining about her legs and feet hours ago.

Helping her climb out of the ravine gave me time to study my handiwork along the opposite edge. Before starting down that side, I'd stripped off fifty yards of fishing line from my spinning reel and strung it ankle high along the crest. The Kevlar high-tech fishing line, also known as braided line, was dark green, almost black, not the semi-luminescent green color of regular monofilament. The stuff was hard to see, and it was strong—four times the breaking strength of equivalent seventeen-pound mono—and didn't stretch. It was a bitch to tie knots in it and nearly impossible to break without cutting, so many fishermen wouldn't use it, but I always kept one spool of it with my favorite reel. The line was barely visible, and it was an insidious setup in the dark, much like the trip wires used on Claymore mines made famous in the Vietnam War. My Kevlar wasn't strung as tight as it should have been, so it may not work even if somebody did walk into it by accident, but it afforded a chance to possibly slow down a pursuer.

We started down the southwestern side of the hill toward the little lake and a finger of water heading north to south from Conmee Lake, certain we'd circled away from a possible tracker. My main concern now was pinpointing Hank and Pete. If I couldn't, there was no purpose looking for their canoe in the swamp. They could bushwhack us at any time. But trying to determine where they were located wouldn't be easy. According to Janeene, they probably knew she had the gun, so they wouldn't walk around with impunity. This was becoming warfare. Sniper warfare.

From above us, toward the high ridgeline, the hiss from a radio boomed in the air. It lasted several seconds, then quit. "Did you hear that?" Janeene asked in a frightened whisper. Her eyes were as big as golf balls.

"Yeah. Couldn't tell how far off. Could have been a long way. Let's move." We bent at the waist and hustled downhill. My guess was we were a good five or six hundred meters above the small lake, and probably twice that distance away from the radio. The noise was too damn close for my taste, and we started moving due west, parallel to the water. Now I knew somebody was trying to track us down, but I didn't know if it was Hank or Pete. My guess was Pete, since I was thinking Hank was either in Lake Suzanette or below us in Brent Lake near the waterfall.

Janeene was gasping. I slung one of her arms over my neck and pulled her toward a thatch of tree branches. "You're doing great," I lied. We ducked under the slumping branch of a cedar tree and she lay down on a bed of rusty brown leaves and needles.

"Don't think I can go much further, Roger. I'm getting really sore."

"You won't have to; we'll settle you here for the night while I run patrols alone." I wiped a smudge of dirt from her cheek. She turned on her side and curled into a ball, pulling her knees almost to her chin. I gently massaged the back of her neck and around her shoulder blades. She closed her eyes and moved against my hand. "That feels good." After a second, she added, "I'm not really a coward, you know, just simply not in shape for this."

"Nobody is." She pulled into a tighter ball, exhausted. Health club workouts did little to prepare one for the torment she had endured today—hiking three miles over steep and broken terrain. Health clubs didn't have sharp rocks, rotten logs, and spiny deadfall to clutter every step. Moving off-trail was a chore, fraught with penalties for one misstep. My greatest worry was that she'd twist an ankle or wrench a knee. Mobility was key to our survival. *Take care of your feet.*

"I served with many soldiers who weren't as brave as you were today."

"I wasn't brave, only scared." She offered a weak smile. "What day is it, anyway?"

"Huh?"

"What day is today? I've lost track."

I looked down at my watch. It was easy to forget about time up here. One day seemed to blend into the next, and the one after that. And since so much of the terrain looked the same, it was easy to become mesmerized by the sameness and forget about time altogether. "It's Thursday, June 27." I pulled my maps out of the daypack and found the one with an overall view. In the corner was a calendar marked by pencil to note the days of my trip. I made an X on the block noted June 27.

"What are you doing?"

"Marking time. I keep a calendar to track the days. Once, years ago, my watch broke. If I hadn't been noting the days, I'd have lost track of time. If that happens you might miss your pickup scheduled with the outfitter. During one trip my friends got confused about the date, and they had to wait at the rendezvous point for three extra days until he showed up."

"What's going to happen to us?"

"We'll be okay, I promise."

She shivered and whispered in a soft voice. "Are they going to catch us?"

"Never. We can hide in these woods for weeks if we have to." I thought of the drone Hank might have but didn't say anything about my fears to her. "There's plenty of water, and we can catch fish." I rolled my eyes at the spinning rods laying on the ground next to her. "If we can give these guys the slip, we'll last until somebody realizes we're missing. They can't track us for long before they decide it's too risky."

She sat up in a cross-legged crouch, eyes burning like stars. "I don't want to die here, Roger."

"You won't. Believe me. I'll take care of you."

She started to sniffle, then wiped her nose on her sleeve and whispered, "I watched you in the woods today. You're like an Apache."

"I'd consider it an honor to be as good as them in the forest. Afraid I'm not."

Although her lips were parched and dried from breathing through her mouth, she looked at her mangled fingernails and said, "I won't complain anymore. Not about anything. Not even about these." She raised one hand to my face. I cracked a faint smile. Her fingernails were splotched with dark red chips of broken paint, almost a polka dot pattern. If she could keep any sense of humor, it was a good sign. Running on high-octane emotions during the day, and surviving, had drained our initial fear of capture. But it had returned the instant we heard the radio. A knot welled up in my stomach. What were the odds we'd get out of this? We had no canoe, no weapons to speak of, and no way to call for help. Our best shot was constant E&E, and I needed her motivated for that.

I pulled out the Baby Ruth candy bars from my fishing vest. "A little surprise. These are for you."

"I only want one."

"Nope. Eat one now and save the other for morning. I can go for days without food, did it in jungle school." Raising the canteen, I took a hefty swig. Ours was full of water from the creek in the crevasse. "But can't make it long without water."

She munched on one of the bars like a chipmunk, nibbling little pieces from the tip. "Drink as much as you want. Stay well hydrated. I'll refill it tonight."

As she nibbled, I grabbed a fishing rod and started unspooling line.

"What are you doing?"

"Getting ready to set perimeter trip wires. We'll need a warning if one of those assholes comes this way." I stripped off sixty yards of the Kevlar fishing line from the spinning reel. It was the same stuff I used at the edge of the ravine, and since the pistol wasn't much protection until a person was very close, the booby trap seemed like a good way to give me a heads-up if someone was nearby.

I cut twenty-yard sections, planning on setting them to the north and northeast. Overhead, evening stars were beginning to dot the sky; I had to get moving before darkness, not stumble around and run into Hank or Pete in the pitch black.

Janeene's head was slumping as she finished the candy bar. She lay down in the burley thicket and made a pillow of the backpack.

"Do your feet hurt?" she asked.

"Killing me. When I get back, I'll take my boots off and try to dry them. Then I'll put on your dry socks." I patted my pockets.

"Sure you don't want to wash them first?"

"Not an issue for me. I'm dreaming of warm, dry socks." Mine were soaked from water in the creeks, and keeping my feet serviceable was my second most important task. "You keep this little nest cozy," I said, gripping her chin, "and no matter what happens, no matter what you hear, don't move from this place. Stay hidden. Cover yourself with pine straw when you sleep." I didn't mention that pine straw would help conceal her from an infrared camera if they had one. "I have to know where to find you, understand?" She nodded.

"You'll be back soon?" she asked.

A wave of acid boiled in my stomach. I wanted to tell her how to survive without me: how to move without being seen, how to hide in the trees, how to find water. There were a million things to tell her, but my tongue was dry with fear. It balled up in my mouth with the pasty spittle of my own waning courage. I had to get back to her. This was no time for bravery. If something happened to me, she was helpless. There was no way to explain my fears, not when she was shivering in the twilight, teetering on the edge of courage herself. She clung to my arm, holding it desperately against her chest. I gently pulled it away. "I'll be back as soon as possible. Get some rest now."

I slipped off to build the trip wire alert system after staring uphill for a long time, purposely veering well away from the route we'd taken up the slope this morning. At this moment we were on the main hill north of the little lake, about nine hundred meters above its shoreline. To the west was the finger of Lake Conmee. It was roughly six hundred meters from our hiding place. I started stringing lines around trees about thirty meters up the slope, tying small branches and dark-colored lures from the fishing vest to the lines. They'd make an ominous racket if somebody walked into them. A warning was necessary to spring an ambush if the chance arose. Getting that chance was what worried me. After Janeene had told me about the GPS devices Hank and Pete had, I wondered if they might have more electronic gear, like night vision goggles. They could be expensive, running upwards of three thousand dollars. They were also small and light enough to be carried easily. Could they have them? If not, it was possible they could have a host of other things, like True Night Vision Binoculars or a Night Vision Pocket Monocular. These devices were under four hundred dollars and with them, you could see about one hundred yards at night. I couldn't even guess what they might have, but one thing was certain, I wouldn't be able to move around in total darkness with any safety.

Back at the pine bough, Janeene was awake. She sat up beside me, huddling against my leg as I checked the pistol. The safety was on as it lay by my right side. "How old are you?" she whispered.

"Too old for this." Every muscle and joint in my body was aching. "I turned forty back in April, but tonight it feels like sixty."

"You must be a good father."

"Huh? Why would you say that?"

"From watching you. . . your patience. Reminds me of my dad. You look a lot like him, too. He has your blue eyes, but his hair is blonder than yours."

Patience was not something I considered one of my virtues. "I am a good father and was a good husband."

She gave me a quizzical look. "Was? What does that mean? You still married?" She looked down at her battered fingernails. "Sorry, didn't mean to pry into your personal life."

"No, it's okay. There's just a long story. . . and it's hard for me to tell it, even after all this time." Thoughts of my late wife

Sherry popped in my head. My, how we had fun in the early days, swimming, sailing, and laughing. She loved to fish. We'd even camped a lot, much like this, but without all the drama. "It's hard for me to talk about her. She's dead."

Janeene stiffened against my leg. *Dead* was apparently not the right word for me to use, although it was the correct description of her condition. Sherry's passing was the last thing I wanted to discuss on this trip, a fact my buddies were adamant about recognizing as we planned the camping adventure. They'd been supporting me since her death, and this was to be my reemergence in the world after almost two years of agony and isolation. I said softly, "My wife died in a terrible car accident, a tragedy really. The person who killed her was arrested and sent to prison."

"Oh my God, I'm sorry Roger. I never should have—"

"Let me finish. I actually feel better about the situation now that I'm back in the world, so to speak. Been hiding in plain sight since October, almost two years ago, when she was struck and killed."

Janeene was silent, and I guessed she was horrified by her questions and my answers, as well as the realization that she'd dug into the pit of my despair. She looked at me with tear-filled eyes. "You don't have to tell me anything. . ."

"Yeah, I do. Coming out of my shell is a good thing, been doing it for the last couple of months, not stopping now. My buddies all know the story, you should too." She turned her face toward me and put her hands up to her cheeks. "Roger, you don't have to explain yourself to me."

I ignored her and started speaking in a quiet but firm voice. "My wife Sherry and two friends were walking down a sidewalk after eating lunch in Buckhead—that's a section of Atlanta that's nice for shopping and restaurants—when a woman driving a van ran up on the sidewalk and hit all three of them.

The driver was running from the police at the time and lost control of the van. Sherry was killed at the scene. Her two friends were seriously injured. One spent months in the hospital—she's still not doing well—while the second one is in a comatose state and may never recover. In many ways, maybe Sherry got the better end of the deal. She was killed so fast she didn't suffer and may not have even realized what happened to her and her friends."

"God, Roger, that's a terrible story. I can't imagine the pain. . . the feelings. . ."

"There's been plenty of hatred in my heart since it happened, but it's time to recover. I attended every second of the trial and helped the prosecutors whenever possible, and most importantly, helped my kids, my twins, deal with the loss of their mother." My thoughts wandered to them. They'd been badly hurt but were brave, probably more courageous than me at times. "We're all doing better, so I agreed to this trip with my friends. We started planning it back in January."

I remembered all the planning sessions and discussion with my buddies, Duke and Larry. The preparations gave me a purpose during the last winter—one I needed to help me open my eyes, heart, and mind to a new future. "Never expected to witness a murder up here. Not in Quetico. Wouldn't have believed it, or thought anything like this could happen if I didn't see it myself. Goes to show you, life is really a crapshoot in a lot of ways."

"I'm sorry you had to see Bobby get shot."

"Not just shot, but slaughtered, and he could see it coming. My wife, Sherry, didn't have the slightest idea what was happening when she was run over. According to Margret, one of the ladies with her at the time, she was laughing and in mid-sentence when boom, their world blew up."

We both sat silent for a few seconds before looking into

each other's eyes. "You know what, Janeene, I'm not giving in to these assholes. They can chase us around the whole damned park, and I'm still not giving up. Life ain't fair. I've been dealt a shitty blow in the past, but that's history." What I didn't tell her was that seeing the execution of Bobby had hardened my heart, not caused me pain or grief, like with the death of my wife. With Sherry I was helpless, wondering for months how that could have happened to her, and why God would allow such a tragedy happen to the mother of my children. Now a cold, vengeful surge of blood flowed in my chest, one that wasn't afraid to admit I could kill again, like I had in the Army. Hank and Pete were the enemy and needed to be treated as such on our battlefield. "We'll escape from here, Janeene, and live to see our children again. Then we can watch these killers be put in jail. That's a promise. I've had enough of the world's bullshit."

Janeene was looking at me with wide, frightened eyes.

I continued, "This trip was supposed to be special for me, first time I've done anything fun in a long time, or that's what I thought when Duke suggested the trip. He helped me through the hard times. Real buddy."

I thought about his questions during his encounter with Hank and Pete. He was always thinking about me, had since the incident with Sherry. "Thank God he didn't come up the top of the waterfall. He'd have probably been killed if he had, but I wasn't gonna let that happen even if I had to stand up and scream my head off at Duke to stay away."

"I'm sorry you got involved, Roger. And I didn't mean to be nosy before," she said, sniffling and wiping her nose on her sleeve. "It's just. . . just that. . . I don't know anything about you and—"

I put a finger to her lips, "You've just heard the key points of my life: a murdered wife, eighteen-year-old-twins, boy and a girl, and guy trying to rebuild his life. It's a simple story. Now it's time for you to rest."

She lay back down on her side. I dug a little trough beside her and had her slide into it, covering her with a thin veneer of pine straw needles. The blackness was enveloping us, draping the hill in a damp, heavy gloom. Somewhere, not more than a thousand meters away, hit men were waiting. Maybe. And they might have the power of a psychic's eye in the dark.

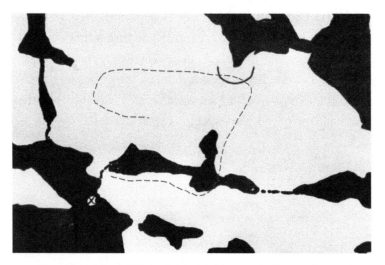

- Map services and data available from U.S. Geological Survey, National Geospatial Program."...

Map 7 - Roger's path from the Waterfall, across The Little Lake, and his Escape and Evasion route with Janeene (medium dashed line). His hiding place is located at the end of the path.

The ravine is located on the map (solid line, U-shaped).

The path from a finger of water in Conmee Lake to Brent Lake is to the northwest of the campsite (dotted line).

CHAPTER SIX

I dozed for an hour—didn't mean to, just nodded off as we lay next to each other in the thicket. When my head cleared, I tried to stretch and stopped in horror. My legs were so stiff they would barely move. My calves felt like torn paper, ragged and ready to fall apart. My toes were so sore they recoiled from the tips of my boots. We'd overdone it today, I realized, trying to massage a cramp from my calf. We'd be lucky if we could walk tomorrow, let alone run if necessary. My only solace was that fear was the best motivator of all and would supply plenty of adrenaline to allow us to make a burst to safety.

My watch showed 10:30 p.m. I found the pistol beside me and cradled it in my right hand, wishing Hank and Pete would just barge into my trip wires and get it over with. *Here's a present, one for each of you.* I rolled over on my stomach, looking out at the lines, but was not able to see them.

"What are you thinking?" Janeene whispered.

"That I'm going to Hawaii when this is over."

"Never been there," she said with a vacant, melancholy tone. Her voice scared me, making me regret my poor attempt at humor.

"Hey, after we get out of here, we'll go there on a trip, a sort of celebration. We'll go to a first-class hotel where waiters and waitresses cater to your every whim. We won't sleep on the ground."

"I'll have a lot to do when I get back, particularly with Angela."

"We'll take her."

"Really? I'd love to take my daughter to Hawaii," she said. "The poor child needs something good to happen in her life. It's been pretty rough so far."

"How so?"

"She's been ill for a few years. The doctors are not sure, but it could be sarcoidosis. It's a lung disease. Usually, it only occurs in adults. In children it's called an early onset version. It's not a major problem, but it's kept her down. That and dealing with my divorce, and her ex-daddy—"

"There's no such thing as an ex-daddy."

She held quiet for a minute. "I wish there was. He and I fight over Angela all the time. It's his parents actually—they adore my little girl, but they make it hell on me. I wish the old bastards would go to sleep and never wake up."

"Not a good way to think about them."

She fell silent again. "You're right. I shouldn't feel that way. They do love Angela."

I couldn't help but think about my own daughter. We'd been battling over my reaction to Sherry's death and the trial that happened afterward. I wanted the female driver to be held fully accountable and face the death penalty for murdering my wife. She deserved what she had delivered, the same as Sherry—not a lesser sentence, which she got from the jury. My daughter Crystal hated the woman vehemently, but held that life had value, sanctity, and that taking another person's life in retribution did not add anything to the meaning or memory of her mother. We were on opposite sides of the moral question, but although we disagreed, we were both heartbroken over the loss of Sherry. "Suppose we'd all like to change some things about our lives. I know I would."

Janeene nodded her head. "Agreed."

A woodpecker rattled on a rotting pine tree nearby and the *rat-a-tat* staccato of his bill reminded me of a jackhammer breaking up concrete. "Sounds like New York," I said.

"Did you live there?"

"Yes and no. I worked in the city but lived on Long Island. Worked so much in those days that I spent too much time in my office and less than I should have at home."

"What did you do?"

"Financial stuff. Trading stocks, bonds, and commercial paper, things like that."

"Why the comment about sounds?"

"NYC is loud—cars honking, sirens blasting, buses and trucks dumping air from their brake systems, hissing like giant snakes. Underground is no better with subway trains screeching on their rails like fingernails on a chalkboard. It's enough to give you a headache. And the city is always being rebuilt. Jackhammers are as common as taxis.

"Come on?"

"Honest. I remember one day walking with a friend of mine. We were jabbering about this and that and a jackhammer nearby was so loud he didn't hear me warn him about an open manhole. He almost walked into a two-foot-wide hole in the street. If I hadn't grabbed him, he would have fallen into the *great beyond* below the city. Down there, in the sewer system, he could have been eaten by alligators or chewed to pieces by rats."

"Really? There's no alligators in New York."

"In the office buildings there are. I worked with some."

"What happened to make you think that way?"

"It's a long story."

"I have time."

"Okay, here's the scoop. Once upon a time I was a managing director for a group of stock traders and salesmen. Some of the alligators were my senior managers and they were involved in misconduct up to their eyeballs. They directed illegal stuff to happen, and several were made to pay huge fines. Two of them went to jail as well, and they turned nasty toward me for talking to our customers. I eventually got pissed off and quit. When that happened, I wound up despising some of those people."

"Think I understand how you feel," she said softly.

A whisk of light from below caught my attention. It was followed by a banging noise, the unmistakable clang of a canoe paddle on a gunwale. *What the hell?* I popped up into a sitting position and searched for the binoculars. My legs were throbbing as I pulled the lens covers off and started scanning downhill.

"What was that?" Janeene asked.

"Stalkers, I'm guessing."

"Can you see through those in the dark?"

"Much better than people think. They work well at night because they suck in light and concentrate it." I couldn't see a thing from here though. "Got to go below."

"Please don't leave me again."

"Have to. Have to know if that's them in the little lake." I spun to her and grabbed an arm. "Remember the rules. Don't leave this spot for any reason."

"Won't budge."

I squeezed her hand and started downhill; my feet were so sore I felt like a person condemned to walking on burning coals. Hadn't gone two hundred meters when the glare of a flashlight broke through the night sky. It was as stark as a lighthouse beacon on the open ocean. Reflections flickered across the water like precious gems tossed on the ground. I couldn't believe my luck. How could these guys be so stupid? I followed the beam with my binoculars back to the source. The faint image of a canoe graced my eyes. It was a ghostly image, like a black and white photo taken in failing light, and the craft was heading toward the waterfall, one person in it. A second ray of light appeared at the precipice. I had a fix on both of them. That beam swung in my direction once, and the light singed my eyeballs as I pulled the binoculars down quickly and massaged my eyelids. My night vision was gone, and I sat like a fool, waiting for the flashbulbs in my head to go out.

Two lights meant two people: Hank and Pete. The idiots had marked their positions as if they had dressed in white shirts and painted red targets on their chests. Why would they do that?

Clattering noises made me guess they were carrying the canoe down the waterfall. It took a long time, but I slipped carefully all the way to the shoreline of the little lake. By that time, nobody was on the precipice, and nothing was in the lake. In the distance, toward their campsite, the trees had an eerie glow. High in the branches, pale yellow light danced and flickered. They must be building a bonfire for me to see it from this range. What in the hell were they doing?

I waited at the shoreline for half an hour before starting back up to Janeene. It was hard finding her; my eyes played tricks on me in the darkness, and my sense of direction was not as sharp as earlier in the day. Once or twice, thoughts of stopping on the hill and sleeping for a few minutes, or a few hours, or waiting out the night and finding her in the morning crossed my mind. But she might panic if I didn't return. It took until midnight, and by the time I reached her my spirit was as sapped as the strength in my legs.

CHAPTER SEVEN

Janeene tapped my hand, causing me to wake up. My eyes were glued shut with a sleepy slime and it took seconds to focus on her face. I barely had the strength to do it. "What time is it?"

She grabbed my wrist and looked at my watch. "Seven-thirty."

"Man, it's late." Sunlight was already dripping through the trees, pouring through tiny patches of open air, and bathing the woods with a golden glow. My muscles ached so badly it was painful to breathe. "I'm pretty worn out."

"Me too. This ground is hard."

I got up on one elbow, fiery pain shooting through my back. "You look pretty good." She did. Her face was etched with dirt and grime, but her smile held genuine warmth. Her spirit appeared in better shape than mine.

"What are we going to do today?" she asked.

"What can we do? Too sore to move if we don't have to." I found my pencil in the daypack and crossed off the date on my map: Friday, June 28.

"You think we should just stay here?"

I rolled over on my stomach and did a poor rendition of a pushup to get myself off the ground. It felt like somebody had kicked me in the ribs. "I need to—"

"Use the bathroom?"

"To say it politely, yes."

"Won't look. Promise."

I sneered, partly a laugh, and partly a grimace from a stabbing throb in my right leg. "Be right back." I struggled to my knees and inched along a short distance to a tree trunk. When I returned, she was breaking the Baby Ruth candy bar in half, putting each piece on the wrapper, which she'd spread out like a napkin. "I want to share this with you," she said.

"No. Told you it was for you." I eyeballed the chocolate morsel like it was a porterhouse steak. Hunger pangs were burning in my stomach.

"I insist. If I hadn't nearly stepped on you in the dark, you'd have had both of them to yourself and you probably wouldn't be in this jam."

"How so?"

"If not for you, Hank would have caught me by now. I'd be dead, and he'd be gone. You'd be safe and eating this candy bar by yourself."

"A pretty succinct theory, but I'm not buying it."

"Why not? You're the reason I'm alive. . . you heard Hank tell Pete that after they buried Bobby, they were leaving. I'm the one who screwed it up and ruined their plans, and got you trapped in the process. I only deserve half of this candy bar."

She was beginning to sound like a child, with short, sweet sentences, and a simple ending to her story. "You feeling all right?" I asked.

"Yeah. I'm so happy to be alive, I could float like those birds up there." She pointed up, where a pair of bald eagles were soaring on the breeze, maybe three hundred feet in the sky. I looked closely to make sure they weren't buzzards or drones.

"Very happy to be alive too," I said. Just didn't have her cheery disposition. We were still trapped, didn't know for sure where Hank and Pete were, and didn't have any idea what they would do next. And I didn't have a clue what tools or equipment they might have. Other than that, and being in the middle of a massive wilderness without food or real weapons, I was inclined to agree. "Your happiness is contagious. I feel better."

"Then eat your breakfast."

"In a minute. Let me run a patrol first." I searched for the binoculars and slung them around my neck, then tried to limber up my calves and thighs, doing half-hearted leg stretches. "How long have you been awake?" I asked.

"Maybe an hour, or an hour and a half."

"Heard anything, like noises from the lake?"

"No."

"Seen anything suspicious?"

"No. Just some squirrels and birds."

There wasn't much else to ask. The situation was normal; I didn't know a damned thing. "How full is the canteen?"

"About half."

"Drink some now, then let me have it. I'll finish it then refill it." I slung it across my shoulder when we were done, noticing a twinge in my right bicep. "We'll have brunch when I get back. Remember the rules."

At the little lake, a flock of mallard ducks was swimming in circles, dipping their heads underwater every so often to come up with a mouth full of aquatic vegetation. They made quite a racket when they pulled off a successful dive. Other than them, the lake looked like it probably had for a million years. No hint of man or his bad habits.

"Can't remember this much soreness," I said to Janeene,

putting the canteen in her lap. I'd already drunk half a container at the lake and refilled it to the brim.

"You should try childbirth. I'm hurting as bad as when Angela was born," she returned. "Maybe worse. I had drugs then."

"Some night fighter's friend would be nice right about now." She gave me an odd look. "That's what we called Tylenol in my Army days." I sat across from her and stared at our candy bar. We both picked up a half and ate it. Slowly.

"What should we do now?" she asked.

"I've been asking that question for the last two days. This is a military operation now. We have a hostile enemy out there. Unfortunately, we don't know where he is or what he plans on doing. I feel a little like a general in charge of an ancient army; often wondered how Napoleon, or Ulysses S. Grant, or any of the great commanders of the past kept their sanity during war. They were never certain where their enemy was or what he was gonna do. They didn't have electronic surveillance gear, like drones or satellites, so they had to send out scouts in horse patrols and wait for reports, and often make war plans with lousy information. It still happens today, getting bad info that is —even with high-tech gear—mistakes occur and the wrong people get killed. So, it takes decisive action at the right time, along with some good fortune, to come out on top. That's what we have to do, seize the initiative at the precise second when it matters."

She looked at me with a blank stare.

"Sorry, I—"

"No, it's all right. I studied a little of that stuff in college."

"Oh yeah. Where did you go?"

"To Michigan State, in East Lansing. I finished in four years, got a degree, but didn't attend graduation, which I regret now. Then I had Angela. I want to get home to her."

My "you will" reply was more of a boast than truth.

"What would a great general do if he were here instead of you?"

"Wake up, and the nightmare would be over."

"We don't have that option." She smiled, flashing her teeth. They were very even and sparkling white, the glow in sharp contrast with the mud-smeared, brown tone of her cheeks.

"It depends on which general," I returned. "Patton would probably charge the campsite to kill them both, or go down in a blaze of glory. McArthur would bypass them and let them rot in place, island hop and live to fight another day—if he had a canoe. I like his idea more, but I think we'd be better off acting like Montgomery, the British general in World War II. They used to say he was too slow deciding anything to be a great leader. He was very cautious and never made a move until he learned everything he could about his opponent, and even then, he dallied, but the English came out on the right side of the war, so he was successful in the end. I think we have to be like Montgomery in this case."

"We're going to sit here and wait it out then?"

"It's our best choice. Time is on our side, not Hank and Pete's."

"Why's that?"

"Because they don't know I'm up here for certain. And I have friends that realize I'm missing."

She thought about that for a second. "What about your canoe?"

"Good question. Hank probably figures it was mine, but so what? I could have drowned two days ago or walked out by now." I told her about seeing the flashlights on the lake last night and the bonfire in the camp. "That's a strange way to act if they thought I was around. My guess is they think I'm gone and they're hoping you'll come back to them."

"I never want to see them again."

"Yeah, but they don't know that. And they don't know we're together." *Bang. I'd left two sets of tracks, mine and hers, near the ridgeline.*

"What's the matter?"

I barely heard the question. *Why did you do that?*

"Roger? Are you okay?"

"Not really. I might have screwed up."

We both sat silently, me thinking about how I needed to be more careful in the future, not make rash decisions that could do more harm than good. "Christ, Janeene, this is like playing a game of three-dimensional Chinese checkers on somebody else's computer. There's more possible outcomes than anyone can fathom." My heart was racing, trying to guess what Hank and Pete were thinking about two sets of footprints. Did they know they had us trapped near Jackfish Point? "Look, one thing is certain: my friends Duke, Larry, and Chuck know I'm missing. By this time, they're probably headed back to a ranger station. If we can hang on for three or four more days, somebody will come back looking for us."

"What if—?" She stopped. The air around us was silent, except for mosquitoes flying around our heads, sounding like tiny helicopters. I swatted the air, chasing a few pests away, glad my friends had decided on coming up here in late June. One time up here in late May, I encountered swarms of deer flies. They landed on us by the thousands when we tried to rest during the inbound trip. When we were paddling the canoes, they left us alone, but when we stopped, it became a horror show; once I looked at my leg and could barely see my jeans. Fortunately, they didn't bite, and we lost them after a day of misery by moving to a new campsite.

I heard more buzzing in my ears, but thought about drones, not mosquitos.

"No more what ifs," I said softly. "Been torturing myself with questions since this started. The only place people will know to look for us is around this little lake and Jackfish Point. My friends know it, and Hank and Pete know it, and if some other campers pass by on Lake Brent, they'll see Hank and Pete's campsite on the outcrop. That will be reported to the rangers if a major search gets underway. Eventually, somebody will come looking here." I pulled a map from my fishing vest and laid it on the ground between us. "If my friends are headed out, we've got three more days to wait. If they're not," I didn't elaborate, "people will be asking about you in five more days, me in eight. Sooner or later, somebody will check around for us. When that time comes, we have to be ready."

She pointed over her shoulder downhill. "What if Hank and Pete come first?"

"We E&E, like yesterday." I poked the map with a stick. We have some ways out of here, but all on foot. Remember, the further we move, the more chance we have to get hurt, and the less chance to be found when help arrives."

She touched a little stream on the map that ran north and south, out of Lake Conmee, no more than three hundred meters to our west. "Couldn't some campers come through here? We could wait by the water and flag them down."

"In all the times I've been up here, I've never used that stream. None of my buddies have either. There may be no way through its portages since it doesn't get much traffic. And even if somebody did pass through and offered us a ride, we'd have to pass right by Hank and Pete's campsite. I don't want to take that chance, for us, or anyone who might help. If by a long shot somebody was headed north, it's a different story, but it doesn't happen much. And I don't know how they would get past without Hank and Pete seeing them." My plan was to check out the north-south stream today. I thought for a second. "Your idea could happen though, if the bad guys were off in the woods to the east in the opposite direction, and somebody came through. But it's a one in a million shot, hate to say."

"This is horrible, Roger. We're trapped, with no way out, and we don't know shit about what they're doing down there."

"Aptly put."

She lay on her back, tears brimming in her eyes. I reached over and grabbed her hand. "Hey, it sounds tough, but look at it this way—there's two assholes down there with a body on their hands and at least one eye witness to the murder. Maybe two. They don't know. And they've got five square miles of woods, hills, and underbrush to search around Jackfish Point. One of the people they're looking for has a gun. I'd guess they're more confused and pissed off than we are." I patted the top of her hand. "Our chances are better than theirs. We'll come out of this in a week; they're going to have to run for the rest of their lives."

CHAPTER EIGHT

Janeene stayed in our base camp when I headed out looking for the north-south creek to Conmee Lake and its portages beside us, expecting them to be visible a short distance from our position. But I was moving slowly and it took an hour to find a good spot to see the water. What I thought was a creek was actually a small lake. The water wasn't moving with any current and it wasn't very wide, a hundred feet at the broadest point, and it tapered into a tiny creek at the south end. The creek made its way into Brent Lake, but it was too narrow for a canoe. It was more like a path choked with green patches of weeds, baby pine trees, and water.

After returning to our hiding place, I laid the map before Janeene and reported what we did and didn't know. It was as confounding as usual. "To get across to the other side, we'll need to use the south end. That brings us closer to their campsite. I wouldn't want to do that unless Hank and Pete were far away. If they realized we were in that area they could use their canoe to move west in Brent Lake and maybe hunt us down."

She studied the map. "Do you think they're still there?"

"Yeah."

"What are they doing?"

"That's the million-dollar question; they're probably sitting in camp wondering about us." We both stared at the map, awaiting divine intervention.

"Staying put is probably the best option," I said aloud.

"Why do you always say that?"

"Because they're the ones with a tight schedule."

She considered this, then said. "What would you do if you were them?"

"Kill myself."

"That's not funny."

"Guess not, but it would make me happy." I tossed in a few snickers as she pulled the canteen to her lips and took a heavy swallow. Her throat was not as dirty as her face and her thin Adam's apple bobbed with the water. I couldn't help but notice the slimness of her fingers, wrists, and arms, and the smoothness of her skin. "How old are you?" I asked.

"How old do you think I am?"

"Maybe twenty-seven or twenty-eight."

"Fat chance. Thank you. I'm thirty-three."

"I thought you said you had your daughter right after college. You said she's six."

"I didn't go right after high school, took a job first as a bookkeeper, went to school nights at a local college, and then transferred to Michigan State."

"Well, you look younger than thirty-three, if it's any consolation."

"And you look younger than forty. You don't have a speck of gray hair."

"I will when this trip is over."

She smiled with those even teeth and looked back at the

map. "You still didn't tell me what you'd do if the situation was reversed."

"If I were them, I'd be thinking about you. They're not certain I even exist. But they know you do, and they'd feel a lot better if...if..."

"If I were dead."

"To put it bluntly, yes."

"So, they'll keep searching?"

"Maybe for a day or two more, if even that long. They accomplished nothing yesterday and they may have decided that trying to find you is wasted effort. You have a good chance of dying out here on your own from getting injured. If you broke a leg in the woods, you might never be found. They probably think the best idea is to hold where they are and wait to see if you come out."

"I'm not going back to those bastards," she hissed. "How could they think that?"

"Who knows what they believe?"

I tapped the paper. "They can read maps as well as you or I can. They realize you're trapped, caught in this area around what I'm calling 'Jackfish Point.'" I pointed at our location and the land around us. "When they found your canoe the other evening, they probably checked around, saw some footprints, and tracked you back to the little lake where I tackled you. They think you are around here."

I let my words sink in as she studied the map. I continued, "They'll probably wait it out for one more day, until Saturday or maybe as long as Sunday morning, hoping you might lose your guts and return to camp. Last night they built a huge fire; I couldn't understand why they'd do that other than to give you a beacon to home in on if you'd had enough of the woods, and to let other campers who might see the fire know this campsite is taken and not to come near. The Fourth of July is coming up. This place will get as busy as it ever gets, even with limitations on camping passes. Much of the year all the available passes for the park are not taken, but on the week of the fourth, in the middle of the summer, they get used. I made the mistake of going into the BWCA instead of Quetico during the holiday period and since there are less restrictions on how many people can be in one site there, the whole place looked like a Boy Scout jamboree. The Canadian park gets busy during the same week, but it's not as bad. I'm guessing they know that."

"So what?"

"So they have problems. They have to try and find you and keep people away from their camp. The longer it takes for somebody to come around, the better the chances you won't bypass them and signal others for help."

"What if paddlers come by and see them?"

"They'll sit in camp and say everything is fine, no problems. When they get questioned about you after they get home, they'll say you and Bobby took off and never returned, and they have no idea what happened to you. Or they'll blame you for killing Bobby—shot him in cold blood. Or they might claim I raided the campsite and killed Bobby in a gunfight. We have no idea what they'll say, but it won't be in our favor."

"So, they'll cast doubt on us. Nice."

"It'll be more than doubt, Janeene, they might report that I killed Bobby and even you after my friends left the waterfall. If they get to the authorities before we do, they can make up any bullshit they want. They'll make us look like the bad guys, or me anyway. This is a dangerous game, one we can't afford to lose."

She shook her head and studied the map. "Couldn't they think we walked through this piece of land here close to Suzanette?"

"I'm hoping they do. I left our footprints heading that way, hoping they would go all the way around. That'll give them a much larger area to search. It'll take time, and they don't have much of it left."

"When Hank and Pete go home without me, won't somebody look for me then?"

"They should. But if Hank and Pete don't go back to Minneapolis or Minnetonka, and let's say they dump their stuff in the woods and go on an extended vacation to Las Vegas, it could be a long time until they get questioned. And when they are, they'll say you and Bobby got mad and left the campsite. You two took off together in your canoe and vanished. Or maybe a guy named Roger Cummings killed you. He was supposed to be around the little lake when you two went missing."

She looked back at the map; her eyes caught in a thousand-yard stare. I'd seen that ghostly glare on soldiers many times. "But that's only one interpretation," I said, breaking her trance. "There's several more."

"Don't want to hear them, Roger."

And I didn't want to go into the details. My gravest thought was that they would recover the naked guy's body and cart it off to some other remote spot, rebury it, and simply disappear. Without a body how could you be sure someone was dead? Television shows and news broadcasts always drove home the point that without a body and a murder weapon, there was no murder case. A person might be missing for years, but unless there was solid evidence of foul play, no charges could be filed. From my rudimentary and possibly incorrect understanding, it took a body and a weapon to provide the right kind of evidence. Although not well-versed in criminal law or investigative procedures or anything related to real police activities, my opinion was that Hank and Pete had to be worried about the burial site. "They found my canoe," I said to Janeene, "so they know I was up here and didn't paddle away. Walked away maybe, but they have no idea if I saw anything or not. From their point of view, they'll be safest if they move the body and bury it at another lake a long way from here."

"But if they're not certain you saw anything, would they do that? They know I didn't see where Bobby is."

"All they know is you're gone. They don't know what you did or didn't see."

Her head bobbed slightly in agreement, but her eyes weren't convinced. "This is all one big question mark, isn't it?"

"My point exactly. We've beaten this to death, so let's wait and see what happens."

It didn't take long to learn their next move.

I heard a canoe paddle banging a gunwale in the little lake before anything else. It was only one tap, like they had been trying to be careful, but the sound of a paddle striking the side of a canoe carries for hundreds of yards. A minute later I heard the faint hissing squelch of a radio.

I went toward the sound, stopping at least four hundred feet above the lake before panning it with the binoculars. Hank was on the south side of the lake aiming his rifle with covering fire as he had when he conducted the assault on our side of the water yesterday morning. I couldn't see Pete, but the sounds of chopping rose up the hill like distant cannon fire. It was a grating noise, metal splintering under the heavy weight of an axe. The guy was breaking my lightweight aluminum canoe into small pieces. They'd damaged it before so it couldn't be used, but now they were chopping it into tiny sections. *Why? To get rid of the evidence?*

Maybe I was starting to guess right in this war of nerves?

Pete worked for half an hour. He'd chop, then stop, then chop again. My canoe was in two-foot sections when I saw it in his craft, piled in pieces in front of his feet to the bow, and from behind him to the stern. Pete paddled directly to the waterfall as Hank walked back and forth along the bank keeping watch. They pulled the canoe atop the precipice and started in the direction of the body. Digging sounds started ten minutes later and didn't abate for an hour. It occurred to me the body wasn't buried that deep, no more than three or four feet. Maybe they had never intended to leave it here, just get it out of sight until they were ready to move? That was my hope anyway.

I didn't go back to Janeene until they had carried the wrapped corpse and the pieces of my canoe down the precipice. I told her what I'd seen. "I think they'll be leaving soon. Their clock is ticking."

* * *

It was a few minutes after noontime, and the heat of the sun gave the damp forest floor a less musty smell. Janeene snuggled against my side as mosquitoes swarmed us from time to time, but they seemed to settle down in the midday heat. I was happy to have an idea what Hank and Pete were planning. My suspicion was they had the body concealed while they were breaking down their camp for a quick exit either this afternoon or first thing in the morning.

I woke up at three thirty, startled by the clatter of a blue jay in a tree overhead. It sang with a barking noise, the *jaay, jaay, jaay* call they make when they're pissed off. A second one in another branch answered. It seemed angry too. As I rolled over on my side to watch the bird, a branch snapped in the woods. Then another, followed by the hiss of a radio. Shit. This time it was close.

Janeene stirred, and I quickly put my hand over her mouth. Her eyes flew open, but my face was inches from hers with a finger crossing my lips, giving her the international sign of *no words*. She nodded her head vigorously, letting me know she understood. I pointed toward the lake and let her go. Staying on my stomach beside her, I searched for the binoculars with one hand while my other hand found the pistol.

It took ten minutes of frantic searching, but I finally spotted Pete stalking up the hill. He was wearing a green-gray hunter's camouflage shirt and matching pants, spattered with flecks of tree bark. I wished he still had the yellow Hard Rock Café T-shirt on his chubby torso. Across his shoulders were backpack straps. In his hands he held a bolt-action deer rifle with a scope.

"One of them is very close," I whispered. "A hundred yards away." She knew better than to respond.

Pete was working his way uphill, crouching every few steps to settle and listen, then rising again and moving. If he'd chosen a route a little further to his west, he would have stepped on us. The guy moved with a practiced ease. He was definitely a hunter. It shocked me how efficiently the chubby guy moved. He was good.

"What's he doing?" Janeene whispered directly into my ear.

"Searching. Be quiet and still."

He couldn't have been more than forty meters from my trip wires. Dammit. I'd considered pulling them in all morning, and regretted being lazy. If he happened to glance down or caught a reflection off the hooks of the fishing lures, we'd be in deep shit. There'd be only one chance to shoot him with the pistol. But he needed to be closer for that, much closer than I wanted.

Gnats were humming in my ears like angry little heli-copters, and Janeene was trembling so hard she actually rustled in the pine needles, but like a bird of prey, my eyes stayed focused on Pete's shape. I didn't move a muscle as he continued up the hill. Gradually, painfully, he began to slip out of sight. He was above us now, at a point where he might be able to look down into the creek and portages I'd scouted this morning. I prayed he hadn't noticed any of our tracks.

A muted voice carried on the gentle breeze. It was a low, mellow whisper, but then the radio crackled. He was talking to Hank. Where was that prick—over in the slough to our west, or below us in the little lake? Ten to one he had his rifle at the ready. Suddenly, the radio squelched full blast. Pete keyed it and rekeyed it three times. Blue jays started clattering, an owl in a tree started hooting, and a crow in the sky started cawing. The noise was deafening. I put my hand quickly back over Janeene's mouth. They were searching desperately for her, using all their tricks to try and flush her out. "They're trying to scare you into running." Judging by her shaking hands, it nearly worked.

Pete wasn't visible any longer, but after the radio ploy I heard him moving. Snapping branches and crunching leaves let me know he was on a mission and in a hurry. The sound got weaker and weaker as I waited, finally gaining the courage to get to my knees and use the binoculars to scout above us. Only branches and leaves filled the eyepieces.

CHAPTER NINE

We never moved after Pete's radio antics. The thought of leaving our lair was terrifying. Janeene and I even relieved ourselves right beside where we were hiding. We'd been lying here for a long time without so much as a whisper, wondering if this was the last day of our lives, which didn't feel good.

"How are we going to get out of here?" she whispered, voice pitifully hoarse. We hadn't spoken for nearly an hour.

"We're not. We're going to hide here until help comes."

She gave me the look a child does when they agree with you without understanding. It had been four hours since Pete passed by our den going uphill; the darkness was now eating its way into the forest. Shadows were growing in the spaces where daylight had been half an hour ago. "They're making one last sweep of this area before they leave. They'll be gone tomorrow. Bet on it." But if real money was involved, the only wager to make was that I'd be dead wrong about the actions these guys might take. Missed half the calls already. Still, what I'd told her was my best guess. They'd try one more pass through the area, hoping to flush her out if she was alive, and get back to the camp before dark. That was the part that scared me most. Getting back. Pete had certainly gone on to the north. Hank had probably continued watching the area from the waterfall with his binoculars, checking in with Pete by using the radio. They'd scoured the little lake area and the western side of Jack-fish Point yesterday, the eastern flank this afternoon. They had to be leaving tomorrow. The body was gone. Janeene was gone. And their time was gone. But Pete still might have to pass back this way to get to his camp.

I wanted to go look for Pete's canoe, but I was rooted to our nest as surely as one is to his ancestry and frightened as badly as any time in recent memory. To be so close to escape and nearly lose your life because you'd fallen asleep was unforgivable. My confidence was shaken.

"Roger, I want you to know I appreciate you helping me."

"Not necessary to say anything."

"Yes, it is. You've risked your life for me. I've been thinking about that all afternoon; I've been a coward all my life, and I can't believe how brave you are."

Brave? How can you call someone cowering in his boots brave? "Why would you call yourself a coward?"

"Because I didn't stand up for my daughter when she needed me. I should have stood up to her father when he bullied her and me, or his parents when they threatened to take me to court for not letting them see her. But I was afraid of losing her and the child support, afraid of everything."

"That isn't cowardice, it's trying to be a mother under tough circumstances."

"Yeah, but when you let people push you into believing your child doesn't need better medical attention, let them sway you into accepting inferior doctors when you think differently, that's not being brave. And it wasn't brave putting up with

Hank's abuse either, especially when his purpose was to humiliate me; I've got a tattoo to prove it. . ."

So maybe the butterfly on her butt wasn't her idea. "Don't see it that way, Janeene."

"How do you see it?"

"Not sure."

"It wasn't only that, I've been a coward in other ways too. Like when you saw me making love with Bobby. I shouldn't have done that on this trip or without telling Hank it was over with him. I should have told him months ago. I intended to. When he won the money, dollars signs popped up in my eyes. And not just for me, but for Angela because the money would let me take better care of her. Maybe we could move to another house and get away from my ex-husband and his family—get away from a lot of things."

"You're confusing cowardice with a lack of honesty. It takes bravery to face the truth. Your situation sounds more like you had to make tough decisions not only for yourself but for your daughter as well. We all face circumstances like that, where being honest and doing the right thing isn't as easy as it sounds."

"I haven't been as brave as I should have, and I'd like another chance."

"We'd all like a second shot. Me included. I'd love a million opportunities to go back and do some things a different way." *What I didn't tell her was the first one I'd cash in on would be to have stayed in my campsite and not come to this little waterfall lake to fish for largemouth bass.*

"You always face up to things?" she asked.

"No. And didn't always act correctly, either." I wasn't really in the mood for conversation but the fear of seeing Pete only meters away during the afternoon had built to a crescendo—and now relief was pouring through us like shots of adrenaline.

The darkening forest comforted me, and apparently, her too. What did it hurt to talk? "I faced a situation similar to yours with my wife, but it wasn't battling over our children—it was fighting over my work schedule and long hours."

"She didn't like you to work so much?"

"Exactly. She valued family time with me and the kids, and I wanted to build a new career, a complete restart. Leaving the Army was hard for me, but she was very happy I left, as there were no more deployments to war zones or other oddball places. She was from a good Italian family in New Jersey, who wanted her to be a stay-at-home mom and cook great meals. Maybe own a restaurant. Marrying a New Yorker just starting a career as an Army officer was not on her family's list of goals. All of us got along well, but they never liked me being in the service."

"How'd you solve the problem?"

"Never did. I left the Army after a little over eight years, even though I intended on doing twenty and making it a career. When the stock job popped up, I jumped in with both feet. And I mean both, as well as my ankles, shins, knees—all the way up to my ass. I loved the stock trading business, could never learn enough. Worked my tail off until late at night and most weekends. It put a real strain on our marriage. Eventually, I came to realize that there would never be enough time to understand everything I wanted to know about the market and stay married, so I relented and became four-fifths of the broker I could have been while keeping my wife happy and my family together."

She looked at me, waiting for me to continue. I searched the woods out to our front instead. "Sounds like you did act correctly when you needed to," she whispered. She slid closer to me.

What she didn't know was, until this very moment, I'd

never spoken so directly about the issues in my marriage with anyone other than my camping buddy Duke, and he only knew parts of the story. I usually avoided the subject altogether, but concluded that fearing for your life lent clarity and honesty to your past.

"What are you going to do when we get back?" she asked.

"Go to Hawaii with you and Angela—told you that."

"I mean really."

"Take a good, hot shower. Shave." The bristles on my chin and neck were beginning to itch. "And probably sit back and think about how good life really is."

"Don't you work?"

"Yeah, but now my job is trading stocks from home. I own enough of them to live off the proceeds if I do it right."

"Must be nice. I have a bookkeeping and accounting job waiting for me."

"And a six-year-old daughter."

"Yes, I do." I was glad she smiled at that thought. She sounded a little morbid before. Focusing on the one thing she obviously cherished above all others might help.

"I'm going to get you back to her soon."

"I know you will. I want to thank you in advance."

I looked back at the forest with renewed interest. Our enemies, Hank and Pete, could be anywhere at this very moment, but it wouldn't surprise me if they had met up and were both traveling back to their camp by canoe. My best guess was that after Pete left us, he continued walking north or northwest while Hank paddled by water into Conmee Lake, using the small waterway to our west. With this plan, they could search the most promising areas, and since they had radios, they could choose a spot on the shoreline of Conmee to rendezvous and get Pete back in the canoe.

But it didn't matter what they did, as long as neither one

came stumbling directly into my trip wires. If I could just make it through the night, we might—

"Hey," I whispered, "where would you take Angela if you could go anywhere in the world you wanted? Hospitals excluded."

"Oh, lots of places. Let me think. . . well, she's never been to Disneyland. I always wanted to take her there after she got old enough to enjoy it. And I'd like to take her to the Empire State Building, never been there myself. And of course, Paris would be nice, with the Eiffel Tower and all. And maybe a trip to. . ."

CHAPTER TEN

I spun the top off my canteen and was bringing it to my lips when a burst of gunfire erupted in the air. *Bang.* One loud shot, then six rapid snaps behind it. They pierced the darkness like bombs from the direction of the crevasse. Canteen water splashed all over my chest.

"What's that?" Janeene cried.

"Gunfire. Coming from above." My watch showed 10:30 p.m.

"Was that Pete?" she asked.

"I don't know. Who else could it be?"

"Why would he. . .? I mean, what would he. . .?"

"I've got the same answers as you. None."

We crouched together, both on our knees, gaping at the darkness. "Jesus, Roger, I'm scared."

"Maybe he saw an animal or is letting us know he's pissed off. I have no idea."

"Those shots were close."

"Not that close. But from the ravine, I think, less than half a click away."

"How far is—"

"Half a click is five hundred meters or a little more than five hundred yards, or about seventeen hundred feet, straight uphill." I grabbed the pistol, slid the safety off, and aimed it at my trip wires, moving my eyes slowly to the left and right, scanning the woods. My night vision was honed from growing used to the darkness all evening. I thought of bolting for Pete's canoe since he was so far away. *Stupid idea.* He could be coming down for it. Or Hank could be waiting at the waterfall.

Six more rapid snaps pierced the air. In a few seconds, one louder bang. What was going on up there? It sounded like a Special Forces ambush.

"Are the shots getting closer?" Janeene asked.

"From the same place, I think."

Six more snaps went off.

"My God, that's a lot of shooting," Janeene exclaimed.

"Yeah. Somebody is desperate or very angry."

She clung to my side, shaking. "Why don't you lie down and rest," I said. "Let me watch the woods."

For an hour I held the position on my knees, alternating looking through the binoculars and just watching with my eyes. Janeene curled up beside me, not asking any more questions. My head bobbed in weariness until finally I lay down on my stomach, facing uphill. Pesky gnats and mosquitoes buzzed in my ears and nose. I cautiously swiped them away, feeling tiny droplets of sweat on my palms.

The gun was under my nose. When I'd doze, my face hit it with a thump, jarring me awake. Imaginary targets danced in my eyes, and it was all I could do to keep from squeezing off a round.

* * *

Dawn approached, washing the sky and forest with hues of foggy gray. Chirping birds and curious rodents rustled in the leaves, sounding like elephants in the frightening calm. I hadn't slept well, just nodded off only to be awakened time and again by my pistol when it tapped me in the face. It took some time before the blackness metamorphosed into misty shades. I aimed the pistol at noises, holding fire while trying to spot a silhouette. Tension cramped my arms and neck.

Janeene was still asleep, oblivious to the chill and mist lifting off the forest floor. Bumping her gently caused her to stir one eye, then the other. "Wake up," I whispered, "You need to do something for me."

"What?"

"Stay awake." I rolled over on my side. "It's first light and I'm going up to the crevasse to check it out."

"Why?"

"Need to know what happened last night. Pete might be down."

"Down?"

"Yeah, hurt. . . injured. Dead maybe."

"What if he isn't?"

"Have to be really careful; that's why I want to go up there now before it gets any brighter. This is the best time of day to sneak around."

She sat up and shivered. "I don't think it's a good idea. We'd be safer if you just stayed here."

"Probably, but I have to know what happened. If Pete fell into the ravine, I might be able get his rifle. Don't think he came by us last night."

"Are you sure he didn't?"

"No, Janeene. Not sure of anything, that's why I have to check it out." There wasn't time to argue in circles. "Look, if he's not up there, we'll wait it out here, okay?" I caressed her face with my hand. "Got to get up there before Hank does."

"Hank? Why will he go there?"

"Because Pete might be in trouble. Those sounded like desperate shots to me last night. If Pete's still up there, Hank will go searching for him. It would be nice to get to that rifle before he does."

"I don't know, Roger. All this sneaking around, this. . . this military stuff doesn't make sense. None of it does."

"Not much has since Wednesday."

"Seems like we've been hiding out for a week."

"Only three days. Today is Saturday. Hey, hand me the backpack, please." I took the master map out after she placed the bag in my lap and scratched another mark on the calendar.

She stared at me like I'd lost my mind. "Your face is full of red spots," she said.

"Damned bugs ate me alive last night." I didn't tell her she didn't look so good herself, cheeks smudged, eyes swollen, lips parched.

"Have to go to the bathroom," she whispered.

"Do it right there. Next to the tree trunk."

She made a face and shook her head. "I can wait till you're gone."

I crouched on one knee, feeling my aching back protest. "Okay. Now please listen to me carefully. I'm going near the crevasse. You stay here and keep watch. Don't move, and don't make any noise. If I should run into somebody in the woods and get spotted, I'll run like hell and scream the word *Atlanta* so you'll know somebody is after me. Might have to run for a long time. But you stay put. This is the only place I'll be able to find you, so stay here, understand?"

Her eyes were narrow slits, and she was on the verge of crying. She huddled in her shirt, wrapping, and unwrapping her arms around her chest. I checked the pistol, making sure the safety was on. "I can leave this with you if you want?"

She looked at the gun like it was a spitting cobra. "I don't want it."

"You know how to use one?" Never thought to ask her yesterday.

"Yeah. I can shoot pretty well. Still, you need it, just in case. . ." Her eyes closed.

"Nothing will happen. Believe me, if anybody's around the crevasse I'll come straight back. Not taking any chances."

"Wish you wouldn't go."

"Have to."

Squeezing her hands between mine helped make my point. "This is one of those things that just has to be done." It didn't seem to appease her. "Listen, the trip wires around us are still in place. If you hear one rattle, it won't be me in them. You just stay down in the pine straw and keep still. One of those guys would have to step on you to find this place, and that won't happen."

"I'm scared, Roger."

"So am I."

I patted her hand again while planning the route. "I'll be coming back to you from the south, right through there." She looked in the direction of a toppled pine tree leaning against another. It looked like an archway. "I'll come right underneath it."

I gave her a peck on the cheek, got up, and moved off to the wires. They were hard to find in the pale light. The lures and twigs were still dangling, the lines intact. *Good.*

Creeping through the underbrush, I stopped every few steps to listen for sounds. The air was still, the forest tranquil. Sound traveled a long way and the *kee-eeeee-arr* call of a red-tailed hawk overhead broke the eerie silence.

It took forty harrowing minutes, but finally the ravine was before me. While peeking around a stump, a branch broke nearby; I bit my tongue, drawing a bead of warm, salty blood. The tiny gash throbbed and I concentrated on sliding my tongue against my teeth, fighting the instinct to dash away at full speed. I made sure the pistol in my hand was cocked and ready to fire.

Inching my head around the stump was an agonizingly slow process, and when I could see past it, I froze. Less than ten feet away was a bear cub. The cub was about forty pounds of matted, dark brown hair. It was sitting on its haunches, swarmed by flies, chewing on the tip of a sapling it had bent over to the ground and broken. The cub stopped chewing and swatted at the air. It lost its balance and tumbled to its side.

My head spun around in all directions. *Where was the mother?* I prayed I wasn't between the cub and her and looked around for the smallest tree to climb. Black bears are excellent climbers, but they stay off trees or branches too little to support their weight. I searched frantically for a thin tree, since there was no way to outrun a pissed-off mother.

Behind the cub came a roar. More of a groan than roar, and the baby clambered to its feet and ran toward the crevasse. It cavorted beside the edge with a small tree branch, then found a pine cone and smacked it around. No adult came to its side. Once or twice the cub walked to the very brink, but it quickly turned aside to wrestle with twigs or branches on the ground. The third time it waddled to the rim, a loud groan bellowed from inside. *Damn. A bear was down in the fissure.* Had Pete shot it? My eyes snapped around the hillside looking for a sniper who might have a bead on me. Where was Pete? My heart pumped wildly as I searched the tree line, fighting a burning notion to skirt back down the hill to Janeene.

Another moan bellowed out of the crevasse. This time the

cub ran to the edge and squealed back, a wailing, high-pitched scream. A sonorous roar answered.

I crept behind a fallen tree and inched toward the rim. Getting within ten feet of the edge, the cub saw me and dashed off, shrieking like an injured pig. It ran twenty yards, turned around and hissed, baring its nail-like fangs. If this call didn't bring the mother out, she wasn't coming. I inched along the ground, kneeled, and peeked over the brink.

At the bottom was a mass of fuzzy, black hair, eyes, and fangs. The bear was lying on her side, head in the creek bed. Blood filled her mouth and I saw huge, soggy circles on her hairy flank. Her nose wrinkled and she raised her head and snarled directly at me. Her eyes were on fire, and she struggled to a sitting position. For an instant I thought she might charge straight up the rocks, and I backed away from the rim, looking for a small tree.

The snarling quit. She didn't come to the top and when I glimpsed over again, she was lying in the same place. I noticed a leather boot sticking out from a boulder behind her and moved along the edge for a better look. A body was wedged between two rocks, sprawled out on its back. The body was dressed in a hunting shirt—Pete's shirt. A milky white thighbone poked out through his pant leg and rust-colored blood smeared both legs and most of his stomach. Lots of it. One arm was bent at an obscene angle. A camouflage-patterned jungle hat covered half the guy's face, hiding his eyes. A glint of light sparkled off a pistol near his other hand. Underneath him, squashed between his backpack and a river rock, was a hunting rifle.

"Hey, asshole," I said. The bear snarled and the cub squealed. The man's head didn't budge. "Hey?" Nothing. I picked up a rock and tossed it near the guy's chest. The body didn't move. A second rock hit his hat and knocked it from his face. It was Pete. His hairless head was purple-blue, and his eyes were swollen shut, bulging from their sockets. A mass of flies and gnats clung to his open, bloody mouth.

He must have stumbled into the ravine in the dark, or stumbled over my trip wires, or was chased in by the bear. Whichever way, it was a gruesome death for the man, falling onto the rocks and shattering so many bones. I wondered if he'd bled to death from the fractures or had been finished off by the sow. Then a wave of revulsion hit me. It had been a long time since the weight of seeing a dead person had settled on my shoulders. I remembered the grotesque, swollen bodies of Iraqi soldiers rotting in the desert sand or in their armored vehicles. I'd accounted for some of those bodies and fell to my knees feeling sorry for Pete and myself. I never wanted to be responsible for the death of another person again, and I had—all because of wanting to fish in the little lake and not keeping my fucking binoculars in their case where they belonged. But this was war, as surely as it was back in Iraq.

Nothing could be done for Pete. My guess was he'd been alive for only half the night. *Why didn't you kill the bear, you prick?* At least I could have pulled his body from the ravine and protected it from other scavengers and gotten his weapons. But with the wounded sow, I couldn't even risk going down to check the rifle. My two bullets might finish her, but what if they didn't? And what if he didn't have any ammo left? He'd certainly fired a barrage last night, most of them probably trying to fend her off. I wouldn't have been able to aim either, lying at the bottom of a darken pit, leg shattered and guts spewing out into my hands. The big sow let out a sad groan. Wish I could end her suffering, but my ammo was too precious.

Out of the corner of my eye I noticed the little cub charging; I jumped back as it snarled and snapped, stopping ten feet away. "Easy, little fella, I'm leaving now, but I wish you all the luck in the world." Without a mother, his chances weren't good.

* * *

I answered as many of Janeene's questions as possible while gathering our gear. "Believe me, Pete's finished. He died during the night. You don't want to know more." Visions of his purple head and mouthful of flies blinded me. "We've got to get moving. Hank might be headed this way."

"But why leave now?"

"Because we can get to a canoe."

"So what? Hank is still out there with a rifle."

Damn it, I wanted to get away from here. "It's time to make a break for it." I jammed the perimeter trip wires and fishing lures retrieved into my fishing vest. In a bullheaded mood, my mind was made up. We had to move. The pistol also went into the pocket of my fishing vest. "We need to save everything. Get those spinning rods and the canteen and follow me down to the little lake."

"Roger, please. Let's stay here."

"No. I've been thinking. If Pete stayed up there last night, maybe Hank didn't come back either. Maybe he stayed in the canoe around to our north. That gunfire happened at 10:30 p.m. They were planning on staying out all night, hoping we'd build a fire or turn on a flashlight, do something they could track to our location. My guess is Hank is waiting for him or looking for him now in the daylight. He could be at the crevasse already. This might be the best chance we have to get out of this place."

"And it might be the best chance we have of getting killed."

"It absolutely will be if Hank comes down the hill with a rifle. I can't hold him off with only two bullets."

"But both of them couldn't find us for two days. How can only one man find us now?"

"Because once he sees Pete, he's going to turn over every

rock until he does. I got a feeling about the guy. Not arguing with you about this."

It took an hour, but finally I found Pete's canoe at the north side of the little lake. It was covered with leafy branches and tucked beside a decaying tree trunk. There were no paddles or life vests, so I recovered mine from the briar patch where I'd hidden them a day before. It was 7:45 a.m., and I was getting worried.

"Roger, what if Hank sees us out on this lake? It's not that big. Won't he be able to shoot us?"

"Maybe. But I'm guessing he circled around toward Suzanette yesterday. Or maybe he went into that finger of water in Conmee Lake. Either way, that's why Pete came up here yesterday afternoon, trying to push us in Hank's direction. That's my best guess."

"Guessing might get us killed."

"It might also get us out of here if there's a gap we can use to escape."

She glared at me. Her hair was a bundle of knots, and her face was grimy with sweat and ground-in dirt. She was Medusa. I held her stare for a minute, locked in a war of wills. "You're really scared, aren't you?"

"Petrified."

"Look, there were two guys yesterday. This morning there's only one. I know that for a fact. It's the first real piece of information we've had in some time. One person can't be everywhere at once; I'm banking on Hank not being down there near the campsite. If I'm right, we're out of here and you're safe. If I'm wrong, we're no worse off than we are now."

I looked toward the waterfall. "This little lake is over half a mile east to west and about a three hundred meters, or yards in your terms, north to south. We'll move along the north shore.

It'd take a hell of a shot to get close to us if he's on the precipice."

"He's a good shot, remember. Said so yourself."

"Yeah, I know, but if something doesn't look right or smell right, we'll go back in the woods and fight it out from there. Okay?" She didn't answer me. "Okay?"

"I think we should go back to the pine bed and wait."

"Then we'll be pinned down. With this canoe we have a chance to move fast."

She crossed her arms and looked down at her feet. She was shivering with fear. She was even afraid of me. "Did you kill Pete?"

"Hell no. He fell in the ravine and died."

She wouldn't look at me. "I'm afraid to cross that lake, Roger."

"Look, I'm tired as hell and every bit as scared as you. If we're going to get out of here, we have to work together. Pull as a team."

"Then why don't you let me be a part of it? You're not listening to me. I'm afraid to go back near that camp."

"Why?"

"Because Hank will torture me if he catches me. You don't know the guy; I do. He's mean, Roger, mean like you wouldn't understand."

I remembered the view in my binoculars when he shot the naked guy, and I remembered certain soldiers in Iraq. "His kind is easier to understand than you think."

I pulled her to my chest, rocking her slowly side to side. "I'll protect you. Get you back to Angela. Believe me. We have to take the canoe."

Her nostrils flared, sucking in deep breaths as she searched for strength. Finally, she answered, "Okay, okay. Let's go."

I helped her into the canoe, then handed her the pistol.

"You hold it." We pushed off from the bank and paddled carefully along the northern shoreline. No one rose from the weeds, no bullets came at our heads.

Looking from the precipice, it was obvious the Brent Lake NE campsite was deserted, or was intended to look that way. The firepit was not smoking and there was no motion of any kind near the tents. The air was listless. Leaves hung like forgotten flags on a windless day. I faced one of the most important decisions of my life. Either traverse the waterfall portage and get into Brent Lake or turn around and hide. An old military saying came to mind: *Victory goes to the one who seizes the initiative.*

Janeene squeezed my hand. "What are you thinking?"

"That even a poor decision executed forcefully can succeed. It's military lingo for, 'let's just do it.'" I pulled the canoe from the little lake and pushed it to the edge of the waterfall, then took the rope, attached it to the bow hook, and wrapped it around a small tree. I lowered it to the bottom, forgetting to look for my sunglasses.

CHAPTER ELEVEN

In Brent Lake, we stopped a short distance away from Hank's camp. A brisk breeze had sprung up in the time it took to lower the canoe down the portage and paddle our way near the campsite. We bobbed in the choppy water. "It's unoccupied," I said, scanning the area thoroughly with the binoculars while considering whether to go there and forage for food or supplies. There were two food packs hanging from trees, a good practice to keep stores safe from pillaging animals. Hunger pangs were plaguing me, and Janeene hadn't eaten anything but a candy bar in two days.

"We might find a gun," she said.

"Doubt it. Food maybe. . . no weapons."

The hammock was swaying. That damned thing had been the cause of all my trouble and I watched it with a malevolent stare wanting to rush ashore and burn it to ashes. A squirrel sat in the netting, rocking it from side to side while chewing a nut. I put the lens covers back on the binoculars, tired of looking at the deserted camp. "Should we try to find something to eat?" she asked.

"No, too risky. Don't feel good about it." At that second, the shrill grating of metal on stone pierced the air. It was behind us. I spun to look at the precipice, then over at the southern portage from the finger of water from Conmee Lake. A silver shape was sliding down toward the water's edge. A guy was pushing a canoe. The nose hit the water with a splash, followed by a guy jumping aboard. One person. I had no doubt that one person was Hank.

"Let's get outta here," I shouted to Janeene, immediately steering our craft toward open water. We had a three- to four-hundred-meter lead. "Hit it. Paddle as hard as you can, gotta move."

We churned full speed ahead, pushing out beyond the land sheltering the campsite and into a blustery wind chopping the open surface of the lake. The sky had cleared completely, not a cloud in view, and a blazing sun bore down. Janeene's paddle clanged against the gunwale as she tried to pull water. My head pulsed as I dug deep troughs, straining with all my might to correct for her shallower strokes.

"Is he after us?!" Janeene yelled.

"Just keep paddling, and I'll see in a minute."

I was afraid to turn around, half expecting to look behind and see Hank's canoe immediately in our wake, magically thrust forward by an ill-tempered water god. I sucked in air with sloppy whistles, blinking my eyes and choking on spray from Janeene's wild strokes. When I turned around, the guy was setting a furious pace, correcting his course, exactly at us. *Shit.* Any glimmer of stupid hope that he wasn't Hank vanished. "Give it all you've got, Janeene. The son of a bitch is after us." But he was now about five hundred meters behind. We'd gained some distance.

Both of us pounded the water with renewed vigor. Her paddling in front helped keep our craft in line, but with less powerful strokes, I had to correct constantly. Two people can normally paddle better than one, but Janeene only counted for half a person. She was already losing power in her strokes. My biceps burned and my eyes stung from getting pelted by water droplets slinging off Janeene's paddle, but I drove forward, forearms ready to explode as huge swathes of water were pushed by my efforts. *If he's gaining, we're doomed in the main channel. We have to get out of his shooting range.* I started searching the nearest shoreline for a landing site.

When her rowing slowed to a crawl, my eyes spun to the rear. Hank's canoe had fallen further back. It was hard to see him in the bright glare of the water since the sun was behind him, but it was obvious the wind and choppy waves had given us an advantage. I squinted and could see Hank kneeling near the middle of his craft, switching strokes from side to side, trying to balance his forward momentum. But he couldn't keep pace, and any error he made caused his canoe to move left or right, blown off course by the wind. He was losing speed. I watched him thrash at the water. *Either he doesn't know how to paddle alone, or he's hurt and can't keep up.* "We're gonna make it."

"What?" Janeene turned with eyes glazed by fear.

"We have to keep pushing, just paddle as steadily as you can. Don't wear yourself out." I stole another look to the rear. Hank wasn't paddling. He was fumbling with something in his hands. "Let's move." I didn't tell her I thought he was getting ready to fire at us.

We pulled with a vengeance, steering our canoe into the deepest chop. Only special sniper rifles are accurate at great distances, and he didn't have one. But a deer rifle aimed properly could still find the mark at a range of five to six hundred meters, especially if he tried to skip bullets across the water or tried to lob a bullet on us and got lucky. Our bobbing in choppy water would make both prospects more difficult, and so I pointed us into the deepest swells.

"Keep your head down and keep stroking," I yelled. "And don't look back."

In the distance I heard a faint pop, then another, but no splashes. *He doesn't have the range.* To my right, a shiny flicker burbled in the water. He was shooting a high trajectory. I heard a few more thumps, then a quick volley of five or six shots, but no splashes.

"What's that noise, Roger?"

"Hank trying to get lucky by using his pistol. Keep pushing and we'll be safe."

She mumbled something, but I lowered my head and forged on. We worked steadily to gain distance. My shoulders felt like burning ropes, filled by smoldering hemp rather than sinew. The intoxicating fire in my joints spurred me. "Keep stroking, Janeene. We're getting away." And getting away was the objective. If Hank had been gaining on us, I would have pulled ashore and taken our chances by either running through the woods or trying to ambush him. But those were terrible choices compared to paddling off to a ranger station. For once, we'd had good luck.

We pulled steadily away from Hank. He must have gotten hurt during the night and couldn't paddle very well. As Janeene had confirmed, he was in his late thirties and looked to be in good shape. Even alone, he should have been able to paddle well enough to give us a real scare. Had to be injured. *Good.*

Half an hour after our encounter he was a distant speck on the horizon. We slowed to an even pace with steady strokes and passed through a narrow channel on the far western side of Brent Lake. I lost sight of him as we turned south, heading for the other campsite on the lake, the one my buddies had used. A sinking feeling in my gut said they had left and gone for help. I'd ruined their trip, but knowing them, they'd go get help for a friend, especially one who'd left for a few hours but didn't return for days.

As suspected, my former campsite was vacant. No wispy trail of smoke from the firepit, no evidence anyone had been here. We always cleaned up our campsites, leaving no trace of our presence for others to encounter or animals to forage. That was how it was supposed to be done in the parks. "Are you going to look up there?" Janeene asked, pointing to the small hill at the landing and the campsite on the top. "Not planning on it, except. . ." Thinking of all the reasons I should not go look, like Hank on our ass, or precious time wasted, and my disappointment if they didn't leave me anything.

"Except what?" she said. My thoughts turned to Duke. I turned and looked backwards and could see about six hundred meters behind me. No canoe on the water, so no Hank. *Maybe Duke left something for me.* "Gotta be quick," I announced, heading toward the site.

When we reached the landing, I spun the canoe around, putting me closest to the land. "You stay in the boat and keep watch. Scream if you see anybody."

Stepping on shore, I went straight to the firepit. They were always the center of life in camp—the place to cook and talk and gather in the evening. Cresting a small rise, I saw a plastic bag on the rocks surrounding the pit and ran to it. Inside were at least ten candy bars, four or five bags of trail mix, a few freeze-dried meals, and what looked like paper. A note. The bag was sealed with one of those zip-tops you squeezed tight with your fingers. It was probably the reason animals hadn't found it—that, and the fact everything left was sealed in individual wrappers, leaving little or no scent. Duke was a smart guy. But I guessed this stuff hadn't been here too long because raccoons, bears, and other marauders had incredible noses. They would have ravaged the whole bag after the slightest whiff. I opened the plastic zipper and pulled out the paper, unfolding it.

The note read:

Roger, we decided you might be in serious trouble. A guy at the lake where you went to fish said he had not seen you. We guessed you saw his canoe at the waterfall and went to another lake. We could not find you in the other places we looked. I tried your cell phone, but no signal. Ours don't work either so we could not call for help. We waited for almost two days. No other people came by, so we left Friday after lunch. We are headed through Darky Lake and then will go to Minn Lake. That should be the best route to find help. Maybe we can find some people or get a signal to call the rangers. Good luck if you find this.

I hustled back to the canoe, carrying the note in one hand and the plastic bag with the food in the other. I shook the goodies in front of her eyes. "My buddies are real troopers. After we get out on the water, we'll have a feast."

We pushed off, heading south. From this direction we could move toward either Darky Lake or Argo Lake. I knew how to get to Darky; we had come through it on the way in. I wasn't sure about the route to Argo from Brent Lake.

"Eat what you want from the bag, even the freeze-dried stuff is pretty good. It might tingle on your tongue and make you want to swallow a gallon of water, but it's yours if you want it."

"I thought you were supposed to cook it with boiled water?"

"Don't think we'll build a fire anytime soon."

She watched the horizon behind me with the binoculars, nibbling on one of the candy bars. "You want one?" she asked, holding hers up in the air.

"Yeah, I could eat a whole Halloween's worth." She dug around and tossed a Snickers bar and then a Hershey bar at my feet. I grabbed them after a few strokes, deciding to admire them for a few seconds before devouring them.

I quit paddling, ate the candy, and moved to the middle of the canoe, using the binoculars to look to our rear. Hank hadn't yet made the last turn, so he had to be maybe seven hundred meters behind, a little less than half a mile—plenty of time for me to think about our route.

We were nearing a point where I would no longer be able to see Hank, or anybody for that matter, approaching us from the north. My view would be blocked by an outcrop of land, so I took a final look and then moved the craft briskly along the contours of the lake, heading southeast, then southwest, and finally slightly northwest. Not being able to see a great distance behind me was worrisome, but in almost all the stretches you could see clearly for at least six hundred meters.

I couldn't remember if the current was heading down-stream or upstream from Brent into Darky Lake. Either way, we had to traverse a portage at the mouth of the river where there was a small set of rapids. "We're going into the river," I said, "straight ahead."

We stopped beyond the first rapids after bumping over rocks and fallen trees, losing speed. Twice, I hoisted the canoe on my shoulders for short runs around logjams in the river. The runs were brief fifty-meter jaunts. At a lengthy section, where the trail ran up a sharp incline through jagged rocks and hanging vines, I posted Janeene behind me with the pistol. "You see him, shoot, then run to me." We never saw him behind us. But we could only see a short distance to our rear. The thick underbrush and narrow width of the river channel allowed us to see maybe two hundred meters behind.

Before we got in the main channel of Darky Lake, I decided

to head north toward Minn Lake, using the narrow waterway connecting the two lakes. My buddies had used this identical route on our way into the interior of Quetico to the Brent Lake campsite, so it was familiar to me.

"Hey, I never asked you before, but does Hank come up here a lot?"

"Yeah. But he said he usually goes into the Boundary Waters, not Quetico. He said he didn't know the Canadian side well."

"Good. We need all the luck we can get."

"Where are we, Roger?"

"We're in a finger of water heading into Darky Lake." It was about a mile in length from the river and its portages to the main lake. I could see about a quarter mile behind me now.

"I came this way since there are several ways out of Darky, but someone would have a hard time finding the portages out. There are also portages that lead nowhere—lakes that have only one way in and one way out, like one called Ballard. If Hank doesn't know this place well and makes a bad guess, he might wander around for a month."

"This the best way to go?"

"We'll find out."

We paddled along the northern shoreline of the finger into Darky. Janeene slumped down in the bow of the canoe. "Rest a while," I told her. Her overshirt was off, tied around her waist. Her halter top was stuck to her back by perspiration oozing off her neck and face, soaking her from shoulders to hips. "Take a good drink, and put some water on this." I tossed my spare T-shirt to her. "Pat it on your face and head. Don't overheat."

"You look as red as a tomato yourself," she returned. I was certainly tired, but more enervated than exhausted. Dipping some water into my hand and gulping it down, I said, "My strength will hold if I keep moving and pace myself." I wasn't so sure about her. "How you feeling?"

She turned around in her seat, the wet T-shirt stretched across her head like a bandana. "Better. I can help again."

"Nice and easy, sweetheart. We're halfway there."

As we entered a narrow section of the finger leading to Darky, I scanned the water behind us. The steady breeze gave the water a constant but light chop, and it lapped against the canoe. Two large, billowy clouds—the first I'd seen all day—towered over the trees far to the east, promising a thunderstorm and respite from the sun. A flicker of lightning danced in the distance, but it was so far away no thunder sounded. It wouldn't hit us.

I hadn't seen anyone today in any of the campsites or out on the lakes and guessed our escape had worked. Hank had a slim chance of following us into the finger of water we were using. If he got confused or lost or couldn't read his map very well, maybe less than that. Finding your way around Quetico was difficult for anyone, even veteran visitors like me who knew some areas by heart. In places I didn't know well, it had sometimes taken hours to find the portages marked on the maps. There were no highway signs and no tollbooths with attendants to ask, and all sloughs of water in the wilderness looked similar, so it was great that Duke and Larry had planned our trip for a section of the park I happened to know well.

As the waterway continued to narrow, I checked my watch, got my bearings, and picked a target point on the cloudless, northwest horizon. At that moment, banging canoe paddles could be heard behind us, and I spun around, picked up the binoculars, and saw two paddlers disembarking the portage area we had just used. They didn't load equipment packs like most travelers do and pushed off quickly. They started slashing the water the second they were in it. They were at best a half mile behind. I didn't need binoculars to guess we were in trouble. But how could it be Hank? And who could have joined him?

"Straight ahead, Janeene. Into the narrow part." I used my paddle as a rudder and swung us to the south side of the finger. We'd be out of sight from them in seconds, and I needed time to determine what to do next. There was no way we'd beat them across the top of Darky Lake and to the river leading to Minn Lake. "Who is that?" she shrieked.

"I don't know. But there are two of them and they're coming fast, straight for us. It might be Hank."

"How did he get another person to—"

"Don't know, Janeene. Just paddle as fast as you can. We can figure out who it is later."

CHAPTER TWELVE

A quick glance to the rear convinced me we were hidden from their view. I couldn't let them see us or get within rifle range if Hank was in the canoe. We had to make landfall and disappear while beaching the canoe on the north side of the lake, so we might still have a chance to use the river leading into Minn Lake. We couldn't afford to get trapped on the southeast or southwest side of Darky. Then we would be stranded for certain.

The waterway started to widen as we approached the actual lake, and I decided to move north. They might see us, but there was no other choice. We paddled hard, as fear is a great motivator and gave us renewed strength. I glanced toward the narrows but didn't see them.

There was a piece of land to our right, and from my perspective, it was round shaped. On a map, I would have thought of it as half a clock. We were at the six position and needed to paddle to twelve.

After hitting the midnight mark, we headed to the far-right upper corner of the lake, hoping a small island would block us from their view. Paddles banged behind us. Bad decision going this way—they could see us. They hit open water in Darky and immediately turned in our direction.

Our canoe plowed into the rugged shoreline, almost capsizing. I grabbed for some of my things while pulling Janeene through floating limbs of driftwood and scampering up some river rocks. Then we tugged the craft up onto the boulders. There was no use hiding it; the followers were eight hundred meters away and closing fast. We had maybe ten minutes, probably less.

"We've got to separate," I said, grabbing her shoulders with both hands. Her eyes darted to the canoe in the lake and back to me. "Listen," I yelled as I spun her around and pointed to our left, "see that swamp over there? It's a little river actually, one we might need to use later." You go there and get in it. Take the gun and hide in the water behind a tree or stump. I'll go up the hill behind us and distract them away from you. You hide there until I come back."

She turned ghostly white. "But you need the gun."

"It won't do any good. He'll have a rifle. My best chance is to run away and make him chase me—far away from you. I can move faster without you. I'll come back though, soon as I can. Stay hidden."

She tried to hand me back the pistol.

"No. You keep it. If he comes near you, blow his fucking head off." I didn't say *or shoot yourself*, but at least she had the option. "Hide down in the water if Hank comes near the swamp."

A paddle banged nearby. "Go on." I pushed her toward the bog. "I'll come back for you. . . promise. Don't shoot me by mistake. Stay alert. Now run." She disappeared in the thick underbrush after giving me the most pitiful look I ever saw.

I dashed a hundred yards uphill, driving for higher ground.

Fallen pine trees and deadfall were strewn all over the hill, blocking my path like police barricades. Picking my way through was daunting, but I jogged left and right and hid behind a tree and waited, gulping in mouthfuls of air. In the binoculars, I could see Hank below, in the rear of the canoe, panning the river rocks with his rifle. The person in front was a kid, a blond-haired teenager, maybe fifteen or sixteen, wearing a Boy Scout T-shirt that said something about a jamboree. He hunkered down as Hank swung his rifle around our canoe.

Hank landed his craft ten meters away from ours. As he hit the bank, the canoe rocked from side to side, then overturned, tossing him and the boy into chest-deep water. Hank kept one rifle above his head and waded onto the rocks, aiming the gun at the hill. He had a second deer rifle slung over his shoulder. It had gotten wet, but a wet rifle could still fire. He shouted something at the boy, then moved toward me under the tree line.

The blond-haired kid struggled to right their canoe. When he succeeded, he pulled it onto the bank and up into the brush. Hank directed him by aiming his weapon at the kid every few seconds. After the boy pulled it further into the woods, he covered the canoe with branches and hid it well. Then Hank had him walk over to ours and tug it back as well. When he was done, Hank joined him and pulled a knife, an Army bayonet, and started jabbing it into our boat. He thrust into the hull again and again, twisting the blade and making jagged tears in the lightweight aluminum that would be impossible to repair with tree sap or anything else we might find. One canoe down, one to go. What would he do now? He directed the kid to cover our wounded craft with lots of branches and leaves so it might never be found.

I kicked some loose rocks and was rewarded with a thunderous crash as stones and soil plummeted down. I rose and sprinted directly uphill, imagining tufts of dirt spitting up behind me and Hank's shots climbing the slope. He never fired, but I ran like he did. Hurdling logs and limbs, I dashed until my lungs blazed. I crested a small ridge, dove beneath a drooping white pine branch, and turned to scout the terrain below. In the distance, the faint *thump, thump, thump* of rotor blades sounded. Somebody was flying a helicopter. Aircraft are not normally permitted over the parks, so it had to be forest rangers or the National Guard. What were they doing?

Hank was searching below, a formidable tracker, dipping in and out of the trees a hundred fifty meters downhill. In front of him was the boy. He was using him like a shield. *You chicken shit bastard.* I had to draw his attention.

Jumping up, I shook some branches and turned and ran for higher ground. A muffled bang sounded. The noise of the rotor blades almost drowned it out, but I knew a shot had been fired. No bullet came near me.

Scrambling over loose rocks and leaving a trail of dust as I ran for another crest, a bullet erupted in the dirt way off to my right. At the next hilltop I crawled behind a fallen pine tree. It was about three feet in diameter, enough to keep me covered.

Down the hill, Hank moved, spinning to his right, and aiming at something. The kid dropped to the ground at his feet. Hank fired a round, then dashed toward the target. When he stopped, he looked at the log he had shot, and pulled the rifle bolt back, slapping his wet pockets for more rounds. He tore through them all twice, then tossed the rifle to the ground. *Dropped the rounds in the lake, didn't you?* Hank unslung the deer rifle on his shoulder, pulled the bolt back, and checked the breech. He slammed it forward and started uphill in a crouch. I wondered if this rifle would shoot after it was submerged in water—not from being wet, but whether or not some trash might cause the firing pin to jam or malfunction. Probably not. I had to assume otherwise. He walked back to the kid who was still kneeling on the ground, and in a blinding flash he smashed his rifle butt on the side of the boy's head. There was no sound other than the helicopter, and the teenager went limp and fell to the ground like he'd been dropped from the sky. My stomach churned.

The swirling rotor blades and whining jet engine grew louder still, crying out "combat zone" in my ears. Pine needles were falling like snowflakes from trembling tree branches. Suddenly, I thought of Janeene. *Don't come out of the swamp.*

I peeked below and watched Hank. He didn't hurry or seem upset by the chopper. Despair overwhelmed me, sucking the wind from my lungs, and melting my guts into putty. I had to signal it, but how? The salty taste of fear dribbled from my nose and drenched my mouth in a cold sweat. I was afraid, a coward. I pulled some Kevlar braid fishing line from my vest, and fumbled like a child to cut several lengths. How could I find a way to alert the chopper? One piece of fishing line was cut to a length of about twenty feet. I looked at Hank again. He was in the same spot next to the Boy Scout on the ground. He now seemed to be hypnotized by the chopper overhead. A second piece of line was cut to about six feet, and I doubled the shorter line back along its length, making it thicker and stronger. I looked around and picked up two six-inch sticks. Below me, Hank was still staring at the sky. I tied the sticks on either end about two feet apart, making handles for a garrote. It was a simple weapon, but it would have to do. I cut two more sections of line and put them in my vest.

Backing away from the log and never taking my eyes from Hank who was still watching the sky above him, I crawled behind another stump and tied a fishing weight to the long piece of line. The rotor slaps were directly over me now, and deafening. Hank was twenty meters away, looking to his left, and I threw the weight into a high branch. He turned his gaze toward me, then away, and I pulled the line. Hard. The branch shuddered curiously out of place like a mysterious hand beckoning help. But could they see it from above? Not with all the rotor wash shaking the highest branches. Hank rushed toward the tree, gun leveled, then dropped to a knee and raised the rifle to his shoulder, aiming at the sky. *Shoot, you bastard.* The helicopter was pissing him off.

I tugged again, and his head popped up over the scope. He inched forward very carefully. He was less than ten feet away now, the barrel of his gun pointed up into the branches. I took a deep breath, wishing I had kept the pistol, then snapped the garrote between my hands and burst toward him.

The rifle barrel swung toward me in slow motion. It was near my right ear when an orange fireball erupted beside my face. The weapon fired, but I kept hurtling forward, smashing into arms, elbows, and the wooden stock of the gun. I rammed him in the chest, knocking him straight backward and down, my knee slamming into his crotch as we fell in a heap.

Hank's face was a foot away, his venomous eyes flickering first in pain, and then with a mixture of fear and hate. With my simple weapon—the garrote, I dove down at his throat, mistakenly pinning one of his hands on the ground beside his face. He squirmed and clawed at my face with his free hand. I gave up trying to choke him and instead punched him hard in the mouth, feeling my knuckle shift painfully in its socket. His fingers were trying to dig into my eye. I rolled my head, snapping the air with my teeth, trying to bite anything in range. From underneath, a jolting shot hit me in the jaw. Lightning bolts flashed in my head, and I tumbled off him to my right. When I looked up, he was crawling at me. I kicked out with my left heel, splattering his nose. Blood and snot sprayed out of Hank's face as it disappeared in a red mist.

He fell backward, and I got to my knees, ready to pounce.

As I launched toward him, his right leg swung. In my stupor, I was too slow, and his boot detonated against my ribs, exploding with a sickening snap. My breath was utterly gone.

Hank rolled onto his stomach away from me, trying to push off the ground as he started to pull a bayonet from a sheath on his belt. Ignoring the searing fire in my side, I jumped on his back, whipping the line around the front of his throat, pulling the sticks with all my might, twisting them around and around, making a choking circle around his neck.

Hank forced himself up to his knees, trying to pull the bayonet completely out. I rode him like a rodeo bull, kicking at his hand as the bayonet fell beside us. He searched for it with his palm on the turf, but I snatched him backward so violently he started scratching at his throat with both hands. Suddenly his right hand shot rearward into my nose. A blue flash shot through my eyes. My nostrils were wrenched to the side, spurting blood down my mouth. I shot my knee forward into Hank's kidney two, three, four times, pulling so tightly blood oozed from the line slicing into his neck.

I screamed, "You think you can break my nose, asshole!" and tugged the wood handles like a cowboy clinging to the reins of a demonic bronco, wanting to shear his head off. His hand flashed backward again, this time straining to reach my eyes. I caught his thumb and first finger in my teeth, and bit, cracking bone while jerking my head left and right. Part of a fingernail floated on my tongue. I pulled the garrote harder still. Hank arched backward and gouged at his neck, scraping grooves of bloody skin as he fought to get under the line. It was half an inch deep in his skin now, and I focused on my hands, twisting, pulling, and wrenching the handles. The back of Hank's neck and ears were ruby red, engorged with blood, ready to burst.

He slumped forward on his chest, his right hand still snagged in my mouth. The other groped gingerly at the line.

My nose was throbbing, numb, and wet, with a warm sticky paste choking my breath. Tears stung my eyes and my vision blurred into a cloudy dream as I tried to squeeze the life out of the creature below me. He was nothing but a thrashing shape as I cinched the noose a final time, grinding his fingers in my teeth while tying a knot. His body twitched doggedly, one shock wave after another.

With his right hand still clenched in my jaw, I grabbed his left, pulling it behind his back. After spitting out his other hand, I took the cut sections of Kevlar out of my vest pocket. I tied the line around both wrists, sitting on his back and watching the blood pulse in his neck. After getting off him carefully, his ankles were bound with more line.

Satisfied he was tied, I kicked him over on his back and straddled him again. His mouth was agape and filled with leaves, his face a mass of blood and dirt, nostrils caked with dusty black soil, and beard full of twigs and pine needles. His eyes were frozen, half-open. On his hip was a knife sheath from the bayonet. It was empty. I looked around—no weapon. But I noticed two bullets in the leaves, and I grabbed them and put them in my pants pocket.

I pulled my Swiss Army knife from a vest pocket and slid a tiny blade under the garrote, cutting a shallow gash in his neck muscles trying to reach the imbedded line. As soon as I cut the noose, his Adam's apple budged. He wasn't dead.

The air was strangely silent, like the aftermath of a tornado. The chopper was gone.

"Gaaah." Hank choked a horrid gasp, leaves and bloody spittle shooting from his mouth onto my shirt. His chest heaved as he sucked for air like he'd just been pulled from a swimming pool, saved from drowning. His lips quivered, trying to taste the air rushing in. I leaned over and picked up his deer rifle, feeling a band of steel wires tighten around my chest. I steadied myself and aimed the rifle butt at his chin. After a minute or so, a more normal color returned to Hank's battered face. "Who's the kid?"

Blank eyes stared up at me. "Who is the kid?" I said again, reinforcing the question with a firm thump of the rifle butt on his chin. "Where did you find him?"

"On Brent Lake. He was. . . was fishing."

"Where? I didn't see anyone on the lake."

"By. . . by one of the campsites."

There were only two official campsites on Brent, the one he had used and the one my buddies and I had used. "Bullshit. The sites are empty." I tapped his chin a little harder.

"I found him and another kid fishing in a canoe. Got no fucking idea where they were staying." He sucked in more air. "Why, what does it matter? I made him come with me."

"It matters a lot. The kid had a Boy Scout shirt on and maybe he had friends. Lotta friends. What did you do to with the other one?"

"Left him on sh. . . shore. I took my canoe with this kid and left." Speaking was a chore for Hank. His breathing wasn't up to par yet and blood and vomit—I could see it in the corners of his mouth—slid back down his throat because he was lying on his back. I had no intention of making him more comfortable and tightened my knees around his chest and pressed the rifle butt down on his Adam's apple.

"Where did you bury Bobby?"

An evil smile grew on his mouth, then a demented grin. "Got. . . got no idea what you're talking about."

"Yeah, maybe this will help you remember." I pressed the rifle butt down hard, choking out the fresh air he was starting to appreciate. I waited until he started to pass out before lessening up the pressure.

"Still. . . still don't know what you're—"

"Save the bullshit. I saw you shoot Bobby and saw you bury him by the waterfall. Also saw you unbury him and move him. Where to?"

The sick smile again. "I don't know shit about anything."

I was within a heartbeat of smashing his teeth down his throat. "Gonna need some better answers here before I get pissed off and take it out on you."

"Bobby and Janeene got lost. We tried to find them and. . . and that's all I know."

"Nice try, but that's not what happened."

He glared at me with lifeless eyes—the eyes of a shark—without guilt or compassion.

I said, "Back to the Boy Scout kids. You see any others?"

"No. They were fishing alone."

"How'd you find me?"

"The boys said they saw a canoe with a man and a woman pass through. Figured it was you. Guess I was right." A partial smile crossed his bloody lips. I jabbed the gun butt in his throat a little harder than I intended. His watery eyes darted around like a pinball machine. "My sense of humor is gone, asshole. You better hope," I hissed, "that you didn't kill the kid. If you did, I'm gonna to come back here and crush your skull."

He didn't answer, just glared.

I got off him and stood, towering over his head and chest. My left side was on fire, burning like a hot poker had been thrust into my lung. It was all I could do to keep from kicking him in the ribs, cracking them like he'd done to mine. Instead, I pushed him with my boot, rolling him over on his stomach, expecting to see the bayonet underneath. It was nowhere to be found. I searched around some more. Nothing.

Suddenly. . . *bam*. . . *bam*. Two loud shots came from down-hill. A woman's scream followed—Janeene's scream. I stepped on the back of Hank's neck. "You got anybody else with you?"

"Fuck you." I lifted my foot and kicked him in the temple, just hard enough to jar his memory, but it knocked him out instead. *Too bad.*

I started downhill holding my side and trying to walk straight, but I keeled over to the left, half-hunching, half-walking, using Hank's deer rifle as a crutch.

Janeene saw me and started yelling. "Roger. Oh, Roger, you look terrible!"

I waved feebly, supporting myself with the rifle. Blood sprayed from my mouth in a frothy, red mist.

She ran at a gallop to my side. "Oh my God, your face. It's all bloody. What happened?"

My head was throbbing, feeling like I was wearing a football helmet three sizes too small. I gently touched my upper lip and nose. They felt like wet tissue paper, swollen more than twice their normal size. "Help me sit." She guided me down to a seat on a fallen log.

"Oh, Roger, I think your nose is broken. And your lip is cut too."

"Not worried about them, it's my ribs. I think they're cracked or broken." I wheezed, coughing into my hand, and spitting up red mucus, praying there wasn't also a punctured lung.

"My God." She started weeping into her hands, looking up at me and staring like I was a circus freak, then putting her face back into her hands.

Feeling more carefully with my fingertips, my lip was split badly. Needed stitches. "I'm okay, bruised and battered, but not dead."

"Is Hank dead?"

"No. He's unconscious, up the hill. Why did you shoot?"

"What?"

"Why did you shoot the pistol?"

"A snake crawled up beside me. Scared the hell out me, and I killed it."

I laughed, a silly, drunken laugh. "Thank God, thought maybe Hank had more friends." Slumping further down on the log, my willpower was fading like a spent candle. "What happened to the helicopter?"

"Took off."

"What was it doing?"

"Couldn't tell."

"Shit. I tried to signal it, but no luck."

"Maybe it'll come back."

"Yeah, maybe." But I doubted it. "Help me up," I said. "I've got to check on the kid."

"What kid?"

"The one Hank might have killed. Come on."

The boy was lying where I'd last seen him. Rusty blood oozed in his blond hair above his forehead. Feeling along his scalp convinced me his skull wasn't crushed. "He's breathing."

Janeene was in tears, standing beside me, unable to speak. "Not sure if we can move him." I was barely able to lift my arms, let alone carry a kid who probably weighed more than a hundred fifty pounds. "We shouldn't risk injuring him more. If we can get help, a paramedic should check him first." She nodded, tears welling in her eyes. "You stay with the boy. I'm going up the hill to drag Hank's ass down here."

"Can you move the bastard, being hurt so bad and all?"

I checked the rifle. There was no round in the breech, but I'd found two around Hank during the fight. The ones now in my pocket. "He'll walk or crawl by himself," I said, loading the round and sliding the safety on the rifle to the on position. "With this, I'm not listening to any arguments." I struggled to my feet, bracing myself with the gun. My hand stung, a knuckle in the middle of my right fist was disjointed. I put the rifle in my left. "Back in a minute."

"Roger, don't. . . be gone long."

"It's just up there." I pointed. "You should be able to see me."

It took ten minutes for me to amble back to our battle-ground. My whole side was aching now, tightening with each breath as if a boa constrictor was wrapped around my chest. I wasn't going to last much longer.

I couldn't find Hank, or more correctly, the place where the ambush happened. I searched around three or four fallen trees and stumps, and finally saw a trampled place in the mat of leaves and pine needles at the last one. Spackles of blood dotted the leaves. Furrows where our boots grooved the dirt during the fight stood out. But there was no one tied up on the ground. *This has to be the place.* I looked to the left and right, under a bush, around a boulder, anywhere he might have crawled or slithered away to hide. Suddenly, I saw some Kevlar fishing line lying loose on the turf. I dropped to a knee, bringing the rifle to my shoulder and sliding the safety off.

The woods were quiet. Nothing was moving, at least nothing out of the ordinary. I scanned the hillside using the scope on the rifle. Dammit, the man was gone—I should have found that fucking bayonet. The bastard must have used it to cut himself free. I waited on my knees, getting accustomed to the sounds of birds, and rustling leaves, trying to hear some-thing different, like a snap or a pop. Nothing. Sweat seeped down my nose, a steady stream dripping off the tip, mixed with blood. *Where is the guy?* The stinging pain in my chest had me ready to faint. I was weary, almost too weak to stand. Could he be circling around back to the canoe, or waiting to ambush me? I swung the rifle in a complete circle, checking with the scope, looking, watching. Finally, I started back to Janeene, wishing I'd killed the man.

"Hank is gone," I whispered. "We've got to get to his canoe."

"He's what?" Her eyes were as large as golf balls, mouth tight, throat muscles twitching as she tried to swallow.

"Gone. Not where I left him." I wasn't looking at her, couldn't. I gazed up the hill, hoping to spot him. "Let's pull the kid down to the water and leave."

"How?"

"Carefully. Get his arm near the shoulder, under the armpit. We'll pull him."

"Roger, I can't—"

"Do it, Janeene. We haven't much time."

I tugged the boy into position, on his back, feet uphill. "Under the armpit," I repeated, and raised one side of him with my left arm. My injured right arm held the rifle a bit unsteady, safety off, pointing where I'd last seen Hank. We shuffled backward, dragging the child between us.

"What happened up there?"

"We'll talk later. I need to pay attention to the forest right now."

We were less than four hundred meters from the water, but it took almost an hour to slide and drag the limp boy through the brush and over rocks. He never awakened, even when we stopped to rest and feel his pulse and breath. His vital signs were good—his head not so much. A bruise covered his face from eyebrows to hairline, an ugly red-bluish thing, streaked with streams of hardened blood. He looked like a bad modernist painting.

Janeene pushed the canoe Hank had used out into the water. I checked the woods with my binoculars, looking for any movement. Getting the kid inside the craft was too difficult for her without capsizing it, and I finally had to give her the rifle to hold while I lifted him aboard. I struggled to get him over the gunwale since I was reduced to one working arm. "Don't hesitate to shoot if you see him." It was the perfect moment for Hank to attack. But he didn't. Probably because she stood like a sentinel, aiming the weapon, ready to fire. There was no doubt in my mind she would kill him if she could.

Janeene went to our damaged craft looking for my things as I covered her with the rifle. When we came ashore, the canoe had almost tipped over but stayed upright. All she could find was my backpack and the bandana she had worn. The fishing rods were gone, possibly sunk, and the life vests and paddles had floated away. One was visible in the water a hundred meters away. In the backpack, were only my maps and a flashlight. She tied the damp T-shirt around the boy's head and put my backpack under him for a pillow. We pushed off from the shore using the paddles from Hank's canoe.

The boy lay unconscious in the middle of the boat as we drifted a short distance through Darky Lake. I could barely swing a paddle; my ribs, chest, and right hand were so sore every stroke felt like punishment. But the sweet smell of safe air poured through my lungs, reassuring me. "We should be okay," I chuckled, giddy with pain.

"You really think so?"

"Yeah, I do."

"What about Hank? If you didn't kill him, and he's gone, then he might—"

"Might nothing. He's got no way to move on water, and no rifle. I beat the hell out of him, and he's wounded worse than me. He's not a threat anymore."

But it wasn't really true. He might still be a menace. The place where I left him wasn't that far from our planned route to Minn Lake, by way of the river and portages on the north end of Darky. If he was bent on pursuing us, all he had to do was make his way to the mouth of the river, ambush some campers passing through, abduct their canoe, and he'd be back in business. If I'd thought about that before, I would have shot him through the foot or broken some toes with the rifle butt.

"Should have killed him, I know, but couldn't. Had the chance, but you don't kill unarmed people." Knowing he wouldn't have done the same for me hit me hard. *I really should have popped the bastard.*

"We need to move south on Darky," I said, "away from Minn and toward Ballard Lake instead. It's a landlocked lake with a steep, short portage. It's an ideal resting place. We can hole up there until somebody comes by and rescues us."

After a long pause, she asked quietly, "What really happened up there?"

"I ambushed Hank. Choked him with a garrote then tied him up. I can't believe he got loose." My breath was coming in short gasps, in between lung spasms. "The son of a bitch cut my lines; I was trying to find his bayonet when you fired the pistol."

"Sorry, I was trying to signal the helicopter, and that's how I ran into the snake. It was sitting on the bank when I climbed out of the swamp. What do you think that helicopter was doing?" she asked.

"Don't know. Aircraft are not allowed to fly over the parks under normal circumstances. But with satellite phones, if you have a true emergency, I hear they'll come to the rescue. Maybe an emergency float plane, but I've never seen a chopper over the park in all my trips here."

"This one had a red cross painted on its side," she said.

"It did?"

"Yeah, but the rest of it was green colored, like an Army color."

Army colored? "Did it hover over us?"

"Kinda. It was over us for a minute or two, but then it moved over the lake, not really above us. It looked like they were searching for something. But it went on that way." She pointed behind us.

I wondered why it went east. There was nothing but wilderness in that direction—more lakes and rivers like we'd been through today. In fact, there wasn't a piece of concrete within twenty miles in all directions. What were they looking for? "We need to keep our eyes and ears open," I said. "If another one comes by, we've got to signal it."

My small daypack was on the bottom of the canoe under the kid's head. "Hey Janeene, there's a flashlight in the pack. Pull it out and keep it with you, just in case."

As she rummaged for it, I slouched back in the seat. The pain in my chest was getting worse. Using the paddle was torture. "Can't go very fast."

"I'll do the work, Roger. I owe it to you."

I tried to laugh, but it hurt too much. My eyes closed, and I sailed off into dreamy clouds of sleep.

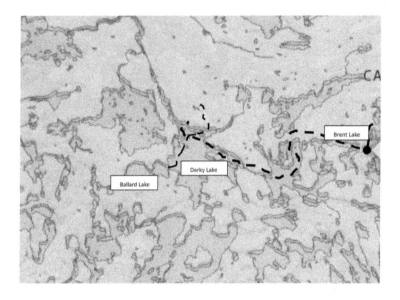

- Map services and data available from U.S. Geological Survey, National Geospatial Program."...

Map 8 - Roger's escape route with Janeene from Brent Lake into Darky Lake (heavy dashed line).

Roger's path away from his canoe where he faces Hank in the woods (small dashed line).

The path leading to Ballard Lake where Roger and Janeene stop. (medium dashed line).

CHAPTER THIRTEEN

The subtle tapping of metal against rocks awoke me. The bow of our canoe was wedged between two partially submerged boulders, bumping gently against them. "Where are we?" I asked, noticing the mellow glow of dimming light in the sky. It painted the trees before me in somber shadows.

"On the same lake, a little farther to the south."

We were maybe half a mile from where I'd fallen asleep. The portage into Ballard was in in view. I recognized it, having been here many times. There were largemouth bass in it and I had *LMB* marked in grease pencil on all my maps.

"I have to rest," Janeene said.

There was a grassy spot in front of us, bordered by gnarly vines, spiny limbs, and granite outcrops. Twenty feet behind it was a short muddy trail leading up a hill. Once you crested the hill, your eyes were rewarded with a splendid view of Ballard Lake. It was worth a trip into Quetico just to fish the place. "Let's get out," I said, trying to rise from the seat, but unable to find the strength to push up over the gunwale. "Stay there,

Roger." She hopped out and pulled the nose of the boat onto the shore herself.

"Afraid I'm too stiff to move."

"You look tired." She waded knee-high in the water, carrying a square object about the size of pillow toward me, coming to where the back of the craft was still out in the lake. "Here, lean up." She put a life cushion under my back.

"Where'd this come from?"

"Found it floating in the water. We only have one."

I settled against it, breathing slowly, painfully. She scooped some water in her hands and brought it to my lips. "More, please." She gave me enough to quench my thirst and patted the sleeve of her shirt against my lip and nose. I noticed drops of blood falling on my chest.

"You're gonna need stitches."

"And a shave." I had raised my hand to my chin and felt a five-day stubble as stiff as copper wire. I knew I looked terrible.

"Heard the helicopter again," she said.

"You did? Where?"

"Over that way, south, near Argo Lake."

"When?"

"Don't know exactly. . . no watch, remember?" She held up her bare wrist. "I heard it for a while before dark, but it moved away, more to our east over Cone and Elk Lakes."

"Wow, you're getting pretty good with directions and the layout of the land."

"I studied the maps while you were sleeping. Found them in the backpack along with the flashlight. I think we should wait here for help."

I was in no position to argue. My ribs had me confined to the back of the canoe and I was so weak and battered that getting out and walking ashore seemed impossible. "Agreed. We wait."

She reached over and stroked the boy's head. "How's he doing?" I asked.

"Breathing, that's all I can say. He hasn't moved or spoken a word."

"Hey, we better prepare for the worst."

"Meaning what? Him dying or Hank coming after us?"

"Both." I didn't tell her about my dreams—Hank and me battling with bayonets, a fight to the death—but I did tell her about my thoughts of him abducting another canoe. It was evident she had studied the maps well enough to understand. She picked up the rifle. "If he comes near us again, I'll kill him. Won't miss." She checked the gun, making sure the safety was on, and slung it on her shoulder. "I'm gonna sit on the shore."

"Pull the canoe parallel to the bank," I said, "That way I can talk to you." She waded back to the bank, tied the bow rope to a tree limb, and edged the nose of the canoe into the water while pulling the rear closer to the rocks. She tied the rear ring to a bush at the shoreline.

She sat near me, legs on the ground and back up against a boulder. The gun was across her lap. "You should have killed him, Roger."

"If it had happened during the fight, it would have been all right. But after I got the garrote on his neck, he passed out and I just couldn't do it. Couldn't kill a man in cold blood."

"After what he did to Bobby?"

"Still wouldn't make it right in my mind," I said, remembering the ember-colored skin of Hank's ears and neck as I straddled his back. If I had been a little slower cutting the line off. . .?

"He's a demon," she said absently. "I knew it the first time he slapped me, saw it in his eyes." She fingered the trigger of the rifle.

"He does deserve to die," I announced, causing her to look straight at me. "But the courts can decide that verdict."

"They should put him in the electric chair, or hang him, after what he did to Bobby and this boy." I glanced at the teenager. He was still lying in the same position where we'd put him on the bottom of the canoe, arms limp across his chest, head on the backpack, feet splayed to the left and right.

I told her, "We should move at first light and sit in the middle of the lake. You can hold that rifle. It'll be Sunday morning; there's bound to be people moving around between campsites or rescuers searching again. This time we need to stay out in the open."

"I thought you said there'd be people here today in Darky, or back there in Brent?"

"Should've been. This is the start of the biggest week of the season. Thought for sure we'd run into somebody traveling on the lakes. I don't understand it."

"There was somebody," she pointed at the kid. "Boy Scouts. Only Hank found them first."

"Young guys like this don't usually travel alone. If he is a Scout, there's bound to be adults, and I'm guessing they're looking for him now. Maybe that's why the helicopter was flying around." It was a reassuring thought, thinking there were more people in our vicinity, that is until I remembered the missing killer. She read my mind. "But nobody's safe with Hank alive, are they?"

"That's one way to look at it." I tried to push forward into a sitting position, but bursts of fire seared my lungs.

"Stay where you are. You and the boy can sleep in the canoe. I'll watch over you from the bank."

"Can you keep yourself awake all night?"

"If I have to. I'm not letting that bastard sneak up on us."

Her eyes were sharp and clear, filled with purpose and grit. I hoped she could remain alert.

My eyes were already drooping again. "I'm out of commission, worthless, or as they say, a straphanger. I apologize for not killing him, or at least breaking his leg or foot. Should've done more."

"You're not cold-blooded, Roger, like you said. I knew that when you captured me."

"I'd hardly say captured."

"Didn't mean it that way. When you saved me—a better choice."

There was about an hour left until nightfall. Swallows were zooming across the water, chasing insects for their evening meal in the hazy light. A loon cried out somewhere in the distance, sounding like it lost its best friend. The lake was perfectly flat, not a ripple on the surface. Until darkness, our canoe would be visible from anywhere across the lake. After that, it would be impossible to see us unless you came right up to our position. "You're going to have to stand guard alone, I won't be able to help much."

"I understand."

I closed my eyes, wishing the stiffness in my chest and the numbness around my nose would disappear. Being in pain had always zapped me of resolve, made me feel like a quitter who simply wanted to lie down and surrender. It was a lousy feeling and needed to be overcome with grit and determination.

"Who is the first person you're calling when we get back?" she asked.

"My kids, Crystal and Ricky. They're staying at their grandparents' house. You?"

"Angela. She's with my parents." She fell silent, but I could hear labored breathing. Suddenly I realized it wasn't breathing, it was crying.

"You all right?"

"Yes." She was wiping her eyes with her shirtsleeve. "I was so scared today, and afraid of dying, it's coming out now." She choked and sobbed for a second then looked up with tear-stained eyes. "I want you to know you helped me today."

"How?"

"To be a braver person, a better person. Looking at you all beaten up makes me realize some people are willing to give everything, no matter what it costs, to help others. A hero. I want to be like that for Angela. I'm going to be like that for Angela."

"I'm sure you will be." I started to tell her I hadn't done anything for her. I'd attacked Hank for *me*, to incapacitate the bastard, strangled him to get the prick out of my life forever, not hers. She'd simply been the beneficiary of my ambush. I wasn't an idol, just a scared trooper who'd done what he needed to do at the time. "Heroes are just people who panic and do the right thing at the right time," I said. I fell asleep before she could answer.

CHAPTER FOURTEEN

I felt something bumping my chin. It thumped again, then my head was forced rearward. A voice yelled as if in a faraway canyon, "Got a live one here, Bagley." A heavy hand was shaking my chest. A blazing inferno grew above my stomach, punctuated by sparks of electricity in all my limbs. I cracked open an eye to see the muzzle of an M16 rifle an inch from my nose. Behind it, two vague camouflage-painted faces peered at me. They turned on a flashlight. I was blinded.

One of the faces lifted a radio to his ear. "I said I got a target here. And there's a kid, the one we're looking for, I think." The flashlight beam fluttered along the canoe, down on the boy. The guy with the radio listened, then answered, bringing the beam back on me. "Can't tell, his face is all fucked-up, but he's alone."

In seconds, my canoe was rocking in the water as one of the soldiers turned around quickly, banging up against the side. "Freeze," he yelled.

"No, you freeze." It was Janeene, screaming back.

He leveled his gun at the tree line. "Who goes there?"

No answer.

"Dammit, who goes there?" Still no answer.

"Hey guys," I said weakly, "it's—"

"Shut up, mister." A hand came to my throat.

"I'm going to ask this only one more time," the soldier pointing his rifle at the forest line yelled. "Who's hiding back there?"

"It's Jan—" The other guy's hand choked off my words. "Shut up, fuck face, or I'm going to ram your teeth down your throat." The butt of his M16 was directly over my mouth.

From the woods, "Who are you guys?"

"I'm asking the questions," trooper number one said. "Now come out here, quickly."

Janeene's cool voice responded. "I want to know who you are. If you don't answer me, I'm going to shoot the person with the flashlight." The chilly tension in her words hung over everyone like a malevolent fog, draping the soldiers in uncertainty. I couldn't believe it was Janeene I was hearing.

"Lady, look—"

"I'm not kidding."

The soldiers looked at each other, the one holding the flashlight saying, "Tell her who we are."

"You got five seconds, fellows."

"We're with the 147th Assault Helicopter Battalion, a Minnesota National Guard unit, and we're looking for some Boy Scouts who got kidnapped. Seems like you got one."

"What are US soldiers doing in Canada?"

"We're looking for some American Boy Scouts. They were supposed to be in the BWCA but got lost and crossed into Quetico. We got permission from the Canadians to search for them. Happens all the time."

Janeene said nothing for a good long ten seconds. "You, holding the flashlight, what's your name?"

"Brookside. Corporal Brookside. Why?"

"I just wanted to hear your voice." The standoff continued. The soldier aiming the rifle started to whisper to the other and I expected a burst of gunfire.

"Janeene, they're here to help us—

A *bear claw grip.* "Quiet, buddy, I'm warning you."

"Okay, guys, I'm coming out."

"Put the weapon down first."

"Okay."

I couldn't see anything, but the soldier aiming the M16 surged out of the water away from the canoe. I heard sloshes and then, "Get your hands off me." I peeked around the guy standing beside me. His flashlight beam illuminated the grassy ground where Janeene lay on her stomach, the soldier astride her back, grabbing her hands. "Hey, leave her—" *Bam.*

* * *

When I woke up the scene looked like the site of a massive automobile crash. White lights were sparkling from ten flashlights dancing around my canoe among the silhouettes of as many people. The shapes passed back and forth in the beams, making the place appear chaotic, like a pack of fireflies caught in headlights. Radios were hissing, and men dressed in combat gear stalked the bank as if a full-scale war was underway. The foul odor of smelling salts was gagging me. I pushed a hand away, needing fresh air.

"You got a name there, fella?" A dark face was within two feet of mine.

"Ro. . . Roger Cummings."

"He's awake," the face in front of me yelled.

Another face came into view. "Hey, partner, what happened?" It was Duke Johansen, my camping buddy.

"Man, it was a nightmare." More faces peered over me. "Where's Janeene?" I asked.

"You mean the lady?" Duke asked.

"Yeah."

"Sitting over there, talking with the soldiers."

"She okay?"

"Appears to be. How are you?"

"Broken up. Ribs, nose. . . whole body feels like shit."

"What happened to this kid?"

"A guy. . . the guy who talked with you at the waterfall, hit him on the head with his rifle stock." I tried to catch my breath. "The guy followed us from Brent and—"

"Easy, pal," a voice I didn't recognize said. "We'll get the whole story after you're out of here." An IV was hooked up to my arm, and everything started to blur. "Let's get him ready for transport."

* * *

Sunlight was streaming through a window beside me, heating the sheets on my bed like beach sand. They were white, everything was white—walls, curtains, ceiling. The covers had a starched, clean feel and I slid my feet on the mattress, basking in the wonderfulness of fresh linen. I noticed a white cast on my right hand over my knuckles and wrist. My head was throbbing, brain bumping up against my skull with each heartbeat, my mind wondering if I was in heaven.

"About time you woke up." Duke was sitting in a chair in the corner, holding a magazine.

"Where am I?"

"Ely, Minnesota. At Ely-Bloomenson Community Hospital. He raised a magazine in his hand, shaking it. "Decent place, but I think every one I've read here is over a year old."

151

"How long?"

"Twelve months or better."

"No, not that. . . how long have I been here?"

"Oh. Overnight. One extremely long night, and another half day. It's almost noon." He tossed the magazine on the chair and came to the bedside.

"Janeene?"

"At a hotel in town. She wasn't really injured."

"Physically, you mean."

"Yeah, I guess." Duke looked at my face and I involuntarily brought my left hand to my nose, feeling the bandages on it and my lip. The skin around the left side of my head was smooth. They'd shaved me. "You have a nasty gash around your lip, and your nose is broken. Cut took four stitches, but it should heal nicely. They made you half-bald, like me, to sew a little wound on the left side of your brick-hard head."

"Thank God for small miracles." My ribs were bandaged too; taped actually, and the adhesive tugged at my skin like sticky fingers. "I can't remember feeling worse. Where's Larry?"

"Back at the hotel. He and I have been sharing watch duty over you."

"What about Chuck?"

"Had to go home, family emergency." Duke's blue eyes were intense, in sharp contrast to the gentle sags of skin on his cheeks and graying hair around his temples. Normally, the gray gave him a calm, grandfatherly look. He was of average height, maybe five feet nine or ten, slightly overweight, but not grossly so; still, usually he looked older than his fifty-six years. At this moment he looked a lot older than that, with eyes that were badly bloodshot, angry. "What's wrong?" I asked.

"I don't like this whole thing," he said.

"Neither do I. You think it's fun being tethered to a mattress with broken ribs?"

"They're cracked, not broken."

"Feels the same to me."

He was dressed in a Black Watch flannel shirt and baggy blue jeans. Other than when we were camping, his normal attire was expensive golf shirts and khaki pants. "Never saw you dressed like a mountain man before, not in public anyway."

"Isn't exactly Fifth Avenue around here, you know?" He pulled his collar up and did a pirouette. "Real comfortable stuff, though."

"Speaking of comfort, when do we get to go home?"

"That's your call, partner." He pulled a folding chair beside the bed and sat down. "You probably don't remember this, but on the way here you babbled a lot of stuff—witnessing a murder, hiding out in the woods, finding this injured kid, and attacking somebody."

"What did I say? Can't recall much."

"Enough to convince the US park rangers and the local police, as well as the Canadian cops and rangers, to keep you around."

"Around? Why?"

"For some better answers." There was an aggravated tone in his voice, uncharacteristic. "There's a cop watching this door, outside in the hallway." He thrust his thumb over his shoulder. "You're technically under house arrest because of the Boy Scout."

"I was trying to help him."

"I know that because I know you. But these people only know you had a missing boy with you."

I remembered the first two soldiers beside my canoe in the darkness. They were frantic, not professional. With my left hand I felt along my forehead. It was rough, scraped, a nice-sized bump swelling against my fingertips. Duke said, "One of those clowns admitted to rapping you on the skull. Slight tap he said."

I tried to laugh.

"I've retained an attorney for you."

"What?"

"I hired an attorney. One here in Ely. . . or from Duluth, actually, to represent you."

"You really think it's necessary? Over a bump on the head?"

"It's not about your head, it's the kid's head."

I thought about the Boy Scout in the canoe. The gravity of his words felt like a barbell, too heavy for me to lift. "You need to talk to your lawyer first, before the rangers and police. He's waiting in the lobby. I think it would be a good idea to talk to him now."

The bed was raised at a forty-five-degree angle. I was almost sitting, and I rolled my head toward the window. It was crystal clear outside, vibrant and warm, but it felt chilly and musty in here. "Why on earth would I need an attorney?"

"Listen to me." he said vehemently. "I may be overreacting, but the rangers, the chief of police, everybody in this town is pretty shaken up over this Boy Scout thing. They found one dead on Brent Lake last evening, murdered, head bashed in, and the missing one with you. There've been incidents up here before, but nothing like this. They want some answers, and fast. So far, all they know is you and that woman—"

"Janeene. That's her name."

"Whatever. All they know is you two popped up with a missing kid and a story about some guys nobody can find. I'm not an attorney, but I understand enough to know when one is needed."

"This is bullshit, Duke. I saved that kid's life. He still alive?"

"Yeah, in a coma. They transported him to Duluth. They don't know if he's going to make it."

I slumped on the pillows, head pounding as if a ball-peen hammer thumped away. Duke had been one of my best friends for years, since my move to Atlanta. We lived in the same neighborhood, played golf and tennis together, and fished whenever we could. He was also a confidante, a guy who knew almost everything there was to know about me. He knew my wife and kids, had helped me with Sherry's funeral, and watched over the twins from time to time. "So, you think I need a lawyer, huh?"

"Absolutely, and if I'm wrong, what would it hurt? From the bits and pieces I've been able to gather from you, the lady last night, and the rangers, nobody is sure what happened. The injured kid's parents have arrived from Minneapolis, and I hear they're already talking lawsuit."

"Really?"

"Yeah. Against the Scouts, you, the equipment outfitters —somebody."

"Christ, Duke, this is a nature preserve, not a soundstage for some made-up TV movie."

"It was, my friend, not anymore. The media has caught wind of the killing and is starting to make a big deal about it. Whenever anything bad happens in the Boundary Waters, Quetico, or anywhere in the Canadian wilderness for that matter, it alarms people. They think bad stuff doesn't happen up here. I remember some Scouts getting lost a few years back, and the recovery effort was enormous. Made the national news in America. And God forbid if somebody gets murdered in a wilderness area anywhere in Canada, it usually makes national headlines in both countries."

A loud knock came on the door. It swung open and a husky man, about mid-forties with a police uniform of black trousers and a long-sleeve gray shirt with stars on the collar, stood in the doorway. He pulled his hat off, revealing thick, brown hair, closely cropped around the ears. Bushy eyebrows dominated his face; under them were squinty, hawk-like eyes. "My officer said you were awake. Mind if I come in?"

"Not at all," I said as Duke rose, and the man walked in. They nodded at each other, acquaintances I gathered. "I'm Chief Bolling," he said, "from the police department here in Ely. Is it okay if we have a few words?"

I looked at Duke. Tight eyes returned my stare. "Can I talk with my attorney first?"

"Certainly. Know him well. I'll send him in." He stepped backward, closing the door.

"You babbled a lot of things last night," Duke said. "If I were in your shoes, I'd have an attorney with me any time I spoke about this."

"I've never doubted your advice before, not while replacing the air conditioner or buying a lawn mower. I'm hearing what you're saying." I pointed to a glass jar on a nightstand beside me. "I really do have to use the bathroom, but I'm too sore to get up." He handed me the jar and I rolled to the side and filled it up. "That's better." I put it on a table beside the bed. Duke grabbed it, holding his nose, and poured it in the toilet.

When he returned, I asked, "Is there a telephone in this room?"

"I don't know," Duke answered. He searched around the nightstands. "There's a phone jack, but no. . ." He went to the closet where my clothes hung. On the top shelf was an ancient rotary phone. He brought it to me while reading the message glued to the front on a sticker, "Local calls only. Long distance requires a credit card." He put it on the nightstand. "What happened to your cell phone?"

"Left it in our camp when I went fishing."

"Here, use mine. This thing probably costs a dollar a minute, if it even works." He handed me his cell phone. I dialed my former father-in-law and his wife, Bernice, in New Jersey. By mutual agreement we had decided that their house would be the best place for the twins to stay during my planned Quetico trip. I liked Harold and Bernice, and we had always gotten along over the years. They knew better than I did how difficult my time in the service was for Sherry, but they harbored no grudges toward me after I left the Army. It was hard to say we were best friends though, but to support their grandchildren and be able to spend time with them, they decided it was best to be more than civil with me. "Give me a minute will you, Duke? And while I'm talking, could you get some maps of Quetico and then ask this attorney in."

CHAPTER FIFTEEN

After meeting my attorney—a stubby, nebbish-looking middle-aged man with curly hair named Jonathan Freidman—I agreed to a retainer fee of twenty-five hundred dollars, and an hourly rate of three hundred fifty for work he performed on my behalf. That was at 12:30 p.m. Duke stayed in the room as we had a two-hour-long briefing during which time my attorney told me there was an extradition agreement between the United States and its neighbor. The long-standing US-Canada treaty requires the offense for extradition to be a crime in both countries. He told me, "Canada is able to extradite persons to stand trial, to impose a sentence, or to serve a sentence at the request of a foreign state or entity that is an extradition partner under Canada's Extradition Act. There's a bunch more language detailing all the rules and procedures, but this is an adequate summary."

"And why do I need to know this?"

He looked directly at me. "Thought you should know in the event you are charged with a crime. I'm not saying you are, or will be, but we must be ready for any possibility."

Dammit, if only I'd left my binoculars their case. "I broke no laws, Jonathan, didn't even take a crap in the wrong place or throw a piece of trash where it wasn't supposed to be. And I didn't bring weapons in where they aren't allowed, or kill anybody in my camping group, or murder one Boy Scout and kidnap another."

"Still, you were in Canadian territory when all this happened, so they have jurisdiction, and if they determine an offense was committed, they can request extradition. Right now, they are being cordial to you by allowing you to stay in Ely." I realized Duke was smart to think I needed representation.

"You have experience with these procedures?"

"A fair amount. I've been involved a few times, but I have friends who are experts in extradition matters who will assist if asked." He paused then added, "Quetico is an Ontario Province Park, and is managed by a superintendent located in the town of Atikokan. The place is about thirty miles from Brent Lake, about as far as Ely is from the same location."

"How did I end up here?"

"The Boy Scouts who got abducted were US citizens who were supposed to be in the Boundary Waters, not Quetico, so when their scoutmasters called for help, the locals got involved, who engaged the National Guard for emergency services. One thing led to another, and a helicopter was dispatched. The Canadians agreed to let it look for the Scouts in their territory, and that's when they found you."

"Sounds like a complicated mess."

"Sort of. But the Ontario Provincial Police force is quite good. They'll get busy on this, too, and sort out who will do what after the facts are clearer. Right now, they agreed to leave you here and let Police Chief Bolling from Ely, and Quetico Park Superintendent Wilkens, try to figure out what happened and who should take the lead in this effort. Unlike Washington, DC, all these folks up here from different agencies get along well and work with each other."

I realized my attorney was sharp after he said he wanted to tape the interview and advised me to tell my entire story without answering questions until I was finished.

That's exactly what I did, spoke nonstop until 4:30 p.m. after Ely Police Chief Ronald Bolling entered, accompanied by a Canadian fellow named Wilkens. He was an elderly gentleman near sixty, tall, lanky, with the good looks and demeanor of Jimmy Stewart, but prone to saying "eh?" when he missed something, which was quiet often. Most of the things he missed happened when I referred to locations on the map spread out across my lap. I pointed out things to him several times and realized after a while he was testing me for accuracy.

After folding the map and putting it on the nightstand, I said, "Hand me that water will you, please, Duke? Throat's dry." He gave me a plastic bottle with a straw inserted in the top. It was difficult to maneuver with the bandages and my numb face, but I'd had a lot of practice earlier this afternoon. My recitation was finally over.

"Now, what questions do you have for me, gentlemen?"

"About a million," the chief answered, obviously annoyed. He'd called several recesses during the afternoon, supposedly for bathroom breaks, but I suspected it was to get people checking on some of the information I was providing at the time. He had a notepad full of scribbles now. "Let's go back to the shooting of Bobby." He rifled through pages, starting at the beginning of my story. "You say you saw this guy—you later learned was named Hank—shoot a man you later learned was named Bobby, in the head."

"That's correct. From a range of less than two inches, like I mentioned."

"Are you certain the man was killed?"

"Don't know how he couldn't have been. The bullet hit him squarely in the head, around the temple."

"And the side of his head blew off?"

"As best I could tell. I could see well through binoculars like I said and spotted a big spray of blood before he keeled over."

"You said an awful lot of things, Mr. Cummings."

I had. Two hours' worth of dialogue, recalling everything that happened, in the order it occurred. Duke had added his part about speaking to Hank at the waterfall.

"Look, Chief, and you, too, Mr. Wilkens, I agreed to speak with you today to tell you what happened as soon as possible, so you could take action to find Hank and the body and do whatever necessary to confirm my story. I want to cooperate fully."

"I think Mr. Cummings has been very generous with his time," my attorney said. "And I think you should have more than enough to corroborate his story with the woman."

"We don't have much to corroborate yet. The woman's statement last night doesn't sound too much like this. And we haven't been able to speak with her today."

"What?" Three voices on my side rang out.

"The lady is feeling very ill, but that aside, she didn't see things the same as you, Mr. Cummings." The room was stone still. The chief was huffing, looking at his notes while Wilkens probed his teeth with a toothpick. Bolling asked again, "Are you sure the man was dead?"

Of course he was. What was the chief asking?

"Janeene had to have known, she was lying on the ground next to where the shooting took place." *But what had she actually seen?* I asked myself. Was it possible Bobby had been shot and she hadn't looked at the wound or the blood on the ground? I remembered her sitting, arms wrapped around her thighs and shins, face buried in her knees, crying. She had to have seen. "I saw Bobby stretched out on the turf, blood pooling from the wound in his head. Janeene must have seen that and. . ."

"Just tell me what you saw, Mr. Cummings. Was the man dead?"

"I'd have to say yes. After the shooting, a second man, Pete, came over to the body, kicked it—it didn't move—and wrapped it in one of those space blankets, a crinkly blue plastic tarp. Then he tied a rope around both ends. If Bobby didn't die from the bullet wound, he would have suffocated in the blanket." Again, total silence in the room.

The chief finally asked. "You saw them bury the body?"

I held quiet for a minute. "No. I saw them carry the tarp into the woods, where I showed you on the map. I *heard* digging, didn't see it, but saw them come out of the forest without the space blanket. As I also stated, I saw them return to the site a day later, heard more digging, and saw them carry something like a body in the tarpaulin down the waterfall."

"Did you actually see the body that time?"

"No."

Chief Bolling rifled his notes again, but my attorney stood up. "Gentlemen, I'd like to call a recess until tomorrow. My client is tired, severely injured as you can see, and needs some time to recoup. I'm sure you have a lot to do." The chief didn't look happy about the statement; Wilkens couldn't have cared less. "Yes, we're busy, but just a few more questions if you don't mind."

"Go ahead," I said.

Bolling wasn't looking at his notes now. "You stated you saw this guy Hank, smack the Boy Scout with a rifle, the same rifle you took away from him after the fight."

"That's correct."

"Did you ever see that rifle dropped in the water after you took it away from Hank?"

"I don't believe so. Hank dropped it in the water before I got it." I recalled him capsizing his canoe, falling in the water with one rifle over his head which didn't get wet, and the second slung on his shoulder, so the stock and breech got soaked before coming up after me. I took the second rifle away from him after our fight. I remembered dragging the boy to the canoe, giving Janeene the captured rifle while I loaded him aboard, then getting in the craft and pushing off. She carried the rifle ashore later, but it never went in the water again. "No, Chief, I don't recall it ever being submersed after the first time."

"As for this guy Hank, do you think he could have gone far after you strangled him?"

"I can't imagine how. He had a deep slice completely around his neck. It was seeping blood, and his nose was smashed, probably worse than mine." I couldn't help touching my own.

"Any other injuries you know of?"

I raised my cast. "He had to have some broken knuckles or fingers, like this. And he lost part of a fingernail. I remember spitting it out of my mouth." The fight was coming back to me a in a blur, him thrashing on the ground as if he were a Brahman bull in death throes, me biting his hand getting ready to bind him up. "He might also have cuts on his ankles and wrists where I tied him with the fishing lines. I wrapped those pretty tight."

"But he cut those off?"

"I'm guessing he did. Saw strands of line on the ground."

"We'll look for the fishing line tomorrow morning," Wilkens suddenly said. His voice was startling, higher pitched than I recalled. He hadn't said two words in the last hour.

"Good," I said. "Maybe you can get DNA or something off the line."

"Maybe."

"Where was the last place you saw the bayonet?" the chief asked.

"On the ground, after I kicked it out of Hank's hand."

"Can you describe it a little better for us?"

"Were either of you guys in the military?"

Both nodded.

"It was a perfect match for the type of bayonet the US Army issued for many years, straight-edged, about a foot long, with a handle guard and a ring that attaches to a rifle barrel. The M14 is the one I remember it on the most. You want me to draw a picture?"

"No need," Wilkens said. "Chief Bolling here has one on his office wall, mounted in a picture frame if I remember correctly."

"I know what you're talking about," Bolling added. "Now—"

My attorney came to his feet. "Gentlemen, I must insist we continue this later. Sounds like we're hashing over points that have been covered."

"One final thing, Mr. Cummings," Wilkens said as he stood, voice deeper than before, "seems you got a better feel for this guy Hank than anyone, so why do you think he didn't kill the woman when he had the chance? Other than his buddy Pete, she's the only one who knew what he'd done."

The question caught me off guard, especially coming from a gray-haired old codger who appeared to be asleep most of the afternoon.

"I guess he wanted to keep her around; she was his girl-friend after all, at least when they started the trip, and she is a good-looking lady. Maybe he thought he could persuade her to keep quiet and—"

"I've got to call it quits, gentlemen," my attorney interrupted again.

"Just wondering, Mr. Cummings. Seems odd to me."

After they left, we huddled briefly and planned on meeting again after supper. "Hey, what was all that about the rifle?" I asked.

"Trying to determine if any of the fingerprints are Hank's, I'm guessing," said Jonathan. "If there are only yours and those of the woman on it, your story could be harder to follow." They walked to the door saying they were going into town for burgers. *Nice.* I was dining on hospital fare, which for me was soft foods like Jell-O, or anything I could get under my bandages and down my raw throat.

I was dozing when Duke and my attorney returned to my hospital room. A night lamp over my head was the only light in the room, giving it a soft, heavenly glow. They turned on the overhead fluorescent lights and my eyes almost exploded. I jolted awake and sat upright. "Sorry," the attorney said. He had removed his striped tie and dark suit coat and unbuttoned the top of his pale blue shirt at the collar. He looked more relaxed, friendlier. "You did an excellent job," he said.

"Simply told the truth."

"But without embellishment. I like that, facts."

"I told Jonathan about your past," Duke said. "Everything I know, even the part about Sherry."

"Sorry to hear about your wife. Terrible thing to happen." The attorney looked down at his hands, waited, then looked up. "The Army part was impressive, though. Former captain, huh? Gives me insight into your account of the tragedy. Straightforward storytelling. And it seems like you are good at hand-to-hand combat."

"Apparently not good enough." I raised the cast on my hand and pointed with my thumb toward my bandaged lip and nose. He smiled, showing a wide gap between uneven teeth. His skin was dusky, with greasy black stubble poking through his chin and cheeks. He couldn't have been more than fifty, but inquisitive eyes belied his age, giving him a younger, vibrant look. "We didn't have much time to talk before," I said. "Tell me a little about yourself."

As both men sat down on folding chairs, Jonathan started, "Live in Duluth, married, two boys, ages twelve and fifteen, happy. Went to Michigan for undergrad and then law school, have a criminal practice."

"Criminal, huh?"

"Yes. I represent clients around Ely and Duluth. Bolling and I are friends, you might say. I handle mostly minor stuff, burglaries, car thefts, things like that. You should think of me more as a public defender than a high-priced counselor. Some of my clients have been extradited when they were tangled up with Canadian crooks, so I've done work with that problem before."

"I wanted him here for his local knowledge," Duke said.

"It was a great idea. I feel a lot more comfortable."

"I do, too," Jonathan said, "after hearing the full account."

"Where to from here, fellows?" I asked.

Both men seemed to shy away, leaning slightly back in their seats. "Don't know," Duke answered. "At dinner tonight we talked and listened."

"Listened?"

"Yeah," Duke continued. "The whole town is abuzz about this thing. Seems like the lady got herself an attorney too."

"You're kidding me."

"Nope. Actually, I heard that early today, that's why I called Jonathan here."

"Glad I had a clear docket," he said.

"Why would she call an attorney so fast?"

"Good question, one you can help us answer."

"Son of a bitch."

"It doesn't surprise me," Jonathan announced. "Scary situation. Think about it: Two people are out in the middle of nowhere. They witness a murder, get chased by mad men, see one of 'em dead in a ravine. And then some Scouts get abducted. You and the lady wind up with a kid after maybe killing the second guy. A strange story to bring forward, for anyone."

"But it's the truth."

"No doubt, after hearing you today, but there's a lot left to wonder about."

"Like what?"

"Like who can identify the person who abducted the two boys? One of the witnesses is dead, the other in a coma, and the remaining Scouts who saw the abduction can't identify the perpetrator. Said they were so far away all they saw was two canoes together. But they did say they saw only one man in the other canoe, and they thought he had dark hair. When they got across the lake, they could only find their one friend, with his head battered beyond belief."

That explained what the helicopter was doing over the lakes, I concluded. The scoutmasters must have used a satellite phone to call for help.

"Look," Duke interjected, "this is why I wanted a lawyer on your side. Since last night, this morning, and supper tonight, I've heard so many theories it makes me sick. People even think the girl was behind it, with Hank, the mystery man."

"How in the hell—"

"You should hear the theories," he continued. "One rumor

is Hank doesn't exist and you and Janeene made up the story about him."

"Bullshit. If they were in the park legally," I announced, "there would be a record of them passing through customs or a park ranger station. That would prove Hank was a real person."

"Easy, pal, I'm not doubting you, just repeating what we heard."

"It should be pretty easy to determine if the guy's real. Janeene knows his full name, family, friends, whatever. And somebody besides her must have known he was coming up here to camp. Hank's almost a celebrity for Christ's sake. He won over eight hundred thousand dollars in the lottery. According to Janeene, everyone was bugging him for money."

"The police are checking on Hank," Jonathan said.

"They're checking on a lot of things," Duke added. "We heard rumors of military-grade drones being used in the area where you said Hank got away. They even have infrared cameras, but other than some moose and a few bears, they've seen nothing yet."

"Hank is an expert with drones," I hissed. "He flies them as a hobby and even uses infrared, I believe." I couldn't remember if Janeene said that exactly. "Anyway, he'd be able to avoid detection by them better than you or me. He knows what he's doing with drones, understands their capabilities and all."

"Did you tell this to Chief Bolling?"

"No. He didn't mention using them in the search area, and the subject never came up."

Jonathan said, "Hank might be capable of evading them. You need to tell the police chief the next time we talk with him."

"I will. What else did you guys hear?"

"We heard a large team of people, including some Ontario Provincial Police, National Guard soldiers, and volunteers

Bolling rounded up, will leave for the sites tomorrow to look for blood on the ground, Pete's body, and traces of Bobby being buried where you said."

"This should all blow over then. They'll find what I said at each one of those places."

"That's not what should concern you," Duke returned. "It's what they don't find that's the problem—like a dead man, a murder weapon, and Hank."

I pushed back deep into the pillows on the bed, sulking. "Dammit, Duke, all I wanted to do was go camping and fishing, not get entangled in a legal mess. I understand the problems, thought of all those things myself hiding in the woods around Jackfish Point."

"Did you? Ever stop to wonder where this leaves you if they can't find Bobby, or Hank, or that guy in the crevasse?"

"It leaves me nowhere. Exactly where I am now."

"It could leave you vulnerable, more so than you would like," Jonathan said softly.

"How so?"

"When your story gets out, families and relatives of the missing people or the abducted kids might try to sue you for wrongful death, negligence, or—"

"This is horseshit; Hank and his friend tried to kill me."

"Did they?"

"Damn sure did. They weren't hunting turkeys out there."

"Maybe not, but it might be hard to prove they were hunting you."

"If you were in the woods with me and Janeene, you wouldn't feel that way." I was fuming. "I tried to help the kid by bringing him to safety. Sounds like I should have left him in the woods, saved myself a lawsuit."

We all sat silently until Duke asked, "Did they ever shoot at you near Jackfish?"

"Already said they didn't. To my knowledge they never saw us there. Pete fired a volley one night when he fell into the crevasse, but that was at a bear, not me. Hank shot at us when we were paddling away from his campsite on Brent Lake. Those bullets are eighty feet down in the water. It's no use, I know what you're thinking; I can't point to a spot on the island and tell the police there's a bullet in this or that tree. I can do it around Darky Lake, but not elsewhere."

The hum of the fluorescent lights was deafening, drowning out my scattered thoughts. I wasn't going to buckle under this. No way. "You guys have done an excellent job of ruining my night, but that was the point, right?"

"Exactly." Jonathan smiled. "I was a psychology major before deciding on the law as a profession. The next round of questions will be very, let's say, intense." After a minute he added, "Only wish I had more real-world knowledge of legal jurisdiction issues. This is a unique case with American citizens on Canadian soil, possibly committing a crime somewhere around an unseen boundary, and returning back into US territory. It might take weeks just to determine which country has jurisdiction to investigate the matter."

CHAPTER SIXTEEN

Three times during the night I awoke, burning with indecision, doubting myself, doubting others, and questioning my reality. By eight o'clock the next morning the misgivings were gone, replaced by the steely resolve that had served me so well in the Army and in difficult times.

Duke and Jonathan arrived at eight-thirty, armed with a bag of glazed donuts, coffee, and a fresh perspective. Sleep had done them well, and they started spouting opinions and perceptions before they sat down. I listened as they postulated, letting them ramble on for a few minutes.

"Put it to rest, fellows."

"Huh?" It was impossible to tell who had responded.

"I've decided to stick to my story straight and true, no concessions of any kind."

"Who told you otherwise?" Duke mumbled, his mouth full with a glazed donut.

"Nobody. And nobody's going to rattle me from the truth. I saw what I saw, acted accordingly, and that's my position. Plain and simple."

Donuts were no longer of interest. "What are you saying?" Jonathan asked, putting a half-eaten one down on the nightstand.

"Simply that the facts are the facts. I'm not worrying about who thinks what, like if my actions were right or wrong, or what a reporter, family relative, or especially an attorney for a plaintiff believes about anything. My story is the final word."

"What brought this about?" Duke asked.

"Nothing but a good night's sleep and a clear conscience."

"I'm not following this," Jonathan announced.

"Try this. Since Wednesday of last week, six days ago, I've been running from a crappy situation—one I didn't bring about, mind you—uncertain what was going on, or why, with no good guess as to what would happen next. My actions were based on what I knew at the time, and what had to be done to keep myself alive. Not about to second-guess myself from this point on. The facts support me better than anything or anybody."

"Sounds like a solid defense to me," the attorney said.

"Defense for what? There's no evidence I did anything wrong."

Both of them sat down like synchronized swimmers. After a minute Jonathan said, "I like that, no evidence to the contrary, nothing pointing to any improper acts on your part."

"What about the Boy Scout?" Duke asked.

"What about him?"

Duke looked at me, "This is hypothetical, you understand, but suppose the lady says you bopped the kid on the head?"

I thought about his question. "Can she prove it?"

"I dunno? Can she?"

"No way, pal, she was hiding in the swamp and couldn't see shit. Did she say otherwise?" My question caused all of us to stop.

"No, she didn't say she witnessed you attacking him; it's

just she didn't understand where the kid came from, how he got into Hank's canoe, or how he got hurt." We were all silent as we thought about the chase in Darky Lake.

I interrupted the quiet. "The Scouts had to be fishing in Brent Lake at a certain time. We were moving toward Darky at that same time and didn't see them when Janeene and I passed through. They had to be either left or right of our course. I could see all the way to the southern edge of the water, our left, and they weren't there; couldn't see as well to the north or my right, because my view was blocked. There were several islands and jutting shorelines with trees obstructing my ability to see north. The kids were probably fishing in that part of Brent Lake. When Hank came after us sometime later, he saw the boys, decided he could use another paddler, and stopped them. He killed one of the Scouts, then came in our direction. When he spied Janeene and me, he chased us all the way to the shore-line in Darky. Once we got on land, we separated. She went into the swamp, and I ran up to higher ground. If Janeene's going to say I hit the kid—and this is theoretical—some fact will be out of place. She couldn't see shit."

"What about the rifle?" Jonathan asked.

"That's a good one. From the questions Chief Bolling asked, sounds to me like there's none of Hank's fingerprints on the rifle stock, but maybe some of mine or Janeene's. Makes sense. We pawed that gun like a treasure. But again, just because I handled the rifle doesn't prove anything. And if Janeene were to claim the boy was struck by me, why would she protect me from the National Guard soldiers? That's a pretty odd way for someone to act if I'd beaten a kid before her very eyes. She'd have been aiming the rifle at me, not the trooper, if that were true."

"Good point," Jonathan muttered.

"Yeah, but you're missing mine. I know the facts. They

can't be denied. We can second guess everything, worry about this or that, and entertain the belief that Janeene will lie for some unknown reason, but I'm not playing that game, even if she does. I'm sticking to my story and living with it. Two years ago, I made the mistake of not believing the facts; I'm not making that mistake again."

Duke looked at me with a forlorn expression. He understood my hidden meaning and more about the heartbreak I had endured than anyone. He'd helped me through that terrible time, and we had an unwritten pact not to discuss Sherry, period, unless I mentioned her first. The right to bring up her memory belonged to me, and me only.

Jonathan stood and reached for his unfinished donut. "I can see you're going to be an easy client to help."

"Only if you don't act like the guests on CNBC who talk in circles, confusing everybody with mindless chatter about the stock market for the benefit of airtime. They beat the issues to death, questioning every angle while getting nowhere, like— well, I'll say it, like lawyers."

"Point taken. You won't have that problem with me."

"Wonderful. Now please tear one of those donuts into little pieces and give it to me. Then tell me what else you two have been thinking."

"After that tirade, I'm not sure we should."

"It's okay. I can play point-counterpoint, just don't want to get lost in the game."

We reviewed my tape from yesterday. Jonathan wound it forward and backward, listening carefully. Duke made notes when Jonathan paused, wanting clarification from me. By lunch we had a stack of issues—things I said that could be misconstrued or interpreted different ways. "I would suggest," my attorney said, "that you only speak to the police with me present. And I strongly recommend that you do not speak to the press."

"No plans to."

"It won't be easy," Duke said. "There's about ten media vans in town as of this morning."

"If I stay in this hospital, reporters can't get in, right?"

"Right." Jonathan got up and stretched. He was wearing the same clothes from yesterday. "If you fellows don't mind, I'm going to the chief's office to check in with them. If nothing is happening, I'm driving back to Duluth. Takes about two and half to three hours." He picked up the tape recorder. "I'll have this transcribed."

"I'll go with you to the chief's office," Duke said.

"Hey, partner, I appreciate you sticking by me."

"Always. Besides, what else do I have to do? Retired, remember." Duke came around to the left side of the bed and shook my good hand. "Just wish I had been able to help when I came to the little lake searching for you."

"You have no idea how close I came to standing up and screaming."

"I can imagine. In some ways you saved my life too. That prick Hank might have shot me if I'd come to the top of the waterfall."

"Never would have happened."

He squeezed my hand tighter. "I'll let you know if I hear something at the chief's office."

"Hey, do me a favor?"

"What?"

"Close those curtains. The sunlight is too bright while my head hurts, especially after grinding it out with you guys."

"You got it." He pulled them tight, casting a sick pallor over the room. "See you later, buddy."

When they left, I called a nurse. My room was on the

upper level of the hospital in the private section. A young woman, about twenty-five with long brunette hair, came to answer my page. I got out of bed and walked to her. "You know who I am?"

"Everybody does. Whole town's talking about the Quetico story."

"May I ask a special favor?" I gave her my most gracious smile, but suddenly remembered the bandages on my face.

She blushed and backed up a foot. "What kind of favor?"

"This is odd, but I suspect it won't be long until news reporters learn exactly where I am; I'd rather not speak to them."

"People are not allowed back in this section without permission. We check them at the nurses' station. There's also a deputy watching your room. He has a chair outside your door."

"I understand, but I noticed a couple times when the door was open, the chair was empty; someone might slip past and that wouldn't be nice for me."

"Deputy Bottelander does like to talk, pretty much nonstop. He's really sociable, but he's a good policeman and always does his job."

"I'm wondering if you could you keep an eye on him for me —keep him in his chair as much as possible to guard my door. I'd give you a special bonus for the assistance."

She was in deep thought, balancing rules and regulations against her better judgment. Before she responded, I said, "You can be like my private nurse. I'll pay a separate fee for the privilege of privacy."

"I'd lose my job if I did that."

"Not if I explain it to the doctor. I'll make a donation to this hospital with stipulations for you and the doctor to get special recognition if you'll agree to help me."

"Doctor McMillian will have to decide this."

"Fine. Would you please ask him to see me when you have the chance?"

As she turned to leave, I asked, "What's your name?" She didn't have a name tag on her white blouse.

"Margaret. Margaret Riley."

* * *

A firm knock came at my door, and Margret said, "A gentleman named Duke Johansen is here. Says he's your friend and wants to visit you. I recognize him from visiting you earlier in the day."

"Thank you, Ms. Riley."

Duke stepped in. "Man, what happened? It's like the gestapo out there."

"A little caution on my part."

"That's a tough Doberman you have guarding the door. Tougher than the cop."

"Yeah, and she wants all the inside scoop before I leave this place."

"Won't be many secrets left by that time."

"Oh?" I sat on one of the folding chairs, being careful with my ribs.

Duke pulled the other around, straddling it and facing me. "The cops have been busy."

"Cops?"

"Well, Chief Bolling, the forest rangers, the park rangers, the Ontario Provincial Police, whoever. There's so many different uniforms and badges around it's impossible to tell which agency everyone is from."

"Okay. The generic term *cops* is good then."

"Anyway, the news flash of the afternoon is that they found parts of a body at the ravine, along with a female black bear that was shot and killed."

"Pete?"

"I'm guessing. They haven't released a name. The body was badly mauled by animals, so they're checking dental records, things like that."

"If they got there, they must have checked the campsite and waterfall."

"They did. No blood at the campsite. Speculation is somebody cleaned it up with shovels."

"Hank and Pete had spades, the fold over type, like military equipment."

"Regardless, there was no blood there, but they did find the hole where you said the body was buried."

"Empty, I assume."

"Correct. They haven't found the body yet."

"It's possible they never will."

"They're entertaining that prospect."

"What about Hank?"

"Vanished. There's an APB out, but he hasn't shown up anywhere inside or outside the parks. By the way, I gave an official statement about him to the chief."

"Saying?"

"Exactly what he and I yelled to each other at the waterfall. Identical to what you told him yesterday."

"You really didn't get a look at him, did you?"

"No. He was hiding in the brush, like you said."

"I wish you'd seen that bastard's face."

"I have. There's a thousand photographs of it all over the chief's office and in the local newspaper. The rangers are covering the parks, giving it out to campers, and looking for him. It's a scary situation out there, causing a major evacuation. People are leaving Quetico and the BWCA in droves."

"Shit, I was afraid that might happen. I could've ended this when I had the chance with Hank at Darky. Should've knocked his head so hard he'd still be on the ground or broken his leg so he couldn't walk away."

Duke wiped his hand across his face. "With that killer on the loose, everyone in the parks wants out, and nobody wants in."

"Gonna be an economic disaster for this town."

"Maybe, but if the reporters keep showing up, the restaurants and motels will do okay."

"Some condolence," I said, thinking the number of reporters was miniscule compared to the number of campers who visited each season. "It's the outfitters who deserve the money, for making the parks accessible for campers and fishermen like us. There's about a quarter of a million people who visit both parks in a normal year."

"Way it goes sometimes."

"Yeah." It was a terrible situation for Pec and others who depended on visitors for their livelihood. Losing July and August would ruin their financial seasons. The hunters who came in September and October to hunt in the BWCA might salvage some of the fall period, but there was no hunting at any time in Quetico, so the summer months were the only time to generate much revenue for that park.

"The hunters will come to the Boundary Waters," I said, "in the fall."

"Would you?" Duke asked.

"For a chance to shoot the bastard, you bet. I'd feel safe as long as I had a rifle. . . and having prey that might fight back, that's a real challenge."

"Different way of looking at it, I'll grant you." He eyeballed me with a strange glance. "I forgot you were in the Army."

"What else has happened?"

"That about covers everything, except for rumors."

"And those are?"

"Mostly that the cops are checking into the backgrounds of Hank, Pete, and the lady."

"What about me?"

"You too."

I bowed my head, thinking this wasn't deserved. "Means they'll rehash the story about my wife. Shit. Was hoping to keep that part out of the news—bad for my kids to hear again and again."

"Sorry, pal."

"Great." I slumped back in the steel chair, feeling the cool touch of metal through my thin cloth robe. Gave me the chills. "This sucks, partner. Couldn't have been further from my mind when we decided to come here for my birthday celebration."

The rotary telephone rang. I had forgotten about it since we plugged it in. I glared at it like it was a Claymore mine. "Get that, will you?" I asked.

He went to the nightstand, picking up the receiver as if it were scorching. "Hello?" After a second, "Yeah, he's here, Jonathan. Hold on." He whispered, "Your attorney." Like I could forget his name.

"How'd you get this number?"

"Wasn't easy. Getting the hospital was, but getting to you was harder than jumping through hoops. Who's Margaret—a CIA agent?"

"No, a nurse at the desk."

"She's in the wrong profession. Thank God she saw me so I could describe myself to her, or I never would've gotten through." He laughed through the telltale crackling sound of a cell phone.

"Where are you?"

"Near Duluth. Couldn't call sooner because my service is poor up there around Ely. Listen, my office has been checking around, and Hank did win the lottery; after taxes he pocketed over eight hundred thousand dollars, and most of it is missing."

"Missing?"

"Yeah. He originally deposited the money in the bank, but a few weeks ago he started drawing large checks, turning the money into cash. There's over seven hundred fifty thousand dollars in greenbacks floating around somewhere. And get this, he had a life insurance policy for a million dollars, payable in thirds to his mother, a child from his first marriage, and a woman named Janeene Morgensen. Know her?"

"You're kidding me."

"Afraid not."

"How did you—"

"I've got friends all over this state." A horn honked followed by Jonathan's voice a second later, "Moron." Then, "Hey, Roger, I'm almost at my office. See you tomorrow."

"Yeah, later." But he was already gone.

"You're not going to believe this," I said to Duke.

He didn't.

CHAPTER SEVENTEEN

The next day, Tuesday, July 2, I planned on resting and putting the overwhelming weight of the murder and the investigation it fostered on hold. I wanted to spend the day in isolation and by taking more than a few strategic naps, since my ribs hurt and my nose stung like it was on fire. That idea lasted all of about ten minutes.

Duke and Jonathan gained entry—no easy task I was informed—to my hospital room shortly after 8 a.m. They were both full of ideas to help me defend my actions in Quetico and give pause to speculations I had conducted any wrongdoing. By lunchtime, our plans had changed, especially after Chief Bolling visited my room to state that no formal charges were to be filed against me at this time, by either him or the Ontario Provincial Police. It was an odd situation the chief noted. "There is no verifiable evidence you committed a crime. The Boy Scouts who lost their friend, the kid murdered by blows to the head near Brent Lake, said they couldn't see the killer's face. He was too far away. They couldn't positively identify him, but they stated the guy had dark hair and was alone in his canoe. After seeing your picture, they said it definitely wasn't you. When you showed up with the missing Scout and didn't have dark hair, we decided you weren't the killer of the first kid. Besides, Janeene Morgensen claims she was in your boat the whole time; said you saved the Scout who was struck by Hank."

"What does all this mean for me?" I asked the chief.

"It means what I said," he responded. "At this time there is no verifiable evidence you committed a crime. We can't arrest you now, but we can request that you continue to recover in the hospital and remain available as a witness. Maybe a material witness."

Jonathan jumped up at that statement. "Are you saying he is a material witness?

"No, not at this time. We haven't classified him as one yet."

I said, "Look, Chief, I want to help however possible. I'm not planning on leaving Ely. "Gonna stay here until I recover which should take a few more days, maybe a week, then we can talk about the next steps. I'll be a witness, plain and simple. You can count on that."

"Be back in a few hours," Bolling said. "You and your team need to talk things over."

After he left, I asked Jonathan, "What does it mean *if* I'm classified as a material witness?"

"It means they can hold you in custody for a period of time. It's like they consider you a suspect in the criminal case but might never file charges against you. They need to hear at trial what you know about the crime, so they consider you material to the case. It's kind of a good thing / bad thing, depending on how you look at it."

"What's good about it?"

"Safety. They can keep you in custody and out of harm's way from the real suspect. It happens a lot in organized crime cases."

"This was no Mafia murder. This was an assault by an asshole, a jealous rogue, who slaughtered a man for no justifiable reason. I can't stay here until a trial starts. I need to be free to move about, go back to my home, take care of my kids."

"I know that, Roger. We'll negotiate terms and conditions after you recover."

Duke, who had stood dumbfounded during the entire exchange, finally spoke up. "Well, that discussion sure scared the shit out of me. What do we do now?"

"We go over everything again, review all our. . . er. . . Roger's information. Find out if there are inconsistencies, anything that was said that could lead to legal troubles for him."

I replied, "I want to help the sheriff and this town. What about a news conference, make use of all the reporters hanging around?"

Duke jumped in, "That's a great idea. You know how reporters are digging everywhere after a story breaks. They'll jump on anything to keep their audience listening. This could be the right time to make a statement."

"We need to be careful," Jonathan said. "Anything misconstrued or misunderstood could lead to legal issues. Issues you don't want, Roger."

"We can ask the sheriff what he thinks about a press event," I answered.

Later that afternoon we did ask him and were told the idea would be well received by him, the townspeople, and Canadians. How he knew for certain Canadians would support such an idea was beyond us, but there was much about the inner workings of the authorities in and around the parks we didn't understand.

* * *

The next night, Wednesday, I slipped out of the hospital behind Duke and Jonathan into an unmarked, windowless van being driven by the chief. The vehicle was stationed near the emergency room entrance, backed up into one of two parking slots. It was innocuous. Although media vans were stationed nearby since I had refused all interviews and never left the building, nobody was watching the place as carefully as they should have. I remembered what it was like to lose sight of your target and imagined the chaos when word of my escape got out. There'd be some ticked-off photojournalists and reporters.

As we neared the van, Jonathan asked me again, "Are you sure about this?"

"Absolutely."

The door to the van slid back, and an officer who looked like Chief Bolling's son held the handle as we climbed into the rear seats.

"Evening, Chief," I said. "He any relation?"

Bolling turned away from the wheel, a wry smile on his face. "Nephew."

I'd gotten to like the chief. He and his staff had interviewed me four more times during the day, albeit they were brief episodes to confirm facts, with Jonathan present on my behalf. I told him about Hank's experience with drones, which surprised him. "I'll tell the technicians; they'll be interested to know this," Bolling said. After a few seconds, he added, "Read about your wife. Sorry about that." I didn't respond, and he seemed to get the message that this was not a topic for discussion. Jonathan said nothing since I had already informed him and asked him not to speak about it to anyone. "You've been a big help in this situation, Roger, and I appreciate your cooperation."

I knew any thoughts of me being involved in foul play had diminished. In fact, during the last interview, I had been treated more like a hero than a villain, as was especially evident when Bolling called me aside at the conclusion and said privately, "That was a hell of thing you did, saving yourself and the lady. Took guts. I'm sorry about the legal problems."

I was too. According to Jonathan, talk of civil lawsuits swirled about like flies at a barbeque. He said it was too early to tell if the action filed about moving the Boy Scout and causing further injury held merit, or if Pete's family had a justifiable wrongful death claim, or there was merit in any of the other scurrilous petitions supposedly about to be filed. One thing was certain, though, I might be trapped in expensive legal predicaments for a long time.

"Anything new?" I asked the chief.

"Not since our last interview this afternoon. Still ain't found Hank; that's the thing that really matters."

"Damn, I wish that guy would turn up," Duke said, "dead or alive."

"We all do," Jonathan interjected. "Won't be a happy ending until he does."

The van rounded the corner at East Harvey Street, turned right on Pioneer Road and went a quarter mile, then veered onto North Pioneer Road at a Y-intersection. "Is this place really secluded, Chief?"

"That's affirmative. It's a private house, belongs to Bill Pec. I believe you know him."

"Not personally. He's been my outfitter for years, but his employees have always helped me. Never met the man."

"You'll like him. Honest fellow."

I wanted to believe all the outfitters were. I harbored an unspoken admiration for the people who lived in Ely, particularly those who ran the camping supply businesses providing equipment and canoes to tourists like me. It was something I dreamed of doing, sort of like a kid wanting to be a cowboy in the Old West.

We pulled up to a driveway fronting a huge house set well back from the road, a shimmering blue-green fescue lawn larger than a football field surrounding it on all sides. "Who mows this?" Duke whispered. "A herd of cattle?"

Bolling cruised up the long driveway to the house. When we were near it, the garage door opened, and the chief pulled inside. None of us got out of the van until the overhead door closed completely. A man wearing a dark blue polo shirt and blue jeans was standing at a door leading inside. He was about fifty, trim, and balding. Well-worked biceps bulged out of his shirtsleeves. This guy could carry some backpacks, known as Duluth packs around here. I noticed the word *Pec's* embroidered on his chest pocket. "I'm Bill Pec," he said, shaking my hand with an iron grip. "Roger Cummings. Is everyone else here?" He stepped aside. "Downstairs in the basement." Duke and Jonathan introduced themselves, shook hands, and followed Pec, the chief, and me down the stairs.

The stairway walls were paneled in rough-hewn cedar, giving the place a dark, rustic feel. The basement walls were the same with mounted fish as décor—bass, lake trout, northern pike, muskies, and walleyes of admirable size—along with a few white-tailed deer heads sporting antlers the size of garden rakes. Two black bear heads graced the mantle above a stone fireplace. A twenty-foot-long bar with a glass mirror behind it was situated at the far end of the room. In the center, was an arrangement of leather chairs and a sofa around a giant coffee table. The tabletop was actually a wagon wheel turned on its side under a one-inch-thick piece of glass. Seven men and two women sat around the table.

Overalls, blue jeans, or denim shirts appeared to be the choice of attire among the men, while the two women favored polo shirts with business names embroidered on them. One wore khaki slacks and the other a denim skirt. I didn't know anybody. Everybody stopped talking and stared at me, probably at the bandages on my face. I stepped into the middle of the room at the edge of the table. Two guys moved their chairs off to the side, giving me the floor.

"I appreciate all of you accepting the chief's invitation to hear me out."

"The sum bitch told us we had to be here," someone said. A few snickers of laughter followed. "But not why."

"He did that as a favor for me," I said loudly, cutting him off. "I'm Roger Cummings, the guy in the news. The one staying in your hospital." The room was so quiet the mounted animals on the walls were breathing louder than these folks. "I want to discuss something with you," I announced, walking along the edge of the table, catching the eye of each person in the room. Two guys backed up, giving me ample walking space. "Please allow me to talk first, without interruption." Silence froze the room.

"First of all, I'm sorry this incident happened in Quetico. It wasn't my intention, but it happened; I realize the full story hasn't been released, but there's been enough bits and pieces floating around to make anyone who reads a newspaper or watches TV, understand a Boy Scout was killed, another was injured, and a body was found eaten by animals. Now the authorities are searching for a man named Hank Kovak."

"That's, we all know," a stocky man wearing overalls said. "What the hell—"

"Please." I thrust my good hand in the air, effectively stopping him. "Let me say my piece and then we can talk." My snarl ricocheted around the room, halting the murmurs, freezing all eyes. With the bandages and my hoarse tone, I looked like a maniac in a hockey mask.

I started pacing again. "The impact on your businesses has to hurt, and it really pisses me off that people who enjoy using the parks as I do, are canceling their trips because this guy Hank is on the loose. Believe me, it pisses me off." At the end of my space, I made an about-face and came back to the middle of the table. Every person in the room was zeroed in on my lips. "You know as well as anyone that if Hank dies out there, he may never be found. Wish that wasn't true, but Quetico's a big place, and if he isn't recovered either up there or somewhere else in this country, people are going to be fearful about coming here, possibly for a long time. Having one person responsible for scaring the hell out of folks and ruining the place causes me more anger than I can express, so something needs to be done about the impact of this on Ely for the future."

"What can you do?"

"Hold on, I'm getting there." I caught each person's gaze again. "Don't have much regard for media hype or the feeding frenzy caused when they jump on a story, but the fact is that people get interested when a tragedy gets plastered all over the newspapers and TV. The media is relentless and, in my opinion, won't stop covering a murder case or other juicy crime until they wear us all out."

A murmur started growing in the room. "Let me continue, please." The noise settled down. "I propose letting the media help us reclaim some of the lost interest in the Boundary Waters and Quetico. If the appeal of the parks were to fade, I'd consider this whole episode a greater misfortune than it already has been."

"How—" this time the voice quelled itself.

"Thank you. What I propose is that I stay around in Ely for a week or two, maybe longer; I should be released from the hospital in another day." I spun quickly around, looking at Chief Bolling. "At this time, I'm free to go home, correct?"

He stepped forward. I hadn't told him I would ask this question. He was taken aback and looked at Jonathan, beady eyes blinking, then back at me. "Technically, you're only a witness now, not charged with anything, but you need to be available. So, yeah, you're free to go home, long as we can reach you. I wouldn't advise trying to leave the country though."

"Thank you." I looked back at the others. "But I don't want to go home; I want to tell my story from here in Ely, and I intend to help the town in any way possible. There needs to be a place to come back to when I want visit the Boundary Waters or Quetico again."

Silence. Then, "How do you propose to do this?" an elderly man with short-cropped white hair asked.

"That's what we need to discuss. Not sure what to do or what difference I can make, but you folks are the business leaders of this town, so you tell me, give me ideas."

"You willing to conduct daily or weekly press conferences?" It was a middle-aged lady with a pale blue polo shirt with the name *Omni Marketing* on the front. "I ask this because I write the marketing material for most of the outfitters in town and have lots of contacts around the state. "And Jean, here," she pointed to the woman sitting beside her, "writes material for our local newspaper, some magazines, as well as promotional stuff for me."

"I'm willing to stay in town and hold news events if it you think it would be useful."

"It might cause reporters to come and stay in town on their expense accounts," a young man in a T-shirt that displayed *Billy's BBQ* added.

"I understand lodging is hard to come by this week."

"Harder than trying to grow tomatoes in concrete," somebody shouted.

A white-haired old man raised his hand, lending civility to what could otherwise become a raucous clamor. "Maybe an exclusive interview with somebody like a Minneapolis TV news station would help. Chief Bolling knows how they can pester the cops and create a bunch of BS people want to read or hear about."

"What about a national news show in the morning?"

The woman named Jean raised her hand. "Might be able to help with that. Mary and I," she indicated the other lady, "have arranged interviews for some local business people and politicians on *GMA*—that's *Good Morning America*."

Another different hand rose up. "How about a book? Or a TV movie?"

I jumped back in. "All that takes time, and I'm not an author or movie maker, but ghost writers or screen writers can help. Hate to bring this up, but if Hank doesn't turn up, that may be necessary for next year." That caused a stir in the room.

"What about a funding website?" a man in his twenties asked. "We could provide info about your story. Start a blog, and write about the investigation, telling the public about all the good things happening in Ely, rather than just the bad. Might make them want to support us with donations for the businesses that get hurt. I got a couple of workers who could start on it."

Bill Pec raised his hand. "I don't know how the others feel, but this is a generous offer, Mr. Cummings—a surprising offer really, and something we need to consider. A lot of people are waiting to see what happens, but my bookings for the rest of July and August are down by fifty percent since the news came out. Folks are just backing out of their plans. We need to think about this, and not make a quick decision."

"Understood," I said. "I don't feel good about playing with reporters, making a game out of them trying to do their jobs, but they set the tone of ethics in the media business, not me. This may not accomplish much because the story might be big news for a week, then poof, it's gone. They say you only get fifteen minutes of fame in your life, and I want mine to benefit the parks, if that makes any sense."

"It does to me," the old man said.

"What did happen up there?" a voice from the back asked.

"Nice try, but that's the one thing I'm not discussing today."

Pec stepped forward, looking around the room. "Guess it goes without saying, but anything we say needs to remain in this room. Agreed?" All heads nodded. He looked at me. "What now?"

I looked at the bar along the far wall. "Let's have a beer and talk among ourselves for a while, then we'll make a plan."

"Good idea. Got some draft Pabst Blue Ribbon and soda pop. Tab's on me." He strode across the room and stood behind the bar and pulled a beer tap and filled a mug.

"You did a good job," Duke whispered in my ear as he rushed to my side.

"Can't tell if it will amount to anything yet." I looked at a glass of suds sitting on the countertop. "Love a beer, only problem is I've never sucked one through a straw before." We made our way to the bar. It was made of planks, those from old sailing ships or warehouse floors. I ran my hand over the polyurethane finish on top. "These planks are twelve inches thick."

"Bill got them from a lumber mill his father owned," a guy about my age with stringy, carrot-red hair announced. "Name's Cliff Walter, run a pack-out place down the street."

"I saw your brochures years ago after contacting the chamber of commerce looking for outfitters to use."

"Family's been here since the 1940s. It'd be a shame to see the company go down the tubes."

"Things shouldn't get that bad," Duke chimed in.

"I'm exaggeratin'—one of my famous charms—but this

town is alive because of the parks. People come up here for other places as well, like the lakes with cottages and boats just south of town, but those are hurting too. Other than newspaper people, the regular crowd is gone, at least for the past few days." Pec pushed glasses of PBR across the bar. I grabbed one and snatched a straw from a holder.

"This is a first." Slurping it, it tasted better than any beer I could remember.

Cliff said to me, "They say you were in the Army. Special Forces. I knew a guy who did that. He was a tough son of a gun."

"Most of them are." Then I realized there would be rumors about me that weren't true; I needed to nip this in the bud. "Wasn't in the Special Forces, hear me now. I was in the Cavalry, the Armored Cavalry and, "If you ain't Cav, you ain't shit."

He laughed. "They also say you're a stockbroker. Is that true?"

"Not really. Now I'm more of a private trader, only buy and sell stocks for myself." I didn't recall reading anything about my latest occupation in the local papers. In this afternoon's edition they had me listed as an institutional trading manager in a New York firm until 2014, when a big investigation almost ruined the company, occupation unknown since then. "Where did you hear that?"

"Got a son who lives in Chicago. He faxed part of this evening paper to me right before I came here."

"What else did the paper say?"

"Said you were a captain in the Army, fought in Iraq, got a wife that's dead—bad accident in Atlanta—sorry to hear about that, and a couple kids. Twins if the newspaper is right."

I admitted nothing about my family, knowing the horrible story about my wife would eventually surface, but I couldn't change history or the pain, and needed to move on. My kids need privacy. "What about the investigation up here?"

"Pretty much the same stuff we been hearin'. One Boy Scout got killed, another hurt, and a mad man is terrorizing the parks." He sipped a healthy slug of beer and licked his lips. "Been hearin' other stuff, too, not in the papers."

"Like?"

"Like the lady slipped out of town this afternoon, and she ain't told the police shit."

"Really?" I thought about what the chief said my first day in the hospital. *Her statements don't sound like yours.* The chief was standing by the coffee table chatting with one of the guests. He and I had some talking to do.

Somebody tapped me on the elbow. "Tell you what I think," an elderly man said, moving alongside Cliff. A baseball cap sat atop his wiry, gray hair, sprouting out at nearly right angles. It looked like he'd stuck his finger in an electric outlet.

"Please do."

"This guy, Hank, is a lowly cuss that crawled off and died under a rock. Problem is, like you said, finding that rock is gonna be a bitch." He punctuated his statement with a quick snap of his beer glass to his lips. He eyeballed me as he downed half the drink.

"If that's true, it's going to be a quiet July," I replied.

"You got that right, mister. I think your idea of staying in town is a good one, especially if you hold a thing like a press conference every day, like the FBI did when that plane was shot down over Long Island in '96. Know that was a long time ago, but I was in bed with a broken back that summer and watched the news all day. Couldn't get enough of it at the time. To this day, I think it was the most coverage of a tragedy in history. Nothing like it now; news seems to come and go too fast when these killings, or riots, or other shit is happening all over the country."

"The FBI has many people working their cases, and a lot of activity to report. I'm only a single person with just one story to tell."

"Do it like you said, piece at a time. Know I'd like to hear what the hell happened out there. Everybody knows about the Scout 'cause they brought the boy in here with you, but I hear tell they found part of a man in Quetico, only it ain't this guy Hank."

I glared directly into his eyes. "At this time, I can't say anything."

"Understand, but if I'm dying to know, others got to be. And the folks that went up there will be back in a day or two; word's gonna get out, one way or the other. It'd be a more powerful story if it comes from the horse's mouth."

"It certainly would." *From a stallion and a mare's lips would be even better.*

The group stayed another hour. I spent half that time talking with Jean, Mary, and Chief Bolling, listening about how to plan for and conduct a news conference. Before the session broke up, we addressed the outfitters, telling them a press event would be arranged soon. I would like to make an official statement clarifying some things while leaving others unanswered.

"Don't do it on the Fourth of July; we got plans!" someone yelled.

"No worries," I answered, striking that day from my mind.

Climbing the stairs to leave, Bill Pec said to me, "You can stay in my guesthouse when you get out of the hospital. You'd have total privacy here. It's yours if you want it."

"Thanks, appreciate the offer and I might stay for at least a couple of days."

"You can use the place until this is over."

In the van I asked Chief Bolling if we could talk before leaving the garage. "Sure. Be wise to do it here." He nodded at his nephew who stepped outside the vehicle. My first question wasn't for Bolling, but for Jonathan sitting beside me. "Have you spoken to anyone about my statement?"

"I have not."

"Who transcribed the tape recording?"

He smiled. "My wife, at home. She understands the importance of client-attorney privilege. She hasn't said a word."

"What does the rest of your staff know?"

Jonathan answered, "Nothing about what you said in the hospital room. I only had them checking on facts about the others."

I looked at the chief. "How much of my interview did you repeat?"

"As little as possible. Wilkens and I agreed on that right away and decided to only tell our people what they needed to know to conduct an investigation. Got two of my men with Wilkens's team, and his guys are leading the search around Brent Lake. The team up there knows more than anybody, but it ain't half of what you said."

"But the team reports to you by radio, right, from the lake?"

"Affirmative. On a secure satellite phone delivered from the FBI, and Wilkens only speaks to me when we're alone. The team tells him what they found, and he tells me."

"When are they due back?"

"I'd guess in under two days."

"We need to conduct a press conference before they return, like we discussed with Jean and Mary."

"That'd be a smart idea."

We all sat quietly in the van. I asked, "Chief, what exactly has Janeene said?"

He studied me carefully. "Too fucking little. Said she saw

Bobby on the ground, bleeding, but she wouldn't say she saw him dead. And she didn't tell us she was sitting in the hammock with the guy, like you did." He paused, thinking. "She also said you came back one morning and told her Pete was finished, but you were—evasive was how she put it, about how that happened. She mentioned she was worried at the time you might have killed him."

"He fell in the ravine, crevasse, whatever."

"I know that now, just telling you what she said."

"Sorry. Go on."

"She also said she had no idea how the kid got his head smashed. She was hiding in the swamp when it happened and found it hard to imagine you did it, so it must have been Hank."

"She's right about that."

"I hadn't told you yet, but we lifted a partial print from the rifle, appears to be Hank's." Bolling turned away from the back seat and glared through the windshield, then said slowly, "In my opinion, she was the evasive one when Wilkens and I questioned her, like she was deciding what information to give or not give us. Kind of pissed me off."

"Was an attorney with her when you talked?"

"Yeah, that ticked me off too." He turned and cast a sideways glance at Jonathan who pretended not to notice. "She didn't have one when I talked with her the night they brought you to the hospital, but I didn't get much from that conversation anyway. She was upset and confused. She had an attorney the next morning."

"Amazing," Duke said.

"Not really," the chief said. "One of the National Guard guys on the rescue mission—a real prick—has a brother who practices law, and he mentioned it to her, scared her; next thing you know, bang, she's got Perry Mason on the case."

"Where's the attorney from?" Jonathan quickly asked.

197

"Minneapolis, they tell me. I got his name written down at my office."

"We can't risk going to the chief's place," Duke said.

"No doubt. Joint is covered with reporters."

I asked the chief, "You know if she left town this evening?"

Bolling didn't flinch. "Couldn't keep her. At this time, she's only a witness, like you, and a resident of this state, with a young daughter I might add. It was in our best interest to let her return home."

"Great," I mumbled. "She wouldn't even let me talk to her, been trying since I first woke up."

"Maybe it's better you don't," Bolling said. He started the van. "You want to go back to the hospital?"

"Yeah. And would you talk with Mary and Jean and see if we can plan a news conference at ten o'clock in the morning, day after tomorrow, Friday, the fifth? I'm sure there are some news people waiting around here that would like to be at the announcement."

CHAPTER EIGHTEEN

I spent the next day, Thursday, the Fourth of July, planning a statement while sitting in my hospital bed. Duke came by early in the morning and we never left the room all day. He was in as much demand by the reporters as I was. Only Jonathan could come and go as he pleased, mostly because he walked out of the building and said he was forbidden to comment, which he was, and wouldn't say another word. His picture had been published in three editions of local newspapers and he was getting all the notoriety he could use in a lifetime with two simple words, *no comment*. Wished I could be so lucky.

"You know," Duke said, "we have a flight back to Atlanta on Saturday night. Our tickets haven't been changed."

"I know. Been thinking about leaving like we intended." Our original itinerary called for rendezvousing with our outfitter for pickup on Friday, July 5, at noon, returning to Ely for the night, and traveling to Minneapolis on Saturday for our evening flight home. A glorious two-week vacation—that had been the plan. "Why don't we just slip out of here tomorrow after the press conference and go back to Atlanta on Saturday?" he asked.

"Think it will be much different there?"

"Huh?"

"Don't you think the reporters will be waiting at our doorsteps?"

"My wife hasn't seen any news people."

"Because we're here."

He clunked down hard in the metal folding chair, bouncing its legs on the shiny linoleum floor. "I used to think it would be pretty interesting to be famous," he said.

"Famous maybe. Infamous is different. Not everyone thinks I did the right thing, remember?"

"When people understand what you did, they'll change their feelings. You'll beat any lawsuit that might pop up."

"I'd like to think so."

"Jonathan thinks you'll win."

"I'd fire him if he didn't."

Duke picked up a copy of the transcript Jonathan brought us. It was marked with yellow highlighter and scribbled pencil notes, comments he had made during our discussions. We'd reviewed it ten times. My account was little changed, just clarified, and intensified. My own copy looked like a crossword puzzle from an old Sunday newspaper. "Suppose this is the right thing to do," I said, repeating a refrain used over and over, "talk to the press."

"I think it is," Duke mumbled, circling a phrase on his paper. "Hey, you said Pete fired a volley of rounds the night he fell into the crevasse?"

"A barrage of single shots. That's correct."

"If Wilkens and his team found the body, then they must have found his rifle."

"Yeah, so what?"

"Then it stands as proof he was after you."

"Somebody might claim he was hunting animals."

"Maybe, but according to your account, he may not have been dead when he hit the bottom."

"Why does that matter?"

"I was thinking, suppose he thought he was firing at you, not the bear, before he fell into the ravine?"

"But the bear was at the bottom, shot at least twice. I saw the wounds."

"He could have shot the bear when it came down after him. When he first started shooting, who knows what he was aiming at?"

"What's your point?"

"My point is that his firing the rifle is proof you needed to be scared of him. He was carrying a gun, one you're not supposed to have in Quetico, and he was chasing you. There are no summer bear hunts in that area. No hunting is allowed in Quetico, period. He was undoubtedly trying to hunt you, not animals. His shooting demonstrates that he was trying to kill something. Maybe the bear came later, after he thought he was shooting at you."

I lay back against my pillows. What none of them knew was I had placed Kevlar trip wires around the top of the ravine. I thought it was a good idea at the time, hoping to possibly cause a pursuer to stumble after hitting them in the dark and maybe fall into the crevasse. If the pursuer found them, he would either walk around the area or cut the lines and take a chance on moving through the ravine. It might have worked on Pete and led to his injury and contributed to his death. I had no way of knowing, didn't mention it during the interviews, and had no intention of reporting my activity now. Janeene hadn't said anything either, and I wasn't sure she even remembered about the setup.

We'd gone around and around on every point we could raise, twisting and tweaking the issues, like attorneys for the defense, only I couldn't see myself as a defendant. "Let's give it a break and stick with Plan A."

Plan A was a simple statement. It would recount the days near Jackfish Point, saying as little as possible, but admitting I'd witnessed a murder, had helped Janeene survive, and had escaped from two men chasing us around Brent Lake. The battle with Hank would be described briefly, noting he was injured, and discuss little else. No questions from reporters would be answered. Jonathan believed I wouldn't incriminate myself by sticking to the script, but he also believed there shouldn't be a press conference at all and that Bolling should make an official statement alone.

We were both tired and hungry. It was suppertime, and Margaret had promised to arrange a meal of grilled pork chops and mashed potatoes. My special nurse had turned into a watchdog and caterer since our discussion. The rotary telephone rang, and I snatched it up, hoping she was calling from the front desk with the meals.

"Roger?"

"Janeene?"

"Yes." Silence. "Can we talk?"

"Sure. About what?"

"The news conference."

"How'd you learn about it?"

"My attorney talked with someone in Ely. I don't know who."

I signaled Duke, pointing hastily at the phone with my good hand and motioning for him to be quiet. "Are you alone?"

"Yeah. There's no attorney with me now. Nobody is listening either. Are you scared, Roger?"

"Actually. . . yes, as scared as I was in Quetico, but in a different way."

"Shouldn't be. You did nothing wrong."

"Tell that to the families who might want to sue me."

"I intend to, if you'll let me."

"What do you mean?"

"That I want to join you in the press conference."

I held the phone beneath my cast, clutching it with the tips of my fingers. The cast was shaking, wobbling from the tension of holding it up and the anxiety caused by her voice. She sounded like she had in the forest: soft, frightened, dependent upon me for strength. "Roger, do you remember us discussing courage?"

"Yeah."

"I told you I wanted to be a braver person, stronger than in the past. I haven't been living up to my promise, and I'm ashamed of myself."

I didn't know what to say. What can you say to a statement like that? She'd run off and hidden and left me to explain what had happened, not vouching for me, leaving me in a lurch trying to justify why three people might be dead. "Why haven't you been talking to me?"

"I was scared. My attorney told me to stay quiet, let him handle the police, the press, anybody who wanted to talk to me. I was alone, and you were so beaten up that. . . that I didn't know what to do, and I listened to him. I barely spoke to the police chief, and I know it didn't seem right to him or you."

"You kind of left me hanging, Janeene."

"I didn't mean for it to happen. The attorney said you'd be fine. I never thought people could sue you for what you did."

"I'm not sure they can. This is all posturing—legal BS, trying to make a case. In the long run it won't work."

"Still, I want to help you, and stand up there with you and tell the story, just like it happened."

For three days I'd been plotting strategy, deciding what and what not to say, mulling over each little detail like one mispronounced word would lead to a prison term. Somehow that didn't seem important now. "I wasn't going to say all that much, Janeene, just give the reporters a quick outline of what happened. The local authorities are still investigating, looking for evidence to prove things the both of us said."

"Let me say it with you, Roger. I owe you that much at least."

The phone was getting heavy, and I switched it to my good hand. "Love to have you with me." I was imagining the two of us on the podium.

"Then I'll come. My father will drive me up there tonight."

"This place is a madhouse. Reporters are everywhere, and there's no rooms to be had. It's the fourth of July, and this place is busy with townsfolk."

"Then I'll come in the morning."

"Wait a second, I have a better idea. Hold on." I put the phone against my chest and asked Duke, "Where's Jonathan?"

"In Duluth. He's driving up in the morning."

"You have his number?"

"Yeah, in my wallet." He pulled it out of his pants pocket.

"Janeene, I'm going to call my attorney, a guy named Jonathan Friedman. He lives in Duluth and—"

"Is he the curly-haired man I've seen in the newspapers?"

"Yeah."

"Will he represent me too?"

I sat, stunned for a second. "What happened to your guy?"

"I don't know and don't care. I'll never speak to him again."

If Jonathan represented both of us, maybe I'd stand a better chance of having any claims against me denied. "I could ask him. I don't know the law very well, Janeene."

"Check with him, please. We were a team once, a good team, and I want to be back on your side."

"Okay, I'll phone him. Maybe you can drive to Duluth tonight, come up with him in the morning."

"I'm at home," she said. "Here's my number." I repeated it aloud and had Duke write it down.

"Jonathan will call you right back." As I was about to hang up, I asked, "How's Angela doing?"

"She's well, Roger. I've told her all about you; she thinks you're a hero."

"At least somebody does."

"I do, too, it just took a couple of days to understand that."

* * *

In the morning I was escorted to the chief's office at 11 a.m. Janeene was waiting with Jonathan. She was wearing a dark gray pantsuit, a trim outfit with a stark white blouse and short-waisted jacket. Her hair was pulled tight along her scalp, held in a ponytail behind her head with a black silk scarf. A touch of makeup gave her face a thin, regal air with eyeliner and mascara making her eyes stand out like shimmering jewels. Any evidence of the blows she had suffered from Hank were not visible, the makeup covering them. "You look beautiful," I commented. I was dressed in a pale blue hospital robe, much like a doctor's outfit, with fresh white bandages and a new coat of plaster on my cast. "Beauty and the beast," I said.

Jonathan said, "I think we should talk about this conference."

"Okay, counselor, fire away. Give us your advice." We listened to his suggestions for ten minutes. "Enough, sir, I understand your point of view. No need for all the legal mumbo-jumbo. I'm going to stick to Plan A like we discussed, with Janeene's support."

"You lead and I'll follow," she said.

Jonathan said, "Roger, you two need—"

"To be unafraid. We are now." Janeene hugged my arm. I put my hand on Jonathan's shoulder, forcing him back into his seat. "We'll do okay."

"Only if you stick to our statement and don't answer questions. Let me do the talking for you two."

"We can live with that."

CHAPTER NINETEEN

The press conference created a major stir in Ely, as well as the state of Minnesota. Media personnel piled in before the scheduled occasion and hung around for a day or two afterward. I read a statement, but answered none of their questions directly, only indirectly through the chief, even though a few of the reporters pestered the hell out of me, demanding responses to even their most outlandish assertions—cloaked as questions I should not ignore. It made me want to yell "foul" in some of their faces.

Janeene sat beside me and never spoke a word. She was stoic and beautiful, but Jonathan was the real headliner as he countered numerous legal inquiries and tilted his responses toward defending our actions. It all came off as we planned.

Our news event was extremely informative but left many of the journalists' questions unanswered. There were no responses for the queries about the killers or their intentions, and it left the correspondents hungry for more information. Some stuck around, hoping to learn and report more about the Quetico murders and investigation, but for many it was on to a different location and the looming stories of the next news cycle.

Chief Bolling came to see me at the hospital the following day. He told me over the phone he had some news that would interest me but said nothing else.

"You did a great job convincing the media you're an honest guy," Bolling said when he entered my room.

"Not all of them, apparently."

"There's always a few assholes who'll try to goad you into reacting to their bullshit questions. I know from experience. Don't worry about it. You did well."

"Thanks."

"Having Janeene at your side and Jonathan speaking for you was a smart move. I think the reporters realized they'll get no stupid or off-the-cuff answers from you."

Bolling took off his hat and pulled a chair close to my bed. My mattress was at a forty-five-degree angle and I could look him in the eye. He seemed to dally, like he was thinking, while he looked at notes in a pad he took out from his shirt pocket. "Wilkens recovered some fishing line near the crevasse, the Kevlar braided stuff like he found where you fought Hank. Don't suppose you know anything about that?"

I froze, deciding whether to claim ignorance, or tell the truth. Honesty seemed like a better but more dangerous choice. "Actually, I do. I was about to string some along the edge of the ravine when Janeene slipped on a rock and called for my help, and I went to her and left the SpiderWire, or Kevlar, on the ground."

Bolling pondered my answer, gazing back and forth between my face and his notes. "So, you didn't use the fishing line to set a trip wire?"

I couldn't answer his question without possibly incriminating myself in the accident that may have happened to Pete if he'd stumbled into my lines. Wasn't certain he had, but who knew? I decided to try and find out what he and Wilkens had found. "You were in the Army, right, Chief?"

"Yeah, the Reserves."

"Then you should know about early warning systems."

"I do, and I also know about trip wires and the like, Roger."

"Well, I intended to set up the lines for early warning. Planned to tie small sticks all along the SpiderWire, hoping to hear a racket if something walked into it in the dark. I did this around our hiding place a little lower down the hill."

"Still didn't answer the question, Roger. Did you set up a trap along the crest?"

"I don't recall finishing it up there." The sheriff eyeballed me with a suspicious glare. "I was in a hurry to help Janeene and might have dropped some line around the crest of the crevice."

"Dropped it?"

"Yeah, I had a wad of it in my pocket and was getting ready to run a barrier line when Janeene yelled. I probably lost it when I went to help her."

Bolling's eyes were incendiary—blowtorches that could burn through any lies I might tell him. "So, you never set a defensive perimeter?"

"Didn't have the time, Chief, as best I can recall. Why, did Pete have any around his legs when they found him? When I saw him dead in the crevasse there was none."

"No, he didn't have any near him, according to Wilkens." After a few seconds Bolling added, "And neither did the sow. But a small cub Wilkens found a short distance away was all tangled up in it. He put the line in his pocket and checked it when he got back. Same stuff that was at the battleground with Hank."

"Must have dropped the Kevlar when I went to help Janeene."

"Why didn't you say something about this before?"

"Forgot, and didn't think about it, or realize it might be important."

We sat in silence, knowing this could be a major point of contention about my actions and the intent to cause injury. Stillness enveloped the room as both of us realized the gravity of the discovery. "Neither Wilkens nor I are gonna comment about the line, unless asked. We're not about to conceal anything, lie about anything, or hide any relevant facts. Since neither Pete or the mother bear were caught up in the shit, or excuse me, entangled in the line, it appears the cub got into it before anything happened." He let the point go, although it also felt like the temperature in the room had dropped by about twenty degrees. I was sweating harder than on a mid-summer day.

* * *

Other news in July didn't help matters for the Ely outfitters. In the middle of the month a major story about the murder of a US citizen, a woman, and her boyfriend from Australia, alarmed many across both America and Canada. The couple was shot on a remote highway in northwest Canada. Another victim, a biology lecturer, was also found slain in the same area, and it led to major manhunt for two teenagers believed to be responsible. I realized the fear of vacationing in the back-country would only increase until Hank and these two teenagers were found. People were scared at the thought of being alone with a killer or killers in the woods. They gave up on Ely because of Hank, and the rest of Canada because of these kids. I knew how they felt; I just didn't agree.

On July 27, there was a reported lightning strike at a Girl Scout campsite in the BWCA, although the actual story turned out to be much different than initial reports. The lightning strike did occur, but it didn't hit the girls directly as originally stated. The news did bring reporters back to Ely. Now the main story was the rescue attempt, where volunteers left for the Girl Scout site during the middle of night and paddled for hours to reach them. It takes bravery, determination, and skill to travel though the parks at night, and the effort was regarded as heroic.

The national networks picked up the Girl Scout story for a night, but by the end of the twenty-four-hour news cycle, it faded. Nonetheless, the negative aspects of the reports emanating from Ely in late June and July took a heavy toll on visitation, causing more cancellations of planned park outings. This was my greatest fear. The parks' supporters and business owners didn't deserve this.

On that same day, a news story broke on television about a rescue in another part of Canada. Apparently, a pilot flying south toward Quebec had engine problems and crashed his plane in a remote area. He was lucky and was also fortunate to be in his predicament for only five hours. He filmed his exploits on a cell phone, and they became a news lead on many US and Canadian television stations. I wished I had a cell phone video of Hank shooting Bobby. It would have gone viral on the Internet and made prime time on network news hours—and my life much easier.

Still, my predicament did get easier when Chief Bolling came to my room at Bill Pec's home in Ely on the last day of the month. I'd been staying in his guesthouse since my release from the hospital on July 8. After my first news conference with Janeene and all the press attention it generated, things had slowed and interest in the search for Hank or the story of life in the parks was vanishing. By late July, the quest to find the killer was old, old news. I'd hung around till the end of the month because my kids were safely ensconced with their grandparents in New Jersey, and they seemed be to very happy there. Harold, the twins' grandfather, had made special arrangements to ensure their safety; therefore, I didn't need to worry about them. And I didn't want to leave Ely and miss the possibility of Hank being found.

"Got something you might like to hear," the chief said, as I followed him toward the sitting room in the basement. It was a moment I'll never forget, Sunday, July 28, 2:06 p.m. "The kid woke up last night."

The kid was the Boy Scout we had all been praying for since his rescue from my canoe. I held my breath. "When you say woke up, did he speak?"

"Nope."

I had been hoping for this for weeks. . . now, my heart sunk, maybe he had brain damage.

"But they think he will. Doctors are giving him time to settle in. Seems he mumbles, though."

"Great." But it was great, and I reminded myself that if the kid could mumble, then he might be able to talk eventually. Any activity at all had to be considered a success. The last time I saw the boy he looked like a victim of a war zone, head bruised and bloody, skull possibly cracked. "When do they think they can ask him questions?"

"Can't tell, maybe today, maybe next week, maybe never. All depends."

I hated the response it depends; heard that word every day trading stocks, and it meant nobody could give you an accurate answer, or at least a good guess at what might happen. "He was in that coma for a long time," I said. "Does that mean anything?"

"How would I know? One doctor said the longer they are

in one, the worse it can be. Another told me he's seen them wake up after ten years, look at you, and start babbling away like they were talking with you a minute ago. Like I said, it depends."

"Yeah, it always does."

CHAPTER TWENTY

The next evening, July 29, I returned home, almost three and a half weeks later than my original itinerary.

It was a warm evening and there was no media attention directed toward me when I landed at Hartsfield-Jackson Atlanta International Airport. It had taken me a little less than three hours to go from Minneapolis to Atlanta, and another sixty minutes to grab an Uber ride and get to my house. It had taken me almost a complete day to go from the Brent Lake murder site to my final location on Darky. Ten miles in the wilderness, a thousand miles in the air—what a difference civilization made. I wondered how long it would have taken to me reach the capital of Georgia from Minnesota in the 1800s by canoe and on foot.

As I was unloading my luggage in the bedroom, the doorbell rang. My camping buddy, Duke, had been back for weeks, and he awaited my return as anxiously as a pet golden retriever.

"Damn, pal, it's good to see you." We were not in the habit of hugging each other—a handshake would normally do—but he gripped me around the chest and squeezed hard with both arms. I returned his hug as violently.

"Suppose you heard?" he asked when we had returned to our senses.

"Don't tell me Hank has been found alive and he admitted all his crimes?"

"I wish, but it's almost as good. Chief Bolling called me while you were on the flight and told me to tell you the kid talked; you're in the clear."

Wow. All this while I'm on an airplane coming home from the forgotten land after almost a month of nothing happening. "You bullshitting me? How could this happen now?" I froze in place, too stunned to continue.

Duke's smile was half a foot wide. Before he could speak, I thrust my hand in the air to silence him. "I need to hear this sitting down, drinking a beer. Follow me."

I went to my den. In the refrigerator behind the bar was a stash of Rolling Rock beer I had bought before the trip to enjoy on my return. The green bottles never looked better. I opened two and motioned for Duke to sit in one of my loungers. He took a swig, sat down, and pulled out the footrest.

"The chief told me the kid woke up around five o'clock this afternoon," he said. "He'd been in and out of sleep these past few days, but he never woke up, just moved his eyes and sometimes his lips. They let him rest and didn't ask him questions. He appeared to be comatose today, then out of the blue this afternoon he wakes up and asks the nurse, 'Where is the guy with the tattoo?'" Duke continued, "She called the doctor, who called the chief, who called some others, who called your attorney, Jonathan. He got there before any questions were asked." I remembered Jonathan lived in Duluth, so he was close to the hospital.

"What came out of it?"

"One key point," Duke answered. "The boy remembered a guy with a snake tattoo on his right arm. Said he had a beard and black hair. He was the one who killed his friend, and the one who made him chase after the other canoe."

This was the evidence I needed to back my story.

Duke continued, "Hank had a snake tattoo on his right arm. He had a beard. When this happened, you had, neither." He glanced at my right forearm.

"Did they show him any pictures? Did they get him to positively—"

"No. They didn't want to push him too hard. They'll do that when he's ready. But the kid did say he never saw anyone else but Hank. He said he and Hank chased another canoe with two people in it, but he didn't see the paddlers. The chief takes this as strong evidence you're totally in the clear, like he's been believin' for some time.

"What did the kid say about getting hit in the head?"

"Nothing. He was silent on that point. But he only saw Hank before that time, not you or anyone else." Duke stopped and looked directly at me. "Chief said it was important that he only remembered Hank, not you or Janeene, or any other person before he went blank. That means Hank was the killer of the other Scout and the one who bashed this boy's head." Duke paused and drank a healthy slug of his beer. "In my opinion, you're out of any danger or liability. But I always thought that, knowing you."

"Hope the attorneys see it that way."

"I don't think there's any other way to look at it. After your press conferences with Janeene, I thought the cops and attorneys backed off because they recognized the truth when it was presented to them. You two were great up there." He smiled. I'd done three more meetings with her, and another four by myself during the month. The number of attendees dwindled down each time as interest waned and other news filled the airwaves. At my conference last week, only two local news writers attended for less than ten minutes. "I knew all the details would come out," Duke announced, "either through the investigations in the woods, or through the kid if he recovered. Looks like our prayers have been answered, at least on one count." He finished his beer with a gulp.

I sat back in my chair, thinking of the issues that still nagged me. For one, a guy named Bobby had been killed, but they couldn't find a body. There was a burial site, but no evidence he had been placed there. He was wrapped in a plastic space blanket so no bodily fluids, hair shafts, or pieces of skin had been recovered. Forensic teams had scoured the site but found nothing except overturned dirt. It was just my word that he had been the guy in the blanket. Janeene hadn't seen the internment, so she couldn't testify to that happening, although she did swear that she had witnessed Bobby being shot, and assumed he was dead. But she could not state unequivocally that he was lifeless, just gravely wounded.

"Still some problems," I said to Duke. "What do you think happened to Bobby's body?"

"Man, that's a tough question. They had to rebury him somewhere else or drop him in the lake. But according to your account, they didn't have much time to pull it off."

I had been chewing on this all month after realizing my original statements were slightly off in reference to time. My thoughts drifted back to the actions on that day. Over the weeks, I'd developed a visual record—a videotape in my head—of all the events, activities, sights, and sounds of those days above the Brent Lake campsite, as well as our escape into Darky Lake. It was like a movie in my brain that could be wound forward and backward, in slow motion, and in minute detail, recalling each second and what I had seen or felt. "They had three to four hours on Friday, June 28 to pull it off. It was before Pete came up the hill at three-thirty in the afternoon, looking for Janeene and me. I didn't watch them during that time."

Duke gaped at me. "No shit. Didn't realize that. When did you—"

I cut him off, not wanting to stop my thoughts and words. "Saw them take something down the waterfall wrapped in the blue plastic tarp, and it seemed heavy, so I assume it was the body of the guy called Bobby. Had to be." I was breathing faster now, trying to focus on the images in my mind. "The rangers checked out the place I showed them on the map, near Jackfish point, and said it looked like a burial site, but empty. The body had been there but they couldn't find it around the campsite, so Hank and Pete had to rebury it somewhere else, or they dumped it in the lake."

"But you told this to the chief already."

"Yeah, I know, but I told them the body had to be close to the campsite area. That's what I thought until today when I started running the events through my head again and again. It never made sense to me how the rangers could not find the body in the water if they sunk it. They had scuba divers search the area, and Brent Lake is very clear. You remember how far down you can see in the water around the campsite, maybe thirty feet in places. A blue tarp would stand out like a beacon in the water," I said more to myself than Duke. "But the lake is huge, and very deep, and maybe they paddled a long way off and loaded the tarp with rocks and let it go. Or maybe they took him out of the tarp, tied rocks to his ankles and wrists, and let him sink. Might be a decade until the body is found." I recalled an experience years before at a different lake when I had been fishing at a remote spot and looked down and saw a body. It was the body of a male deer, a buck with a complete set of antlers, a ten pointer. It was in about twenty feet of water, and it spooked me with its ghastly stare. The animal was perfectly preserved, no sign of injury, and I wondered why it was in the water. It was springtime, so hunting probably wasn't the reason. But it could have been shot the preceding fall, and the cold Canadian waters might have kept it frozen. The shock of seeing such a beautiful creature staring up at me from its deathbed stuck with me even after all these years. I wondered how Bobby would look if we found him.

Duke said, "I think your theory about them reburying him in the woods around Brent Lake makes sense."

"I thought so at the time, but now I'm not so sure, according to my recently revised timeline." I looked at Duke and pointed to my head with my finger. "They had between three and four hours to bury him."

"You can go a long way in a couple of hours."

"Yeah, but you can't go a long way, dig a hole at least six feet deep, six feet long, and maybe three feet wide in a short time. You remember how hard it is to dig a hole up there? With all the rocks around, it can be almost impossible. Could take a day to carve out a site to bury a man. And it has to be at least six feet down, or the animals will find it for sure. If I wanted a body to disappear, I'd go deeper than that, thinking the first place they'd buried him was way less than six feet down. That scared them so they moved the body when they had the time."

"I remember the ground around the lakes and understand your point."

"In my opinion, they either sunk him in the lake, or buried him in soft ground, like a swamp."

"Interesting conclusion, Roger. Which place do you think they picked?"

"A combo of both. Sink him in a swamp near a lake, a deep swamp, so the body would settle into the muck and never come up—just get buried further and further down over time. That's my best guess. It's what I would do if I were in Hank's shoes."

I remembered the small lake where Janeene had hidden her canoe after her failed escape attempt. "Son of a bitch." The place looked more like a pond than a lake, at least on the maps. I'd never been in it during any of my trips, just wouldn't go to a place that small and out of the way from a main route of travel. No outfitter had ever marked a map for me with an *LMB* or any other fish initials for this tiny place. Remembering the pond's location on the map, I wondered where its source of water came from. By an inbound stream that wasn't marked on the map, or internal springs bubbling up from the bottom, or maybe a swamp-like dribble of water from the hills nearby? It would be a great place to stash a body. I'd tell the chief to look there the next time we spoke. "But that's just one of many problems, partner."

"Oh?"

"The biggest problem is Hank. Why can't they find him? They've had an army of people, like the US and Canadian forest rangers, National Guard troops, Ontario Provincial Police, Ely Police, and a ton of volunteers searching for more than a month now. They've used dogs, drones, search teams, and satellite surveillance, and they haven't come up with shit. Nothing. Nada. Not a thing. A guy can't just disappear. He had to leave a trail somewhere. Hurt as badly as he was, he couldn't travel very fast."

"Take it easy, Roger. They're gonna find him sooner or later."

"Sooner is my wish."

I got up to fetch another beer. "You want one?"

"Yeah, after your rendition of June 28, and Hank still missing, I need something to settle my nerves."

Duke drank a quarter of his bottle while I downed half of

mine. "They need to find this guy, or we'll have to sleep with one eye open," I said.

"Why would you say that?"

"You kidding? My name and face were plastered all over the newspapers up there. Same for Janeene, and you, too, if I remember correctly. You got mentioned a couple of times for sure." I was huffing now. "If Hank should manage to get out of Quetico, he could decide to take revenge on us. I'm sure he would on Janeene."

We both sat in silence, ruminating.

"The man is dead, partner."

"I'm praying he is."

"Anyway, I am glad you're back home," he said, casting a more upbeat note into our conversation. He appeared relaxed, able to enjoy himself, but I caught a tinge of concern after my remark. "Have you talked to Janeene much?" he asked.

"Yeah, every other day or so. She came to see me a couple of times while I was in Ely. Joined me for some of the news interviews. I'm starting to like her."

"Like? Anything more to it than that?" He smiled with a wry grin.

"No, we're just talking. . ."

He quickly said, "I think she's very calm, and her demeanor impressed me. What do you mean you're talking?"

"You know. . . consoling each other. When you've been through an experience like we have, it either drives you apart, or pulls you together. We're kind of getting closer."

"What's she doing now?"

"Taking care of Angela, being a good mother, and working as an accountant. That's about all there is to report."

"The press been bothering her?"

"They did back in early July, but it's tapered off. She's more worried about Hank getting out of Quetico and coming after her than the press people haunting her. He's the real question mark in her life, and mine, too, I might add. They need to find the asshole."

Duke stood up and walked toward the television mounted on the wall of my den. "Okay if I turn it on? I haven't heard a peep about the BWCA since that Girl Scout thing a coupla days ago."

"Go ahead."

As he pushed the button I said, "People in Ely are having a hard time recovering from the press coverage up there this summer. Visitors are not coming to the Boundary Waters or Quetico like in normal years."

"Yeah, it's too bad. The townsfolk are nice people," Duke reminded me.

We watched the television channels dedicated to twenty-four-hour news programs. After a minute he looked back at me and asked, "You're not looking right. What's bothering you?"

"The crevasse."

"What?"

"You know, since I moved through the crevasse or ravine, whatever, and Pete appears to have stumbled into it and got killed by the bear, some people might try to hold me responsible for his death. Pete's relatives certainly do." I hadn't told Duke about the Kevlar trip wires and wasn't going to now.

"That's not what the authorities think," Duke reminded me. He was right. The police had concluded that Pete was hunting Janeene and me with his rifle and had probably walked into the ravine in the dark. But he could also have been chased by the bear and fallen. Nothing was certain. No charges were filed against me, but that hadn't stopped Pete's relatives from considering a wrongful death lawsuit, according to a news report. "Your lawyer thinks it's a baseless claim."

"He's supposed to think that."

"Everyone I talked to up there thinks the same thing—you're a hero, remember? You rescued Janeene from a monster, saved a kid's life, and fought a murderer until you were almost killed yourself."

"Yeah, that's fantastic, but I might be facing lawsuits, and all I wanted was to have a great time in the park and catch some fish, and let the twins spend some time with their grandparents." No mention by me of trying to forget Sherry's accident.

Duke wouldn't let me swim in the vat of self-pity. "You'll come out of this on top, believe me. What other problems you got?"

"Other than two dead people, one of whom is missing, and a third guy I wish was dead, but may not be and is missing—nothing of any magnitude."

"Good way to look at it. Things could always be worse. Remember, if you need me, I am always here to help."

"Thanks, pal. Wonderful use of clichés."

CHAPTER TWENTY-ONE

The next morning, I woke up missing Ely. Up there, the twists and turns of the investigation and the search for Hank allowed me an intimate perspective in the case. Now I felt distant, especially after learning about the kid in the hospital from my good buddy in Atlanta. The drama of understanding what was happening in the search for Hank was engrossing, and in Ely I'd been part of an inner circle of those informed by Chief Bolling of any developments on an hour-by-hour basis. He had six deputies in his department, and they were a close group, very tight, and although there were few revelations in the last week I was there, being in the inner circle came with the reward of knowing you would be among the first to learn any news. It didn't matter if the facts were big or small, inconsequential, or monumental, you would be told. By leaving, I'd missed the most important moment of the month—the kid waking up, and more importantly, him identifying Hank. *Man, what I would have given to be in that hospital room.*

I also missed Janeene. She had a remarkable memory for

tiny details, as I'd noticed during our time discussing my maps around the Brent Lake campsite and Jackfish Point.

The last time I saw her she looked hopeful, and the shine in her eyes was bright. Still, she was terribly frightened by the possibility that Hank may still be alive and moving through the park, since she thought he was capable of avoiding the searchers and police to come find her at her home in Chanhassen. She whispered to me during our last phone call a day ago, "I'm selling my house. My uncle on my father's side, Dan, owns a home in Eden Prairie. Dan is sick with lung cancer, and I can stay with him as long as I want and help with his care. He needs some family around. His wife died several years ago, although he does have a nurse that's like a sister to him. Still, I'd like to help him."

"Be enough space for you and Angela?"

"Yeah, Dan's place is big, plenty of room for us while my house is up for sale. My agent thinks it'll move before school starts for Angela. I'll buy a new house next spring. Dad is helping me with all this."

"Sounds like your father really takes care of you."

"He tries. Been that way for as long as I can remember. He's not rich, but he does okay."

"What does he do?"

"He and Dan own several gas stations, a couple of laundromats, and a dry-cleaning place in Eden Prairie. They've been partners since high school. I do their books."

Janeene and I hadn't spoken since that conversation, and now my calls only landed in her voicemail.

* * *

More than a week at home did nothing to calm the storm in my head. I tried to resume a semi-normal life while remaining out of view, but it was difficult.

The only time I was not invisible was in my own neighborhood—funny how that worked. Friends at the country club in my subdivision all knew the story or had heard parts of it and wondered what version of it may have been true. It felt peculiar walking around the club's areas, like the men's locker room, the golf course, tennis courts, or the dining rooms. People I didn't know, or didn't know well, huddled and whispered among themselves while sneaking looks in my direction. I understood now how any level of fame had its price. A level of notoriety based on my wife's unfortunate death and my accidental involvement in a newsworthy murder story only increased my sympathy profile. To say I felt uneasy was an understatement.

But the spotlight on me faded quickly. In the time since I had returned home, nine days now, much had happened in America that caused alarm and made everybody watch others more closely. In less than a week's time, forty-six people had been gunned down in El Paso, Texas, half of them killed, and another nine people murdered and seventeen wounded in Dayton, Ohio. People were shell-shocked and wary of others, and not certain if they were safe to go shopping or have dinner and drinks with friends. Still, a few eyes were focused on me wherever I went in the neighborhood, and they seemed to be wondering if Roger Cummings was a victim or a hero.

Other than my time with Duke, which was for a few hours on some days and minutes on others—he had a wife, grown kids, and four grandchildren—I was going into a turtle shell, only able to poke my head out when it felt safe.

After advising Duke of my plans to visit the twins and their grandparents, I left for New Jersey at 8 p.m. on August 6 and drove straight through to Harold and Bernice's place. It took 19 hours, but it seemed like days to me. College for the twins was starting at the beginning of September, in a about a month. Crystal would be in the freshman class at Princeton, and Ricky was attending Rutgers. This was a major reason why I agreed that they should spend time with their grandparents during my extended stay in Minnesota. They were used to New Jersey from frequent visits over the years.

I spent hours talking with Crystal and Ricky, assuring them that every part of me was fine, physically, and emotionally. Part of that was false, but they didn't need to know I was concerned about their safety. Harold and I had a side discussion during my stay in Ely about Hank's disappearance and his possible threat to me as well as my children. Harold had been a city councilman for three terms after a successful law practice and was well-known by many retired and still-working cops. He'd arranged to have several friends unofficially provide surveillance while the twins were visiting.

"We need to set up a budget," Harold said to me as we sat in his den after dinner. "I have a few guys watching over the twins, but we need to pay them." Harold and I agreed to chip in five grand apiece to support any security measures we, or he actually, deemed necessary. Harold didn't waste money, and he could make sure the budget was well spent. "The kids are worth a lot more than that to both of us," he said. Although they didn't know it, Crystal and Ricky couldn't have been in a safer place.

After a three-day visit, I prepared for the return trip. "You two haven't been banished to Grandma's; I can fly you home and pick you up at the airport anytime you want."

"I know, Dad," my son said. "I want to come back before school starts up here. I need to see a few of my friends and old teammates before they take off to their colleges."

"You miss your buddies? I asked, remembering how close they all were in high school.

"Yeah, but we all said our goodbyes in May and June during the graduation parties and all the stuff after that. We knew we'd be drifting away, so I'm ready for Rutgers. I've already met three or four kids around here who are starting there when I do."

I looked at his sister. "And you?"

"'Bout the same. There are two girls in this area, right down the street actually, who are starting at Princeton when I do. Grandpa knew about them and introduced us. We met at Willie's Café and have been hanging out together since. It's been fun, like starting school a little early." She gave her brother a wink and said, "Ricky's been gawking at one of them. Got the hots, I think."

Ricky snorted a half laugh, which he did when he disagreed with his sister.

"Okay," I said, "pick a date and we'll make a trip back home happen." I looked over at Harold, who was watching intently as I said to Crystal, "I think it would be a good idea for you two to travel together. Can you guys do that for me?" She hesitated, then said, "Let me work it out with Ricky. Can we let you know tomorrow before you leave?"

"Sure."

On the drive back home after the visit with my children, I called Janeene several times, but only got her message recorder. Even though it was Saturday, August 10, I tried her office as well as her cell number. No luck. We'd spoken several times during my ride up, but they were short sessions.

It was midday now and I was on Interstate 85 in Durham,

North Carolina, headed back to Atlanta. I hit the call button on the car phone system and dialed Duke.

"When are you due back?" he asked before I could speak.

"Maybe six hours, with luck. All depends on traffic."

"Well, I got news for you."

My forehead shrunk down over my eyes, thinking I had been outdone again. I'd spoken to Chief Bolling less than two hours ago, and nothing had changed. No Hank, no Bobby, no nothing. "What kind of news?"

"Insurance info."

"Insurance?"

"Yeah, remember talking with Jonathan Friedman about Hank's policy for a million dollars?"

That discussion with my lawyer was back in July. "Yeah, a third of the money would go to his mother, his ex-wife, and Janeene."

"According to Jonathan, who called me yesterday looking for you, that was changed. Now it's a fifty-fifty split between Janeene and his mother. The ex was written out in May."

"No shit?"

"That's what he said. And he told me the policy will only pay off if Hank is proven to be deceased."

"That might be impossible."

"Yeah, I know. My friend said a certificate of death is needed to pay any claim. It's very hard to get one if a person is missing. With no body or proof of death, it could take between five and seven years until a person is presumed deceased, and even then, a death certificate isn't issued automatically. You might have to present evidence in court to have one issued. But my friend did say that without that, the policies don't pay off. The death certificate acts as proof of loss for the insurance carrier."

I said, "So you're saying since they haven't found a body,

there's no proof Hank died. No one will collect on his policy, at least not for many years, if ever."

"That's how I understand it, Roger.

I honked at a fool in a little foreign car drifting into my lane. "Good thing for hands-free calling," I yelled, pushing the horn repeatedly. "Need one hand on the wheel and one on the horn to keep these idiots from running into me."

"You have car insurance, don't you?"

"Yeah, it and just about every kind of insurance there is. Spend way too much on a product I never use." Neither of us spoke for a few seconds.

Duke continued, "It can take as long as seven years to resolve this situation! If they find Hank's body next year, and he died from getting killed by a bear, the claim is paid then and there. If they find his body, and he shot himself in the head, the claim is paid after two years. If they don't find his body, it might be seven years until Hank's mother can go to court to have him declared dead. Even then, it could take years after that to get the court to make the declaration. I just want you to know how long this can hang out there."

"Appreciate your efforts in all this, but knowing you, there must be a hidden purpose."

"There is. Jonathan informed me, and he told me to tell you: Hank's brothers are really pissed about the delay in getting any money for their mother and have been making threatening statements toward Janeene, her family, and you. Nasty stuff. Jonathan heard that from the brothers' attorney. It may be bunch of bullshit. . . threats often are, but you need to be aware of the possible danger."

"Thanks, pal." I wondered if Janeene was aware of the change in the beneficiary clause. Maybe Jonathan could call her and check it out, see if she knew.

"You want a beer if I get back at a decent hour?"

"Love one. It's been lonely around here without the local hero around."

"The local sideshow, you mean?"

"Nope. I stand by my statement."

* * *

While crossing the South Carolina and Georgia border I decided to call Chief Bolling. He was briefly in and out of his office on most weekends, so the desk clerk told me she'd try him at home. If he could talk, he'd call me back.

No call came until I was nearing the intersection of Interstates 85 and 285 in Atlanta. "Hey, Roger, you wanted to talk to me," Chief Bolling announced at full volume on my car phone speaker.

"Yes, sir, I was wondering if you've had a chance to check out that little pond that I mentioned to you last week."

"No, haven't been back in that area yet. Not staffed like we were before when you were here. I'm afraid the civilian helpers are dwindling in size as well. We still get some volunteers to go out in the bush, but nothin' like the first week or two. Besides, the Ontario Provincial Police are officially in charge now."

"I've been thinking about Brent Lake again."

"Never a good sign," he lamented.

"Been trying to figure how far Hank and Pete could have gone in three and a half to four hours to get rid of the body and get back near Janeene and me."

"Why?"

"Because that's all the time they had to do something before Pete came up after us."

"You told me that already."

"Yeah, but what I didn't tell you, because I wasn't really concentrating on the timeline, was they couldn't have buried

231

the body in that time, at least not six feet down, and made it back before three-thirty that afternoon. They had to drop the body in the lake or in a swamp. I'm guessing a swamp. We never concentrated on that before."

There was silence on the line. He came back in thirty seconds. "So, this is your reasoning on Janeene's pond?"

"Precisely. But there are some other places they could have used, like a slough directly south of the campsite. When you look on a map, it looks like someone making a pistol with their hand, using their finger and thumb."

The chief replied, "I know the place. When you were here, you felt pretty certain they dropped the body in Brent Lake."

"Yeah, I did, but since the divers couldn't find anything, and you can see forever in Brent, I've changed my mind. I got to thinking that maybe Bobby's still in the tarp in a swamp. In dingy water, where he'd be hard to see. I should have realized it earlier."

"We'll take it into consideration."

His enthusiasm didn't impress me. "How are the other searches going?"

"They're not really going, like I said. After all the manpower we threw at it in July and no results, the desire to keep pushing is growing weaker by the day. Hell, we checked miles of bush that first week and didn't find shit, other than the beat-up canoe where you fought the guy. Even the military drones couldn't give us a lead on Hank. You did a good job of pointing the Canadians and our folks in the right direction, but Hank and Bobby are like ghosts."

I concentrated on traffic, which was creeping along, not wanting to yell at him at the top of my lungs—FIND THEM. Bolling was a good cop and kept all things in perspective. "What's happening in the parks now?"

"Not much. Trips are way down, but a few are still going.

People are starting to use guides again." Guides had always been available in both parks, but most people rarely hired them. Many campers were experienced or were young guys who wanted to go with their buddies to fish and drink whiskey or were Scout groups that had many knowledgeable adults to oversee the excursions. Guided trips were pretty rare, but they could be arranged through the outfitters. "There are usually two guides in a group now, and although guns are not allowed in either park, nobody's checking."

I said, "Guides make sense to me, then somebody can watch at night."

"That's the reasoning. It's good for the fellas in town, gives them some work, and gives me extra sets of eyes in the BWCA for sure. Wilkens, the boss man up in Quetico, has the same deal working. But there are fewer trips up there. Still, he has some of his people going in and out every week checking all the rivers, streams, and creeks around Argo Lake, Darky, and the river back to Minn Lake from Darky."

His comment made me think about that entire section of the park. "I don't understand how Hank could have dodged all the people that trekked around those places."

"Lots of woods north of Darky Lake, and around That Lake, or Wink Lake. My guess is he headed off in that direction. He'd be a bitch to find if he crawled down into a bear den or under a big rock and died. Even the infrared drones wouldn't see him. He stopped for a second. "Look, Roger, you see how hard it was to find that escaped convict in Tennessee, and he was right in the area around the prison with hundreds of troopers looking for him. He hadn't really gone far. If the guy hadn't robbed somebody's outdoor refrigerator and got himself videoed on a wild game camera, he might still be on the run."

I remembered the news reports about it in July. It was hard to argue with the chief's logic. "Where to from here?" I asked.

"We keep looking. I'll send teams to the places you mentioned, but it won't be any time soon. Maybe by the end of the month, maybe by the end of the season."

"That's all I ask."

"Well, if that's all, then I won't tell you—"

"Tell me what, Chief?"

He paused for effect, then said, "The money Hank supposedly had in cash has not turned up anywhere. Not in his father's account, mother's account, ex-wife's account, ex-girl-friends' accounts, or anywhere else. Seems to have vanished, according to the feds. To me, that means Hank has either gone with it, or he hid it where no one can find it, and he's dead. I'm betting on dead. I don't think he made it out of Quetico, or ever will. We may never find his money."

"Thanks for the update."

"My pleasure." He paused a few seconds, then added, "You did well to escape from the guy and save the lady and the kid. You need to look in the rearview mirror and say *so long* to Mr. Hank Kovak."

"Wish I could."

CHAPTER TWENTY-TWO

Duke was standing in my driveway when I pulled in. "Got to get out of the house, pal, the wife and grandkids are driving me crazy tonight."

"You're not babysitting them, are you? Don't want to find out they set the house on fire while you're visiting me."

"No. . . no, the wife's doing that. It's just the noise, it's earsplitting. Someday you'll have the same problem, women and loud grandchildren."

"It won't be exactly the same in my case."

Duke looked at me with a reddening face. "Sorry, partner, didn't mean to bring up reminders of Sherry. I talk too much."

After regaining his composure, he asked, "How's Harold doing?" He and Sherry's father, Harold, who had played a major role in the funeral preparations since she was to be buried in New Jersey, had become quite close during that time —a friendship that was still strong.

"I keep him informed about Quetico and the search for the body and Hank. He shares my concerns about safety, especially for the twins."

"Yeah, Harold's a good guy and pretty shrewd, if you ask me."

"He's still a major player in local politics, so he's got former cops and other buddies keeping an eye on the kids. He sends you his regards and told me to tell you he'll call you in the next few days."

"Great, love to hear from him."

Duke and I had a Rolling Rock beer in my den after I unpacked my things.

"Got any plans for September, other than seeing Ricky and Crystal off to college?"

"Might have," I said, not trying to sound coy. He missed my intonation. I was thinking about a visit with Janeene, and replied, "A guy I met at a stock trading conference several years back, Jerry Milner, lives in Minneapolis. We talk on the phone at least two to three times a month, or anytime we're interested in the same trade. Jerry's an excellent options trader, much better than me, and he's offered to host me at his home anytime I want to visit with him and learn more about his style. He wants to understand more about my knack for playing earnings events and winning buckets of money."

"Now you sound like a salesman."

"Sometimes you have to be." I pictured Jerry. He was ten years older than me, not married, and confined to a wheelchair. He was wealthy from trading stocks and writing books, and he had an entourage of employees who assisted with his daily living needs. "You can stay for a night or a month," he told me once. "I've got a section of the house in the lower level I haven't seen in years. It's yours if you want it but give me some advance notice so I can have the crew get it ready for you." I'd mentioned him to Duke as we landed at the Minneapolis airport for our trip to Ely and into Quetico this summer. He must have forgotten my comment or he would have quizzed me endlessly about Jerry and his trading style.

Duke turned on the television in my den. I was nearby in the kitchen, which adjoined the den by way of a serving counter. Looking for a dinner entrée in the freezer, I could vaguely hear the announcer as he said, "This just in. Breaking News." The newscaster's report was impossible for me to hear clearly, but I could hear my buddy fuming at his report. "This is crazy," Duke yelled, gazing at the screen. "There's no reason to allow civilians to be walking around with military-grade weapons. This has got to change so we all can feel safe wherever we are—Dayton at a local bar, or El Paso at a Walmart. Crazy world we're living in. Seems nobody's safe anywhere."

"What happened this time? Another shooting?"

"No, just more information about the suspects—they both were heavily armed. The innocent folks in both tragedies thought they were in safe places."

"Yeah, that's why it surprised me to see the murder at Brent Lake. I'd always thought the parks were safe, maybe not from black bears, but from people anyway. Never thought a shooting would happen up there."

"Me either, buddy, breaks my heart to lose the beauty and solace of the park. It's too special a place to suffer from the same horseshit we have in the real world."

I always felt honored to be allowed into Quetico, like it was hallowed ground meant to be savored by deserving outdoorsmen and to be respected for the way it allowed nature to prosper, unaided by man. That criminal Hank damaged it. *But Quetico got its just due. It's the last place Hank will ever see.*

"You going fishing in the morning?" Duke asked.

"Yeah, early, in the pond. Want to go?"

"Can't. Got plans with the grandkids." Then he said, "Tell

me that story again about the barn owl you saw at the pond last year. You remember it?"

I ignored his question and thought of the white-faced bird flying silently from a tree branch to snatch my lure floating on the water's surface. It grabbed it in its left talon then banked into a hard turn, all the while staring directly at me. I jerked the plug instinctively, hoping the owl wouldn't get impaled by the hooks on the lure. That would have been a disaster. But the wooden bait dropped back on the water and the bird perched on a branch, ten feet away, questioning me with those piercing eyes. Its gaze never left me. After thirty seconds it flew off without a sound—never heard a wing flap.

I said, "If you had been with me that morning, you would have seen it yourself."

"Wish I'd been there."

After a few seconds, I added, "Yeah, but luck doesn't work that way. Good stuff and bad stuff only seems to happen when you're alone. Kinda like Quetico."

It was after 9 a.m. when my cell phone rang as I was casting an ancient floating plug, a Hula Popper, toward a fallen tree. I'd been fishing in my neighborhood pond since before 6 a.m. Early morning was my favorite time of day to catch bass, and I'd already landed a dozen, when the call came. I reached into my tackle box to pull out the phone. It was Janeene calling.

"Hey, lady. What's up? Been trying to reach you."

"I got a call this morning," she said. Her voice was tentative.

I waited a second, "From whom?"

"A friend of Hank's." Silence filled my ears.

"I thought you changed your number after the trip."

"I did, twice."

I sat in the sunshine just starting to invade the shadows, but suddenly felt the dimness enveloping me. "What did the caller say?"

"He claimed he was a loan shark and that Hank owed him money and he wanted some from me. Said I was on his life insurance policy and there would be plenty of money."

"He did?" I didn't think news about the insurance was common knowledge. I wasn't sure until this very moment that Janeene was even aware of the paperwork's existence. "Is this the first time you've heard about the policy?"

"Hank never told me, but I heard rumors about it when we were in Ely. I thought it was just gossip, so I didn't mention it to you. I don't know how to determine if it is true. Who told you?"

"Jonathan. He heard it from one of his lawyer buddies in Minneapolis. He can confirm if it's really in place, but it might be true," I answered, not wanting to reveal the precise details of the coverage.

Her breathing was husky. "Do you know anything about it? Anything for certain?"

"A little, but I can't vouch for the accuracy of my info. It's supposed to be a million-dollar benefit, payable in thirds, to you, his mother, and his ex-wife. But it might have been changed, leaving just you and his mother on the plan. I'm presuming that someone will have to verify all the details to make sure it is valid and up-to-date for payments required and such."

"I don't know what to think about this," she said.

"You shouldn't think anything. Not now. I'll talk with Jonathan. Wait until he confirms that the policy actually exists, reads the terms, sees you named as a beneficiary, and makes sure it's legitimate. Even then, it may never pay off—if Hank pops up somewhere. If he doesn't, it might take at least another seven years until he can be considered deceased, and a certificate of death is released."

"Are you saying he might be alive?"

"No, no, I'm not even considering that a possibility. You're missing the point. Hank hasn't been found dead, so no claim will be paid until he is." I realized I shouldn't have mentioned my reservations and needed to change the subject. "Did this caller threaten you?"

"Not directly. He seemed a little anxious after he started talking, like he realized he was making a mistake, so he said I should gather some money, but then he hung up. I saw a call-back number on my phone and rang Chief Bolling's office and gave it to his clerk, a woman named Martha."

"Good. What did she say?"

"Said she'd contact the chief and people in Minneapolis and have them check it out." She held silent for seconds. "The caller scared me, Roger. I was getting Angela ready for church. I don't need this, for me or for her."

"I understand. Is this the only time since you changed numbers?"

"Yeah, I got a few obscene calls after I first came home, but they ended after I got a new cell phone and a different service provider. They started again and I changed my number a second time. Since then, nothing, until today. I don't like this."

"Don't blame you."

She was silent as I sat and looked at the water in the pond. "This is never really going to end, is it, Roger?"

"Don't say that! You've got to be strong, like you were up in Quetico. Bolling believes Hank is dead. Hell, everybody thinks he's a goner, and I'm coming to that same conclusion. He may have some relatives who are pissed off at you and me, but they don't want to go to jail for threatening us or bothering you."

"I still have Angela to worry about."

"I understand."

"How can I protect her? How can I keep her safe from people who make threats?"

I watched a great blue heron stalking quietly along the shore. They were patient birds of prey that could strike like rattlesnakes or stand still for hours when they were on the hunt. They had the option of when and where to pounce. Reminded me of trackers like Hank and Pete. "Janeene, remember, I told you I wanted to go to Hawaii after this was over? To celebrate."

"Yeah, but I don't think it's over."

"Well, I do. And I say we go. Can you leave after Labor Day?"

"That's just over two, three weeks away, Roger, I don't know. Angela starts school in a week and I just don't think we can go."

"She's only starting the first grade. She'd miss a few days, so it's not like she'll ruin her academic future." I looked at the calendar on my cell phone. "I can fly to Minneapolis anytime. Maybe I'll go to Ely to talk with Bolling, stay a few days at Pec's house, check out the situation, and then come and get you." I was thinking out loud now. "I can stay around Chanhassen for a while, then we can go to Hawaii, stay in Kona for a week, then I'll get you home."

"I don't know, Roger, I'm scared right now. Let me think about it. Not sure this is a good time for me."

I didn't like the hesitation in her voice. "We could put a trip off until Thanksgiving or Christmas, if you want." I paused and started thinking about my real reason for wanting the trip. It had nothing to do with a vacation. "We need to talk about us, either at home or in Hawaii."

"I think so too."

"Don't like hearing you've been scared by some stranger."

"I'm okay, just caught by surprise. I could tell by the guy's voice at the end that he was more worried about what he said than I was."

"Good. Maybe Bolling or his friends around Minneapolis can track the guy down."

"That'd be nice, Roger."

The silence between us grew, and I hoped she might say something but she didn't. "Okay, forget about Hawaii for now; it's probably a bad idea. When can I come see you?"

"Don't you work?"

"Not every day. Normally I'd be playing the market in the mornings, but August is typically a tough month, and this year it's been horrible. The China trade war talks are spooking investors, and the chaos in Washington has people on edge too. So, no, I'm not working at the moment."

"Lucky guy to be able to pick when you want to work."

"It's not luck, just that relatively stable environments are better for trading. I can trade in crazy times, but it means having to stay glued to the computer screen and keep my gains and losses on a very tight leash. Besides, I haven't had the interest lately, because of my. . . our trip into the park."

She was quiet before saying, "We were lucky, Roger. I understand that now better than ever before. I'd like to see you whenever you can visit. I think about you all the time."

"I'll make it soon. Talk to you tomorrow."

After ending the call I pulled my small fishing boat from the water and loaded it on its trailer, since my interest in fishing had vanished after my discussion with Janeene. Ropes that held it firmly on the transporter had just been fastened when Bolling called, surprising me.

"What did the feds say about the call to Janeene?"

"Hold on there, Roger, we're not people like in the TV shows. Folks don't jump around between commercials and come back with answers."

"Sorry, Chief, it's just that it aggravates the hell out of me that somebody would try to scare her in a phone call."

"Me too. I got the Chanhassen office working on the number now. They'll get back to me by noon."

I looked at my watch, it was 10:22 a.m. here, so an hour earlier there. Waiting a few more hours for answers was no problem, and there was no point asking him anything else about the call. I changed subjects. "Thinking about coming back up there to visit you after Labor Day."

"Oh? That might be a good idea. We could use another press conference to bring people back into town, but it might be necessary before Labor Day."

"Why?"

"About an hour ago, I learned that Wilkens's guys found something yesterday." My heart started to pound. *For a country boy, this guy sure could deliver some drama.*

"Okay, I'll bite. What did they find?

"A T-shirt."

"What kind? Did it have any writing on it?"

"I'm looking at photographs now that were faxed in last night. Looks like Rock something, like Rock Hard. . ."

I cut him off. "Rock Hard is a water-soluble putty that you use on wood to make repairs. Does it say *Hard Rock*, like in Hard Rock Café?"

"I'd say so, looking at the other pictures. The top is in bad shape, torn in the middle of the front, and dirty from mud and water. But I see all those words, Hard and Rock and Café. They're not all together because of the tear."

"What color is it?"

"Hard to be certain; it's been covered in muddy shit, but I'd say yellow, judging from the photos."

"I saw Pete wearing that T-shirt when he and Hank

confronted Bobby at the hammock, right before the shooting. I remember it clearly."

"How do you think it got into the river in between Minn Lake and Darky?"

"What? Is that where they found it?"

"Apparently so."

"Wow. I've got to think about this." He let me breathe for half a minute, enough to let my blood pressure come back to normal.

We were both silent as I recalled the shooting and the aftermath. The videotape was playing in my head again.

"Are you sure you saw Pete in this?"

"Absolutely. He had it on when Bobby was killed, and when they went to bury the body. Where exactly did they find it?"

"Near Minn Lake. Pulled it out of a mud bank on the side of a creek. Wilkens thought it might have belonged to Hank.

"I wish it was his shirt, but this one was Pete's. Still, it would be better if they had found the asshole Hank in it. Where is it now?"

"The CSIS – Canada's version of our FBI, is testing it in their lab."

"Hey, Chief, if it's any help, when Pete came up after Janeene and me, he was in a hunting shirt and not the Hard Rock Café T-shirt. I remember wishing he still had the top on because it was yellow. He would have been much easier to spot than with a hunting shirt."

"Gotcha, Roger."

"One other thing, I realize now that Hank may have gotten much further toward an escape route than I've been guessing, he might have slipped into Lac La Croix from Minn Lake, and from there he could be anywhere."

"We've been considering that prospect as well."

* * *

Later in the day I returned a phone call from a former Army buddy who lives near Columbus, Georgia.

"You owe me some personal time, Roger, been too long since we got together. If I'd known you were going to ignore me like this, I'd have never saved your ass in that swamp. Let's get together and go fishing, tomorrow."

I'd tripped while crossing through a swamp at Fort Stewart, Georgia, on a night training mission, and swallowed a mouthful of nasty water. Gagging and snorting up phlegm was probably not going to lead to my death, but it didn't matter to my buddy. He was a hero and I owed him for pulling me up to my feet. Forever.

I drove to West Point Lake in LaGrange, Georgia, eighty miles south from my home, and rented a fishing cabin at the marina.

CHAPTER TWENTY-THREE

The drive back to Atlanta was lonely, and painful, especially after spending the evening drinking too many bourbon Manhattans with my Army comrade, who told me his son was having a baby—my buddy's first grandson—and my morning listening to my fishing guide known as Motor Mouth due to his knack for *talking nonstop*. My head was pounding, and worse, I was accompanied only by my thoughts, which wandered all over the mental map of life. The brain has a way of creating a minefield of doubts. The drive home wasn't fun.

During the ride, I called everyone in my contact list. Many calls were unanswered, but it didn't stop me from trying to reach people, again and again. Duke answered a little after two in the afternoon. "What's up, buddy? You coming home?"

"Yeah, I'm on the road now, near Newnan on I-85. Should make it by dinnertime, but you know how it goes."

"Boy, do I. Took my family to a Braves game last night. The new ballpark is great, and the grandkids had never been there, but usually you can get in and out of the area without problems. Parking was easy because we had special passes, but there was an accident on 285, so we got stuck in a mess for hours."

"I'll be using the same highway this afternoon; hope I have better luck."

"Can't have worse."

"You up for a beer tonight? I need to stop the pain in my head."

"You betcha."

"Hey, have you heard from Chief Bolling? I know he likes to tell you things before me."

Duke laughed. "Yeah, he's sprung a few surprises on you. But no, I haven't heard from him in over a week. Why don't you call him, and let me know if there's any progress?"

"He's next on my call list." He wasn't. Janeene was, but Duke didn't need to know that.

If it was 3 p.m. on the East Coast, it was 2 p.m. in Minneapolis. I called Janeene, hoping to catch her at the office, but just got her answering message.

The next call went to Chief Bolling. He did answer. "Got some news to report," he said, before I could even say hello.

My breath froze, remembering I was speaking with drama man. "You trying to make me have an accident?"

"Drivin' again? You become a long-distance trucker when you got back to Atlanta?"

"No, just taking a few jaunts to get some chores done and keeping up with old friends."

"Know how that goes." He paused, then in a deep and official voice, said, "We found a blue plastic tarp, like the one you saw Bobby wrapped up in."

I slowed down and pulled into the right-hand lane where my racing heart would be easier to manage if the need arose. "From your description, I assume there was nothing in it."

"You would be correct in that assumption. But the lab

might be able to tell us in another day or two if there had been a body in it, and if that person was Bobby Johnson."

Johnson. In all the time since the murder, I hadn't heard Bobby's last name. *Poor guy.* It must have been announced during the press conferences or printed in the newspapers; I just didn't remember it ever being spoken by anyone. He deserved more respect from all of us—more respect than had been given to Hank Kovak. We all knew that bastard's full name.

Chief Bolling added, "The Canadians found it near the pond where the lady left the canoe. The place you told me about couple a weeks ago. They finally got a team to check the area out."

"Damn, Chief, if they'd gotten to it sooner—"

"Hold on. As I told you before, we don't find things like in Hollywood movies. It takes time and effort to investigate, especially miles out in the wilderness, and we're in short supply of support. It's not like down there in Georgia where they have a lot of people to help. You see all those Coast Guard guys crawling around on the hull of that ship in St. Simons Sound? I couldn't believe it. They cut a hole right through it to get a guy out."

I waited for his temper to calm. Mine too. I liked the man and didn't want to jeopardize my best connection in the entire investigation. "Yeah, I saw the story and don't know how they're going to get the boat off its side—was an auto transport ship, longer than two football fields and full of cars. Mercedes, I think." After a few seconds I added, "My apologies, Chief, I appreciate the difficulty, and your efforts."

"I understand. If the situation were reversed, I'd want some answers too. And fast."

I thought about Bolling's first name. I'd never spoken it, but knew it was Ronald. It had been listed in the papers and was printed on a nameplate on his desk. He told me once, "My first name is Chief now, goes with the territory."

"Was the tarp in the water?"

"No, it was about a hundred yards from the pond, stuffed under a log and buried under dirt. If an animal hadn't rooted it out, it never would have been found. Guess is that the tarp had a stink, so a black bear or some other creature dug it up and shredded it, trying to forage for food. Thing is torn up pretty badly, like an animal with claws would do, but the Canadians think they'll be able to test it for blood residue, or hair samples and the like."

"When was it located?"

"Day before yesterday. Wilkens called last night when the crew came in from the site before any news could leak." *Wilkens, the Canadian ranger, was a smart old codger.*

"But no sighting of a body?"

"None. They looked around and checked out parts of the pond, but there were only two people on the team, so they couldn't do much more than that. They say they're going back with a bigger squad."

"When?"

"Within a week or two. I'm gonna lend them some fellas here in Ely—scuba divers. The back end of the pond is a swamp, like you suspected. It'll be shitty work, but our folks can use the money, so they'll walk and crawl and dig around in the muck. If Bobby was sunk in there, they'll find him is my bet."

I was silent, thinking about the place on the maps. It fit the plan Hank and Pete might have tried, to submerge the body in a spot not too far away, but out of the normal travel routes. "Your guys need to get back there ASAP."

Bolling was smoking hot and breathing hard. He needed a few seconds to simmer down. "Can't push Wilkens much harder, but I'll try to light the fire under his ass by making my fellows available next week."

"Sorry to piss you off, Chief, but if they discover the body, I'm coming back up there."

"That'd be a good idea. You can make a statement. There's plenty of folks that want to hear what you have to say. We could use some activity in Ely, especially from out-of-towners who rent rooms and eat in restaurants."

"I'll call Bill Pec; see if he can put me up in his spare room."

"You do that, and take care of yourself, Roger. I'll keep you posted on anything we find."

I waited five minutes to let my mind grasp the facts of the conversation with the chief, and to think about my next move. There was no real question concerning whom I needed to talk to next.

Janeene answered with a quiet voice, like she was waiting to hear who was calling. I thought my number would show on her cell phone, but you never could be sure these days. "Oh, Roger, I'm so scared all the time, I wish I'd never gone to Quetico." Her comment startled me.

"Something happen I should know about?"

"No, not really, just have spells, more like moments of anxiety when I'm worried about me, Angela, my family, everything. The nervousness comes and goes. I'm scared about what might happen if. . ."

"We all have those feelings, Janeene. I get 'em too." I knew she was worried about Hank.

"I didn't mean to bother you with my worries. Where are you?"

"South of Atlanta. Should be home in an hour and a half. You can talk to me all the way home."

"I can't talk that long."

"Why not?"

"Because I'm at work."

"Then toss in a few words like overhead accounts, or tax liabilities, anything to make it sound like official chatter."

"You have an odd sense of humor, Roger."

"Yeah, I do. Always have."

Thinking about the chief's report I quickly babbled out, "They found a blue tarp near where you left the canoe; if it turns out to mean anything, I'm coming up to Ely to see you, and meet Angela and your family."

My words caught her by surprise, but she focused on the discovery, rather than on my visit. "Really? They found a tarp? Does this mean they found Bobby?"

"No, just the plastic he might have been wrapped in. They don't know for certain yet if it's the one we're looking for."

"Jesus, Roger, I can't believe he got killed because of me." She was silent and I heard a mewling noise, like she might start crying. This conversation was beginning to veer away from my intended purpose, and I didn't want her to feel grief, only joy at the discovery. *Had to get her back on track.*

"You're not responsible for murder, or anything that happened, only for a little thoughtlessness at the wrong time." I let her think about my words. "Listen, Janeene, you've got to stay strong for Angela and your folks. I want to come up to Minneapolis and meet them."

"When?"

"Soon." I thought about the team Bolling would be sending into the park to help Wilkens, but it sounded like it might be a while until that happened, maybe a week or two, but Janeene didn't need to know it would take that long. A lot had to get done before I visited Ely or Minneapolis again.

"That'd be wonderful, Roger; my family has been dying to see the guy I talk about all the time."

CHAPTER TWENTY-FOUR

The flight from Newark to Atlanta that was bringing Ricky and Crystal home was due to land around 1 p.m. I was looking at the display board in the main terminal and saw their flight number—ARRIVED. The words were posted in white letters against blue panels beside the city of departure. A side panel showed the date and time; it was August 14, 1:05 p.m.

I wandered around the baggage claim area then moved toward the giant escalators that brought people up from the caverns below to where the trains stopped to let people off to exit the secured areas. I spotted the kids, waved and was immediately rewarded with large smiles and looks of relief as they exited the security zone not far from the baggage area.

"Flight okay?" I gave Crystal a hug with my left arm and shook Ricky's hand with my right. "Yeah, no difficulty getting on or off the plane," he said. "I'm hungry. Nothing to eat on the plane but pretzels."

"Delta was always a peanut specialist in the old days."

"Wouldn't know, Dad."

"You want to eat in the concourse?"

"Yeah, I can't take another step without some chow."

"Let's get the bags, then we'll eat." I squeezed Crystal. "How are you doing, honey?"

"I'm fine, Dad, just glad to be home." She was dressed in shorts and a long-sleeve shirt. The shorts were khaki, the top a shade of pale blue. She was glowing and tan, like she'd been sprayed in a body shop from head to toe with a paint gun of suntan lotion that worked to give her skin a golden sheen. "Wish I had your skin."

"You always say that."

"'Cause I mean it." My complexion was fair, the result of a heavy touch of Irish on my side of the family tree, and my hair was reddish blond. My daughter, on the other hand, had gotten her silky skin, good looks, shape, and strikingly blond hair from my wife. She was beautiful, as was my son. He was a male version of Crystal, but a half foot taller, a hundred pounds heavier, and on the muscular side. He didn't get much genetic impact from me. His face gave him away as a friendly guy who should consider acting as a career. He certainly didn't have my stiff chin or cold blue eyes, or my frigid demeanor.

After lunch we headed home, stopping at the local grocery store near the house to buy a few things they each liked. I knew it was better to buy what they wanted and would eat, rather than push my preferences and be left with a refrigerator of old leftovers after they were gone. Buying their favorites kept the house happy with the warm smell of food, whether it was from boiled hot dogs or oven-heated pizza. Sherry always had meals cooking and I loved the smell of a lived-in house.

That night as we were sitting on the back deck after eating, the conversation turned serious. The bone-in ribeye steaks that were cooked on the grill were now only meatless shanks. My portion had been generous, Crystal's immoderately small, and

Ricky's unimaginable. The roasted potatoes in herbs and garlic butter were gone, as was the leafy green salad with sliced black olives and red onion. Even the lemon cheesecake with meringue and blueberry sauce was seriously damaged; none of us normally liked dessert. But everyone was hungry for answers, so the food halted our discussion about my trip to Quetico like a copperhead snake stops a hunter on a game trail. I'd pushed the most serious questions about my experiences off in my previous trip to New Jersey, during the latest the phone calls between us, and on the ride home. With their reluctant acquiescence, I had only discussed parts of the saga with them since it happened. But that ploy would no longer work, so it was time for full disclosure.

Ricky started the questioning. "Dad, you've got to level with us. You think Hank Kovak is really dead? Or could he come after you? Or us?"

"You two came loaded for bear, huh?"

"Grandpa was very watchful while we were there," Crystal said. "I know you guys talked about us when we weren't around, and I noticed his police friends near the house a lot. I even saw one when I was out with my girlfriends."

I glanced back and forth between Ricky and Crystal, concluding it was a joint effort to quiz me. Neither wanted to do it on their own, but as a team they had the power to pursue answers. And they wanted them. It was time for me to explain a lot of things. "First, let me say that I love you both. Everything I did in Quetico was intended to save me or others, and get back to you guys—whatever was necessary to make that happen."

Ricky said, "Dad, this sounds like one of your military speeches."

Silence hung over the patio like a summer storm had come and gone, leaving a sultry silence in its wake. "Sorry, we know you would've done everything you could, but we don't understand any of the details. You haven't really told us anything." It was Crystal, wanting to learn more.

After a few seconds I said, "You've both seen my press conferences on television or videotape, so you know the basic facts. All of which is true. What you don't know is that there's still a hunt to find Hank, the guy who shot the victim. That hasn't changed, but another piece of the puzzle will be determined soon."

"Another piece? Are they going to find the guy or not? Tell us something to make us feel safe."

"Safe?"

"Yeah, safe, like knowing we aren't about to be attacked," Crystal shrieked.

"You two have nothing to worry about! The killer knows nothing about me, and certainly nothing about you two."

"Bullshit, Dad. Information about you was plastered all over the TV news, in the newspapers, and on the Internet. There was plenty written about us too. We're guessing that's why you had us stay with Grandma and Grandpa all summer." Ricky had never cursed at me before, and really hadn't now—he was just calling me out on the facts.

"I don't like the use of that language."

"Sorry, Dad, but you have us really scared."

I glanced back and forth at both of their faces, narrowed eyes focused on me like radar antenna. "Okay, please listen carefully." I brought them up to date on my talks with Chief Bolling about the Boy Scout waking up, where Bobby's body might be, and the information he provided to me, including the discovery of the T-shirt.

"Could this guy Hank, or his body, be somewhere near Darky Lake or Wicksteed Lake or any of the other lakes in that area, like Minn Lake, or Wink Lake?"

"Possibly. I guess you've been studying the maps." I said to Ricky.

"We both have," Crystal returned. "If he's alive, could he have gotten into Lake Lac La Croix?"

Her question startled me. "There's no evidence he has. The police, the rangers, and the sheriff are all watching possible exits from the parks. Bolling thinks the guy is dead. At this point, I'm inclined to agree with him."

"So why were Grandpa's friends watching us so closely?"

I thought about denying that they had but decided I shouldn't deceive them anymore. Still, I was not about to tell them that two of the retired cops were on the flight with them, had pictures of Hank Kovak in their pockets, and, at this moment, were sitting in Duke's driveway across the street in a rental car watching this house. Harold had checked in with Duke. "You know how your grandfather is, he still thinks he's in charge of saving the world."

"What if the guy isn't dead?"

"That's why we have to stay vigilant." My words were treated with silent stares.

After a minute Ricky asked me, "Are we safe in this house? Will we be safe at our schools?"

I was heartbroken at the question. Never could I have imagined a simple camping trip could lead to a situation where my children feared for their safety. How could I have been so stupid as to put them at risk?

"Wait a minute," I said, "let's respect the facts we do know before we scare the crap out of ourselves for no reason." I reviewed a list in my head to mull over with them. "First, Hank was in terrible shape when I last saw him, and he wasn't capable of outrunning pursuers for very long. They were on his trail in less than two days. I'd give him a one-in-ten chance of evading the searchers if he was alive. If he crawled into a bear den or other such place, he had an excellent chance of dying and not being found by them. Second, the money he had in the bank from winning the lottery that had been turned into cash was about seven hundred fifty thousand dollars. It hasn't surfaced in any account belonging to anyone possibly related to Hank.

"You didn't tell us that," Crystal said.

"There are a lot of things I didn't tell you," I said, giving her a fierce glare. I continued, "There's no evidence that Hank ever came out of the park. I repeat, no evidence. No one has seen him in any of the park areas. No one has reported seeing him in his hometown. No one has reported seeing him hitchhiking across the country. In fact, no one has seen him anywhere since I last saw him, and that was almost six weeks ago." I paused for a breath, "You can't survive for that length of time injured and without food. You'd find drinking water, but for food you would have to hunt or trap animals or catch fish. With no weapons or tools that would be very hard."

I waited to let my words sink in, then said, "Fourth, there have been no confirmed phone calls from this guy to anyone for two months, since he went into the park." Ricky started to ask a question, but I put up my hand, stopping him. "Last," I was on a roll and did not want to lose my thoughts, "at this time, there is no evidence that Hank had accomplices in his hometown. By that, I mean other than his brother who has made threats through an attorney, Hank did not have a friend or even an acquaintance who was so involved with him that such a person would take it upon themselves to get revenge for his death. The authorities have interviewed many people, and although there is talk of a wrongful death lawsuit against me for possibly causing Pete's death, it appears to be based more on speculation than anything else. Nothing has been filed so far, and nothing may ever happen. If a suit is brought, I'll fight it all the way as hard as I can, as hard as I fought in Quetico." I let my breathing slow and wiped a drop of sweat from my forehead. "Bolling and the others think I have little to fear from them or their families." I was winded. "You two have even less to be worried about."

"But there are some people who could sue you, or kill you? Wonderful. I didn't realize that before," Ricky offered.

"Nobody will hurt me, son, or either of you two, I promise you that." My bravado didn't go over too well, but at least they knew I was ready to defend them, if necessary.

We all took a minute to think about what had been said and what it meant.

After an uncomfortable pause, which felt like an hour, Crystal said, "Who is this woman, Janeene, and what does she mean to you?"

I was frozen in thought. *What should I tell them? What can I really say?* "Janeene lives in Minneapolis. She's there now." I looked at Crystal, "We are friends, nothing more than that, but I do like her, and we've gotten close since the escape."

"When you say close, like close with thoughts, maybe dating?"

"No, not like that at all." My eyes averted her glare.

"How could you, Dad? It's been less than two years since Mom died!"

I roared back, "I'm going to have to move on sooner or later."

Crystal wiped her eyes. "I can't believe I'm hearing this." She sat in silence for a few seconds. "You seeing her anytime soon?"

"I'm thinking about it." My thoughts wandered to the park where I'd first seen Janeene and Bobby. They'd been making love. And she was supposed to be Hank's girlfriend! How could I explain that to anyone, let alone my children? In some ways, I didn't want to like Janeene. But I thought again of the bravery she had shown during our plight, and afterwards. Still, I had my doubts about her sincerity, honesty, and certainly her loyalty to a supposed lover. But who wouldn't leave Hank?! No answers came to me. "I might see her soon, and I might not. Can't honestly tell you at this point."

My answer didn't assuage either of them. Ricky let out an "Oh Man!"

What they didn't know was that Janeene and I had been quite coy about the hammock incident. When we told our stories about the murder, we purposely left out the part about a sexual encounter—maybe on purpose, maybe by accident, but certainly not through collusion. We never agreed to leave that out, it just happened. Later on, we agreed it was nobody's business but ours, a private secret in this tragic event. Hank would be pissed off at Bobby even if they were only kissing, and probably would have killed him all the same. *We'll never know*. The part about being next to each other in the hammock in bathing suits was repeated many times; it just didn't mention that the version was false. Actually, both of them were naked, and she wasn't beside him but was on his lap, facing him, and they were joined at the hip. So, I had some decisions to make. Tell the whole story, tell only part of the story, lie, or say nothing. Lying had never been a practice in my early life and didn't feel right then or now. So that was out. Telling the whole truth was also out. The whole truth would ruin Janeene and would end any chance she and I might have of a relationship, or even a simple friendship. Saying nothing was not an option either, too much had already been said. The only choice left was selective telling, revealing the part of the story that people needed to know to take action and leaving the rest to imagination. That's the option Janeene and I had chosen before, and the one I would choose now. "I'm thinking about going back to Ely to talk with

the sheriff and others like Bill Pec, and then go to visit
Janeene. I haven't decided yet."

"You'll do this after we're off at school?" It was Crystal
looking in my eyes.

"Don't know. . . might go up there before Labor Day, maybe
after." I had memorized their move-in dates for college. Ricky's
was on August 31, and Crystal's was the third of September.
"I'm going with each of you for your first day at school, just like
in kindergarten, junior high, or high school. Nothing's changed,
I'm sticking with you guys for the rest of time whether you like
it or not." From the way they rolled their eyes, I couldn't tell
which way they felt.

CHAPTER TWENTY-FIVE

The week passed in a flash. The kids were busy with friends they hadn't seen all summer, and in truth, may never see again when everybody departed in different directions for college or whatever they were planning to do after graduation. I remembered my high school friends, but other than at reunions, they were rarely in my life. A few of my good buddies in high school didn't attend the reunions at all, and I hadn't seen them since our graduation ceremony on the football field. It was a bittersweet fact of life that some things changed—not for better or worse—just changed. This was also how I felt about Crystal.

In talks with her during the week I could tell she was growing up and growing away from our family, or what had been our family for many years. Not that it was a bad thing, since I believed she was allowing the memory of her mother and me to be a distant, vague, but pleasant thought. She asked several times, in both direct and obscure ways, about the lady and her daughter. I gave her equally pointed and obtuse answers. At one point she said, "Come on, Dad, you know what I mean." This caused her to laugh.

On August 19 at four-thirty in the morning, we left for New Jersey driving my overstuffed Jeep. It was a trip that would change our lives forever. I knew this because I'd made a similar trip twenty-two years ago when leaving home to attend college, never to return. My folks sold our house after my freshman year and retired to Florida. They both passed away a few years later from fatal bouts with cancer. Never saw my old neighborhood again, except once when I went back just to look at the high school house. A premonition hit me leaving the driveway now—*my son and daughter might never live here again.* Each of us would change in the coming year, not for good or bad; we would just be different. My sanguine attitude was lost on both my passengers, one of whom was fast asleep and the other listening to classical music with earphones. It shouldn't be hard to guess which one was sleeping. My neighbor Duke would certainly know the answer. I reminded myself to call him on the drive up at a more reasonable hour.

We arrived in New Jersey on schedule for a late night supper and were greeted with a wonderful meal of homemade spaghetti, complete with large hand-rolled meatballs stuffed with mushrooms and green peppers. It was one of Grandma Bernice's specialties. She had many.

On Wednesday evening we were the guests of honor at a surprise party hosted by all the relatives living in the state. And I mean all of them. Aunt Carmona, almost ninety, danced for an hour, swaying while holding Crystal's hand. It was a huge moment in an immigrant's life when their prodigy attended college, especially one as prestigious as Princeton. It was a surprising memory I will always cherish.

I left for home on Friday morning, promising to be back a

day before Ricky started school at Rutgers on the last day of August.

* * *

On Monday, August 26, I answered an early call from Chief Bolling. He got right to the point. "Wilkens's team found Bobby's body yesterday in the pond you told us about near Brent Lake. It was a good thing, because testing of the blue tarp proved inconclusive, and we wouldn't have kept looking around that spot if you hadn't kept pushing us to check it out."

I remembered the chief told me last week the blue plastic sheet that had been buried under two feet of dirt was torn to smithereens and had probably been licked clean by predators. But it was apparently crucial to finding Bobby Johnson, because without it, the retrieval would never have occurred. "There are some legal details to work out," he said, after announcing the discovery.

"Like what?" I asked.

"Well, like the guy is a United States citizen found in a foreign country and maybe murdered by an American national, for starters. Jurisdiction is at question, or at least for who might prosecute a case—if there's gonna be one—and who has claim to the body for purposes of investigation and other such issues. Right now, the Canadians are in charge."

"I'm not good at legal matters, that's why Jonathan is my attorney. What I want to know is are you sure it *is* Bobby, and who's going to determine the cause of death?"

"Yeah, dental records have confirmed that it's him. We got them weeks ago, and Wilkens's investigators checked them first, before they started an autopsy. It ain't done yet, and it will take a while because the corpse was pretty ugly, being buried in the mud and all for two months, but there was enough evidence to support what you said. Wilkens told me it was obvious when looking at the skull that he had been shot at close range—blew half his head away—and he was probably dead in seconds. Your account adds up, at least from what we know now."

"I was backed up by Janeene."

"I'm aware of that."

"Does she know?"

"Thought you might want to break the news."

"Thanks, Chief, appreciate the decency." I thought of Bobby's family, and immediately thought of mine. There would be years of agony after news like this, the death of a close relative. "I realize this is a good day for me and Janeene, but I suppose it's a difficult time for Bobby's family and friends."

"Expect it is, haven't spoken to them yet. The search team only found the body yesterday, and Wilkens just called to fill me in on their activities. None of this has been released to the public, but I expect it won't take long for leaks to spring up. My divers are still in Quetico, but they are due back tomorrow evening. They'll blab for sure. Takes nanoseconds for scuttlebutt to circulate around Ely."

"Maybe we can beat them to the punch."

"Huh?"

The idea of a news conference flashed in my head, but I wanted to know more about the body. "Hey, Chief, did Wilkens say anything about the corpse, like how it was hidden, anything like that?"

"He said the guy was naked and sunk with a backpack loaded with rocks. They bound it to him with ropes. It worked pretty well 'cause he was down about five feet in mud." I wondered whose equipment was on Bobby. They might have used Pete's gear and that could explain why his Hard Rock Café T-shirt wound up near Minn Lake. They would take anything personal out to avoid evidence they had been involved. Hank might have put the top in his bag. I told Bolling about my idea. "We'll see if we can figure out who the knapsack belonged to. You have a good nose for stuff, Roger."

I looked at my watch. It was 8:45 a.m. "I'm coming up today. I can be there in Ely before supper. What about holding a news briefing tomorrow?"

"Kinda quick for travel arrangements, don't you think?"

"Apparently you've never been in the business world; I've traveled on shorter notice than this for more years than I care to remember."

"Touché, Roger. But I do like the idea of getting out in front of this."

"Talk with Mary and Jean. They did a great job back in July with the events. Get them working on a plan. And if you would, call Bill Pec, please. See if he can take me in tonight. I'd appreciate it very much."

"If he can't, I will." His generosity caught me off guard.

"Thanks, Ron."

"Stick with Chief, suits me better."

I made a reservation for a 1:10 p.m. fight to Minneapolis, then called a limo company, one I had used for many years and was very reliable. Next, I called Duke. He said he wanted to go, but I talked him out of it since I was planning on seeing Janeene. "Guess I'd just be a left foot anyway," he said.

Janeene was harder to reach, and I was told she was in a meeting when I called her office, but the receptionist said she would give her my message.

On the ride to the airport, I phoned Jonathan. He was in a conference, but an emergency message I left with his secretary caused him to call back ten minutes later, and I told him my about plans.

"We'll do a press conference tomorrow," I said. "Not sure when or where, but it will be in Ely, probably in the same place we used before. I'm trying to reach Janeene to tell her about the body and about the conference so she can attend if she wants."

"Very short notice for a woman with a daughter and a job, but it would be excellent if she could join us. She adds a touch of sympathy to the abduction theme."

"Yeah, and her statements have sure turned to out to be good for me." I thought how different it could've been if she had refused to join our team like she'd done after our rescue from Darky Lake. Suppose she had decided to side with Hank and Pete, and said Bobby had been killed by me, and held that I had bopped the Scout on the head or alleged that I kidnapped her instead of sheltering her. After studying the events of the trip in exacting detail, I realized how good fortune had been on my side. Janeene really was the key. Her corroboration of my testimony set the tone for the investigation. I was innocent of any crime, but out in the wilderness with no witnesses, the truth might be impossible to determine. Jonathan had discussed various scenarios with me many times, especially the part Janeene played in establishing my credibility. "Hey, Jonathan, have you been watching the Epstein story?"

"How can you not? It's been in every broadcast this summer."

"Ever wonder how that guy could have done so many things with so many people and yet there was no rock-hard evidence of wrongdoing? As long as there is no video proof or recorded conversations of the accused breaking the law, or signed paperwork in the matter of financial dealings, you can't prove shit."

"Yeah, but look at it the other way. We're a nation of laws, and we live by them. It swings both ways. Take your situation, for example. You explained what happened, what you did, and why you did it. Sounds quite heroic and reasonable to me. But others may not feel the same way. Still, they had no video camera out there either, so they would have to prove beyond a reasonable doubt that any action you took was not what you said, or that your actions were wrong, or criminal. If they can't do that, then they have no case either. There needs to be hard proof—undeniable, unassailable facts to find someone guilty of a crime." He stopped, huffing like a freight train.

Jonathan had recited many excellent points and I appreciated his opinion about my actions, and his deep interest in the case. "I'm calling Janeene to see if she can attend the press meeting. You might need to bring her up with you."

"I can do that, Roger. Just let me know."

* * *

Janeene called as I was awaiting departure on Concourse A in Atlanta. "Hey, lady, got some great news—well, sort of great." I paused, thinking she could take it two different ways. "They found Bobby's body."

"Oh Roger, that's. . . that's wonderful." She paused, sounding weepy and choked up after the true meaning settled in.

"I want you to take it as a positive, sorry he's not with us any longer, but. . ."

"No, it's okay, Roger, I've been thinking about what you've said; it's not my fault he was shot. I feel guilty about, but not responsible for what Hank did. I can hold up."

"Can you attend a press conference with me tomorrow?"

"You mean in Ely?"

"Yeah, I'm flying in this afternoon, getting ready to board a plane any minute."

She fell silent, and I could imagine the wheels turning in her head. "I have to talk to my boss."

"Jonathan can meet you in Duluth, if that's any help."

"It is. I can ask my father to drive me there. What time is the event?"

"Hasn't been decided, so it's any time you can make it. I'll stay with Pec or the chief tonight, and if you're coming, I'm sure. . . no, I'm positive we can hold it until you arrive. Without me and you, there's no news conference, just an announcement, and the town of Ely wants an event."

"Have to work on my arrangements."

"I'll tell Jonathan to call you in an hour or two. Can he use this number?

"Yes."

"I can stay for a while after the meeting."

"Please do, Roger. We need some time to ourselves."

After I landed, a message sounded on my cell phone. It said a Pec driver would look for me outside the baggage claim. He would be carrying a sign that said PEC OUTFITTERS. He would drive me to Ely and to Bill's house. I was glad to learn they still thought well of me.

CHAPTER TWENTY-SIX

The press conference was scheduled for 3:30 p.m. That gave Chief Bolling time to arrange the meeting site, and to advise all the other authorities involved in the investigation. It also provided time for Jean and Mary to notify all their contacts in the news business, as well as giving Janeene and Jonathan time to connect in Duluth and drive to Ely. I also suspected the time was chosen to allow visitors to arrange for accommodations in Ely if they so desired. More news was rumored to be available the next day, or the day after, depending on autopsy results, lab tests, and other information to be provided by Wilkens and the Ontario Province Police. I laughed, thinking about Bolling's ability to inject drama into any topic he deemed appropriate, and to cause guests to congregate in the Ely area to support local companies.

The chief asked me to be ready to answer questions from reporters, and I agreed; Janeene was sitting beside me as a potential backup witness. "We're not going to use her unless it is necessary, and even then, we might not let her speak," Jonathan said, looking directly in Bolling's eye. "And I'd rather

Roger only answers questions from you, not reporters." They nodded at each other in silent agreement.

In the presentation room Jonathan sat to Janeene's right, while I sat on her left. We were at the front of the room flanking the chief and three of his officers. Janeene was dressed in an off-white outfit consisting of linen slacks and a silky over-sized shirt, which was also pale white, with a loose-fitting collar. Her blond hair was pulled back in a ponytail, giving her a smart, stylish appearance. But she looked intimidated, and I squeezed her hand, saying, "You don't have to say anything; Jonathan can speak on your behalf." She didn't argue.

The conference started nearly fifteen minutes late. The chief made the official announcement about recovering the body with myriad technical details about where it was found, who recovered it, who possessed it now, and what was to be done with it in the future. He made extensive comments about the legal issues of the case. He also thanked all the participants of the operation, especially his scuba team and his counterparts from Canada. He talked more than forty minutes without entertaining questions, which aggravated the press corps. "We'll get to your questions later," he said every time a reporter tried to interrupt.

He concluded by summarizing every discovery that had been made to date, then offered an introduction of Mr. William Anderbeer. *Who?*

"Mr. Anderbeer would like to make a statement," Bolling said, astonishing everyone, including me. I remembered Jonathan telling me the Boy Scout had a Swedish name, but I'd forgotten it.

Anderbeer was over six feet tall and looked very lean and fit, weighing about two hundred pounds, and no more than forty to forty-five years old. He was blond-haired and quite tan —an imposing figure, albeit appearing to be good-natured because of a warm smile. He was dressed in a business suit but had been way off to the side, so I thought he was an attendee.

He stood and walked to the middle of the room in front of the chief's podium and faced the crowd. "I want to take this opportunity to personally thank Captain Roger Cummings and Miss Janeene Morgensen for saving my son. As a former Army Corporal I appreciate the phrase, *leave no man behind*. What they did under dire circumstances to bring Billy to safety has to be considered a true act of sacrifice and valor. My wife and I and all the Scouts in our troop are grateful for their bravery and determination. They have given us a reason to look forward to the next dawn. I might add that Billy is recovering quite well at this time. His physical wounds have healed, but emotional scars remain. His memory of all the actions gets clearer by the day, and he misses his friend Jacob Guteling, the boy who was killed by Ha—I'm not going to repeat the name." He bowed his head, then looked up with tears in his eyes. "We appreciate all the hard work done by Chief Bolling, his teams, the US forest rangers, support personnel from the Minnesota National Guard, and finally the Canadian forest rangers in conjunction with the Ontario Provincial Police." He turned from the crowd and looked directly at me. "I salute you, sir." He snapped to attention and offered a brisk salute. I was stunned but stood and returned the salute like I had done so many times in the Army.

The room was strangely quiet after the speech by Mr. Anderbeer. Chief Bolling noticed the awkwardness and shouted loudly before anyone could react, "We're taking a ten-minute recess and will answer questions then. Restrooms are in the rear."

I helped Janeene to her feet as Anderbeer approached us. He hugged her and shook my hand. We spoke for several minutes, and he noted that Billy had stated that he knew Hank had struck him. No doubt in his mind. And yes, he should make a full physical recovery. His son identified Hank from photos of his face and tattoo. He did not know who Janeene and I were, but he sent his thanks for our help.

Ten minutes later Bolling called the room to order. "I promised you a question-and-answer session, so fire away."

The questioning was intense and enlightening, as the reporters asked every imaginable question and were not satisfied with puny answers.

"Who killed Bobby?" someone yelled.

"Why was Bobby killed?" another screamed. There was a litany of similar questions. Chief Bolling acted as the emcee of a bad version of a town hall meeting. He did an excellent job answering questions, while not allowing reporters to directly quiz Janeene or me. I did answer questions from Bolling, though, mostly those about our evasion in the woods above the little lake, or our escape from Darky. Jonathan answered any questions about possible criminal allegations against me or Janeene, or lawsuits that could be brought, and generally convinced the reporters that no valid actions had been filed to date and no charges should be filed against us.

At 5 p.m. the session was called off, not because all the questions had been answered, but because Bolling was growing weary of answering a slightly modified version of a previous question. Given enough time, it was apparent to me that reporters could travel full circle with their queries and end up back where they started.

As Janeene and I were preparing to depart, Bill Pec came to our chairs and said, "If you two will follow me, I'll take you out the back and over to my house." Reporters were jostling nearby to try and talk with us, but we followed Pec behind the podium area and out a rear door. A young, dark-haired man was behind the steering wheel of a large Dodge Ram pickup truck, and a husky guy was standing next to the rear doors holding a handle. It was Bolling's nephew. He opened it and hustled the three of us inside to the cab's rear bench seat.

On the way to his house, Pec told us the chief needed to go to his office to answer a boatload of messages that required his attention and would join us for dinner later in the evening. "We have room in the guesthouse, or you can stay in our main house," Pec said to Janeene, "if you prefer. It's no problem."

"How many bedrooms in the guesthouse?"

"Four."

"Then I can stay in the guesthouse with Roger. If I could handle him in Quetico, there should be no difficulty here in Ely."

Pec smiled, "Okay, supper at 7:30 p.m. then, in our dining room."

Jonathan drove up a minute later and unloaded Janeene's luggage from his car. "Are you staying the night?" I asked him.

"No, got to get home to the wife and dictate some notes. There was a lot said today that I need to think about." He held up a small recorder. "Please call me in the morning; after ten o'clock would be good, Roger."

"Will do."

I carried Janeene's luggage into the guesthouse and got her settled in her room. After a quick cleanup, we met in the room adjoining all the bedrooms. It was a large area with two couches, four chairs, and a big screen television. It also had a bar, although not as large as the one in Pec's lower-level basement of the main house.

"That was quite an event," she said, sitting down in one of the chairs. "More unruly than I expected, and Anderbeer's statement nearly made me cry. That and the salute was touching."

"I thought so too. Took me by surprise." I walked to the bar. "Do you want some wine, a cocktail, or a beer?"

She smiled, "A sparkling water would be nice."

I poured two plastic bottles of water into glasses, added ice cubes, and brought one to her. Drank half of mine in one toss. Responding to Bolling's questions had dried my throat like a desert creek bed.

"You were courageous today, Roger. I was impressed by you."

"You're making me blush, and I almost lost it with Anderbeer myself. But he made me think about what's important in life. This whole story has caused me to do that many times."

"Me too."

I watched her throat as she tilted her head back slightly and swallowed a sip of the water. It was a thin, elegant neckline. Much too soft and gentle to have undergone the horror she went through being dragged back to the tent by Hank at Brent Lake. A full picture of her torment developed in my mind but disappeared in an instant. *I needed to change the subject.*

"We can talk for a while," she said, "then we should get ready for dinner. It was kind of Mr. Pec to invite us for dinner. He's a nice man."

"Yes, he is."

After a pause I said, "We need to talk about us. Maybe we can do it after dinner. Or maybe we should put it off until I drive you home tomorrow."

"I think tomorrow would be better, but you decide."

After some thought while looking at her face, I said, "I'm struggling right now, have been for the last year and a half. That's after when. . . my. . . my. . ."

"When your wife passed away?"

"Yes."

I remembered telling Janeene the whole story when we

were hiding near the little lake but reminded myself now that anybody in the country who read a newspaper or watched television would know the basic story about the accident. It had been this way in my neighborhood in Atlanta, at the local grocery store, even at the church I attended, for the last year and a half. Everyone knew the story of poor Roger's wife.

"I'm looking for answers, although that isn't the right word, more like a direction in my life that gives it meaning. I don't have one right now." She gave me a strange look. "I need to redirect my focus on something, somebody, or somewhere, and it needs to be done now."

She stared, studying my face and realizing I wasn't insane, just lost, like a momentary light had blinded me. "Why now?"

I might have opened my private door a little too wide, letting her see inside the man called Roger Cummings. But once the door was cracked, it might as well have been kicked wide open. "My wife and I were always happy together, and completely faithful, but we were fighting during the month before she got killed." I stopped trying to find the right words or phrase and walked around the room. "I regret that now."

Janeene said nothing, making me believe she just wanted to listen without comment. She watched me move around the couch.

"My wife occasionally drank too much wine, mostly with her girlfriends. Not enough to behave poorly, but she'd get tipsy from time to time, and let things happen that weren't good."

"What kinda things?"

Her eyes were zeroed in on mine. "Nothing like having an affair. And I didn't cheat on her. We loved each other. . . and would have until the end of time. It's just that time ran out—her time ran out."

"What things happened that weren't good?"

"She let our dog get run over, and I was pissed off about it."

"Your dog?"

"Yeah, a silky terrier, and a hell of a guy. I cherished him, but he was her dog, all eleven pounds of him, and he would fight to the death to protect her. She loved him because he was pure—no faults you could complain about—and he would comfort her in ways nobody else could. Sparky was his name, but he died in New Jersey when she was visiting her parents. He got run over by a car one night when Sherry came home a little too happy after being with friends and let him out go to pee and he walked into the street. I was really mad at her about Sparky and I was still upset with her when she died. Feel horrible about that."

Janeene said nothing and waited for me to continue.

"Since the woman I once cared about is gone—my dog, too —I've been floating around, looking for a landing pad."

Janeene's eyes were brimming with tears, and she took the tips of her fingers and wiped them across the bottom of her eyes to keep them from dribbling over. "I'm sorry for your pain."

"I'm not living this way anymore." I looked directly into her eyes. "Sorry if I upset you; I didn't mean to, just wanted you to know the real story, not what's been reported in the newspapers."

CHAPTER TWENTY-SEVEN

"Are you really thinking about moving to Minneapolis?" Janeene asked, as we drove my rental car to her place in Eden Prairie. It was after ten o'clock in the morning. We'd bid Bill Pec and Chief Bolling goodbye after a late breakfast with them and had been driving away from Ely for an hour. "I thought your talk about moving was just being nice to me."

"It is about being nice to you, but it's also about being good for me." I clutched the steering wheel and looked at a highway sign, guessing it would be another two hours until we reached Minneapolis. We had plenty of time to talk. "I've always liked the city, all of Minnesota for that matter, and entertained thoughts of moving here many times. It's been a dream since my first trip into the BWCA. I want to catch another big muskie, maybe a few giant northerns, and of course a dinner plate full of walleyes. That's all I'm saying."

Janeene smiled but was quiet and looked out the passenger side window. She glanced at me and asked, "You committed to finding out?"

"Yeah. I have a friend in town that might let me stay with him while I mull over all the options."

"Think you can stand the weather up here in winter?"

"No problem for me. I like ice fishing."

She glanced back out the window and finally looked back in my direction. "I would love to see you more often." Her voice was softer now, almost a whisper.

I reached over and clutched her left hand in my right and gave it a squeeze. Her hands were warm, on the small side, and very smooth, like the feel of velvet. "I need to see you as often as possible. . . to figure out if . . ."

"Figure out what?"

"If it's possible for you and me to make a go of it, you know, more than just people helping each other after a nasty episode."

She sat in silence at my clumsy remark then turned her palm up and squeezed me back. "Roger, I do have feelings for you. They started the very first morning when I saw you working so hard to protect me, to keep me safe, and get me back to my daughter. My emotions have only grown stronger since we met."

"Good thing. We met in a wrestling takedown, as I recall." She laughed. "Seriously, Janeene, I want to be near you for my own reasons."

"Like?"

"Like I'm starting to really care about you. Might be falling in love."

She blushed. "I sort of feel the same way."

We drove for half a mile in silence, Janeene looking out the side window at the scenery and me looking at traffic in my lane.

My cell phone rang loudly through the car speaker system. The call was from Jerry Milner, my stock trading friend. "Hi, Jerry."

"Hey, Roger. You ready to accept my offer?"

"I'm in the middle of deciding that now."

"What do I need to do to convince you it's a great idea?"

"Promise to teach me all your secrets about playing stock options."

"I'll educate you about options, show you all my tricks if you teach me everything you know about earnings events. That's a great deal for both of us."

"Sounds fantastic, can I let you know later today or tomorrow?"

"That's fine," Jerry said. "I can have the place ready by next week. Thought about what you asked, and all you need to cover is the cost for my housekeepers to clean each week and do your laundry. We'll talk to them when you arrive and determine a fair price."

"Okay by me. I'll only need the place until maybe Christmas. I won't be there all the time, just a week or a few days, then back to Atlanta for a while, something like that."

"You can keep any schedule you want; we'll work it out after you decide. But I think it's a great idea for both of us—a win-win situation."

"I do too. Can't wait to get back on the screens, trading again, and making some money."

I punched the dashboard button and disconnected, then glanced at Janeene before checking the road to my front. What I didn't tell her was that Jerry's offer was a reason for me staying in Minneapolis, but not the only one. I was worried about Hank. He was a ghost who posed a threat to both of us, a malevolent force who lived at the edge of night and invaded my dreams. Bolling and I had made a pact that he would keep me informed of any nugget of information about the man. Until he was found, or enough time passed, he could still reappear in our lives like a demonic monster—a real or imagined menace floating beyond the horizon. It was a chilling thought to harbor, and not one she needed to hear about from me.

We rode in silence for a few miles, Janeene still looking out the window at the trees and hills beside the road. "He's still bothering you, isn't he?" she asked.

"Who?"

"You know who."

I hadn't allowed his name to cross my lips in days, trying to forget the hate in his eyes and the smell of his breath when he tried to kill me, or when I had the chance to end his life. I should have killed him when I had the chance. *Stop saying that to yourself.* "I'm not worried about anybody, especially Hank, if that's what you're thinking."

"He worries me."

"I know he does, but he shouldn't. He's just an evil story for the parks, a predator who vanished and might rise again to strike anyone—a true asshole, one who wants to kill Boy Scouts, his friends, and haunt his enemies. But I want the legend to be: HK, a killer who got what he deserved for hurting others and died alone in the wilderness by the claws and teeth of animals. That's what I want."

She turned and looked at my face. I could only look her way for a second, then turned to watch the road again. She mumbled, "You really think he's dead?"

"Yeah, I do. If he hasn't turned up by this time, he's a goner. My guess is they'll find his body, or parts of it, next year, somewhere north of where we fought."

She let out a hiss, loud enough it could be heard over the road noise. "I want to believe you, Roger. I'm just worried for myself and Angela. If that bastard gets out of the park, he'll find me. He left some stuff at my house before we went into Quetico. He'll want it back. If he's alive, he's coming after his things. Trust me."

"What kind of stuff?"

She glanced at me. "A couple of duffle bags with hunting clothes, camping equipment, and some fishing tackle. One of them had an old drone in it.

"Where are they now?"

"Gave it all away. I had to clear everything out before putting my house up for sale. Charities will pick up all kinds of things when you move, then decide what's worth keeping or not."

After a few seconds of silence I said, "I never really asked you, and in some ways don't care, but why did you get involved with Hank in the first place?"

She looked down at her hands, fiddling with her nails and replied, "I was out with some girlfriends at a bar about six or seven months ago, and he came up and started talking with us. He didn't have a beard then and no tattoos, and he seemed nice. One of my friends got interested in him and he hung around for most of the night, but after she left, I started talking with him. One thing led to another, and we dated the next week. I wasn't in a relationship at the time—hadn't been in a real one since my divorce—so he caught my attention at a good moment for him."

My interest in Hank was just a pretense to get her talking about the guy. I needed to learn more about him—his habits, his likes and dislikes. At this point I really knew very little about the man. I waited, looking at her, wanting her to continue.

Finally, she did. "He seemed to be nice at first. He had a good job, made great money, had a nice house, and was actually a big shot in his company. We were only friends really; then he won the lottery. That changed him. He wanted to see me more often and kept giving me gifts like clothes and envelopes with money. He claimed he wanted to marry me, but it didn't take long for me to realize he was. . . how can I say this. . . a dishonest person. He had two other girls on the side. I learned that from one of his coworkers at an office party, and I decided it was over long before we ever went into the park; I just never told him." She paused, then added, "He was one big mistake in my life at a time when I was weak. He scares the hell out of me to this very day."

I focused on the highway, watching a truck ahead slow down for an exit ramp. "You can stay with me in Atlanta if you're worried. I have plenty of room. The monster won't know anything about me or where I live." Then I remembered Hank heard my full name from Duke at Brent Lake, and recalled what my kids had said about getting information. It wouldn't take long to check a few newspapers about the park incidents and do a search on the Internet to confirm some critical facts about me. *I'm less hidden than he is.*

"I can't leave, my life's here. Angela starts school soon and my mom is ill. I have to stay close by and I need to help my father with his businesses, do his books. I can't move away from here, Roger."

"Maybe you misunderstood. I'm not asking you to leave your home, but you can come visit me anytime you want." I honked at a Mercedes sedan slowing in the left-hand lane. It moved over and we shot past. "You'd love Atlanta. Why don't you come for a short visit?"

"When?"

"Next week, next month, whenever. I have to go to New Jersey this Thursday and stay until the third of September, but any time after that is okay."

"Why go there?"

"Thought I told you—to see my kids start college. Get them and all their stuff into their dorm rooms. Hey, want to join me?"

"I can't, Roger. I'd have to plan for a trip, make arrangements for Angela, take vacation time; there's a lot to do. I'm not like you—wealthy, or a person with no real job."

"I'm not wealthy, Janeene, but comfortable, and I have a job —trading stocks. I've just been screwing off since June."

We traveled in silence a few miles down the road when Janeene said, "There's something you need to hear about Hank." She lowered her voice enough for me to know bad news was coming.

"Then tell me." I moved into the right-hand lane.

She looked at me, then back out the side window, then at the vehicles in front of us, and finally back at the side of my face. I didn't move my head, but I could see her by just shifting my eyeballs quickly to the right and back. "One thing you should know, just so you understand, Hank was impotent."

"Impotent? You mean he was a limp dick?"

"Yeah, he couldn't get an erection if a team of strippers danced in his lap."

I turned my head to the right and saw her looking squarely at me, eyes on fire. "The bastard had problems, lots of problems, emotional and physical, and he couldn't get it up for months. I got tired of his excuses, knew he was cheating on me anyway from the work friend, and then realized he was damaged goods. His sister told me the story of him getting an infection from some woman he dated on the side, so there were at least three other people he was seeing besides me. Her confession woke me up about him. He wouldn't give me the attention I needed because he couldn't, and even if he could, he wouldn't have because he was an asshole. I made a huge mistake getting involved with him, but—and you need to hear me now—I never really cared about him, and certainly never loved him, and wish to God I had never allowed him to be in my life."

I paid attention to the road. "I'm guessing the story about him raping you in the tent was bullshit?"

"He tried but couldn't." She looked down at her hands. "I needed you to feel sorry for me at the time. I would have died in the park if you hadn't saved me. I'm sure of it."

"You didn't need to feed me bullshit to make me help you. I saw what Hank did to Bobby. I'd have gotten you out of there without the lie."

"I know that now; I didn't then."

We drove in silence for a mile, then I said, "Good thing we didn't report the false rape to Chief Bolling. I don't like lying to authorities for any reason."

"But you didn't tell them about me making love with Bobby. You must have seen us. You told them we were only kissing."

"I wanted to protect you. By the time we got out of Quetico I was starting to like you and didn't feel it was necessary to tell people things they don't need to know. They needed to know Hank shot Bobby, not that you two were naked." This discussion was veering too far away from my intended purpose. "I never said anything about what you were or weren't wearing. More importantly, though, I didn't mention the tattoo on your ass cheek to anyone."

She snapped her eyes, glaring at me. She waited half a minute before calmly stating, "The butterfly was a mistake. I did it because Hank pestered me after he got the snake on his arm, and he challenged me to prove I was loyal to him. At the time, I pretended to be because of the lottery money, so I got one where it wouldn't be seen, except by certain people. It's within my panty line. You can't see it in a bikini." After a minute she added, "I get the feeling you think less of a person if they have a tattoo."

"You really think that?" I couldn't understand why anyone, anywhere, at any age, at any point in human history, would disgrace their body by putting a lousy painting or rendition of an object on their body and not be able to wash it off. It struck me as completely asinine. "No, I love shitty artwork."

* * *

We didn't speak again until we were driving on HWY 212 nearing Eden Prairie. It was midafternoon and traffic was moving at a steady pace. We were within fifteen minutes of the house where Janeene was staying, the one that belonged to her father's brother, Dan.

"I will admit, though, the canvas for your butterfly is absolutely spectacular."

She smiled, but still looked a little bit pissed off. "Are you going to stay around until you have to go to New Jersey?"

"I can, or I can fly home tomorrow before going there."

"I'd like to see you tonight, and maybe tomorrow as well." She reached her left hand for my right and gave it a little squeeze, looking at our fingers. "I've been selfish all my life and able to get away with a lot over the years. In my experience, pretty girls have abilities others don't, and I've taken full advantage of those powers with the men." She looked up at the side of my face. "I respect you and I'm attracted to you; we deserve a chance." She patted my hand. "Wanted you to know that."

In my mind, respect was one thing, love another. To be successful in a loving relationship, I always thought there had to be a little lust—a touch was enough. There always had been in mine. I felt that same tingle now whenever I looked at Janeene, but at this moment it made me wonder if she knew how to play that card better than I could handle her skill to use it over me. She needed to feel the same about me or have the same weakness I did with her.

A highway sign for the Courtyard Marriot Minneapolis/Eden Prairie was on the right side of the road. I called the phone number listed on it and made a reservation for two nights.

"You sure?" Janeene asked when I finished the call.

"I'm not sure of anything, but there's a way to find out. I'm sticking around for a couple of days."

Before we got to her house, we made several more decisions. Some were ridiculous things, like what to put on the pizza we would order for dinner. I voted for sausage, meatballs, onions, green peppers, and mushrooms, while Janeene voted for cheese, spinach, basil, and tomato sauce. Angela, I was told, liked the same things as her mother, so we ordered two small pies for the ladies and a giant one for me. When I learned Janeene's father would be at the house with a couple of friends while he was watching Angela, I ordered two more pizzas like mine. Didn't want him or his buddies to go hungry, even if it turned out I couldn't stand the guy. Janeene assured me we'd get along well, but you never know, and women often misunderstand men. That's been my experience anyway.

We also decided to celebrate our triumph in Quetico by agreeing to go to Hawaii for a Christmas or Valentine's Day vacation. Janeene voted for the February date, because she liked spending Christmas and New Years with her family and friends. If we were still interested in each other by February, we might go then. The vacation had provided inspiration during our saga in the wilderness, and the timing would allow us to see if we really cared for each other. Time has a way of settling out the differences between lust, love, boredom, or contempt. Any of those outcomes were possible, but my heart felt inspired. Time would also allow me to learn about her family in Minneapolis and decide if I really wanted to move to Minnesota. Now there was a conceivable purpose for a move.

At supper that evening, I decided her father was an interesting man. That's the best way to describe Alex Morgensen.

At five feet ten inches tall and nearly two hundred fifty pounds, he looked sort of like a buffalo that could run over you before you had a chance to escape. But after talking with him you soon realized he was a gentle man and not prone to temper tantrums or outbursts of his personal point of view. He often said very quietly to the people he spoke with one-on-one, "What do you think?"

Only seven people were in the room—six-year-old Angela, whom I fell in love with instantly; Janeene; me; a nurse who attended to the brother, Dan, who owned the house we were in; the father, Alex; and Ray Pintubu, a family friend and owner of several gas stations across town.

My most enlightening discussion was with Dan and Ray. I learned more about the gas station business than could be gleaned from reading a book. When Dan went to talk to his nurse, Ray continued to chat with me. "What's your occupation, Roger, if you don't mind my asking?"

"I trade stocks for a living."

"Like with a brokerage company?"

"No, I used to, or something similar. Now I just trade for myself."

"You must have nerves of steel. I can't even look at my quarterly statement without having to take a crap."

"Yeah, there are some scary times. But if you watch carefully, move slowly, and follow specific rules, you can play the market and not lose your mind."

"It's losing my ass that worries me."

"Ha, know the feeling quite well. You must have challenges in your business."

"Do I? You can't imagine the problems." He sipped his beer and said, "The main difficulty is finding good workers— those who show up when they should, can keep their hands out of the till, and treat the store as if it were theirs. It's

287

almost impossible to find people that meet those requirements."

From observing gas stations over the years, I could imagine the troubles. "Do your stations sell food and all the other stuff? Are they what people call convenience stores?"

"Yeah, that's the problem. Lotta times people pay in cash, and it has a tendency to disappear somewhere between their wallet and our cash registers."

"How much cash moves through a given store each month?"

"I've got two places," Ray said, "but on average I'd say each one does about three hundred thou a month, and about a fourth or fifth of that is in cash. It's getting less and less each day because of debit and credit cards, but there's still a lot. I'm certain a good chunk of it gets ripped off before it hits the till. But sometimes it works in reverse. More money shows up in the register than is printed on the receipts I count. Those are good days."

I never realized how much cash moved through these businesses on a daily, weekly, or monthly basis, and how tracking all the currency was so difficult. It sounded ripe for abuse. "What about your margins?"

"Razor thin on gasoline, which is the majority of the revenue. On other things like cigarettes, donuts, and candy, the margins are good, but the turnover can be slow. Stuff can stay on the shelves for weeks."

"How many do Alex and Dan own?"

"Oh hell, they're big time compared to me. I think it's about five gas stations now, and some laundries and dry cleaners." He sipped his beer again. "What problems do you have in your work, my friend?"

"Trying to live in two places at once and testing the waters around here."

He looked at me with a strange glance. "I wish you well, sir, wish you well."

As I was getting ready to leave, Janeene said with a sweet smile, "Maybe I could come to visit you for a weekend and stay for a Friday or a Monday. I love short trips and four-day work weeks."

"Just give me the dates, and I'll book the flights."

"Will I see you tomorrow?"

"If you want. You know where I'm staying."

She looked at me like I was a cold drink on a hot summer's day. "I do want to see you, Roger, more than you can imagine."

"I have a vivid imagination."

"I'll come to your hotel for breakfast in the morning before work." The house was still busy, but not chaotic, and we were off to ourselves in the foyer. She leaned in toward me, and I put my arm around her waist and pulled her closer. Our kiss was magnetic—our first real kiss. It made me want more. She beamed with those white, even teeth, a smile made for a toothpaste commercial, and said, "Please call me after you wake up; I've gotten used to your voice in the morning." She kissed my lips again.

CHAPTER TWENTY-EIGHT

After breakfast with Janeene, I went to meet my stock trading friend. Jerry Milner's house sits atop a knoll in Edina, and resembles an English Tudor-style mansion, surrounded by flower beds and picturesque gardens. It looked like a postcard of a British Inn.

The private section in the lower level of his home was huge, consisting of five separate rooms including a full kitchen, a master suite, a master bath, an entertainment room, and finally a library and study area filled with books. An elevator served the floor from above.

On a massive desk was an internet modem. "I can have it activated," Jerry told me. "No one uses this area now. My nephew lived here years ago, but he got married and lives in LA now."

I knew from his bio he had no children and wasn't married now but had an ex-wife. She perished in the commercial airliner that was shot down over the Ukraine in July of 2014. I made no comment, thinking that like me, he had experienced things in life you'd rather not discuss.

"Try the place for a month, Roger, and we'll see how it goes with you and me working together. I'm thinking we'll meet in my office on weekdays when you want to get in trades and play the market. Doesn't have to be every day, or even every week, just whenever you want. I'll watch you, and you watch me. We'll see what happens."

"Should work," I said, walking around the entertainment room. "This place is great, almost a complete house. Need to give you some rent or I'd feel like I'm cheating you."

"You only need to take care of the staff. They'll buy your groceries and cook for you if you want, and do your laundry, take out the trash, vacuum, whatever. You decide."

"Is five hundred a week okay? Should be enough to cover normal stuff like coffee and eggs, and some groceries like meat and a few potatoes. If I want something special, I'll pay for it separately."

"That's more than what I was thinking, but it's up to you."

"I think five is fair, so it's settled. I'll be back next week or the week after that. I'll let you know when."

"Fine. My folks will have the place ready."

I shook his hand. "At least I know what the ante is for my trades each week." I took a final gaze around the room, thinking this place was a great hideaway. "Let's watch CNBC and Bloomberg TV and you can give me your feelings on the mood of the markets today, see how close we are in our reasoning."

"Can do. You know this could really be fun. I haven't traded with a partner in twenty or thirty years."

I picked Janeene up for an early dinner on my way back from the visit with Jerry. We had cocktails and dinner at a restaurant next to my hotel and then retired to my room until it was time to get her home. We had a wonderful evening.

* * *

An early flight to Newark on Friday morning made me get up at 5 a.m., but it gave me plenty of time to drive to Morristown, New Jersey, and help Ricky load my rental van with clothes, computer equipment, sports gear, and a ton of other stuff I could barely imagine a college kid needed.

The next day, Harold and Bernice, along with Crystal and a few of the relatives that lived nearby, went with us to Ricky's campus at Rutgers. He was recruited to play lacrosse, a sport I had also played in high school and college, but Ricky developed much better stick work than I ever had and deserved to be in the dorm reserved for college athletes. Our group helped Ricky carry piles of his belongings up to his new room. It was chaotic meeting other students, their parents, and supporters who choked the hallways and parking lots unloading their precious cargo. Nobody mentioned the affair in Quetico and I guessed they didn't know. I noticed one of the cops Harold had retained sitting quietly on a bench watching activities outside the building.

Sending my son off to start a new challenge and seeing him happy about the idea was a highlight in my life, but there was still a twinge of fear in me. A vague emotion gnawed at my gut. *Could he be in any danger?* I couldn't bring myself to believe he was. If it was established that he was at risk, then I could act, but instead I was frozen by uncertainty. I felt the same about Crystal but couldn't let a feeling on my part affect their lives. We needed to find Hank or his body.

"I'll be back in a couple of weeks to see a football game and check your grades," I told Ricky. The grades didn't worry me, but the Rutgers' football team was another matter. Unfortunately, the lacrosse season didn't start until the spring, so I'd have to wait until then to see a game. Didn't mention my concern to him about his safety.

Princeton didn't have a move-in day until the third of

September, but essentially the same group of family members joined the event. More, actually, since Sherry had been a family favorite with her stunning beauty, warm smile, and casual air of elegance. Crystal was a picture of her mother, and two of the older women cried as they hugged her over and over, saying she had made her mother proud.

Crystal stayed with me for the last few minutes of our visit. She whispered in my ear, "Dad, I want you to know I love you, and will support any decisions you make. Please keep your promise to Ricky and me. Stay safe, and stay alive to see your grandchildren." She started to sniffle, and I hugged her tight. She added, "And please keep me informed about what you're doing. I don't want to learn something from friends, or the news; I want to hear it from you, so I'll help if I can, especially if it concerns the lady. I need to know you love me, and that's the best way to show it."

"Then that's what I'll do, sweetheart."

She turned to go, "Love you, Dad.

"Love you too."

* * *

Before I took a flight to Atlanta on Wednesday, the fourth of September, I talked with Harold about the twins' safety. We each agreed to kick in another five thousand dollars for their protection. "I get a lot of mileage for the money," Harold told me. "Even with the trip to Atlanta, a rental car, hotel rooms, and few bucks to the guys, we've got nearly two thousand left in the original kitty. The guys are really frugal, and they don't charge much for their work. I think they actually like being back on watch, rather than staying retired. Another $10K in the pot should be more than enough carry us until next year. By the way, tell Duke I said thanks for his help."

"Will do."

We talked about the general surveillance plan. Harold told me his cop friends said the best way was to watch for a few days in the beginning of the school sessions, make sure no suspicious characters were studying the kids, and back off. Come back and check around each week until Kovak, or his body, was found. "You can help them by staying on top of the search and letting me know the status."

"I will. I'm going home for a day or two, checking in with Duke, then flying back up to Minnesota. I have an idea about how to light a fire under Chief Bolling."

"Just remember, Roger, the cops are the good guys. Don't get pissed off when they're slow to dig up facts. They're usually under heavy pressure from every direction, especially when killers who aren't in custody are involved." Harold had apparently learned some valuable lessons as a city councilman.

CHAPTER TWENTY-NINE

Chief Bolling met me at Bill Pec's house when I arrived at five o'clock the next afternoon. I'd flown up after getting the sheriff to agree, very reluctantly, to listen to my idea about conducting a brainstorming session concerning the whereabouts of Hank Kovak. He also stated he had a deputy, Karen Per-Olof, who was knowledgeable about the technique and would join us for the discussions.

Three people—the sheriff, his deputy, and Bill Pec—were sitting side by side at a table in Pec's study, across from me now. Mrs. Per-Olof was about thirty, dark-haired, and looked very attractive in her nice-fitting uniform. "She doesn't take crap from nobody," Bolling told me on the phone. "Her husband owns a gym here in town, and she works out like a demon—probably stronger than him. Karen will be good for our group. She studied this stuff in college and will know if you're feeding us garbage and wasting my time."

I didn't realize brainstorming was taught in school as my training came at work after Lean Technology grew popular with many business executives. When my employer at the stock trading company hired a consulting company for a six-month contract, I became the inside expert in Lean deployment and supported the process after they departed. Brainstorming was only a small part of the overall system; however, it was adaptable to many situations—like this one, generating ideas about how this bastard could have eluded us for so long.

I started the process by stating, "Since we haven't found Kovac or his body, I want to consider how he might have gotten out of the park, and if he did, where he might have gone. That's why I'm here, to support the effort to find him."

"You can't be involved in looking for him, Roger. You're a private citizen and you have no right to take any action in an active investigation." It was Bolling. "What you did in Quetico was admirable, but still questionable, and you're lucky the lawsuits have been dropped, or deemed as not winnable."

"I'm not going out looking for him, Chief, just helping with the analysis of his disappearance."

"Your best action is to go home and forget everything. Kovac is dead, anyway, in my professional opinion."

"Easy for you to say, Chief. You don't have any skin in the game."

"HELL I DON'T! Ely is my town, a place I love, and I haven't been able to squash the bullshit about this bastard in over two months. The city got its financial brains beaten out this summer and we're in a bad situation because of it, no matter what you think—no skin, my ass."

"Sorry, Chief, didn't mean it like it sounded. I'm just worried about my kids and Janeene and her daughter. It didn't come out right." I lowered my voice and slowed my delivery. "Still, you and all the rangers, the Canadians, the soldiers, whoever, haven't accomplished the objective of determining the whereabouts of one Hank Kovak, dead or alive. We can't afford to wait on the off-chance this assassin will come out of the wilderness or his hiding place and ruin our lives."

"The damage has already been done, Roger, at least in Ely, whether he's croaked or not." It was Bill Pec speaking in a solemn tone. "We're damned near out of business since July. I'm not sure what you are asking us to do."

"What I think we should do is sort this out. Granted, he could be dead, and chewed into tiny pieces we might never find. Maybe we'll find his bones next year, maybe never, but we need to put that possibility off to the side for now."

There was palpable tension in the air, and I needed to be careful, like Harold had warned me in New Jersey. I said in a calm voice, "What we need to concentrate on at is how he could have escaped. I've been thinking about this a lot and focusing on possible escape routes. Didn't really do that before; instead, I was buying the line that he was probably rotting in a cave north of Darky and would be found, or parts of him, sooner or later. It made sense to me, until recently when I had to put two kids in college with the thought that a killer could be stalking them. Scared the hell out of me." I stopped and looked each one in the eye.

"What I propose now is the four of us develop a scenario where Hank got away, how he did it, who helped him, and where he could be staying. If we can't come up with a believable story, then I'll quit trying. My flight home has been scheduled for Sunday afternoon. That gives us this evening, tomorrow, and part of Saturday if needed, to work on my hypothesis. If we get nowhere, I'll wait it out until next spring."

Bolling stood and loosened the tie of his uniform, and I could sense he was angry and needed to cool off and relax. "Look, Chief, let's assume he got out of Quetico somehow. Who helped him? How did they know where to pick him up? Where is he hiding now?"

"We did that investigation back in July, remember? I personally requested cooperating agencies to check out his family, friends, co-workers, ex-wife—anybody who might have known something. We drew a blank in all those inquiries."

"Did you ever find the lottery money?"

"No, I told you that, and we haven't seen a trace in anyone's account."

"What I'd like to do is sit down with a map, plot a course to Minnetonka, which is where Hank is from, and determine how he, or any of us facing the same situation, would have made our way to that location. And we can start by deciding he hid the lottery money in a place only he knew about, recovered it, and is using it now to pay for his freedom."

Bolling said, "I'm not accepting the premise he escaped. We've considered this all summer, and it's gotten us nowhere."

"Yeah, but this is different. Let's make the assumption he escaped. How hard did you or the other departments really examine that possibility? From what I remember, you were concentrating on finding the asshole in the woods between Darky, That, and Wink Lakes, using drones and search teams. You expected to find him. That was your major focus, and the other stuff, like how he could escape, was not really on your mental radar. You had him trapped in the woods, or so you thought. Let's try a different approach. That's all I'm saying."

Pec got up and went to a small refrigerator behind his office desk. "Anybody want a drink?"

"A beer," I said. "But a root beer; you have one of those?"

"You're in luck. Chief? Deputy?"

"Same." Bolling looked like he had mellowed in the last few minutes, but I could tell he was angry at his failure to find Hank. He probably took some abuse in town and maybe from the other departments involved in the searches. The Canadians would understand, since it was their territory and they knew how hard it could be to find someone up there in the wilderness, but not locating a culprit was a lawman's worst nightmare.

"Just some bottled water would be fine for me," Karen said.

"You folks help me start an analysis technique; it's called brainstorming. I used this process in business and it's the best way to develop a range of possibilities. The rules are simple—there is no bad idea. Just blurt out what you think, and I'll write it down, and none of us can be judgmental about what anyone says. We'll grade the ideas after we've drained all our thoughts and go from there."

I rose and walked to an easel Pec had beside his desk and carried it to the center of the room. It was loaded with paper three feet high and two feet wide. "You have some markers, Bill?"

"Think so." He went to his desk, rummaged around in the drawer, and handed me three in different colors. I wrote HANK ESCAPED across the top of the first page.

"Okay, I'll start," I said. "Hank called a friend on a cell phone to pick him up in Minn Lake." I wrote it on the pad below the header and numbered it one.

Bolling said in a loud voice, "Service is not good up there, so that was not possible. And we checked with the provider for records on Kovak's call log. Nothing." The chief looked at me like I was a fool.

"I know, but in this exercise, we write everything down, without judgments or deletions, and come back to evaluate them in the next section."

"Waste of time, Roger."

"What if Hank brought another person's phone into the park? A person you didn't know about, and got enough signal to send a message? It could have been like three coughs, or sneezes. Something that wouldn't make sense to you or me or mean much on a call log," I answered. Bolling looked surprised.

"The purpose, Chief, is to get every feasible idea on paper first, so we don't leave anything out, then come back and decide whether it's good or bad." He nodded in silent agreement. Karen smiled.

I posed a second hypothesis. "Hank had a satellite phone with him and called a friend to pick him up in Minn Lake." I wrote it beneath the first statement. This time Bolling made no comment.

Pec said, "HK, that's what I call Hank 'cause I don't like to use his name, is under a rock, dead near That Lake." I started to write it down but stopped. The comment was out of order because I'd noted on the top HANK ESCAPES, which was the premise of this exercise. This statement didn't fit. I glanced at Karen, and she waited for my move. I pointed to the header at the top, "Your statement doesn't work with our hypothesis, Bill, want to try another?"

"No, let me listen for a while until I catch on."

I announced, "HK had a plan with Mister X to pick him up at a specified place and a specified time before he ever went into the park." I wrote it across the page.

"I'm getting the drift of your process," Bolling said. "Still, seems kinda crazy, but what if HK, let's call him Asshole or Mr. A for short, never intended to come out of the park until much later on, like after we would have been done conducting search-es." I wrote the idea down and tore the page off the easel.

"Can you put this on the wall?" I asked Bill. "Tape it at eye level so we can read it easily."

"The Hard Rock Café T-shirt found in the creek near Minn Lake meant that HK was heading out in that direction," Bolling said. It was added to the next list.

We started another page, and another, eventually filling twelve of them with ideas. Deputy Karen started adding ideas after listening to her boss and Bill make a few. Near the last page was an idea I had written out—Mr. A had prearranged for a person to meet him at a specific time and a specific place before he ever went into the park.

After listening to the chief and Pec's ideas and comments, Deputy Karen listed a thought near the bottom of the last page. Mr. A had arranged with his pickup person to not use any of either park's official entry points or ranger check-in stations and leave his vehicle in a hidden location before paddling to a specified rendezvous point, on a specific date at a specific time.

A final point, which I had written on the last easel sheet, was that a person supporting Mr. A was probably not a close friend or coworker and was possibly someone he had hired. He was not a family member, as they had been evaluated by authorities and were not considered to be involved in his escape.

The next day, Friday, I spent the entire day and evening reviewing all the ideas and began classifying them as feasible or not feasible. I was at it full-time since my arrival while Bolling and Deputy Karen had duties to perform, and Pec a business to run, but they spent two hours Friday afternoon and early evening working on our analysis and winnowing our beliefs into conceivable outcomes. Deputy Karen helped me write a conclusion Saturday morning before both men joined us for lunch in Pec's guesthouse.

Through a process of elimination and evaluation we came to several undisputable conclusions—if HK was not lifeless and decaying in the forest, he had escaped by staying hidden in a cave or hollow tree trunk, to avoid the drones, and was probably a good distance west of the area that had been the primary target of the search teams. We now postulated he had concealed himself between Wicksteed and Minn Lake, on the west side of the river-like waterway between Minn and Darky Lakes. This area was not searched in detail by personnel, or by anything other than an occasional drone or helicopter flying overhead as they progressed to the main search zone. The fact that the Hard Rock Café T-shirt was found on the west side of the waterway, almost at the confluence with Minn Lake, reinforced our hypothesis. It was unfortunate it took nearly six weeks, until August 11, to locate the clothing item. Otherwise, the attention of the search teams would have shifted in that direction immediately.

We also concluded that when the heavy influx of search personnel left after almost two weeks of rigorous work, if Mr. A survived, he remained hidden during all or most of that time, then moved carefully to a prearranged pickup point at a specific place and was met by a person who did not enter the park in an authorized manner. No communication was necessary to pull off the rendezvous. No permits were used, meaning there would be no record of this person entering or leaving the park at any of the ranger stations. This person then smuggled Mr. A out, probably by canoe and/or motor vehicle to an undisclosed location, which could be in Minnesota, or somewhere else in the United States, since we considered travel across international borders too dangerous to attempt. There was plenty of money available to support such a plan.

All this analysis only meant something important if in fact Mr. A survived the ordeal. If he was dead, it didn't mean shit, or was wasted time, like Chief Bolling said. But it gave me renewed focus for keeping Janeene and her family and my kids safe from this fiendish villain possibly hiding in the woods somewhere in Minnesota or the US.

"I still think he's a carcass, a skeleton a lot farther west than where we were searching, but I concur with your logic. You make some excellent points," Bolling said.

"I agree," Pec added. "Roger, do you really think he

this pickup? Seems to me, if this is true, he would have o kill Bobby ahead of time before the trip."

"Not necessarily. He might have arranged the pickup just to have a backup plan in case something went wrong, anything at all, with what he was planning to do. Or maybe he called this person after he killed Bobby by using a sat phone we haven't found or know about? Who knows? Maybe he planned to execute Bobby, maybe not. Maybe he planned on murdering him and Janeene? There's no way we can know what Mr. A was thinking. Hell, he might have been considering killing Pete for all we know. And it doesn't matter what the bastard thought; we're just assessing how he might have escaped the park, if he did at all." I quit talking and studied their faces. They looked grim. "I'm satisfied knowing there was a feasible way, although not a highly probable one, that he used to elude us and make it to safety. That's all I wanted to achieve."

CHAPTER THIRTY

After lunch, as I was driving toward Minneapolis, I called Jerry Milner and learned the area in his basement was thoroughly cleaned and ready for my arrival.

"You can use it tonight if you want," he told me. "I have an engagement in Sacramento I've had planned for months and will be there for several nights. I should be back by Monday or Tuesday, though."

"You sure it's no problem?"

"Not at all. I'll tell Alfred, the headmaster, that you're arriving this evening."

"Headmaster?"

"It's a joke between everyone on the house crew. Three people work in my home, doing everything from cooking and cleaning to mowing the lawn and fixing faucets. Alfred's been around the longest, and he's the leader of the pack. The others listen to him more out of respect than anything else and gave him the nickname."

"In that case, I'll ask for him when I drive up."

"Do that. He can show you where to park in the garage and

how to maneuver through the hallways to your rooms. Anyone gonna be with you?"

"Hadn't planned on it."

"It's okay with me if you have guests. It's your area."

"Thanks, Jerry."

"See you next week, Roger."

"Have a great trip."

I called Janeene and she was thrilled that I was staying in Minneapolis tonight after the Ely brainstorming session. We'd been talking all week, but my plans were uncertain from day-to-day, and I had considered going to Atlanta after the meetings and then coming back here next week to visit her. Since Jerry's house was ready, it gave me a new option.

"Please stay, Roger. You can join us for dinner at Dan's house tonight. I forgot to tell you before that it's my mother's birthday and everyone will be here for supper. She's the only one you haven't met. Mom looks forward to meeting you, but she doesn't know it might be tonight."

"Well, then I'll have to be there to surprise her, won't I?" After a second, I asked, "What can I bring? Wine? Flowers?"

"Flowers would be wonderful. She loves roses."

"Any particular color?"

Janeene thought for a second. "White or yellow. She likes red on Valentine's Day, but not so much in the summer."

"White they shall be."

My unexpected introduction couldn't have gone any better. I was an immediate hero with the family as soon as I entered the house carrying three dozen white roses in my arms and walked directly to Janeene's mother and presented them. Caught totally off guard, she wittingly fawned over me again and again, even asking to sit beside me as we were waiting to be seated for dinner. "When Dan comes down, he'll sit at this end," she pointed at a chair. "My husband will sit at the other end, and I want you right next to me."

Angela, tugging at my hand, said, "I want to sit next to Roger, Grandma."

"You can, sweetheart, there's plenty of this nice man to share."

A minute later, a tall, burly guy carried Dan down the stairs to join us for dinner. He put Dan in a chair at the head of the table and we all moved around to take our places. Three ladies were clamoring to sit beside me—Janeene, her mother, and Angela. Fortunately, there were four chairs on each side, so Angela could slide in between Janeene and me on my right.

"Can't get up and around like I used to," Dan said, after he had been gracefully placed in his seat at the table. "Mickey can lift me into bed, or into the tub, like I'm a toy."

Mickey weighed at least three hundred pounds, mostly muscle. "He looks like he could lift you and this table at the same time," I noted. The brothers got a good chuckle out of that. Mickey didn't even crack a smile.

"He was an offensive lineman with the Golden Gophers a few years back," Janeene's father said to me.

"Ah, a nurse who hails from the University of Minnesota. Well, strength is a good quality to have for this job," I announced. Everyone agreed.

We had a great dinner of corned beef and cabbage, a favorite of Janeene's mother, and a meal they had every year on her birthday. The roses, which were the center of attention in the middle of the table, allowed me to have an extra dessert—a vanilla ice cream sundae with salted caramel topping and chocolate sauce.

After dinner, I had the chance to talk privately with

Janeene's father. "When did you hire Mickey? Last time I was here there was a female nurse."

"Yeah, there was. Her name was Ruby. She was great, but she couldn't lift Dan. That started to be necessary in the last few weeks." He gave me an odd smile and added, "Besides, Mickey's as strong as an ox, has a concealed weapons license, and works for a company that offers protection services in addition to nursing. After talking about it with Janeene, I decided it was a good move for both of them."

I couldn't have agreed more. "What do you mean protection services?"

"Mickey's company has armed people with gun licenses, who come around at unannounced times to check on him and make sure everything is all right. They check out the house coupla times a day." I wasn't aware of this arrangement and wondered why Janeene hadn't mentioned it to me. It was a great idea, though, similar to what Harold and I had arranged for the twins. Seemed like there were more people who were concerned about the possibility of Hank escaping from Quetico.

After her folks left and Mickey carried Dan up to his room, Janeene led Angela and me to her part of the house in the upper level of the three-story structure. She had a multi-room suite: One room had a couch, chairs, and a big screen television, complete with a large picture window overlooking a spacious backyard. Two other rooms served as bedrooms, each with full baths attached. The final area held a small refrigerator, microwave, and a two-burner hot plate.

"This place is great. How long have you been here?"

"Since my house went on the market in early August. Closed last week, by the way."

"It did? You didn't tell me that. What'd you do with your stuff?"

"Dan let me put it in his basement. Got rid of everything I really didn't need or want anymore. Surprising how much junk you can collect over the years."

"My house is the same way—went from four of us to just me. The place is way too big for one person and stuffed to the gills with junk the twins don't want anymore."

"Sell it and come live with me." She smiled at my shocked look.

"I'm considering it." Shocked her right back. I leaned toward her and kissed her full on the lips. She hugged me tightly and wiggled against my chest. I wanted to make love to her and end the game we had been playing for months, but it wasn't the right time or place. Maybe soon.

"I've got to get over to Jerry's place before it's too late."

"You have to go? You can stay here if you want." She bit the tip of my earlobe. "I can sleep in Angela's bedroom with her."

I laughed. "I promised his headmaster Alfred that I'd be there before 11 p.m. to meet him." I got up and pulled her to her feet and kissed her again. "You feel safe here?"

"Yeah. Mickey's around all the time, and he's got backup," she said. "Another guy from my dad's store is supposed to take Angela to school and back every day, starting this Monday. She's not riding the bus anymore."

"Good idea. See you tomorrow?"

"You better."

I gave her another kiss and she walked me down the stairs and through the main entertainment area adjoining the kitchen, through the garage and over to a side door where my car was parked. On the way out, I noticed Mickey studying the backyard through the kitchen window.

CHAPTER THIRTY-ONE

At ten o'clock Sunday morning, I was drinking coffee at a kitchen table that was in my part of Jerry's mansion. Albert, the headmaster, had been thoughtful enough to stock the cabinets in here with essentials like coffee and sugar and load the refrigerator with a few necessities like creamer, milk, and eggs. I needed to write a check to Jerry for the monthly amount, four times five hundred dollars—always liked to pay my obligations ahead of time.

Sunday mornings were usually study time for me and had been since I was a young trader—quiet times when no one would normally bother me. I was studying a stock chart on my laptop, noting the four-, nine-, and eighteen-day triple moving average crossovers, when a call came to my cell phone. It was Chief Bolling. "Hi, Roger. You have a minute?"

The heaviness in his voice caught me off guard. "Never too busy for you, Chief, even if it is a Sunday. What's up?"

He seemed to hesitate, but then said, "Heard a strange story, one you may not like." I remembered his nickname, the drama man, which Duke had joked about during our early days in Ely.

"Go ahead, I can handle it."

"Seems an officer who was working the Golden Valley fire last Monday, the second of September, caught wind of an odd story. The fire happened around midnight, so it was actually Tuesday when the investigation got underway—that's when the officer picked up the strange report. The officer's supervisor was told about it this morning and called me. I discussed the situation with my people, and we decided you needed to know."

This didn't sound like the Sheriff Bolling I'd come to know, talking things over with other people and feeling like he needed a consensus to tell me something. "Excuse me, Chief, but you're not making a lot of sense right now. Odd story? Strange report? A cop talking with some guy?" Bolling could scare the hell out of you with just a sentence or two. "You missed your calling; you should have been a horror movie scriptwriter."

"That's funny, Roger, but this info is something to consider, not necessarily worry about." He stopped and waited before saying, "The officer who filed the report stated he was approached by an older man near the fire site who just walked up to the barrier tape and started talking with him and—"

"Barrier tape?"

"Yeah, you know, the yellow stuff marking a crime scene or an area where we don't want people walking around touching evidence." I had broken his chain of thought by interrupting. Wouldn't do that again. "Please go on, Chief."

"They were just talking away about the fire and the body they found in the burned building and the fellow casually mentioned that he saw someone resembling Hank Kovak."

"WHAT?"

The chief quit talking, but I could hear his labored

breathing in the telephone mouthpiece. "Did this person actually say he saw Kovak at the scene of the fire?"

"No, the guy made a remark to the officer that he saw someone resembling Kovak's description near the blaze, about an hour earlier." I waited, saying nothing, hoping he would continue. "The observer mentioned he was standing behind the police tape when he noticed a guy who looked like Kovac. He'd seen his photo in the newspapers back in July and recalled the man's eyes. He wasn't certain it was Kovac, and he said the man had a bandana around his neck and thought that was odd for this time of year."

"Bandana? Could use it to cover a scar. I don't remember it ever being reported that I used a garrote on Hank."

"It wasn't. That info has been kept confidential by me and Wilkens. Neither of us ever said anything about the Kevlar fishing line being used as a weapon. In fact, we never mentioned finding Kevlar at all."

"You certain about that?"

"Absolutely."

I waited as long as I could before speaking. "You said it was the eyes that alerted this guy?"

"That's what the man said. But the person he observed was clean-shaven, no beard, and he had long, stringy gray hair. Those parts don't add up, but according to his account, he was about the same height and weight as Kovak from what he could tell from the newspaper stories."

I remained silent, thinking about Hank. His snake tattoo wouldn't be visible if he wore a long sleeve shirt, but he did have dark, brooding eyes, and I recalled them quite well. An image of his face in my binoculars appeared, along with a view of the spittle and blood in his mouth when he was lying underneath me in the woods. I should have killed him. *No, you should have broken his leg and made his escape impossible.*

"Can you talk with this person or this observer again?"

"I wish. The officer thought he was just jawboning and didn't get a name or a phone number. It wasn't until later that he thought it through and decided to report it to his supervisor. That's when I got called. I know folks in the Golden Valley department."

I let my emotions calm, thinking the cop who heard the story was incompetent for not acting on the information and requesting an official interview, or at least getting a name. But I could only blame myself for Hank not being found. It was me who let him get away instead of disabling him. "Hey, Chief, I was under the impression you believe Hank is dead, somewhere north of Darky Lake."

"I do, and it stands to reason," the sheriff snorted back at me, "because that's near where you last saw him and where we hunted the crap out of the woods with the drones and search teams. Alive, we'd have found him. As a corpse, though, he could have been eaten in days. Any number of critters could make an entrée of him, like wolves, coyotes, lynxes, bobcats, cougars, foxes, or black bears. Even if he crawled into a cave, they'd have gotten him."

"Still, there's no proof he died, is there, Chief?"

"No, Roger, there isn't, and you know all this. Except for finding the Hard Rock Café T-shirt, which doesn't prove shit, we've never located any hard evidence establishing what actually happened to him."

"Are you saying that after this report, now you're thinking he might have gotten away?"

"Hell no, but it's a possibility, you know that. After the brainstorming meeting, you know it's feasible—not real likely, but still not impossible. Without a body or physical evidence, there's no proof he died. We haven't really searched the park since we found Bobby, and campers don't go up there as much in September as they did in July and August." Bolling was breathing hard. "I just wanted to let you know what we heard about HK this morning."

"Shit. This just isn't going to end, is it, Chief? We'll be haunted by this dirtball forever."

"I don't know what else to tell you, Roger! We discussed letting you know, or not telling you anything, and decided it was best to keep you informed. You were in the Army, you know what war is like, how you can never know enough about the situation or let your guard down. I'm not happy we don't have answers, but you need to know what we heard." The chief slowed to catch his breath. I'd never heard him rant this much about the case and realized he was as worried and angry as any of us with the lack of closure about the son of a bitch.

I told him, "You know, Chief, if the guy who reported this was a friend of Hank's and wanted to scare the crap out of us, this is a good way to do it. Even if he's just some dickhead who wanted to start trouble, it's the same story as in Quetico—no witnesses, no proof, and nobody to substantiate anything.

"Didn't think of it that way, Roger. You make a good point."

CHAPTER THIRTY-TWO

Three hours later, I was sitting at Dan's dining room table again, the one where the birthday party had been held last night, telling Janeene the story Bolling had told me. "The unidentified guy told this story to a cop less than a week ago, on Monday or Tuesday."

Her eyes were narrowed to slits. "Jesus, Roger, do you realize how scary this is? I won't be able to sleep tonight."

"This is an unconfirmed report. It could all be bullshit, or maybe the old man was mistaken." I didn't tell her about the bandana.

"Or it's one of Hank's relatives or friends who wants to scare me and my family. It happened this summer. You remember that phone call, when the guy said he was Hank's loan shark and wanted money?"

"I remember it clearly."

"It worried me to death for days. This is the same thing, and it's really horrible when you don't know what or whom to believe." She rose from her chair, and I noticed she was shivering. "If it was him, he's coming after me, you watch."

"Why do you keep saying that? What makes you think he won't just disappear and take off to some distant place. He knows cops all over the country are looking for him." I realized that's not a correct statement anymore. There was no search under way any longer. "He's got to know the police are on the lookout for somebody fitting his description. He'd be crazy to take a chance he might be recognized."

"You don't understand. He is crazy and filled with hatred and the need for revenge." I looked at her face; normally it cast an almost carefree glow, but now it was plagued by worry and eyes that broadcast a deep-rooted fear.

"You think he wants revenge for you playing around with Bobby?"

She almost sneered at my assertion, catching herself at the last second and saying, "You kidding? You think that creature cares about Bobby or me? All he cares about, if he makes it out of the park, is his money."

"I'm not following you."

She looked at her hands, then back up at me, and then down again. "I don't want you to get mad at me. I should have told you before, but Hank left five hundred thousand dollars in his camping gear at my house." I was aghast, stunned.

She waited for me to talk, and when I didn't, she continued. "I had no idea it was there until I was getting ready to clear my place after deciding to sell. I found it while pulling his stuff to the driveway for pickup by a charity. Almost didn't look inside, and the money would have gone to a church or some food bank, but I did, so I've got it."

I waited a little longer for her to explain further, but she stopped speaking. "Where's the missing part?"

"What part?"

"Bolling told me there was supposed to be over seven hundred fifty thousand stashed out of sight."

"I didn't know that, and it doesn't matter. Five hundred thousand was all there was in the duffle bag. He'll want this money back no matter what, and he'll kill me to get it." She started to sniffle.

"Christ, Janeene, you've got to turn that money in."

"Why? Why do I have to turn it over to the police? He paid taxes on it. It was his to do with as he pleased. . . and he left it at my house, like he wanted me to have it."

"I don't think that's what he intended. This isn't right."

"What's not right about it? I'm the one he slapped around when he was angry, the one who tried to get him to see a psychiatrist, the one who tried to be on his side. I deserve the money as much as anyone, and he left it in my house. I'm using some of it to pay for protection for my family."

"Yeah, but he didn't tell anyone, especially not you, about hiding it in the duffle bag. He was planning on getting it back when he came home from the camping trip."

"Guess we'll never know, will we?" Her eyes were ablaze with fear and anger, and she was shaking. I cradled her in my arms and just let her whimper for a while.

"Where is it now?"

"Hidden where no one should find it."

I thought about how she could hide the funds, and more importantly, use them without raising suspicion. "Am I correct in assuming you moved the money, or will move it, through your father's businesses?"

"You're partially right. I'm his bookkeeper, remember?" I considered her comment and realized she might just give the cash to her father and let him dole it back out to her over time for her services or as special fees or as one-time, tax-free gifts of ten thousand dollars, which could be paid to someone on an annual basis.

"You can hide $500K in your dad's companies?

"Easily."

She also had the sale of her house and the cash made from that transaction to give her enormous financial room to maneuver. Still, I didn't feel good about the knowledge she was withholding information, and HK's money, from the authorities. This put her, and me by default, in jeopardy of conducting illegal activities. I had some thinking to do.

"I feel like Angela and I deserve to keep it as payment for Hank nearly ruining our lives. Believe me when I say it's buried so well it will never surface."

"That's what Hank thought when he tried to hide Bobby's corpse."

"The money has already been taken care of. You don't need to know more."

This was a sharp lady, I realized, rocking her back and forth in my grasp like we were slow dancing at a nightclub. But she was no special FBI agent, or a woman who could kill people like some bullshit female agents portrayed on TV. "Can you and your father afford to hire more security? Just for a few months."

Her eyes snapped up, suddenly filled with wonder. "That's a good idea, Roger, I'd feel a lot safer if we had someone watching over my entire family."

She said, "I'd like for you to go with me to a firing range and practice shooting a pistol."

"We can do that."

"And I'm going to have my dad arrange for an armed escort for Angela when she goes back and forth to school each day—not just one of his employees. I can't tolerate the thought of that monster kidnapping my daughter."

Later that afternoon, I spoke with Chief Bolling only to learn there was nothing he could do but talk to his friends in Golden Valley and other departments around the state and ask them to report anything they heard about HK. They had all received notices about him in early July, but since it had been months since the Quetico events, he was no longer a top priority. The constant issues of daily crimes, accidents, and other tragedies demanded the full-time attention of most police forces.

CHAPTER THIRTY-THREE

Jerry returned from his Sacramento meeting on Monday afternoon. We were enjoying an evening meal together in his spacious dining room while I told him about all the events of the last few days. He'd been apprised of the situation related to the park murders since they happened, and he was always interested to hear the latest news.

"I'm taking Janeene to a firing range in Chanhassen tomorrow. It's a private facility, but open to the public on weekdays, and we can rent handguns and purchase ammunition at the pro store on-site. I'm looking forward to it."

"I know the place, but hell, you don't need to rent pistols, Roger. I've got over thirty in my collection, along with about as many rifles. I'd love to have some of them fired. They don't get used enough."

"That's generous Jerry, but—"

"No buts, I insist you shoot them; you're doing me a favor." We finished the New York strip steaks we were eating, and one of the house staff, a heavyset man of about fifty, cleared our place settings. As the man left for the kitchen, Jerry leaned over and whispered to me, "Robert is retired military, a former ranger. He damaged his feet in a bad landing in his parachute and gets disability. But there's nothing disabled about the way he can handle a pistol, or rifle for that matter."

"Glad you told me."

After supper we went to Jerry's gun room, and he offered to loan me the use of any of his firearms, minus a few collector versions he did not fire.

"It might be a good idea for you to choose these," he said, offering up two identical pistols. They were Colt 1911 Gold Cup Lite semi-auto pistols .45 ACP, with five-inch National Match barrels, and their clips held eight rounds. "This way you and Janeene can have identical guns. . . be easier to teach her."

"I don't need to give her lessons; she's a pretty good shot already."

"She might like the light weight and size of this gun then."

I took hold of one of the pistols, made sure the clip was not in, and checked the breech to ensure it was not loaded. I swung my arm around the room away from Jerry, aiming at imaginary targets. "Love the feel of these. A Colt 1911 was on my hip in the service, and I also have a General Dwight D. Eisenhower commemorative model at home. You should see the twenty-four carat gold inlays on the barrel and hand-grips. Never been fired, though, since it's a collector's piece now."

"You can send me photos. I imagine it would be hard to bring up here on an airplane," he laughed.

"No doubt."

"You can keep one of the guns in your bedroom while you're here. The other you can loan to Janeene if you think she'll be safe with it." His tone was more serious.

"Thanks, Jerry. But maybe I should pay you for these."

"No way. They're not that expensive anyway. I have more

than a thousand rounds in the safe and you can use those free of charge. Just clean the guns after you fire them."

"I'll replace any ammo we use."

"If you insist."

"You're not worried with all the weapons—sorry, your firearms—around your house?"

"Still thinking in military terms, huh?"

"Hard habit to break, especially when holding one of these." I pointed the pistol toward the far wall.

"All the guns, except four, are kept in this secure room. Each of my crew keeps one in their possession at all times. I have a pistol in my nightstand drawer. Being eccentric, sort of rich, and stuck in a wheelchair requires me to need my staff members to have special capabilities. You already heard about Robert. The other two are almost as good."

"I'll keep that in mind if I come home late."

"You can come and go as you please, just don't look like a burglar sneaking around in the bushes after dark."

Janeene shot well and drew the attention of many of the men at the range, not because her shot groups on the paper targets downrange were particularly well-placed, although they were, but because she was one of only three women there at the time and was without a doubt the best-looking lady some of them had ever seen. I overheard that comment a few times.

"Good shooting," I said as a way of a compliment. "Had many young soldiers in the cavalry who couldn't aim as well as you. You would have made a good MP." The look on her face convinced me she didn't understand. "MP stands for *military police*. You would have qualified as an expert marksman or markslady if there is such a word."

We put our borrowed pistols in their carrying cases after cleaning them and got ready to leave. "I want you to see the place Jerry rented to me. It's much like the setup you have with Dan, except we'd be alone. Can you come by now?"

"Actually, this would be a great night to have you over to my place. Angela has a doctor's appointment for her lung disease in the morning. She and Dan are staying with my mom and dad tonight 'cause the office is right near them. She'll miss school tomorrow, but her teachers know that, and Mickey has the night off. It's the first for him in a while; he needs the break."

When we got to Dan's house, I took one of the empty pistols inside in a plastic gun case. I left a box of ammunition, along with a fully loaded magazine in the case but not inserted in the weapon. I pulled the slide back, cocked the hammer, and pushed the safety to the on position, then hid the tote on a bookshelf in the large entertainment area adjoining the kitchen. Nobody but the two of us saw where it was stashed behind a group of science fiction novels.

* * *

A warm stream of sunlight slipped through the windows and awoke me as it reached my face. I was in bed, naked and on my back, with Janeene's right leg slung across both of mine. The bed covers were thrown down, almost off the mattress, because it was very warm in her bedroom. I peeked to my right and admired the shape of Janeene's thigh and calf while noticing the perfect profile of her foot. Her toenails were painted a bright turquoise green, and they made me smile. I sat up twisting to my right and glanced at the especially pleasing view of her behind, noticing the butterfly.

We were sleeping on the king-size mattress in her bedroom.

She stirred and woke up suddenly, squeezing my body with her legs and arms. After a minute of reveling in the warmth and sweetness of her grasp, she popped up and said, "Got to go potty." She told me it's what her daughter said when she needed to use the toilet, and it had become a habit.

I chuckled at her comment as she released me, and I got up and followed her into the bathroom. She was in the water closet, so I turned on the shower to let it warm. When she came out, we traded places. She was under the spray when I returned, and I joined her for a quick rinse, which turned into a long, wet kiss, which turned into a slow, slippery, sensual gyration. She leaned forward against the wall, and I gathered her breasts into my hands and rubbed up against her butt cheeks, while kissing her neck and shoulders. As we were about to get serious, she said, "Let's use the bed; it's safer."

We toweled off and rushed to the mattress. As we lay down, she spun around and insisted on a kneeling position, offering me a close-up view of her butterfly. As I tapped my finger on the shape, she said. "Make it fly like last night." I did.

Afterward, Janeene went to the kitchenette and made coffee. She brought steaming mugs back to the bed and we sat up by propping the pillows behind our backs. The nightstand clock showed 7:30 a.m. She turned on a TV mounted above a dresser on the bedroom wall and selected a local news channel to learn the weather forecast for the next few days. But the main story was the remembrance activities of September 11, 2001, or 9/11, as most people referred to the day. There were photos of the twin towers burning and a view of the crash at the Pentagon.

Janeene snuggled against my side. "Those were bad attacks. . . really sad events for all of us. You ever see anything that terrible when you were in the Army? Anything that really scared you?"

"Many times." An instance came to mind that was as frightening as humanly possible. "Once I was a passenger in a helicopter that crashed; it wasn't a big collision like you see on TV with fire and explosions, but one where the chopper lost power less than a hundred feet above our landing zone. We autorotated into the sand and hit hard enough to seriously screw up the helo, but nobody really got hurt, except for some nasty bumps and bruised egos." I didn't really like talking about my time in the Middle East, and changed the subject. "When do you need to get to work?"

"We have some time until I have to get ready." She snuggled closer. "Think you can handle two times in one morning?"

I kissed her full on the lips and ran my hand across her chest. She had her answer.

As Janeene was showering and getting ready for work, I thought about September 11, the anniversary of the attack on the World Trade Center. You couldn't fly anywhere after nine in the morning on that day eighteen years ago. I was twenty-two when it happened, just out of college the spring before, and visiting a friend of mine in Los Angeles when the news broke. I was as stunned as everyone and remained stranded in LA for the weekend as all flights were cancelled. I remembered watching the video of the plane crashing into the first tower. What an accident. Then the second plane hit! We were under attack. Suddenly my cell phone rang. It was Chief Bolling.

"You know what day it is?" I quizzed him before he could announce the reason he called.

"Sure do. We fly our flags at half-mast on this date every year. I seem to recall you telling me you joined the Army about that time?"

"I did. I was in ROTC in college and graduated the spring before and went on active duty in October of 2001."

"You wanted to go to war?"

"Yes and no. I got married later that year, and my twins were born in the next. But I was pissed off at Al-Qaeda, so even though we had a family, I was ready to fight; I served in Iraq after the second Gulf War."

"Never heard you talk about it."

"Other than with my Army buddies, I don't discuss those times. They're private—thoughts you can only really share with people who experienced what you did. I don't mean to be short, it's just the way I feel."

"You learned some good stuff in the Army, and you survived in Quetico because of your training. I respect your service, Roger."

"Thanks, Chief, but you didn't call to talk about my Army days. What's up?"

Bolling was silent like he was thinking and finally said, "You've seen the background info on Kovak; he had both an undergrad degree in mechanical engineering and a master's from Purdue, so it's more than interesting the guy who was found dead in the fire last week was also a Purdue grad, and an engineer."

"No shit. You're sure about this?"

"Yeah, but there's no evidence they were friends or anything, but there is evidence they both attended a local engineering meeting at the same time." I heard papers rustle as the sheriff looked through his notes. "They went to something called ASME back in May and June of this year."

"American Society of Mechanical Engineers," I told Bolling. "What could this mean?"

"Probably nothing. Maybe they were just math geeks who went to the same meetings, or maybe they were simply friends and nobody knew it, or maybe Kovak went to the meeting and tried to recruit this guy for something. All we know is they were both at the same meetings at the same time, and there's suspicion about the deceased's death; it doesn't appear to have been caused by the fire."

"What's the suspicion?"

"You know I can't tell you that, Roger, even if I knew. The only reason I mention this now is because of the possible reported sighting of HK. I'm keeping you posted, like I said."

"Thanks, Chief. Not sure if this makes me feel better or worse." I decided not to say anything to Janeene.

CHAPTER THIRTY-FOUR

I spent the rest of the day studying stocks with Jerry in his monstrous office. During the second week of September, there weren't many companies reporting quarterly earnings. The busiest months for earnings reports were January, April, July, and October.

"I understand what you're doing, Roger, only I don't appreciate which companies you play, and why."

"Like anybody dealing with the market, I can't give you a precise explanation, other than to say that over the years, I've learned certain companies will under promise and over deliver with regard to specific numbers, especially earnings estimates. There are three tech companies I follow that are reporting next week. I'll write up an opinion on each, explain it to you, and make a small trade in the direction I expect the stock to move. You can accept my opinion or not, but if you do, you can place a small options trade in the same direction, and we'll see what happens."

"Damn, Roger, your approach is as about as obtuse as mine, and maybe even harder to explain."

"Yeah, but this will give us a chance to check out the other guy's logic; see if it works in practice. It's what we need to confirm, and we'll know in a few weeks if our methods are as good as we think or we're just fooling ourselves."

* * *

I called Janeene around five o'clock in the afternoon to see how the appointment for Angela turned out, whether her sarcoidosis had gotten better or worse, and to learn if Dan and Mickey were due home soon. Everything was fine, and the men were back at the house. "You want me to pick up something for dinner?"

"Yeah, how about Chinese? You know what we like."

"I do. What about your father or his brother? Will they join us?"

"Dad's staying at his house tonight, and Dan is already sleeping." They won't join us, it'll just be you, me, and Angela."

"What about Mickey?"

"He only eats special meals. Lotta salads and fruits, along with big steaks."

"Okay then, I'll see you around seven."

* * *

After our supper of moo goo gai pan and chicken fried rice with scallions, Janeene left me downstairs while she got Angela ready for bed. I took the opportunity to talk with Mickey. He was standing in the kitchen quietly observing the backyard. At over six and a half feet tall, he had a slightly better perspective of the grass than me. His cheeks were rosy and contrasted with his pale skin. "How long have you been a nurse?"

He didn't turn to look at me, just kept gazing around the

yard illuminated by a bank of floodlights. "About four years. Since pro football didn't work out, I'm glad I got a degree in something I could use to make a living." He turned a dimmer switch on the wall to the right and the glow lessened, giving the yard a mystical radiance. "You're the one who suggested hiring somebody like me, right?"

"Correct, and I want to figure out if it was a good decision." I purposefully left my statement open-ended.

He paused before giving his reply. "I've been in this dual role of caretaker and protector since graduation from college. I've taken karate and judo lessons since high school, can bench press over five hundred pounds, and have an even temperament which serves me well in this profession. I have a license to carry a concealed weapon and I like this work and will do everything possible to keep my clients healthy, happy, and safe." He gazed directly at me. "Anything else you need to know?"

"Is the weapon in a holster on your left ankle?"

He glared at me, then half-smiled, "Yeah."

I stood directly in front of him and returned his gaze, tilting my head slightly to the rear to stay steady on his eyes, and asked very slowly, "Have you ever shot anyone? Can you fight with a knife? Could you kill a person?" I saved my favorite for last. "Can you box?"

His answer wasn't immediate, like he was remembering. "Wounded a guy once in the arm when he broke into my client's home. I don't do well with knives, don't like blades. A pause, then he continued, "I could kill a person if they were a definite threat but would rather wound 'em." He thought for a few more seconds. "Never have boxed, but it'd be handy to learn."

I moved to a huge island in the center of the kitchen and stood next to it. It was so large it had two sections with drawers and cabinets and an open space under the middle of the countertop. "I'll teach you someday. I like training heavyweights; they're slow."

He almost cracked a smile. "That's me."

"You've gotten a briefing from Janeene's father?"

"Yeah, he's the one who retained me, or I should say our company."

"He show you photos of Hank Kovak?

"A bunch, from newspapers, and I've memorized every nook and cranny of his face."

"You got any help available to you?" I already knew the answer but wanted to hear his opinion.

"Yeah. In our company we keep a scout on call at all times, a guy who floats around between assignments and checks on the worker bees. He's been here earlier, and he'll check again later tonight. Our scouts are badasses; you don't want to mess with one."

"I'm worried about Kovak—we call him Hank, HK, Mr. Asshole, or Mr. A for short. Saw him slaughter a man for what I consider to be no good reason. Expect he'd do it again if he thought somebody was a threat to him or he didn't like them, or any of a dozen reasons that wouldn't make sense to you and me. The guy is dangerous because he's hidden, not because he is unpredictable. As to that part, I predict if he is alive, he will try and hurt Janeene or her family sooner or later." I waited while he absorbed my words and meaning. "You okay protecting her? You're not gonna chicken out if that asshole comes blasting through the front door, are you?"

He looked me in the eyes. "I heard you were in the Army, former boxer and all, a tough guy, but I can stand my ground against you or anyone."

"Good, 'cause I need to know we have a trooper—a man who does what he says and lives up to his promises—in our corner at all times."

We both took deep breaths and walked around the kitchen, satisfied we'd withstood the first attempt to scare each other. I pulled an eight-inch chef's knife from a drawer. "Why don't you like these?"

"Just never did."

"Knives frighten you?" I swung it around over my head and across the kitchen island. He watched it cautiously.

"Kinda. It's the thought of it slicing into my arm or stomach, cutting through muscle and veins, that. . ."

"I'll show you a few ways to protect yourself from someone wielding a blade, a method to disarm them." I pulled a plastic spatula from a different drawer and held it above my shoulder like I was going to stab him. "This is the worst way for an attacker to use a knife, but the most common." After handing it to him, I had him approach me from that same position; I sidestepped the spatula and put him in an arm brace. His arm was thick and hard to control. "This is only an exercise, mind you, just to give you an idea how to respond." I was glad he didn't resist too much because he would have been almost impossible to overcome.

"Understand, sir." We got untangled and he asked, "You learned this in Army training? You're pretty good."

"I did it in hand-to-hand combat drills—liked it as an exercise, but the instructors could kill amateurs like you and me in no time; they're true experts. Only learned enough to allow me time to pull out my pistol and shoot my opponent."

He smiled for the first time, revealing a sizeable gap between his front teeth.

Janeene came down to the kitchen and said, "Angela's asleep. You want to watch TV with me upstairs?"

"Yeah, for a while." We retired in her area before I went back to Jerry's place.

* * *

A constant question plagued me throughout the night, or in those moments when I was half-awake and not able to float back into a full sleep. If Hank had escaped, and that was a big if, was he really capable of planning a revenge attack on Janeene? I didn't want to think about the criminal, but my thoughts couldn't be stopped. It happened to me on occasion—I got in a dreamlike state where I'd awaken and be thinking normally, then I'd drift off and start hallucinating while staying suspended in a half-conscious haze for an hour or more. Sometimes, when these episodes occurred, I envisioned killing people in self-defense, but was never slain myself, although I was often in harrowing situations. Instead, I would awaken just prior to my impending doom, sweating and breathing hard, and the nightmare would be over. Such occurrences were not frequent, and they were never enjoyable.

I realized now, especially after Bolling's news about ASME, that Hank was probably brighter than we all anticipated. When he talked with Duke at the waterfall, he stayed hidden so he couldn't be identified. Smart move. If Janeene and I had been killed, he could have easily left the park and denied knowing anything about Bobby's murder and Pete's unfortunate accident and been absolved of any suspicion. He could have lied his way to freedom—if he'd been able to kill us.

I guessed Kovak wasn't well connected with criminal groups, like an international drug lord would be, nor had enough money to retain a top-notch hit man to ferret out either of our locations. Bolling told me once, "It takes big, big dollars, a pile of money, to hire real pros. Anyone HK might employ would be a lower tier thug, a slug really, capable of turning on him in an instant. He'd probably have more concern about his own safety than we do for Janeene and her family, and it might be best for him to just lay low and forget bothering her."

How long he would maintain that stance—if he was even alive—was hard to estimate. What Bolling didn't know, that I did, was that Janeene had five hundred grand of his money. HK wasn't fully funded, so his ability to employ highly-skilled killers was less than good; in fact, it was poor—lousy even. But I figured he'd do anything to get his money back and punish her for taking it from him. I wrestled with these thoughts for half the night and finally had to conclude there was nothing I could do other than remain vigilant and prepared, and hope the bastard, or parts of him, like an arm or a leg, turned up in Quetico next year.

CHAPTER THIRTY-FIVE

"I'd like you to come to my high school reunion, it's next weekend, on Saturday night," Janeene said, as she and I were lounging on her couch while Angela watched cartoons on the television.

"What's the date?"

"September 21, a week from tonight. It's our fifteenth."

"Fifteenth?"

"A little odd I know, but I've got some good friends and we like to get together whenever we can. We do this every five years."

The date reverberated in my head while reviewing plans for football games at Rutgers and Princeton, as well as any earnings dates I had planned with Jerry during the coming week; I also thought about my recent discussion with Harold about the safety of my twins. All was good on that end. "In that case I'll fly to New Jersey on Monday and visit with my kids for a few days. Neither one has any big events on the weekend of the twenty-first, so I'll get back here by Thursday or Friday and go with you."

"Don't understand how you can fly around that much, Roger. I'd hate it."

"Been doin' it all my life, since college anyway." I was thinking out loud now, "Might also be a good time to dash home and talk with Duke about my house."

"What about your house?"

What she didn't know was that I had talked to Duke about overseeing the sales process with my listing agent, Mitch Eagle, another buddy who lived in our neighborhood. "Might sell it. Haven't decided yet, but I'm considering it."

Janeene beamed at my comment.

We celebrated the reunion with Janeene's former high school friends at a hotel in downtown Minneapolis. It was a great event, and a wonderful chance to enjoy a family affair. That's what the flyer called it, *A Family Affair*, as guests were encouraged to bring their children. While the adults dressed in suits and dresses for dinner and dancing, the children had a special meal and were entertained by members from the local dance company and the cast of a comedy troupe in an adjoining room —an open area so parents could see their youngsters. The kids were having as much fun as we were, more actually, from the sounds of laughter coming from their room. Angela was in bliss, dancing and singing with the others. I was meeting many people for the first time, and enjoyed their company, but didn't get the belly laughs from their words like Angela and the other kids did from their newfound friends. It was a spectacular night.

In the morning we ate a great breakfast in the lobby restaurant, then said goodbye to Janeene's friends and drove off for Dan's house.

"I'll call Mickey," Janeene said, dialing a number and getting an answer from him. "We're coming back now. Is Dan doing okay?"

His response was, "Everything's fine." They talked for a minute.

"Mind if I speak to him?"

"Why?"

"Just want to say hello." She handed me the cell phone.

"Hey, Mickey, do you like to fish this time of year?"

"Only for crappies or yellow perch."

"Sounds great to me. See you in a while."

"Fishing? What was that all about?" Janeene asked.

"If he'd answered only walleyes, I'd call the police." She looked at me like I was nuts. "Just a little code he and I worked out."

"Sometimes I worry about you, Roger."

"I worry about you all the time."

She looked too weary to haggle with me any further, so she lay back against the headrest and pretended to doze, but then reached back in her pocket for her cell phone. "Need to call my father and hear how Mom is doing today."

She called him and learned things were not rosy on that end. It was a brief conversation, but he was talking loudly, and I could hear most of what he was saying. After hanging up, she pleaded with me to stop by his house before we headed to Dan's place. "Mom's okay, nothing to worry about, but she's not been resting well and would like to see Angela." She looked at me, "It's on the way, and we won't stay long, trust me. I'm pooped."

We pulled into the driveway and up to the house. Her dad was standing in the garage and was clearly visible since the door was open and the light was on inside. It was his habit to watch his guests arrive in this manner. He didn't wave at us like he normally did, but he looked fine. I opened the car door for Janeene, then got the sleeping Angela from the back seat and carried her toward the garage in my arms. As we got there, a twinge of fear flashed in Alex's eyes. Stepping inside, I quickly learned why.

Before I could put Angela on the floor, a pistol was placed roughly against the back of my head. "Just keep walking and keep the kid in your arms. Do anything funny and I'll shoot her." I didn't recognize the voice. Could this be a robbery? "Carry her inside." I did as instructed.

Once we were indoors, the garage door was closed. A family room was before me, as was the silhouette of a man in a flesh-colored hood, with holes for the eyes, nose, and mouth. The hood distorted his face as he stood over Janeene's father who was on his back on the floor. He yelled at me, "You drop the kid, and I'll blow your dick off." It was the voice of Hank Kovak! He was aiming a pistol at my crotch, between Angela's legs. I hunched and pulled her a little higher in my arms. "Good, now I know you understand, and I've got a better shot." After a second, he said, "Maybe I'll have you hold her for an hour or two, then blow your pecker to pieces when you let her fall." He laughed—an evil sound.

"Hey, bitch, you been poking this wimp?" Hank was looking at Janeene, who was kneeling now and attending to her father on the floor. The asshole must have smacked him on the head with his pistol before we entered the room. He was unconscious and blood seeped from a gash on the top of his skull. She dabbed at the wound with her sleeve.

In the corner of the room, I saw a second guy on the floor, facedown, hands tied behind his back and ankles bound together, probably the security person from Mickey's company.

"I'm talking to you, sweetheart."

"I hear you." She kept dabbing at her father's cut.

"So answer me."

"What do you want, Hank?"

"Hank? Who is he? What do you think I want?"

"A life? A brain?"

"Real funny. I'll shoot your daughter a couple of times and see how you talk to me then."

"You hurt anybody, or even touch us again, and I'll never tell you where the money is."

Hank made a sound like he'd been wounded, and I noticed a vile, but careful change in his voice. "Oh, so now you think you can play the part of a tough bitch. We'll see how strong you are when I shoot all of you, not enough to kill you, just make you suffer and watch each other in pain." I shuddered at the sound of those words, wishing I could put Angela down and choke the bastard until his eyes bulged from his head.

"Not kidding, asshole. You touch any of us again, and your money will burn before your eyes."

Hank looked around the room like his cash was hidden in the walls and he could imagine the area in flames. The other guy, who also had a similar hood over his head, was standing against the door leading into the garage. He was the one who had put the gun to my head. He announced, "We need that money. No way we can walk out of here without it, I'm not in this for ashes. My partners will be pissed off too."

"Don't listen to her," Hank said. "I'll cut her fingers off if she doesn't talk, then start carving on Angela. We'll see how tough she is with her daughter bleeding on the floor."

"I'm not bullshitting you, Hank. You hurt anybody, and you'll never find the money. I'll keep the secret until your newfound friend here kills you." She looked toward the unnamed man standing at the door. "I can already tell he doesn't trust you."

"Shut up, bitch." Then, "You better get us moving toward the money. Where is it?"

"Not here. I'll tell you only if you leave my family alone. They can't identify you."

Hank looked at me. "Put her down over there." He pointed toward a couch across the room, and I placed her carefully on the furniture. The child was fast asleep and hadn't heard anything, and it needed to remain that way. Hank kept his gun aimed at me while his accomplice taped Angela's mouth. She started to wake up, but the fellow turned her on her stomach and bound her wrists behind her, then her ankles together. I heard a faint moan but guessed she'd fallen back asleep or passed out.

The guy rolled her father over so his face was on the floor and tied his wrists and ankles. He straddled him and taped his mouth. When he finished, Hank told him to check the house again.

When the guy returned, Hank asked him, "The wife still sleeping?"

"Yeah. Knocked out cold from the dab of chloroform we put under her nose before. She'll stay that way for hours," he answered.

"Where's the money, Janeene?"

"I'll tell you after we're driving away from the house."

Hank looked at her family in the room, and I thought he might pick one person and try to threaten her into talking.

"Not kidding, Hank. Touch anyone and you're not getting an answer from me."

"Wanna bet?"

"THE MONEY IS AT DAN'S HOUSE, HIDDEN. Take me there and I'll get it."

Hank's partner sounded off at the news. "That's what we wanted to hear. Come on, Kovak, let's get outta here and get the dough. That's what matters, not these people. You can come back later and chop them up into little pieces if you want to."

"Let's go," Hank said to us. He motioned toward the door to the garage. Hank loaded Janeene and me into my car after tying my hands behind my back with rope and stuffing a rag in my mouth. I was on the rear seat lying on my side as ordered. Hank got in the front and sat beside Janeene, who drove. In the open section between the seats, I could see him as he kept the tip of his gun barrel against the lid of a full plastic water bottle and aimed both at her stomach. Hank ordered Janeene to drive slowly in order to keep his partner's car right behind her. I noticed her looking in the mirror; she could see me between the seats. He had her call the brother's house as we got near it.

Mickey answered. We were within three minutes of reaching the place and Janeene was giving him instructions about what to do when we arrived. I inched upward while pushing the rag out of my mouth with my tongue and finally got a chance to mouth the word *walleye* to her in the rearview mirror. She noticed and asked Mickey what was available for lunch. He said there was a full menu. "Is there any walleye in the freezer?" she asked. "No," he replied.

Hank said, "Drive up to the garage doors like we're gonna unload." We stopped at the first one. Janeene pushed the opener and a door lifted as we parked. His partner parked behind us and got out. He had a pistol in one hand and a full plastic water bottle in the other. "Watch out for someone ready for us," Hank said to his accomplice.

Hank looked at Janeene, then me, "Walleyes, huh? Get out and walk around to the rear." As I did, he cut the rope binding my wrists. "Now open the trunk and pull out two bags, one for each hand." After I tugged Janeene's suitcase from the pile of luggage and put it on the ground, I pulled mine out and then carried them both by their handles, one on either side of me, and headed for the door leading inside the house. "Hold on," Hank said, "let Driscol go first. His partner looked around at Hank like he was pissed, then slowly and quietly opened the door into the house. He stepped inside. As we were about to enter there was a loud thump. It caused us to halt in place. Seconds later a crash happened, sounding like something had fallen over. Driscol came back to the door.

"Big guy in here thought he was gonna plug me, but I got him first."

"Why shoot him?" Janeene shrieked.

"'Cause you warned him, bitch, that's why," Hank answered.

She started to whimper, and I thought her bravado would fade. It had kept us alive this long and was working to our bene- fit, but I realized it could all head south in an instant. Driscol pulled her by the arm inside the house. Hank followed me in, his gun leveled at my back. In the kitchen, Mickey was sitting on the floor near the windows overlooking the backyard. He was bleeding from a wound near his right shoulder. It didn't appear fatal, but it had to hurt. There was no weapon around him on the floorboards. Maybe it was still in his ankle holster.

Driscol held up a nine-millimeter Glock handgun. "It was his," he said to Hank. "I also got his cell phone. He was trying to call somebody." He pulled off his hood.

"Check it," Hank ordered, pulling his off also. Driscol looked at the screen. "Call didn't get answered."

It was clear now we were not going to survive. Mickey and I could definitely identify the intruders, but our memories were easy to erase with a bullet. Only Janeene might be worth keeping alive for a while until Kovak got his money.

"Who were you calling, fat boy?" It was Hank, looking at Mickey.

"The office. No answer."

"We need to get out of here, fast," Driscol said. "We don't want to get trapped here. He could've hit a notification key or some other signal."

I was holding the luggage in both hands at my side and looking at the huge island in the center of the kitchen, and noticed a salad partially prepared on the countertop beside some plates and glasses. Hank spun suddenly and hit me with his pistol under my left ear. My jawbone popped like it had been broken or dislocated and I fell to my knees, toppling the suitcases beside me. "Is this the prick who nearly killed me in Quetico?" he screamed at Janeene. "And you've been fucking him?" He kicked me in the stomach and my wind was gone. "I'll beat him to death right before your eyes if you don't give me my money fast." To reinforce his point, he hit me on the top of my head with the butt of his gun, causing a rivulet of blood to drip down my face. I was ready to pass out.

Janeene shrieked, "Okay, you bastard. Hit him again and you won't get anything. I swear."

"Big talk from a woman who dates puny little wimps. Look at your boyfriend now." I noticed a shadow on the floor and winced from an impending blow.

"Stop! I'll give you your money." She was pleading with him now. Her leverage was gone, not a good sign for Mickey or me.

"Janeene," I whispered, "don't—"

The barrel of Hank's pistol was suddenly placed against my left temple from above. I fell off my knees and sat on my butt on the floor next to one of the suitcases. I was sitting in the open space between the two pillars of the island. Under it I could see Mickey across the room lying in blood but still conscious. Hank said to Driscol, "Start our car and turn it around so we can leave fast when I get the money. I'll take care of these people." I heard a door open then close and guessed Driscol went outside.

Mickey motioned with his eyes for me to search around under the island. He looked to my left and tilted his head. On the floor a foot away was an eight-inch chef's knife sort of hidden by a piece of luggage. Mickey must have been using it to chop up lettuce for his salad. Hank was still holding the pistol against my left temple, and I waited.

Janeene said, "Leave him alone. I'll get the money."

"Where is it?" Hank demanded.

"On the bookshelf. In a box."

"Make it quick, and no funny stuff or I'll shoot you and this pathetic bastard."

I felt the barrel of the pistol leave my head and guessed the gun was being pointed at Janeene as she moved to the wall of books and started rummaging for the box. She wasn't in my view, but things were falling with loud noises as she searched for the gun case I had hidden. Hank said, "Put it on the counter so I can see inside."

She came to the counter and put something on the top. Maybe she could load the weapon hidden in the box in time to save us but I doubted it would work. I knew better than anyone what it took to load a weapon, cock it, aim it, then shoot. Hank moved slightly away from me. When he did, I reached for the knife with my left hand.

"How much is in there?" Hank asked.

"A little under two hundred thousand," she replied.

"Two hundred thousand. Where's the rest?"

"What rest?"

"Three hundred thou is missing."

"There was never that much, only two hundred thousand in your duffel bags." After a short pause, she said, "I used some. . . a little, maybe two or three grand, but that's all there was."

After a second, he said, "Bullshit. Maybe I can beat an answer out of your boyfriend."

He was standing above me, and I swung the knife up with my left arm and jabbed it into something soft.

"Dammit," he screamed. There was a loud crash on the floor behind me and then a flood of warm fluid hit my neck. It was bright red and drenched the suitcase and the floor to my left.

Two deafening blasts shook the room. Mickey's eyes widened and I heard something heavy fall behind me. Janeene sprinted past me running toward the door to the garage and threw it wide open. "Stop!" she yelled, but an engine revved up and tires squealed. My head wobbled toward the floor and darkness surrounded me.

CHAPTER THIRTY-SIX

Something hit me in the nose once, twice, and was starting to piss me off. I was on my back on the floor, and it reminded me of the rescue in Darky Lake. "Hey," I said, flailing with my right hand at a blur in my face and a terrible smell in my nostrils. The floor was covered with blood to my left side.

"He's awake," said a voice I didn't recognize.

"Let me talk to him." Janeene knelt down beside me. "Roger, can you hear me?"

"Yeah, what happened?"

"I shot Hank."

"You did?" I assumed it was Mickey who got him somehow. Then I remembered Driscol holding a nine-millimeter handgun belonging to Mickey. It was confusing but I realized Janeene was saying she fired at least one of the shots that rang out. Through the gap in the island, I could see a man attending to Mickey. He was bending over him and holding a large cotton wad near his right shoulder. "Who are these—"

"We're from the company hired to protect you folks," a

voice from above me said. "Mickey got through to us before he was hit."

Janeene was kneeling over me now and gently dabbing a large bandage on the top of my head. "Jesus, Roger, you really took a beating." She helped me to a sitting position. My stomach hurt from the kick by Hank and suddenly I felt very ill and threw up on the floor and the suitcase beside me. Vomit mixed with the blood on the surfaces making a smelly mess. "Sorry," I mumbled, looking at the slimy mixture, not really talking to anyone.

"WHERE IS THE AMBULANCE?" Janeene shrieked.

"It's on the way, ma'am. We called for one as soon as we got here, right after calling the police. All we heard from Mickey was that he needed backup. Didn't say why. Shit, never seen a situation like this before." His voice was queasy as he knelt alongside Janeene. He sounded like he might be ready to puke himself. "This is the worst backup I've ever been on."

"You called my father's house?"

"Yes ma'am, like you wanted. No answer, but I told the cops to check on him." He started the dry heaves.

"You're not really helping here. Why don't you go over there and assist your partner," Janeene ordered.

He got up and moved over to Mickey. It would take at least two people to lift that giant onto a stretcher anyway.

A loud siren sounded nearby and grew louder and louder until it was in the driveway. In seconds the room was filled with people, and I winced and drifted off into darkness.

* * *

I never passed completely out and was only vaguely aware of my surroundings and the people trying to help me. My head was pounding so hard my skull was about to explode. Trying to talk during the ride to the hospital was nearly impossible with the siren wailing and the vehicle swerving from side to side. Nobody would tell me anything about where we were going, who was going with me, or what had actually happened at Dan's house. The ambulance stopped at the Fairview Ridges Hospital Emergency Room to allow me to be taken inside for treatment.

A semiconscious zombie could have answered the questions from the medical staff about the events that landed me here better than I could. After three or four unanswered queries by an admitting nurse, they gave up. In short order, an x-ray of my head and neck confirmed no cracked skull or broken bones, although my jaw had been almost dislocated by Hank's blow beneath my ear. It was swollen and felt like a golf ball had been placed in my cheek. Fortunately, I hadn't lost any teeth since the strike was below my gum line, but my tongue explored every inch of my mouth over and over, confirming and reconfirming my assessment.

Emergency rooms are never fun, but this unit was good to me because the attendants put me in a private room after the x-rays and I immediately fell asleep.

Regaining my senses, the room was a complete mystery to me. I awoke in a hospital gown and felt my heartbeat increasing while trying to remember how I'd gotten here. My clothes had been removed from my body, and they were hanging on a hook on the wall. They hadn't been cut off, so how they managed to get there was hard to imagine.

Gradually, I recalled the trip in the ambulance and other things about the events of the past twenty-four hours. It was a little hazy, and although I felt much better than before, the face of Hank Kovak came through. Did I hear he was dead? I looked at my watch, 7:15 a.m.

A nurse came into the room and offered me breakfast, which consisted of plain white toast without butter, ice water, and black coffee. She could not or would not answer any of my questions, and shortly after she left, a young male doctor walked in with a clipboard in his right hand. "You'll be released in a little while," he said with a slight Spanish accent.

"You think that's a good idea?"

"Yeah. All the tests have come back negative; you're in decent shape. Maybe a slight concussion, and certainly a headache for a day or two, but there is no swelling of the brain, so you can go home this morning. We try to keep people here in the ER for as little time as possible, and since you seem to have a rather hard head, you appear to be fine." He added a smile with the last sentence. He was short and slim with dark hair and a slightly bent nose, which made me think someone without a sense of humor, like me at the moment, had punched him in the face, or he had been an athlete before medical school? "You ever box?"

"No, but I did play football, or what you call soccer, in high school and college."

"Explains the nose."

"Yeah, I suppose so." He laughed and reached up and stroked it. "The police want to talk with you. You up to it?"

"I don't know. Give me a minute to think." The last time I was in a hospital Duke insisted on having an attorney present, and Jonathan Freidman had been an excellent counselor and had served me well. Maybe I should call him now.

A minute later Chief Bolling poked his head in the door. "Hi, Roger, mind if Captain Fisher and I come in?"

"Should I have Jonathan present?"

"Don't think it will be necessary. We just want to clear up a few things before your friend, Jerry Milner, takes you to his house. If you get worried, we'll stop talking and you can call Jonathan."

I nodded at him, and he entered the room accompanied by a tall, thin officer in a uniform similar to his but with a different shoulder patch. The man was about fifty with blond, thinning hair and graying sideburns. I was pleased to see Bolling.

"Okay, we can talk after you guys tell me about Janeene. She okay?"

Captain Fisher answered. "She is at her father's house with him, her daughter, and her mother. Everyone is doing well. She told me to tell you to call her when you can."

"How's Mickey?"

"He is in another part of this hospital. . . lucky guy. The wound wasn't that bad, bullet went right through without hitting any of the shoulder bones or the rotator cuff. It wasn't a hollow-point round like Kovak had loaded in his gun or else it would have been a different story. He should recover pretty quickly, they tell me."

"That's great news."

Glancing at Bolling and then toward me, Fisher said, "I understand you two have met before."

"We've been acquaintances since the tragedy in Quetico."

"Every time I see you in a hospital, you look like crap, Roger." Bolling's eyes were bloodshot, which I imagined was the result of being informed last night about my recent activities and probably driving to Eden Prairie at that time or early this morning.

"Thanks, Chief, appreciate you reminding me of my poor luck."

"Luck isn't your problem; staying out of battles with criminals is."

"Battles?" Fisher apparently didn't understand our humor,

so the chief filled him in on my stay in the Ely hospital last summer. "I'm beginning to believe Roger here likes combat; he tells me he wins most of his fights, but I'm starting to wonder."

"Only like a fair match with boxing gloves, not handguns or knives."

"By the way, Captain Fisher and his people will conduct the official interviews. They have jurisdiction, but they think you and I are friends, so they're just being nice by allowing me to be here."

Captain Fisher took the cue and pulled a notepad from his shirt pocket. "Can you tell me what you remember?"

"Very little. Right after I walked in the room with the luggage, I got smashed in the neck, just below my jaw."

"Who hit you?"

"Had to be HK. He was behind me."

"Who?" Fisher didn't understand the use of the initials HK. Only Bolling and I knew we both had developed the habit of referring to the asshole by anything other than his given name.

Bolling said, "HK stands for Hank Kovak. It's sort of a nickname we use for him. The other is Mr. A, short for Mr. Asshole."

Captain Fisher made a note in his pad. "After he hit you, what happened?"

"I fell to my knees and grabbed my head."

"Do you remember reaching for the knife?"

"Not really, but I remember seeing it on the floor; then I got hit again and things went kinda blank, and I can't recall much after that."

"Did you hear any of the discussion between this guy Hank Kovac and Ms. Morgensen?"

"Please call her Janeene. What discussion?"

"The one about the box from the bookshelf."

"No."

"Did you hear them arguing?"

"No. Like I said, I was about ready to pass out."

"When did you pick up the knife?"

"Don't know. At one point it was in my left hand somehow, and I swung it up and behind my head. That's all I remember." After a few seconds, I added, "You guys will have to tell me what happened after that."

"We understand you cut Kovak's femoral artery with a kitchen knife," the captain said.

"Did I? Wasn't certain what happened, only saw blood spurting out on the floor beside me. I couldn't feel much with my arm or hand, I was numb from my neck down."

"Tell me what you remember after seeing the blood on the floor."

"I vaguely remember puking, but that might have been later."

"Puking where?"

"Everywhere. Vomit sprayed all over the luggage."

"Sounds nasty," Bolling commented.

The captain motioned at Bolling to stop him from making comments and proceeded to ask more questions, most of which I could answer, but chose not to, or to evade with partial answers, pleading total ignorance to any question he posed that involved events after the second blow to my head. This was my *get out of jail free* card. Everyone could see I'd been bashed violently on the skull—nobody could be expected to precisely recall anything after getting hit that hard.

The concept was accurate in theory, but not in reality. I remembered everything—every sound, word, smell, or action that happened in that house—but they weren't getting anything from me; I was done dealing with Hank Kovak and all his bullshit. He'd been a fixture in my life for no good reason since late

June, and that was about to stop. "After the second smack on the head, I can't be certain about anything." I looked at Chief Bolling. "What can you guys tell me?"

Captain Fisher glanced at Bolling and said, "You tell him; since we've talked to the others, it's okay to fill him in on the basics, just tell him the stuff we've already confirmed."

"Okay, here's the story, Roger. HK and this person, Driscol, who was picked up this morning at his residence, ambushed you at Janeene's father's house. He, his wife, and Angela are pretty shaken up, but doing well." Bolling rubbed his thick, dark hair, and continued. "Mickey Reynolds, the nurse, got your call and was phoning his company when the bad guys showed up. Driscol got the jump on Mickey and wounded him, but he saw you get smacked on the head a couple of times by Hank's weapon." Instinctively I reached up and put my hand on the top of my head. It was covered with a thick bandage, much like a skullcap.

"Mickey saw Janeene get a box from the bookshelf. He couldn't see inside it, but heard Hank ask about the contents, and Janeene answer him. He couldn't hear the exact words of either person; however, he saw Hank pointing his pistol at Janeene. At some point Hank staggered backwards, probably when you cut his leg. He was aiming his gun at Janeene. She pulled a .45 out of the box and fired off two rounds in self-defense and killed him. That's what we've been told."

I thought about what I'd heard in the house and distinctly recalled hearing Janeene tossing books off the shelf searching for the gun case, and I remembered Hank asking about the money in it when she placed it on the top of the island. But nothing was said about the pistol in the box. I'd been worried she might not be able to load the magazine in time to protect herself from Hank, but that was apparently not the case. If she had time to load the clip, pull the slide back and charge the weapon, aim, and shoot, what was the asshole doing at that time? My suspicion was he was grabbing his thigh after I stuck him with the knife and he dropped his pistol. *He was unarmed when Janeene shot him.* I recalled hearing a loud knock on the floor before the shots, but I said nothing to them. "What did Mickey say?"

"Only that his view was partially blocked, but the last thing he could see was Hank aiming at Janeene, then bang, bang, two shots and Hank keeling over. He thought Janeene might have taken a bullet. He didn't know who fired at whom."

"She facing any charges?"

"Not at this time," Captain Fisher said. He paused and looked at me for a reaction, which I didn't give. I wasn't about to provide any extra information in this go-around with the law. "The gun she used was one you borrowed from Mr. Milner. He told us you and Janeene were allowed to use it, and that you both knew how to shoot safely."

"That's correct. We practiced a couple of days ago, fired it at a shooting range near Milner's house."

"We heard about that. Seems Edward Driscol, the guy with Kovak, saw you two there. He was at the same place that day." It was Captain Fisher talking.

"How do you know his full name?"

"The rent-a-cops at the house almost ran into him as they were driving to the scene. Traffic was pretty light, and they identified the car that barely missed them—the color, the make and model, and about half the numbers on the license plate. Janeene gave us the last name, Driscol, from hearing Hank say it, and a physical description of the guy. When the information matched up with a man named Edward Driscol, we learned he lives on Goodners Lake. It's near the town of Marty, and his place has been sequestered as of this morning. There appears to be evidence Hank Kovak was staying there.

We'll know more after the lab tests and the questioning of Mr. Driscol."

"Is HK dead?"

"Yeah. Shot twice in the chest, one round in his heart," the captain said. "Seems you taught your lady friend well."

"Janeene was already a good shot, just needed practice." I ruminated over the thought she had killed the asshole, and I really didn't know what happened, or how, or in what sequence. "Couldn't see a damned thing from where I was on the floor."

"We know," Fisher added, looking at his notes. "We got the full account from Ms. Janeene Morgensen and Mr. Mickey Reynolds." He consulted the notepad again. "After Hank knocked you on the head, he pointed his gun at Janeene and was about to shoot her over the money in the box."

I wondered about the money, like how much was in the box, and whether Mickey had heard the actual discussion or not, and if the authorities suspected there was lottery cash in the gun tote. But I didn't want to ask them anything about it —directly."

"Shoot her for money?"

"Yeah, there was a little over two thousand dollars in loose bills in the gun case." I said nothing, thinking about the amount she told Hank was in the box. Big difference. "Dan Morgensen said he always keeps that amount of cash or more from his gas station businesses in the house," Fisher said. "Mind if I ask you something?"

"You can ask, but all I remember is what you've already been told."

Fisher looked back at his notes, appearing satisfied, but said, "Did you see or hear anything that gave Ms. Morgensen a reason to shoot Hank Kovak?"

"Other than he was a murdering dickhead with a grievance

against her and wanted to chop off her fingers and then cut up her daughter, no." He looked at me like I'd lost my sanity. "Sorry, Captain, didn't mean to lose my temper."

"It's okay, we heard about those threats. Anything else you can add?"

I touched the bandage on my head again. "Couldn't see much from the floor, and the pain was so sharp, I couldn't concentrate on words."

"I understand, Mr. Cummings. Mr. Milner's driver will take you to his house for some rest. We can talk to you again there, right?"

"Certainly. Will I need my attorney present?"

"It's up to you, but I don't think it's necessary."

He nodded and left, but Chief Bolling stayed behind. "You should be okay, Roger. Nothing you did should cause you any legal trouble. I spoke with Jonathan Friedman, and he thinks the same thing."

"What about Janeene?"

"Case of self-defense, I'd say. Mickey made a formal statement that HK was aiming a pistol at her. It was loaded with hollow-point bullets when it was checked, so the threat was real. There's no evidence she did anything other than protect herself."

"Will you call Jonathan and tell him I want him to represent her, just in case there's any wrinkles."

"Can do."

Chief Bolling dawdled at the foot of my bed, then said, "We learned this guy Driscol attended Purdue at the same time as Hank. They're looking for links between HK, Driscol, and the guy found dead in the fire; might be more connections there than we thought." He paused then walked to the side of the bed. "You know, Roger, I thought all that crap about writing words and ideas on paper and picking through them all and coming up with theories was a bunch of bullshit, but now I admit you were more on the right track than not."

"Thanks, Chief, I know how tough that must be for you to admit." I smiled and held out my hand. He shook it. "Truthfully, I wish I'd been wrong," I said, while patting the top of my skull and the bandages carefully. "It's tough being an old hardhead."

"I imagine it is."

CHAPTER THIRTY-SEVEN

Jerry Milner and I tried to visit Mickey before leaving the hospital but were told he was being evaluated and it would be some time before the workups were completed. We decided to phone him later in the day and left.

Sitting in the back seat of Jerry's Cadillac Escalade with him while Robert, the former Army Ranger, drove us, made me feel like royalty, or a politician. I wasn't used to being chauffeured in a private car and enjoyed the chance to talk with someone while not having to pay attention to the road. "How long have you owned this SUV?"

"Got it last year. Might trade it in and get another one after the results we turned in last week." He was referring to our recent stock trading success. Although I'd gone to New Jersey and Atlanta during that time, I'd spoken with Jerry several times each day after making a few stock and options trades. We got in and out of four short-term positions, and between us, we'd earned about twenty thousand dollars each.

"You planning on staying in Minneapolis this fall?" he asked me.

"Maybe. And I might be around this winter, too, if I can go ice fishing."

"We usually get out on lakes in early December, after a good freeze. I've got a friend who has an icehouse on Minnetonka; it's a blast spending a day there, catching yellow perch and crappies. Great eating. They plow the snow to make roads you can drive on to reach the cabins on the lake. Even have street signs, just like the green ones with white lettering on normal roads. Great tradition around Minneapolis."

"I'd like to go. Can Janeene come along? Her family used to ice fish on a lake near them."

"Sorry, it's men only on my trips." After a second, he asked, "How's she doing, by the way?"

"Don't know, haven't talked with her. Bolling told me she and her family were all okay, at least physically. I'll call when we get home. . . or back to your house."

"I don't mind if you call it your home. Can be for another year if you want."

"Appreciate it. I'll stay for another month or two for certain, then decide what to do before the winter."

"That's fine, just let me know so I can keep the staff informed."

We stopped at the main entrance and were escorted inside by Jerry's driver.

* * *

My phone calls to Janeene were not answered, but my messages asked her to call as soon as she could. I was sitting in my computer area eating lunch when the phone on the table rang. It sounded like an alien creature; I hadn't heard a landline ring in months, since my stay in the hospital in Ely. "Hello."

"Roger, are you okay?" It was Janeene.

"Yeah, I'm fine. . . well, actually pretty beat up. I've got an ice bag on my head, but no cracked skull or broken bones, just some stitches. What about you?" After a few seconds of no response, I asked, "Why didn't you call me on my cell phone?"

"I'll explain later, but I need to know if you understand what happened at Dan's house."

I didn't say anything, giving her enough time to ask me other questions or think about what she was requesting of me. She was absolutely silent. Finally, I said, "What's to understand? I was hit on the head, almost knocked out, and must have stabbed HK in an artery above his knee. That's all I remember. What about you?"

She was quiet, and I could hear her breathing in the mouthpiece. "After you were hit, I pulled the gun case from the bookshelf, and Hank got mad; I thought he was going to hit you again. When he looked down at you, then back up at me, he tried to aim at my face, but I fired before he could. Twice."

I waited before speaking, holding my breath, and talking quietly, "Heard the shots, but didn't know what happened. Bolling told me you killed him."

"I had to. Before he got me."

Wow. She'd left out a few facts—important details—like Hank didn't have a weapon in his hand at that instant. I heard his gun hit the floor behind me after his leg was slashed, and I'd left the pistol in the box unloaded for safety reasons to avoid someone reaching in the case and accidentally pulling the trigger. To fire the weapon, she'd have to push the safety to the off position, then either pull the trigger to allow the hammer to release or uncock it with her thumb, snap the magazine in place, then charge the gun by loading the breech after pulling the slide back and letting it go. It took between five and ten seconds before the weapon would be ready to fire. If Hank was aiming at her, he could've squeezed off a round in that time.

"Did you ever open the box after it was put on the bookshelf?"

"I didn't, but maybe somebody else did?"

Like whom? Nobody but the two of us should have known where the gun was unless she had told Dan or Mickey. I didn't ask that question, deciding to hear what else she had to say.

"Was the gun loaded?"

"Had to be, or it wouldn't have fired."

"Was the safety on?"

"No, it was off."

Now I suspected her story was not the way it happened, but who could argue? Mickey certainly hadn't contradicted her story, and he had a much better view than I did, or so I thought. But he was lying on the floor also, so perhaps he couldn't see above the countertop, or he had closed his eyes from the pain of his shoulder wound. Either way, he didn't refute Janeene's account; could be he was siding with her presumed story because like me, he would have been slaughtered if HK hadn't been killed. My guess was that he claimed no knowledge of their discussion—that he couldn't hear it—like I did, and let Janeene's account be the one that mattered, and she claimed self-defense. That was the explanation that counted to the police.

But I knew better. HK was not aiming at her, because he dropped his gun when I cut him with the knife; I heard the loud crash behind me and knew Janeene had time to load her weapon, aim, and shoot the unarmed bastard. That was the only way it could have happened. At that point, it didn't matter if her gun was loaded or not; HK wasn't armed, and she had plenty of time to prepare, aim, and pull the trigger. I sensed she had no remorse about killing the man, and it sent a chill down my spine. "Just glad you weren't hurt," I said.

"Had to protect myself. . . and you. There was no choice."

She seemed to be waiting for me to discuss the shooting further, or at least I got that impression and was sure she'd defend her actions and continue to claim the weapon was loaded and Hank was ready to shoot her. I wasn't about to argue with her account of the incident since I was on the floor nearly comatose and could claim ignorance of anything he or she said. Besides, the monster threatening her, her family, and me and my kids, had been purged from our lives. That was the one positive thing about this situation. The man was gone, finally and completely—no more wondering if he'd escaped the parks and was stalking us.

Janeene had made a choice, a desperate and determined decision, intended to terminate a killer who had no scruples. He undoubtedly would have murdered Mickey and me, as he indicated to Driscol before he ordered him from the room to start their getaway car. He probably would have taken Janeene with him as a hostage to abuse and torture, if I hadn't stabbed him in the thigh.

My actions hadn't been as resolute as hers when the chance had been presented in Quetico. There was no doubt I should have incapacitated HK by at least shattering his foot or leg with my rifle butt, if not outright killing him by choking him to death with the garrote during our fight. If I had, we wouldn't have been terrorized all these weeks, and we wouldn't be in this dilemma now, so the blame for her having to kill him was on me, not her. Nevertheless, I found it hard to justify murdering an unarmed man, even if he was the most heinous villain imaginable.

Silence filled my handset and there was an uneasy pause before she said, "He deserved it after what he did to Bobby, my father, and you." She was quiet for a second. "And he threatened my daughter. That was too much. He couldn't be allowed to... to continue to scare us."

Without saying it, she was imploring me to stay silent about her account of the shooting, and to forgive her for a cold-blooded murder. I gave her time to slow her breathing, deciding to change the subject. "How's your mother?"

"She's fine. Slept through it all and we haven't told her much. And please, when you see her again, or the others, don't speak about the attack at Dan's house. We really shouldn't say anything about it to them. They've suffered enough."

I fully understood now; her intention was to keep discussions about the shooting of HK between just the two of us, and nobody else. I said, "There's not much your family needs to know anyway." The need-to-know phrase hung in my mind, like a faint reminder that there were times in one's life when silence was the best remedy, if you could live with your decision. Apparently, Janeene could. I wasn't certain how it would settle in with me.

Without knowing why, I suddenly thought about the insurance policy. Had no idea if a person who killed the purchaser of a policy would still collect the proceeds, especially if the recipient was the person to conduct the slaying. I didn't care about the money but realized the fact that the death had been in self-defense created an interesting proposition, and one the insurance and legal scholars would have to determine, not me. At the time of the gunfire, I assumed Janeene was not thinking about such matters, only that she deserved the right to be free of the man, and now she was.

"Can you see me tonight?" she asked.

"Where are you staying?"

"At Dan's house. We got his old nurse back, and she's taking care of him."

"I'm feeling better and should be able to drive, and I do want to see you. We need to discuss a few things."

"Like what?"

"Our future."

"We can discuss that in bed."

Visions of butterflies bounced in my head. "Not sure I'm ready for that. Let me rest this afternoon, and I'll come to your place this evening."

"I'll be here, Roger. Been waiting for you all my life."

* * *

Hanging up, it was time to for me to examine the soul of this lady, as well as my own, and make a decision about our lives going forward. It had to be done now, before I got involved further and made a mistake by either staying or leaving and regretting the decision in either direction.

I'd never had difficulty with questions about morality. My military service had been predicated upon following legal orders and having the courage to decide whether one was lawful or not. If an order was deemed not permissible, it could be ignored, and the violation reported. It was pretty simple to me, although at times it could get very challenging trying to determine right from wrong, especially in a combat zone where your soldiers were being fired upon and possibly wounded or killed. Fortunately, I was never faced with the situation of being ordered by a superior to conduct an illegal action or had to investigate the suspicious death of a prisoner at the hands of my troops.

I did, however, have moral and ethical problems as a civilian. Senior personnel in my stock trading company sponsored illegal activities. In that case, my decision had been to disobey the directives and hold my ground. I had no difficulty justifying my honorable position in those matters. In the end, I won, but it took a toll on my friendships as well as my beliefs about the honesty of some of our managers and coworkers.

With my late wife, Sherry, there'd never been problems about morals or ethics. We'd grown up together from our teenage days and had understood one another from our first year onward. We were both moderately religious, dedicated to each other, and conducted our lives with respect for others as well as the laws of society. We loved our children and raised them to value us, others, and the greatness of America. Most importantly, there was a loving calmness in our relationship that lasted almost to the end, although it was stressed after the death of our dog. Having a touch of anger pointed at her by me just before her accident was a mistake I would regret for the remainder of my days. But at no time in our marriage did I question her morality, honesty, or humanity. If my wife hadn't been a casualty of a senseless crime, there was no way I was ever going to leave her. I never intended to be in this situation again in my life—choosing whom to trust and love.

Sherry had been the polar opposite of Janeene. That was proven in the showdown with HK, when Janeene displayed no moral concerns about the appropriateness or inappropriateness of her actions, only that she needed to protect her daughter, her family, and me. It doesn't take long to see a real person in times of extreme duress. Janeene was a fighter, with no qualms about winning when she needed to, in any way she could. The words, *whatever it takes*, crossed my mind. Many soldiers who served under me had the same attitude. She might have made some poor choices in life, and some I wouldn't have, but she defended those she loved with all her heart. And she'd saved my life. . . I couldn't ask more of anyone than that.

But the question remained, was she a cold-blooded killer?

Without meaning to summon them, the events of the kitchen battle began replaying in my head. It was like remembering a dream, one slightly out of focus, fading in and out of reality. I recalled being on the floor after getting struck in the jaw and neck and falling down on my knees. Neither Hank nor Janeene could be seen from that position, and after the second blow I was reduced to sitting on my butt, nearly unconscious, and unable to focus my eyes. But I could hear things.

Mickey said he didn't observe them clearly for the entire encounter, just parts of it, but maintained he'd seen Hank aiming at Janeene's face after she'd retrieved the box from the bookshelf. That might have happened. I thought I heard Hank's gun hit the floor after I stabbed his leg, but never spotted it anywhere around me. The countertop was full of plates, glasses, and silverware, so something else could have fallen off as Hank groped at his wound. It was possible. And there was no absolute proof Janeene was changing the facts, only my suspicions, but then again, I recalled Captain Fisher telling me in the hospital that there was several thousand dollars in cash in the gun tote. Janenne told Hank there was nearly two hundred thousand dollars in the case, but there was no money in it when I'd left the pistol inside. Dan Morgensen might have put some cash in there, and he might have loaded the weapon. Her version could be correct. But why all the discrepancies about money? What really happened to Hank's lottery winnings?

When it came to the matter of Janeene being a crafty accountant, it was undeniable. But when it came to the matter of Janeene being a cold-blooded killer, it was questionable and could be entirely wrong. There was no doubt about Hank Kovak's status, however. He was a killer and as heartless as a rattlesnake. I witnessed the execution of Bobby Johnson—saw his head explode from a bullet to the temple. And HK had killed a young Boy Scout for no good reason other than to steal his canoe. He'd also smashed another Scout's head with his rifle butt, which could have killed him, but fortunately did not. And although unproven, he might be involved in the death of the engineer who attended an ASME meeting with him. That put Hank's scorecard as: two definite slayings, one possible murder, inflicting severe injuries on me, Janeene's father, mother, and one Boy Scout. He was also the reason Mickey had been wounded along with another bodyguard at Janeene's parents' house, and he'd threatened Angela and Janeene herself. On balance, if Hank had been tried in court, he'd have been convicted and sent to death row, or sentenced to serving life in prison without parole. He was an asshole, and undoubtedly got what he deserved.

My quandary wasn't about Hank, but with Janeene. I'd fallen in love with the woman and needed to understand what she'd done in the kitchen. Either she killed him while he was unarmed, or she hadn't. I'd never be certain about the shooting —it could have happened as she claimed, or she could have deliberately pulled the trigger on a defenseless villain. I imagined myself in the situation and thought if Hank had dropped his hand below the countertop to point his weapon at someone on the floor, he could've quickly raised the pistol and aimed it at my face. If he did that, I'd have blasted him into another world, like Janeene did.

My cell phone rang, and I picked it up while looking at its display screen—my camping buddy from Atlanta. "Hey, Duke, glad you called, I'm thinking about selling my house and moving to up north."

"Might not be such a good idea, Roger. I just got a call. . . some weirdo said to tell you, 'This ain't over.'"

That made up my mind. I was moving to Minnesota.

ACKNOWLEDGMENTS

Although I began writing this manuscript in the early 1990's, it wasn't until I met a member of the Atlanta Writers Club in the fall of 2018 that I became interested in the possibility of publishing my work as a novel.

After attending a few general sessions, I joined the AWC in late 2018 and began attending local chapter meetings in Roswell, GA. These meetings provided the spark that re-ignited my interest in writing, and more importantly, introduced me to writing in such a manner that publishers would consider my work for publication.

Our local members, Jeremy, John, Olga, and Jan, to name few, were instrumental in listening to my readings each month, and making comments aimed at improving the pace, tone, or setting of the chapter. I listened carefully, adopted many of their recommendations, and cannot thank them enough for the meaningful advice they rendered. If I missed mentioning some-one, and I'm sure I did, I apologize for a poor memory.

If not for the Covid 19 Pandemic starting in January of 2020, I would have never missed a local meeting. I enjoyed them immensely, especially joining the others for lunch after a morning session. But by March of 2020 it was clear that remote meetings were the wave of the future. Unfortunately, my skill at using Zoom-like programs was not honed, so I frequently missed local meetings in the next few years. But the impact the group had on me was monumental. In May of 2022, during the AWC Conference, I received an offer from Running Wild Press and Rize Press to publish STRANDED—and this during an interview on Zoom!

I wish to thank Diane Lisa Kastner for selecting my work for publication and for appointing Angela Andrews as my editor. Angela was magnanimous in her approach to meeting our goal, and she was a true pleasure to work with on the project. The editing process came at a difficult time for me – as I was relocating from one state to another, but Angela made it wonderful experience. I realize now Diane has built an exceptional organization. The people I have had the pleasure to deal with during the selection, editing, and publication process are truly
      outstanding   individuals.   This   includes   Evangeline Estropia.

The final people to acknowledge are the folks who introduced me to the Boundary Waters or Quetico Provincial Park and travelled with me to those sites during our adventures. This includes buddies Barry, Joe, Doug, and Terry, as well as my father, William, brother Lindsey and his lady friend Gisele, and brother Patrick. All of us had memorable times in the Land of the Great Pierre.

ABOUT RUNNING WILD PRESS

Running Wild Press publishes stories that cross genres with great stories and writing. RIZE publishes great genre stories written by people of color and by authors who identify with other marginalized groups. Our team consists of:

Lisa Diane Kastner, Founder and Executive Editor
Cody Sisco, Acquisitions Editor, RIZE
Benjamin White, Acquisition Editor, Running Wild
Peter A. Wright, Acquisition Editor, Running Wild
Resa Alboher, Editor
Angela Andrews, Editor
Sandra Bush, Editor
Ashley Crantas, Editor
Rebecca Dimyan, Editor
Abigail Efird, Editor
Aimee Hardy, Editor
Henry L. Herz, Editor
Cecilia Kennedy, Editor
Barbara Lockwood, Editor

Scott Schultz, Editor
Rod Gilley, Editor

Evangeline Estropia, Product Manager
Kimberly Ligutan, Product Manager
Lara Macaione, Marketing Director
Joelle Mitchell, Licensing and Strategy Lead
Pulp Art Studios, Cover Design
Standout Books, Interior Design
Polgarus Studios, Interior Design

Learn more about us and our stories at www.runningwild-press.com

Loved these stories and want more? Follow us at runningwildpublishing.com, www.facebook.com/runningwild-press, on Twitter @lisadkastner @RunWildBooks

RUNNING WILD
RUNNING WILD PRESS